More Than You Dreamed

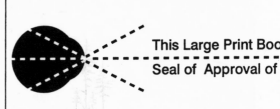

More Than You Dreamed

Kathleen Gilles Seidel

Thorndike Press • Thorndike, Maine

LP

10-92 Thorndike 17.95

Library of Congress Cataloging in Publication Data:

Seidel, Kathleen Gilles.
  More than you dreamed / Kathleen Gilles Seidel.
    p. cm.
  ISBN 1-56054-495-3 (alk. paper : lg. print)
  1. Large type books. I. Title.
[PS3569.E5136M6   1992]   92-19388
813'.54—dc20   CIP

This book is a work of fiction. Names, characters, places
and incidents are either products of the author's
imagination or are used fictitiously. Any resemblance to
actual events or locales or persons, living or dead, is
entirely coincidental.

Thorndike Press Large Print edition published in 1992
by arrangement with Pocket Books, a division of Simon
& Schuster, Inc.

Cover photo by Alan LaVallee.

The tree indicium is a trademark of Thorndike Press.

This book is printed on acid-free, high opacity paper. ∞

for Marlene Drucker

A grateful mind
By owing owes not, but still pays, at once
Indebted and discharged.

— Paradise Lost

Acknowledgments

Do male authors thank their babysitters? I must. Christi Morris was here when I was breaking sod; Elizabeth Mitchell rode in for a gallant last-minute rescue. Manning the fort in between were Meagan Vilsack, Suzanne Thulin, Davis Roberts, Katie Kirkman, and Lacey Gandy. The hospitality of Laura Brookhiser, the little girl next door, provided countless hours of unexpected work time.

After eight books, you run out of things you know about and have to write about what your friends know about. Fortunately, I am blessed with many knowledgeable friends. If I have not completely disgraced myself writing about film, it is a tribute to Lawrence and Kathleen Karr who were generous indeed. Casey Stuart read my Civil War material, and Bill and Gerry Ely escorted me around Winchester. Anne Stuart nursed me through many odd literary adventures. Catherine Healy introduced me to her friends who proved much too fascinating to write about . . . at least in this book. Alison Barschdorf, while not knowing how long film will survive in a freezer or when American G.I.s were first captured by Germans, always knew who would know.

Other friends provided insight into the animal kingdom: Barry Levine knew about chickens, Pamela Regis knew about horses, and Faye Zucker knew about group therapy.

From *The Pocket Books Guide to Movies on Video*. Ed. Michael J. Brockhiser and David Ternisky. 3rd edition. New York, 1992.

Weary Hearts

N.R., 128 m., 1948

Bix Ringling (Phillip Wayland), Charles Ringling (Booth Wayland), Alicia Burchell [Mrs. Charles Ringling] (Mary Deas Wayland). Directed by Oliver McClay and produced by Miles Smithson. Screenplay by Bix Ringling and William Casler.

Second only to *Gone With the Wind* as the most popular Civil War drama, *Weary Hearts* tells the story of two brothers who flip a coin to decide which one will ride with the Confederate cavalry and which will stay home and raise horses. A bittersweet love blossoms between the brother who stays home and the other one's wife.

This is the last of Oliver McClay's movies, made when his talents were fading. Much of the movie's enduring appeal has been attributed to the work of William "Cass" Casler, the editor and co-screenwriter. Casler later went on to win Oscars for his direction of *Nancy* and *Mustard Lane*. *Weary Hearts* was nominated for Best Picture, but lost to Olivier's *Hamlet*.

One

She didn't have to ask who he was. She knew. It took one heart-stopping glance. He was Phillip Wayland.

Were the shadows of the Dracaena palms playing a trick on her? No, there was no question. He had the dark, curl-tousled hair, the sharp cheekbones, the full lower lip. With a face promising everything in gallantry and dash, the man on Jill's doorstep was Phillip Wayland. He couldn't be anyone else.

Except Phillip Wayland was a character in a movie made forty years ago; even the actor who had played him was long dead.

So he probably wasn't Phillip Wayland. But still . . .

"Miss Casler?"

Miss Casler? This man — or at least his face — had been the heart of all her girlhood dreams, the secret intoxicating crush of her preteen years. Time after time he had come down off the screen to smile at her, to crush her in his arms. Why was he calling her *Miss Casler?* Why wasn't he sweeping her off her feet and taking her to whatever starry land in which fervent adolescent crushes dwelt?

11

" — Doug Ringling, and I got your address from — "

How Jill loved that movie. She had lived it, breathed it, imagined herself in it, living in Civil-War Virginia, a world of gleaming spurs and perfumed rosebuds. When she took her Pony-Club lessons, riding her obedient little pony around and around a sawdust-covered ring, she was, in her own mind, not a quiet child with blond braids and a black velvet riding cap, but a girl-Phillip, braving the pounding rains that had come rolling in across the Appalachians, mastering a powerful steed whose breath was hot and whose flanks glistened. When she would lead her little pony back to the stable, she would be driving a string of fine Virginia thoroughbreds into a dark clearing of the Massanutten Mountain, hiding them from the plundering Yankees.

Even when she no longer wanted to be a girl-Phillip, she still loved the movie. Now she wanted to be the girl for Phillip's boy. He was everything a new-awakened girl could want. He had glowing eyes, courtly manners, and dark hair that danced in the wind. His sun-browned hands closed firmly around the leather reins, and his commanding legs urged his horse into a gallop. When he came on the screen, Jill would hold her breath and feel her mouth grow dry. Then, at night, she would dream about the times when he would come down off the screen.

And now he was standing at her door.

Except, of course, he wasn't. This was someone else. He had been talking to her, and she didn't have a clue as to what he had been saying.

"I'm sorry," she apologized. "I was absolutely in love with you when I was twelve . . . although I suppose it wasn't really you."

"No." He smiled, and it was — oh, God — Phillip's smile, Phillip's long, lazy smile. "It was my uncle Bix you were in love with. When you were twelve, I was afraid of girls and had zits."

"Don't *say* that. Speak softly, you're treading on my dreams."

It was not like Jill to blurt out her adolescent fantasies to strangers. She was not a person who talked about herself. But she couldn't help it. How could she not be honest with this man? She had known his glowing blue eyes so well, she had loved them for so long.

She shook her head, laughing at herself. "Have I frightened you? Except for these occasional lapses, I really am a well-adjusted person. Can you take that on faith long enough to come in for a cup of coffee?"

"If you show me where to walk, so I don't tread on any more dreams than necessary."

He followed her inside. At the moment she was living in a two-bedroom bungalow on the palm-treed grounds of the Holmby Court, a small luxury hotel off Wilshire Boulevard in the Westwood section of Los Angeles.

A pair of oyster-colored damask sofas faced each other at one end of the bungalow's living room. Jill gestured to Phillip — no, no, he wasn't Phillip. Good heavens, what had he said his name was? She hurried to the triple windows that took up most of the far wall. Scooping back the edge of heavy damask drapes with one hand, she found the cord with the other. The curtain's rings rasped along the brass rod, and the bold California light flooded into the room. The sunlight made a bright stage of the little seating area. In its center sat this man. He did look like Phillip.

How fun was this. If Phillip Wayland really had knocked on her door when she was twelve, she would have been self-conscious and awkward, embarrassed and painfully young, a child to the man. But now she was twenty-eight, and he seemingly only a few years older. This could be truly grand.

14

She sat down across from him, moving a big bowl of tulips so that she could see him better. "I ought to be embarrassed" — but she was not — "I went so starry-eyed when I saw you that I didn't catch your name."

"Doug. Doug Ringling."

She could have guessed the Ringling part. "You said Bix was your uncle. So are you Booth's son? No, I'm sorry . . . Booth, that was his name in the movie. I mean Charles. Are you Charles's son?" *Weary Hearts* was about two brothers, Phillip and Booth Wayland. The parts had been played by real-life brothers, Bix and Charles Ringling.

"Actually not. Bix and Charles had a little brother. He's my father."

"There were three brothers?" None of the *Weary Hearts* publicity — and Jill had read it all, every blessed word of it — had mentioned a third brother.

"He was just a kid when the movie was made," Doug explained. "He never came West, so — "

"Don't tell me you grew up in Virginia?"

"Ah . . . yes." He was surprised by her interruption. "In the Valley, the Shenandoah Valley."

"The Shenandoah Valley? How wonderful." Jill clasped her hands over her heart. This might be getting sillier and sillier, but

15

it was also getting better and better. *Weary Hearts* was set in the Shenandoah Valley; Jill had always thought of it as a magical land, sparkling with small stone churches and apple orchards rising over the crests of green hills. Now this man who looked exactly like Phillip said he had grown up there. "You didn't ride horses, did you?"

She couldn't help herself. She had to ask that. Phillip had been a born cavalryman.

He shook his head. "No. I played basketball. I look like Bix and I'm built like him, but I'm taller."

"Are you? I suppose that's good." Jill didn't suppose that she sounded very convincing. "What can I get you? Coffee, tea, something soft? I don't think I have any beer or wine, but I can call for some."

He refused. "I don't want to take any more of your time than — "

"Do you get tired of this? People falling all over themselves because you look like a character in a movie? Or do most people have more dignity than I seem to?"

"I don't mind. Folks in the Valley do idolize Bix because he died young, and maybe if I hadn't had things I was good at, then it might have been tricky . . . oh, well — " He broke off, dismissing what might be a very complex psychological issue with a wave

16

of his hand. "The people I know are used to me. But your falling all over yourself does make it easier to get to my point." He drew some papers out of the breast pocket of his blazer. "Have you seen this?"

Jill took the papers. They were folded, but she could guess what they were. There were only two reasons why someone who looked like Phillip Wayland would knock on her door. He might have come to sweep her off her feet and make all her prepubescent fantasies come true. Or he was here to talk about *Weary Hearts*. While Jill's devotion to the movie was as irrational as any twelve-year-old girl's flowery dreams, she did have some reason to claim the movie as her own. Her father had edited it and had helped write it. That was why, in the days before VCRs, she had been able to watch it as often as she liked. Her father maintained a screening room in their home, and the studio let him take a copy of the movie whenever he asked.

Made in 1948, *Weary Hearts* was a Civil War movie. While not quite *Casablanca,* it was right up there with *It Happened One Night* and *It's a Wonderful Life.* Everyone had seen it, and everyone loved it. It was not a classical masterpiece, it was no ground-breaking work of art. It was just a good, solid, romantic movie that had been enter-taining people for more than forty years. Recently there had been an article in *The Journal of Popular Film and Television* about the making of the movie, a story whose two key figures were Bix Ringling, Doug's uncle, and William "Cass" Casler, Jill's father.

The original idea for the movie had been conceived by Bix Ringling, a young contract writer for one of the big studios. He had done the initial treatment, which the studio took through script development, then de-cided to produce. Although the film eventually turned into one of the studio's biggest money-makers, the production had initially had a very limited budget. Assigned to direct had been Oliver McClay, an aging alcoholic, and none of the cast had more than "featured player" status.

Bix's brother Charles and Charles's wife, Alicia Burchell, had been among those con-tract players, and the gimmick of casting them along with Bix in their real-life rela-tionships had been the modest production's one source of interest.

As limited as the studio's expectations had been for the picture, Oliver McClay's rough cut was disappointing, so disappointing that the studio had considered not releasing it.

Then Cass Casler, Jill's father, came into

the story. He had been an editor under contract to the same studio. Too well paid to have been included in the picture's original budget, he was interested in its fate. Both he and Bix were from the Shenandoah Valley, and *Weary Hearts* had been set there.

So when Bix's love song to the Valley was about to be buried, Cass stepped in to try to undo Oliver McClay's mistakes. Working first with the script, he restructured the movie's narrative, coming up with such a compelling story that the studio was willing to put the film back into production for extensive retakes. The cast and crew returned to the Shenandoah Valley for reshooting, and Cass wove the new footage into the old. This version of *Weary Hearts* was an instant success at the box office. It was nominated for Best Picture and decades later was still so popular that it was one of the first classic films successfully released on videocassette.

Cass's work on *Weary Hearts* had been a turning point in his career. It was the first clear indication of his enormous cinematic talent, which later became part of the studio's trademark. Never again did he play the editor's safe, anonymous part. From then on he was a director, responsible to his own vision.

He ultimately made twenty-eight movies,

including his Oscar-winning *Nancy* and *Mustard Lane,* but Jill knew that *Weary Hearts* had always been special to him, not just because it had been his stepping stone into direction, but because, alone among his movies, it had been set in the Shenandoah Valley.

Weary Hearts ought to have launched Bix's career as well, but his part ended tragically. The day after the filming of the new material was completed, he, his equally talented sister-in-law Alicia Burchell, and a number of the crew members boarded a small plane on a foggy night. The plane crashed into the Blue Ridge, killing all on board. Of the principal actors, only Charles Ringling, who had been cast as Booth, survived. In order to play the starving Confederate soldier, Booth had had to lose a great deal of weight quickly. After the shooting was over, he stayed in the Valley until his mother's cooking got his weight back up.

Recently a freelance writer named John Ransome had discovered in Cass's files Bix Ringling's original treatment for *Weary Hearts.* Bix's material was, Ransome asserted, a routine, even mediocre action-adventure war story without a trace of the final version's haunting love story or of Phillip's agonizing choices. It would have made a very ordinary blood-and-guts war movie. Cass had taken out the blood and had added heart. His contribution, Ransome concluded, had been even more extensive than anyone had thought. He had added everything that made people love the picture: the emotion, the romance, the bittersweet ending, all those had come from Cass.

Jill smoothed her hand across the top sheet of Doug Ringling's copy of Ransome's article. The photograph on the first page, dulled by the Xeroxing, was the movie's most famous still — Phillip gripping his sister-in-law, Mary Deas, by her shoulders as they stood in front of the burning barn. On the next page, Jill knew, would be a photograph of her father, her brilliant, devoted father. She didn't turn the page. He had been dead for two years, but it still hurt.

He used to tuck her into a corner of his deep chair and tell her stories about his boyhood home. He told her about the Valley's sweet limestone soil, its wooded hills and gently rolling farmlands. The Valley had been the "grainery of the Confederacy," sheltering Stonewall Jackson's fifteen thousand men, paralyzing fifty thousand hard-worn Yankees. Cass had spoken of the Valley proudly, longingly.

Jill's eyes stung as she thought about her father's death. She felt her lips tighten, her throat close. She blinked quickly. There, on the sofa across from her, was Phillip. *Phillip will understand. He knows what it's like to lose someone, he knows what I've been through these two years.*

Suddenly this man having come wasn't funny and delicious. It was strange, unsettling. He was a stranger to her; she had to remember that. There was no reason for him to understand her any more than would any other stranger.

She spoke carefully. "What can I do for you?"

"I realize the movie was made before you were born, but did your father ever talk to you about how it was made?"

"A little, but it was a difficult time for him." Jill willed her voice into an even cadence. "His first marriage was breaking up. All I remember was him speaking well of your uncles, especially Bix." Actually, Jill didn't recall her father ever mentioning Charles, the brother who had played Booth. "He said Bix was a true gentleman, which wasn't something he said about many people."

"Did he ever say anything to contradict this article?" Doug gestured to the papers still in Jill's lap.

"No." What an odd question. "He certainly

didn't dwell on his own role as much as the article does, but he wouldn't have." Cass had never been arrogant. He hadn't needed to be. His pictures had always been popular with moviegoers, and his reputation among the critics was as steady as anyone's ever was. "Why do you ask?"

"How interested are you in this movie?"

Did he always answer a question with a question? "It got me through puberty," she answered lightly. "I owe it a great debt."

He was sitting forward now, his elbows resting on his knees, his Phillip-Wayland eyes in direct contact with hers, confiding, urgent. "Great enough to help me find out what really happened?"

Bells went off, clanging, screeching warning bells shrieking at the base of Jill's skull. This was not Phillip Wayland who would sweep her off her feet and understand all her troubles. She had to keep that absolutely clear. This was a twentieth-century man with his own twentieth-century agenda. She didn't know what he wanted from her, but clearly he wanted something.

She was curious, but she was determined to be cautious. She happened to be rich, and rich people were manipulated enough. "What do you mean? Is there something wrong with the article?"

"I don't know for sure."

That was crap. He certainly believed something or he wouldn't have come here. "But?" she prompted.

"But my family tells a different story."

First he reviewed the "official" story. The movie had been shot in March and April of 1948, with the location work having been done in the Valley during April. Shortly thereafter the studio executives had rejected the rough cut. During June and July Cass had helped draft a new script. The movie had gone back into production in August. Only part of what had been shot in March and April had been used in the final version.

Jill knew all that. She listened politely, growing more uneasy. What did he want from her? She wished he would get to the point.

He continued. "My grandfather — Bix's father — told me that when Bix and everyone were out in the Valley the first time, they were doing things that the studio had no idea they were doing."

That did not seem remarkable. Jill had been on a number of movie sets where the actors and crew were doing all manner of things that the studio or production company had no idea they were doing — usually cocaine.

But she didn't suppose that was what Doug was talking about. "Such as?"

"Such as filming a different script."

"What?" Jill sat up, caution gone. Filming a different script? She couldn't have heard him right. "That's not possible."

"Is it really? That's what I'm trying to find out, if this is possible."

"If what's possible?" She stared at him. "The cast and crew filming one script while the studio thought they were doing another?" That was too strange to be true. She leaned back against the mounds of tropical-colored pillows, almost laughing, relieved that this was so ridiculous, that this wasn't anything she would have to deal with. "What script would they have been filming? *King Lear*?"

"No, it was a script that Bix had written, but that the studio had turned down . . . or was sure to turn down. It was work that he really believed in, that he was determined to see filmed. So he decided — "

"Wait a minute," she interrupted. "You're serious, aren't you? You believe this."

Doug nodded.

"Then start at the beginning."

The beginning, he told her, was in a German prisoner-of-war camp. Bix had been captured at Kasserine Pass, and during this confinement his thoughts had turned homeward, to Virginia.

"Bix was born in 1920," Doug said. "The Civil War still felt very close; he would have grown up on Civil War stories. People of his generation were always surprised when they found out that their parents weren't born until long after the war was over."

So it was inevitable that his mind should turn to that war, and he endured captivity by creating characters and planning a story set in Civil-War Virginia.

He escaped from the camp. An injury to his hand kept him from returning to combat. He was instead assigned to Army Signal Corps where he did chores for Frank Capra, who was making the *Why We Fight* series. This introduced him to the world of movies, and after the war he took a job as a writer at one of the studios.

"He was first assigned to a number of low-budget horror films and then polished up the men's dialogue on bigger pictures," Doug said, "but nights and weekends he was always working on what really mattered to him, this Civil War story."

When he finished the screenplay, he started showing it to friends. Apparently everyone who read it loved it, but nobody thought that the studio would touch it. It wasn't commercial enough.

"You have to understand Bix. He escaped from the Germans because he was smart. He was crafty, that's probably a better word for it. He was Tom Sawyer. When he wanted something done, he got it done even if he had to go in through the back door, through a cellar window. He had a scheme for everything."

The scheme he crafted for *Weary Hearts* was his most ambitious ever. He set aside his first script and wrote a second one, the treatment for which was later found in Cass's files. It was every war-movie cliché strung together, but it could be made cheaply — Bix had learned a lot from his work on the horror films — and so the studio decided to do it.

"Now, I don't know the logistics of this," Doug said, "who he told and who he didn't. But some little group of them all agreed that they would actually film the first script, his 'secret' script. Apparently it was magnificent; everyone involved really believed in it. Bix had made sure that the characters' names and the settings were the same in both scripts so they could do it without the studio knowing."

Jill could feel her head shaking, her long blond hair brushing her shoulder blades. This was not possible. Having the characters' names and the settings the same would hardly have been enough. In those days the studios exercised great control over their productions. There were committees, budgets, contracts, a producer, a director, an editor. There were shooting schedules and call sheets. Even on location, there were daily reports from the unit manager and the director, giving California counts of how many pages had been filmed, how many feet of film had been used. There would have been no way to keep the studio from knowing what script was being filmed. Absolutely no way at all.

"So have you read this other script?" Jill asked. "The one they supposedly filmed?"

Doug shook his head. "No. Apparently all the copies were on the plane with Bix and Alicia when it crashed."

Jill frowned. "That doesn't make any sense." She wasn't being argumentative. It just didn't make any sense. "They came out in August to film new material. There'd be no reason to bring the April scripts back with them. Maybe one copy or so, but certainly not all of them."

"I don't know," Doug admitted. "And most everyone's dead — Bix, Alicia, and a lot of the crew died in the plane. Oliver McClay, the first director, Miles Smithson, the producer, and then your father . . . they've all died."

"Your uncle Charles is still alive, isn't he? What does he say?"

"He says it's all true, but he doesn't know what was in the script. He says he paid attention only to his own part; that was his technique as an actor."

"That's not so unusual." At last here was something plausible. "That's the way Elizabeth Taylor worked, only reading her own lines. But without a script, without anyone who was a part of your 'little group,' how do you know the story's true?"

"You can tell from the movie," he said. "Things that would have been filmed in April, had they been shooting the war-movie script, were obviously filmed in August."

"Such as?" Jill could hear how cool her voice sounded. She was closing herself off, growing too polite, radiating disinterest. She didn't much like herself when this happened, but it was necessary sometimes, a rich girl's classic defense.

"The depot scene," he answered.

In the final version of *Weary Hearts*, Phillip rode with Mosby's Rangers, a Confederate guerrilla troop, only once as they looted and burned a Federal depot. But the original treatment — the "war movie" script Doug was calling it — had Phillip riding regularly with Mosby.

"So surely," Doug said, "the depot scene, as part of the first script, would have been shot in April."

"I'd think so," Jill responded.

"Well, it wasn't. It was shot in August. I know the Valley, I grew up there. I know what April looks like, and I know what August looks like, and that was August."

"Maybe they had to reshoot it for some reason." But as soon as she spoke, Jill knew that she was wrong. The burning depot was the most expensive scene in the movie. They wouldn't have reshot it. Maybe on a *Heaven's Gate* budget, but not on *Weary Hearts'*. Her father might have stood the scene on its ear in the cutting room, but he wouldn't have reshot it.

"So what was the problem with the rough cut?" she asked. "Was it still that McClay did a terrible job?"

"No, just the opposite. It wasn't bad. It was too good. The studio executives, the producer, all said it was too challenging, too innovative, that it just wasn't commercial enough."

So the studio killed the film because it was too good? Jill couldn't believe that.

Things didn't get suppressed because they

were too good. The very literary, arty films might get scant distribution, non-existent promotion, but if they were truly fine, the films did get made. That something was too good was the excuse of people who had written boring screenplays. Agents had a whole vocabulary to avoid alienating new writers. "Too literate" meant a screenplay was too pretentious. "Too well-written" meant it had no plot. "Too intellectual" meant that the characters were uninteresting.

If the rough cut really had been a masterpiece, the studio most likely would have let it go through. They hadn't spent much money; why not take the gamble?

Moreover, if the script really had been something important, her father would have fought to preserve it. Jill was sure of that. He had started his professional life as a professor of English at the University of Virginia. Throughout his life he retained a professor's commitment to history and to the integrity of art.

The memory of his face again filled her mind: his thick silver hair, the narrow aristocratic features. He had had primary custody of her since she had been five, and even after she had moved into her own home, they saw each other regularly, spoke on the phone almost daily. She knew him far, far better than most women knew their fathers. He wouldn't be on the wrong side in a battle like that.

But that was apparently exactly what this Doug Ringling was saying. Not only had Cass edited the final version, he had done so much work on the new script that he had shared the screenplay credit with Bix. John Ransome had been praising Cass for having universalized this routine war movie . . . but if Doug's story was true, Cass had commercialized a masterpiece.

But Doug's story wasn't true. It couldn't be. If the studio executives had gone to a screening of a rough cut to find that an unauthorized script had been shot, they would have fired everyone on the spot. From the producer Miles Smithson on down, everyone involved would have been on the street.

Suddenly Jill could stand it no longer. She was not going to listen anymore. This was a preposterous story, a fiction nurtured by a family who had lost a son. To have a son captured in the war, escape, and then only a few years later be killed in a plane crash along with his brother's wife must have meant grief beyond even hers. Of course, the family would have found it comforting to believe that Bix had written a masterpiece. Jill could understand that, she could forgive it, but she wasn't going to believe it.

She looked at Doug Ringling. It now seemed so odd to have someone who looked like Phillip Wayland sitting behind a big bowl of tulips. Here was a face that promised everything in gallantry and dash on top of an open-necked Oxford cloth shirt, khaki slacks, and a lightweight navy blazer. It was incongruous. No, it was more than that, it was creepy. She wished he hadn't come.

It was easier to speak if she didn't look at him, if she didn't have to think about how much he looked like Phillip. There was a little pattern woven into the oyster damask covering the sofa. She focused on the spot where the pattern disappeared beneath the shoulder of his navy blazer. "If you're asking me if I think this is possible, I don't think it is." She stood up, and he had no choice but to do likewise. She shifted her gaze to the watercolor landscape hanging on the wall directly behind him. "The studios simply had too much control then."

"Well, if you think of anything," he said as he pulled a card out of the side pocket of his blazer, "here's my number."

Jill took the card and walked him to the door, saying good-bye awkwardly. This had seemed so sweet and funny at first, a figure appearing out of the mists of her adolescent dreams. But he had turned out to be a real man with a ridiculous story. Cass would have never done what Doug was accusing him of.

She looked down at the card he had given her. There were two phone numbers, one for day, one for home; they were handwritten on a yellow file card. Who was this Doug Ringling that he didn't carry preprinted business cards?

She moved to the little Queen Anne lady's desk that was along one wall of the tiny foyer. The florist who had brought the tulips into the living room had designed a richly scented bouquet of white auratum lilies and the pale green flowers of a tobacco plant. Its fragrance carried well, giving the air of the foyer a fresher charm than potpourri ever can. But standing close to the bouquet, Jill found its spicy perfume of nutmeg and vanilla a little overpowering.

Why had he come?

As a girl she had managed to block out the fact that other people watched the movie, that others might have felt as strongly about it as she did. She had cherished a myth of exclusivity, enabled by the fact that she usually watched the movie alone in the screening room of her father's big house. The movie was hers; Phillip was hers. When the camera pulled in for a tight close-up, those deep blue eyes were looking at her.

And now Doug Ringling had the nerve to take those same eyes, that same soft lower lip, everything, and parade the whole package around for the world to see.

Perhaps it wasn't fair to blame him for wanting to take his face with him when he went places, but he had alternatives, hadn't he? He could have locked himself into an iron mask as Richard Chamberlain had done in that movie, hiding the key in some place known only to her. Surely that's what any sensitive and gracious man would have done.

Why had he come? To tell her that her father had been a studio hack? *Here, Cass, when you've got a free moment, would you trash this movie? It's great, but we need better box office.* No one would believe that, not for a moment. She pulled open the little desk's single drawer and dropped the card inside. Why was she saving it? His story was so ludicrous. She couldn't imagine that she would ever want to see him again.

Doug Ringling could accept things. That was one thing he knew for sure about himself, that he could look reality in the eye and offer to buy it a beer. You had to be that way, he had always said, when you spent four years hearing that you were one of the finest defensive players in the history of A.C.C. basketball, perhaps in the whole N.C.A.A., and hearing, with the very next breath, that you didn't have a prayer for a pro career.

From eighth grade on Doug had known that however well he played in college, that was going to be it. He could play defense well enough for anyone, but he couldn't shoot up to pro standards. He had always known that. He accepted it.

When the cards had been dealt, Doug had gotten a good hand. He was tall and quick, he was smart, and he looked exactly like his handsome uncle Bix. But the card that gave a fellow the ability to get a round ball through a round hoop had been dealt to someone else.

In its place had come a card labeled "Personality." He was witty, he was articulate. He could lead other men, he could inspire. It was this personality that had made him such a success as a coach of college teams. He had long ago accepted that this had been the trade-off, to play or to coach. Had he been able to stack the deck God had been dealing from, he wouldn't have changed the order of the cards.

So it had taken him about twenty seconds

to accept the fact that Jill Casler did not believe him. It was even more than that; she was uncomfortable, even hostile. That was too bad, he thought as he fastened the seatbelt in his rented car and pulled out of the Holmby Court's elaborately landscaped parking lot. It would have been nice to have her help. But it didn't feel like a major setback, and it certainly wasn't going to stop him. He believed there had been a secret script shot in April, and he was going to find out what was in it. You didn't get to be a head coach at a Division I college by letting other people write the rules.

Declaring a story ludicrous, not worth considering for one instant, was one thing. It was another to forget it. Jill found that she wasted most of the afternoon thinking about Doug's tale. The more she thought, the more insulted she grew on her father's behalf. Doug hadn't accused Cass outright of anything — he had hardly mentioned Cass's name — but she could only infer one thing from what he had said: If the rough cut had been splendid, a true work of art, Cass would have been masterminding the destruction of something fine. She wished Doug had been more direct. She wished he had openly accused Cass. Then she could have defended him.

By evening the concierge had gotten a copy of the *Weary Hearts* video for her. The bell-boy who brought it over offered to help her with the VCR, but Jill had learned at age eight how to use an editing machine. A VCR was nothing.

The bungalow's video equipment was housed in a long, low cherry credenza. Jill slipped the tape in and sat cross-legged on the floor. She pulled one of the small coral-colored pillows on her lap and leaned back against the love seat, watching the screen. The notice from the FBI about video piracy flashed on. Then the well-remembered music rose and the credits began, those familiar names — Miles Smithson, Oliver McClay, Bix Ringling, Charles Ringling, Alicia Burchell — rolled across the sweeping pictures of the Shenandoah Valley, the white clouds, the willows at the river's edge, the woodland hills.

Jill hugged the pillow. She usually loved these credits, the beautiful landscapes with the overture's promise of the bittersweet joys to come. The music always lured her into the movie's magic, enticing her into its world. At least, it always had before. Now, as the rich bass line swelled and the percussion section took up the stern tattoo of horses' hooves, she found herself thinking not about the thundering herd, but about Woody Allen.

He could do it. He could create a dummy script to dupe his money people, then film some other script altogether. He worked in secrecy, barring the press from his sets; he didn't always show the complete script even to the actors.

But Woody Allen had his own production company. He wrote, directed, and starred in his own movies. The studio with which his company had a contract let him work in such secrecy because he always brought his movies in on time and under budget. Then the movies made money. That was the source of his independence. No one else had that kind of control, even today. Certainly no one in 1948 had had it. Back then everyone was an employee of the studio. The studio system was designed to keep track of everything that happened.

Jill looked back at the screen. Booth had already ridden off to join Turner Ashby and the Black Horse Troop. The Yankees had not come yet, but Mary Deas was growing drawn and worried, and Phillip —

Was Doug really taller than Phillip? Yes, of course he was. Jill could see that. And his cheekbones were a shade broader, his jaw just a bit different. Phillip was saddling his horse. Jill peered at his hands, trying to remember Doug's hands.

This was no way to watch the movie. She wasn't involved in the story. She didn't care about the characters. All that interested her about Phillip was his resemblance to Doug. *If he's ruined this movie for me . . .*

She fastforwarded to the depot scene, the one Doug had claimed would prove that the studio's script had not been the one filmed. Jill watched it for a moment and instantly felt vindicated. It proved nothing. Doug Ringling did not know nearly enough about how movies were made.

It is routine for an editor to splice together footage from a number of different takes. Viewers never know to what extent a scene has been pieced together unless a mistake is made. When Judy Garland first meets the Scarecrow in *The Wizard of Oz,* her braids are long. As the two characters talk, her braids suddenly become short. They switch back and forth between short and long throughout the scene. Retakes and pick-up shots of the scene were made several months after the initial filming, and the continuity girl had not noted how long the braids had been first time around.

In *Weary Hearts* the costly exteriors of the burning depot were all night scenes. They showed little of the landscape, whether in

April or August. Only Phillip's postdawn ride back to Briar Ridge showed the trees and fields that Doug claimed dated the filming to August. But the two halves of the episode could have easily been filmed months apart. Doug's "evidence" meant nothing.

Jill hit the reverse button to rewind the tape. There was not one thing to support his story. And so, she told herself for the second time this day, that was the end of that.

Two

Of course, it wasn't. All night Jill repeatedly woke up to the most pointless thoughts. *The director, the continuity girl, and the cameraman would have to know, but if the sets, costumes, and characters' names were the same, would the designer or the sound men need to know?* She kept trying to figure out how someone who wasn't Woody Allen could have done it.

Or why they would have done it. Miles Smithson, the producer of the movie, hadn't had his own production company with a contract to provide the studio with so many movies in so much time. He was an employee of the studio. His office was on the lot; he reported to the executives who could have fired him in an instant.

Everyone involved in a deception such as this would have been risking their careers hourly. No other studio would have hired anyone who had been fired for this kind of duplicity. What could have been in that secret script to make it worth taking such risks? Doug said it was magnificent, but would that have been enough to bind the "little group" into a conspiracy that could have ruined their professional futures?

Assuming, of course, that there had been a conspiracy in the first place. Jill didn't believe so . . . although, for a person who didn't believe, she certainly couldn't keep it out of her mind. At four A.M. she sat up, switched on the bedside lamp, and admitted that she was obsessing.

She was not the sort who usually gave into obsessions. If she lost a filling or had a tooth that ached, she was perfectly able to keep her tongue from probing the pain until she saw the dentist. She really was capable of being very sensible.

It was just, she told herself, that Doug Ringling had caught her at a bad time.

Four weeks ago she had lost her house. It had been a little two-bedroom cottage off Topanga Canyon Road near the Pacific Coast Highway. A towering pile of mud had rumbled down the hillside, uprooting trees, dragging down electric poles, sweeping away two houses, one of which had been Jill's.

She had been out of the country at the time, but her neighbors had alerted her father's office, and his former secretary had sent out a moving crew. With the mud approaching fast, there had been no time to give them instructions. They had saved what they would have saved from their own houses:

43

the stereo, the televisions, the VCRs, all of which were insured and easily replaced. They did get Jill's clothes, her modest accumulation of jewelry, and her father's two Oscars. They left behind her Rolodex, her calendar, and her kitchen drinking glasses, having no way of knowing that these ordinary-looking glasses were startlingly valuable, as they had been used on the set of *Casablanca*. She had inherited them from her father who, decades ago, had roomed with someone who was a prop boy on the *Casablanca* set. Cass's roommate had lifted a box of glasses simply because he had needed glasses, and despite their value to collectors now, that's how Jill had used them, to drink from.

Jill was determined to be all right about having lost her house. She always refused to attach any sentimental importance to objects. Her mother was a compulsive shopper, and, as a result, Jill loathed accumulating things. If there was any woman able to cope with losing most of her belongings, she told her concerned friends, she was.

Nonetheless, it had been an unsettling month. She had had to reconstruct her Rolodex, and almost all her friends — children of the Hollywood famous or celebrities in their own right — had unlisted phone numbers. Losing her calendar had been an even greater problem. Her mother had suggested that she be hypnotized in an effort to remember her appointments. Jill had chosen not to, concluding that if her presence at some event was truly essential, someone would remind her of it.

Life was finally starting to seem normal again, but odd moments would catch her off guard. She would reach for a particular shade of lipstick, then remember it was at the bottom of a huge pile of mud. She would want a certain book, she would picture exactly where it sat on the shelf, she would want to run over to the house and pick it up . . . then she would remember that the house, the shelf, and the book weren't there anymore.

It was a little like after her father died, and she would think about calling him or dropping by the big Bel Air house. Then she would remember and all the hurt would start up again.

Of course, losing her house hadn't been nearly as bad as losing her father, but it hadn't been one of life's better experiences. So it certainly wasn't the best time to hear that someone with the face of a Confederate horseman thought that her father's reputation was undeserved.

The next morning Jill drove to her father's

office. This was not the office of his production company; that had been closed after his death. The two people working in this office had managed Cass's investments during his lifetime and now ran the estate for Jill.

A true Southerner, Cass had believed in land and had plowed every dime he ever made into California real estate. He had two sons by his first marriage, men so much older than Jill that their children were her age, but Cass had provided for them in the punishing settlement made during the bitter divorce from his first wife, Ellen. He did set up some very generous trusts for the grandchildren, whom Ellen had not allowed him to see.

"I'm not going to leave a thing to the boys," Cass had told Jill. "That's what their mother has been telling me for twenty-five years, and I'm not going to disappoint her. I shall leave something to their children, which will make her hopping mad, but if fortune smiles upon us, she will die before me and be spared the agony of knowing that I am capable of doing the right thing."

A glint in his eye suggested that making Ellen mad was half the reason he was setting up these trusts.

So Jill, the only child of his short-lived second marriage, inherited the bulk of his estate. This left her beyond every euphemism of "comfortable" or "independent." She was flat-out rich, way above the ten-to-twenty million dollars of the "moderately wealthy" and solidly in the ranks of the "truly wealthy." She was, on paper at least, a centi-millionaire several times over.

No one observing Jill's life would have a clue that she had so much money. Like almost every truly wealthy American, except for the late Malcolm Forbes, she lived quietly, having neither a yacht nor a private plane, because having yachts and private planes complicated one's life, breeding worries about staffing and logistics. Only the moderately wealthy bought yachts, planes, and flashy jewels. Only the moderately wealthy needed to show off; the truly wealthy had nothing to prove.

This money came from her father. From her mother, Melody, Jill inherited her willowy build. She had a dancer's body — tall, with elegant, tapering fingers and a swan's graceful neck. She had narrow shoulders, and her breasts, waist, and hips moved with lithe, flowing curves. Her legs, identical to her mother's, were her best feature, gloriously long with a line of trim strength behind the glowing, tanned skin. Her height was in her legs, the extra inches naturally giving her the look other women achieved by hiking their leotards up to their hipbones or wearing high heels with their swim suits.

She had her mother's blond hair, which she wore long, sometimes swinging loose, sometimes clipped back at her neck. Facially she resembled neither of her parents. Melody was classically pretty with the even, delicate features of a Greek statue. Jill had a stronger jaw, more definite cheekbones, fuller lips. Her mother's look was delicate, Jill's was engaging. This was consistent with her casual clothes and her informal, friendly manner, both of which disarmed anyone who had gotten his ideas about rich people from the behavior of the merely moderately wealthy. The truly wealthy were often rather nice.

The Casler Properties offices were in a complex of low, Spanish-style buildings a few blocks off the Hollywood Freeway. A red-tiled arch led into a courtyard that had recently been paved over for parking. The space nearest the main door was prominently marked "Reserved for Miss Casler." Somebody else's white Mercedes was parked in it. Jill managed to squeeze her own American-made car between a pair of Porsches that were each angled across two spaces.

Currently employed by the estate were the two people Jill trusted more than anyone on earth. Ken Sommerston, an attorney now more involved with real estate and investments than with the law, was a good-hearted, genial man. The estate's secretary, Lynette Shepherd, had been with Cass longer than either of his two wives. With graying hair twisted into a hairnet at the back of her head and glasses, which she wore suspended from a chain, she looked like a grammar-school librarian, but she was an exceptionally competent woman. Her memory was superb. If Cass had ever told her anything about the making of *Weary Hearts,* she would remember.

Both Ken and Lynette were always delighted to see Jill, having known her since the day she was born. As soon as Jill opened the door to the fourth-floor suite, Lynette, presiding over the outer office from a large mahogany desk, flipped a switch on the intercom. "Ken, Jill's here." Then she came around the desk, holding out her arms.

In a moment Ken was with them, he, too, kissing Jill's cheek. The file folder he was carrying caught in her hair.

Smiling, she untangled herself. "I suppose this is something you want me to sign."

"It's the inventories for the insurance claims." He was filing for her mudslide losses. "Do you want to go over them? See if we've forgotten anything?"

How was she going to do that? Only by picturing in detail each room of her lost home. On the table opposite the front door had been a tiny watercolor framed in gilt, standing on a little easel. Next to it was a vase that her friend Susannah Donovan had given her. Was either of them valuable? Jill didn't know. They had been lovely, that's all she had cared about. What about the arrangement of dried flowers and sea grasses in the vase? Her mother had brought in a florist to design it specifically for the vase; it picked up some of the colors in the painting. Like many things Melody purchased, it had cost the earth. Should that be listed on the claim?

Jill did not want to have to think about each and every one of her lost possessions. Getting every last dime out of the insurance company wasn't worth it. She shook her head. "I'm sure you're close enough."

She sat down on the sofa across from Lynette's desk. She was glad to be there. After taking her to see the empty mudland that had been her house, Ken had planned on bringing her to his own home, but she had asked to come here. The offices felt warm, comforting, full of her father's presence.

Cass had not opened it until he was quite affluent, and the furnishings revealed that. Although the rooms were washed with Southern California's straw-colored light, they were decorated as if they were in Williamsburg or Richmond. The large, square reception room was dominated by a dramatic Jacobean pattern of scarlet and navy flowers on a parchment background. The fabric covered the camelback sofa and the rolled-arm wing chairs; it had also been fashioned into deep fringed swags over the windows. The inner offices had gentler toiles, airy designs of vines, ferns, and birds in white and faded blues.

In the midst of this steady dignity, Doug Ringling's story seemed hardly worth talking about. But Ken and Lynette had taken seats on the wing chairs and were looking concerned, waiting to hear why she had come.

"I wanted to tell you about this visitor I had," she said. "He was a nephew of Bix Ringling. It was the strangest thing, but the nephew looked exactly like him."

"I think we knew about that boy," Lynette said. Even after so many years in California, her accent still whispered of North Carolina. "When the studio was putting on all that whoop-la for the movie's fortieth anniversary, they wanted him to come to the publicity events dressed up like Phillip, but he wouldn't do it. What did he want from you?"

To stomp all over my most cherished fantasies.
"He had an odd story about the movie."
She related it as he had told it, leaving out
any judgments on Cass's role, but even so
she felt a little disloyal. Why was she both-
ering to explore this any further? Why
couldn't she forget it? "I know neither of
you was with Cass then, but did he ever
say anything?"

Ken shrugged. "I don't think so."

Lynette took a moment, but then had to
agree. "He didn't talk to the two of us about
what was happening in the production office.
He certainly didn't say anything about the
movies he had done in the past. He wasn't
one to insist that you admire his work all
the time. But you know we have the files
on that movie over here. Do you want me
to get them?"

That was why Jill had come. For a year
after Cass's death, despite her refusal to become attached to the objects in her own
life, she held on to her father's papers. She
paid for storage space and for someone to
assist the scholars and writers who wanted
to examine the material. But as it became
essential to screen the people with a genuine
critical interest in the papers from those who
wanted to pilfer valuable autographs, Jill was

prevailed on to donate them to the University of Southern California. The Doheny Library there already had Arthur Freed's and Mark Hellinger's papers as well as the MGM script library and the Warner Brothers' production and personnel records.

She secretly wanted to give them to the University of Virginia — she thought Cass might have liked that — but Frank Capra's papers were in Connecticut, David Selznick's were in Texas, Dore Schary's were in Wisconsin. Jill knew that she could best serve the travel budgets of film historians by keeping Cass's papers in California. He himself was always practical about things like that.

She had felt a wrench at turning the papers over and so had thrown her emotions one completely irrational bone — she had kept copies of everything relating to *Weary Hearts* and to *Nancy*. *Nancy* had won Cass his first Academy Award. It was Jill's second favorite of his movies because she had spent so much time with him on its set.

As Cass had produced *Nancy* himself, its files were bulky, covering every aspect of the film, from the story-conference notes through the detailed budgets to the distribution contracts. There was much less material for *Weary Hearts,* as Cass had been an employee of the studio at the time.

So Lynette was able to carry the *Weary Hearts* files back to the conference room in a single armload. She laid them on the glossy table and left Jill alone.

Jill had looked through this material when copies had been made the year before. As she remembered, the only script-related items were a copy of Bix's first treatment, the one that had prompted John Ransome's article, and a copy of the "Script As Shot," a version constructed after the movie had been completed. An "As Shot" script told nothing about the process of making a film; it detailed the result.

Some of Cass's editing notes were in the file, as were drafts of a few of his memos to Miles Smithson. Jill read these carefully, but they were all dated late August and September, after the filming had been completed. There was nothing from the June and July period during which Cass was helping to redraft the script. Jill imagined that that material had been left in the studio files.

She was coming towards the end of the stack of folders. She knew that what remained would be more contemporary, including, for example, the copy of the studio's plan for promoting the video and of the press release in which they announced that they were donating all their original camera negatives on nitrate stock — of which *Weary Hearts* was the best known — to the Library of Congress. The studio's publicity department had forwarded both of those to Cass as a courtesy.

Jill picked up the next folder from the stack and flipped it open without reading the tab. What was inside was structured as a letter to the studio on Cass's letterhead, but it was clearly a multi-page contract. Jill started to read. It was an option contract. On May 24, 1959, Cass had taken out an option on the rights to remake *Weary Hearts*.

Jill stared at the contract. Cass had never been involved in the remake of a movie. He had always had plenty of ideas, plenty of new material. But this contract suggested that he had wanted to film another version of *Weary Hearts*. Jill was astonished; she had had no idea.

She pulled open the conference room door, calling for Ken and Lynette. She held out the contract. "Did you know anything about this?"

Ken took the contract, glancing at it quickly. Lynette moved close to him so that she could see too.

"No," she said, "but we wouldn't have. This was all production office business."

"Do I understand it right?" Jill asked, although she was reasonably confident of her

55

ability to understand a contract. "Cass was thinking about remaking *Weary Hearts*?"

Ken nodded, then moved over to the conference table and looked through the rest of the papers in the open folder. "And he kept renewing it, fifteen, sixteen years, it looks like. He didn't let it lapse until the mid-seventies."

"That wasn't like him," Lynette said flatly. "He didn't tie up money in things he didn't have definite plans for. I do know that much."

"But why did he option it in the first place?" Jill wondered. This was really surprising, Cass thinking about remaking *Weary Hearts*. The mid-seventies . . . John Travolta as Phillip? It didn't bear thinking about. "Can you see remaking that movie?"

"No," Ken answered. "But don't trust me. I was a hundred percent sure that *One Flew Over the Cuckoo's Nest* was the one book that could never be made into a movie. That's why I worked for Casler Properties, not Casler Productions."

Generally there were two good reasons to remake a movie, neither of which Jill could see applying to *Weary Hearts*. Sometimes there was something new to be said about the movie's plot or setting; one reason that *A Star Is Born* kept getting remade was that people kept having new things to say about Hollywood. But if Cass had had something new to say about the Civil War, he had never told Jill about it or mentioned it in any of the interviews he had given — and she had read every one of those.

The other reason for remaking a movie was to improve on the original casting. But just as no one would want a different Rhett Butler, a different Citizen Kane, or a different Rick and Ilsa, so too were the parts of Phillip, Booth, and Mary Deas fixed in people's imaginations. Bix and Alicia had been killed before the movie's release, and Charles, in his grief, had never acted again. With none of the three actors ever appearing on the screen after this movie, they had become the roles, the parts defining them, they defining the parts. Jill would not be the only one who found the idea of recasting a sacrilege.

She was shaking her head, feeling her hair sweep around her shoulders. "I just don't get it."

"Maybe it was that he knew how crazy you were about the movie," Ken suggested. "And he wanted to keep anyone else from remaking it."

"That's a nice idea." And it really was. "But when he first took out this option, I hadn't been born yet. He hadn't even met

Mother. Technically he was still married to Ellen, even though they were separated and she was living in Virginia. Maybe that's it. Do you think he did this because it was his only movie set in the Valley?"

"No," Lynette said bluntly. "Cass was sentimental about a lot of things, but not money. He threw away an awful lot of money on this option over the years. He must have been planning on remaking it. I don't know anything about what prompts a person to remake a movie, but I'd swear that Cass had it in mind."

Jill was more puzzled than ever. She knew her father; his behavior had always seemed consistent, explicable. This was odd. "I'm going to call some of the people who used to work in the production office."

She sat down with Lynette's massive Rolodex and gathered the numbers of former Casler Productions employees. Over the next two days she spoke to all of them, and if any had ever known about Cass's option on these rights, no one remembered. Certainly there had been no significant discussions or plans.

The last person she spoke to was Walt Schneider, a story editor. He confirmed everything the others had said.

"You know the movie," Jill then said to

58

him. "Can you think of any reason to remake it?" This was someone whose narrative imagination her father had trusted.

"Not offhand," Walt confessed. "I don't see how you could update it. You couldn't set it during World War II. It's about staying home with the war on your doorstep. You could go backwards to the War of 1812, which isn't something anyone is the least interested in. Or you could see it in a Vietnamese village. Booth-the-Cong bravely sets out to waste Charlie Company. That would be a real box-office smash, wouldn't it?"

Jill agreed that *Weary Hearts* told from the point of view of the North Vietnamese was not anything she'd wait in line to see.

Of course, if Doug Ringling was to be believed, that was the problem with the movie's first rough cut. Not enough people would have waited in line to see it.

And, in fact, his story did provide the one plausible explanation for Cass's secret interest in remaking the movie.

Cass would have seen every foot of film printed from the April shoot. He would have read every version of every script. If what Bix had written was a masterpiece, Cass would have known.

His option would have included the rights

to all the preliminary material. Perhaps it wasn't the "Script As Shot" that Cass would have remade. Perhaps it was some other script altogether, a script with the same settings, the same characters, a similar plot, but different enough to be thought a masterpiece.

Jill was now determined. She was going to find out if there was any truth to Doug's story.

She would not have persisted had it remained a question about his family, whether or not his uncle Bix had written a masterpiece. As much as she had once idolized the character Bix had played, the question of how good a writer the man himself had been did not feel very urgent to her.

But she cared terribly about what kind of man her father had been. That did feel urgent. Perhaps with time she could have learned to forget Doug's innuendos about Cass's character. But what was going to explain why, year after year, her father had quietly renewed the option to make the movie? And why, after fifteen years of renewals, he had stopped?

She wanted answers.

"So did you meet her? Did you actually lay eyes on her? Does she really exist?"

Doug dropped his suitcase down on the

worn linoleum floor. He knew that Randy's first question would be about Jill. "I met her. I laid eyes on her. She really does exist."

"Does she look as good as her pictures?" Randy asked, even though he had been in the midst of a phone call when Doug had come into the kitchen of the old farmhouse the two of them shared.

"Much better."

"Is she as rich as they say?"

"Now, how on earth could I know that?"

Jill, although only a few weeks older than Randy, was his aunt, his father's half-sister. Randy had never met her; Randy's father was the only one in the family who had. Nonetheless, the Casler family were all enormously interested in her. She had gone to the Academy Awards with the actor Payne Bartlett this year and had had a total of four seconds of camera time. A video tape of the hours-long ceremony had been passed up and down the Shenandoah Valley so that everyone could watch those four seconds in slow motion. It was fun to be related to a person who went to the Academy Awards.

But Doug had always suspected that the Caslers were perfectly happy to be related to Jill without bearing the burden of actually knowing her. She was rich; everyone she knew was famous. Who didn't assume, in some secret corner of the heart, that the rich and famous would not be very interested in one's own little self? Even Doug, who had had his own share of fame — although notoriety was probably the more apt term — had put off visiting the wealthy Aunt Jill until the end of his stay in California.

"Tell me everything," Randy went on. "You might as well practice on me. You know your sisters will hang you by your heels until they get it all out of you."

"Why don't you finish your phone call first?"

"Oh." Randy looked down at the open receiver in his hand. "It's just my mother." He put it back to his ear. "Sorry, Ma, I got to go. Doug's back." He listened for a moment, then held out the receiver. "She wants to talk to you."

Obediently Doug crossed over to the phone, forcing himself to keep a blank expression. He found Randy's mother very hard to take. Her speciality in life was putting other people in the wrong.

"Douglas." Louise Casler's voice was cool. "How was your trip?"

"Very pleasant, ma'am."

"I heard Randy ask you about his father's sister. I suppose she was quite curious about the family."

"No, not a bit," Doug was pleased to report. As far as he could tell, she was oblivious to them. He had told her that he was from the Valley; it had not occurred to her to ask if he knew any of her relations. They might think about her all the time, but she did not seem to ever think about them.

"Well," sniffed Louise. "What kind of manners is that? Not to ask after your own family? I hope my children would acquit themselves better than that."

"I'm sure they would." A conversation with Louise was never over until she was clearly in the right, so Doug always aimed to put her in the right just as quickly as possible.

"I suppose you spent all the time talking about the movie," she said, as if that were some grave lapse on Doug's part instead of the actual purpose of his trip.

"Yes, but she didn't know anything."

"I don't know why you thought she would."

"I don't either, ma'am," Doug answered. "I don't either."

"I don't imagine that her father was a very communicative parent."

"I suppose not," Doug agreed.

How Louise could have known one thing about Cass Casler's parenting, Doug didn't

63

have a clue, but he had seen Jill's face when she had spoken about her father. Cass might not have been a communicative parent, but he certainly had been loved.

Actually, Doug was disappointed by how little Jill had known about the movie . . . how little everyone had known about it. He had gone out to California with the notion that a rough cut was like a draft of a manuscript, something that could be preserved intact. But apparently there was a single "work print" that the editor cut and slashed; it changed every day. Parts of the version of *Weary Hearts* that the studio executives had rejected would have been incorporated into the final film.

So what happened to the parts that they didn't use? he had asked.

No one seemed to know for sure.

The movie had been made only forty years ago. Forty years wasn't all that long in Virginia. His grandmother probably had stuff in her deep-freeze that was older than that. But it turned out that forty years was a lot longer in California than it was in Virginia.

So he had gone to Jill.

But she wasn't going to help. And there was no reason why she should, why anyone should. His own family had lived with Grandfather's story for years; none of them had ever thought to investigate. Doug hadn't either, until this spring. It had never upset him that Bix's talent had gone unacknowledged, that he was known only as an actor, not a writer. Sure, it had seemed a shame, but not nearly so much a shame as was his death, and there wasn't a thing to do about that.

Then, this spring, Doug's own reputation had crashed, splattering itself across every sports page in the nation. He had come to the Valley with nothing to do. He started helping Randy with his poultry business. It wasn't bad work. He liked physical labor, he enjoyed learning about Randy's high-tech equipment, but he was used to coaching college basketball, a job that consumed every breath, every hour. He needed more of a goal.

The old family stories about *Weary Hearts* kept flitting through his mind as he watched the little conveyor belts chug by with their string of warm, smooth white eggs. With his own reputation lost, it seemed a real crime that Bix hadn't had more of a chance to establish his own. Suddenly this came to seem like something Doug could do for him, this uncle whom he had never known, this uncle whom he so resembled. Doug could reclaim Bix's achievement, he could insist that the truth be told. He could do for Bix what he was unable to do for himself.

Outside the master bedroom of Jill's bungalow was a small flagstone patio set off from the hotel grounds by a low white railing and a screen of lush plantings. Jill always preferred being outdoors, so on the morning after she had talked to her father's story editor, she carried the bedroom phone out to the patio, clipped it into the outside jack, and sat down at the glass-topped café table. She was going to spend the day on the phone.

She was not indulging in idle gossip. Although Jill did not have to support herself, she led a busy, productive life. She had considerable abilities. Although not blessed with her father's narrative gifts or his visual imagination, she did have his sense of structure. She could instantly discern how something was organized and, almost as quickly, identify what in that particular system was not working properly. She was systematic, thorough, and efficient. Had she not inherited three high-rise office buildings and the land under two shopping malls, she could have earned her living as the office manager of a big, expensive law firm full of tense lawyers and cantankerous clients. She would have done a splendid job.

As talents went, it was not a magnificent one, but it was hers, and, driven by her British nanny's stern precepts against idleness, she put it to good use.

She had a very large circle of friends. Those she had grown up with were, like herself, the children of important and powerful film-industry figures. Others were people she met through them — young writers, actors, and producers, all determined to become important and powerful film-industry figures in their own right.

So it was an interesting, animated group. It was not the sanest. There were some pretty high-strung characters; someone was always in some crisis or another. And when there was a crisis, people called Jill.

She was good at calming everyone down. Earlier in the spring an actress on location in Kenya had been about to walk off the set. Jill knew both her and the director. With the production blasting through its budget, the director asked Jill to come out to Kenya and talk to Alexandra. Jill did. She knew a lot about psychology, having done considerable reading on the subject since her father's death, and with her eye for structure, she was able to see that on this particular set the lines of communication were structured all wrong. People who should have been colleagues had slipped into parent-child roles. Jill would have never dreamed of offering a diagnosis of other people's emotional blind spots, but she said enough that the movie got made.

She was good at getting things done. Many of the girls she had gone to school with were now in the young-Hollywood-wives set and were active in charity work. Jill sat on the boards of several small foundations. She was of greater service when people attempted things beyond their skills. Last night she had gotten a call from some friends who were organizing a big outdoor AIDS rally and fund-raiser. They had never done anything like this before, and they were desperately behind schedule.

Jill had helped such friends often enough before that she had all the skills and contacts of a professional fund-raiser or event coordinator. She spent six determined hours on the phone, arranging for permits, contracting for security forces and portable toilets, browbeating sign painters and musicians, accomplishing more than her friends had in weeks.

She spent another hour reading drafts of the minutes from the meetings of two boards she was on. Then her attention was free for *Weary Hearts*. With the same organized thoroughness that she usually brought to other people's projects, she made a list.

She called John Ransome, the author of the article that had apparently sparked Doug Ringling's search. Ransome might well have heard hints and rumors about the rough cut, none of which he could substantiate well enough to print.

But he hadn't. He was friendly and forthcoming; no freelance journalist specializing in film would want to alienate the daughter of an important director. But the only surprise he had for Jill was that Doug Ringling had called him before visiting her.

She wasn't entirely sure how she felt about that. "What did you think about his story?"

"His story?"

Ransome sounded bewildered. Jill realized that she had spoken rashly. "Why did he say he called?"

"He said that he was a nephew of the two brothers, and he was curious about the script for the April shoot. A *Roots* sort of thing. It sounded like normal family curiosity to me."

So Doug hadn't told Ransome about the secret script. Jill wondered why.

She looked at the list of questions she had jotted down before making this call. "Your article said that the studio has lost the script shot in April." Studios tended to do things like that. "Did you look for any of the footage from the rough cut?"

"I checked the card files," he answered. "There wasn't a thing, but I didn't expect there to be."

"What about the paperwork — the budgets, the schedules, and the contracts, all that?" Jill asked. Without the script or any of the actual footage, the best evidence of whether the approved script or some secret one had been filmed might be in the paperwork. Certainly the documents would all have to superficially conform to what would have been generated by the approved script. Much of it might have even been fake; dummy schedules and dummy budgets created to fool whoever needed to be fooled. But some of it had to be real. If Oliver McClay had filmed the cavalry battles that were mentioned in the treatment but not used in the final movie, then somewhere there were invoices for renting all those horses. If no one paid for horses who can die on command, then the scenes wouldn't have been filmed. "Did you go through any of that material?"

"Lord, no." John Ransome was unapologetic. "What a bore that would be. This was a pay-by-the-word article, not my life's work."

Jill agreed with this, too. Looking at the

paperwork would be boring, but it was a chore she was prepared to undertake. She was also planning on duplicating his examination of the studio's card files. Those files were supposed to list the location of each reel of stored film, giving both the vault and shelf numbers, but those files were never accurate. Ransome's quick check easily could have missed something.

A number of searches for film footage had been undertaken in recent years. In the best-known cases, the missing footage had been trimmed out of a finished film because the movie was too long. Exhibitors wanted to be able to run two shows a night so *A Star Is Born, Lawrence of Arabia,* and *Lost Horizon,* among others, had been cut after their premieres. These cuts had been made by someone with economic rather than artistic goals. The result was often a choppy film with inexplicable references to scenes that had been dropped. It was hardly surprising that people who loved movies wanted to restore these mutilated films to their original full-length splendor. Their passion — their obsession — was something Jill had always sympathized with.

Sometimes rumors grew up around scenes that had been filmed, but not used in the final film. For years people had whispered that the "Jitter Bugs" number had been cut from *The Wizard of Oz* because that old vaudeville ham, Bert Lahr, playing the Cowardly Lion, had been so marvelously funny that no one watching it would have ever looked at Judy Garland. What fan of vaudeville would not want to see that footage?

What John Wayne fan wouldn't want to see the half-hour taken out of *The Alamo?* And who wouldn't want to see the "masterpiece" version of *Weary Hearts?*

But such desires were rarely gratified. Jill knew that Ronald Haver had spent a month looking through the Warner Brothers vaults searching for the twenty-seven minutes from *A Star Is Born.* He found a complete sound track, but he had not been able to find very much of the film. In the end he had to remount the production using the long sound track, filling in the missing visuals with stills and even some new photographs.

The restorers of the full-length *Lawrence of Arabia* had the opposite result. After hunting through four hundred pounds of unlabeled footage, they had found the film, but not the sound track. The edited scenes did not correspond to the script so the restorers had hired a hearing-impaired couple to lip-read the footage and had the now-aging actors rerecord the lines. Then a sound engineer remixed their voices to restore them to youth.

But as incomplete as these searches had been, at least those people had been looking for material cut from finished movies. Finding raw footage was even more unlikely. The "Triumphal Return" sequence from *The Wizard of Oz,* during which Dorothy had the others return to Oz with the witch's broomstick, had been cut early in the editing process. None of that footage survived. The "Jitter Bugs" number had been cut after the first preview. Although it had taken five weeks and eighty thousand 1938 dollars to film, all that has ever been found was the sound track and a home movie taken by the composer. At least that was enough to show Bert Lahr had not stolen the scene from Judy Garland.

Jill knew that the chances of anything surviving from the rough cut of *Weary Hearts* were even more remote.

Since television started buying feature films, some producers saved a little more footage in case the movie had to be recut for length or moral concerns. Then, for the few years when the "Bleepers and Bloopers" shows were popular on television, footage that showed major stars making embarrassing mistakes was saved. But, for the most part, the pounds and pounds of film left over from a production were junked.

For any excess footage to have survived for the forty years since *Weary Hearts* had been made would have been extraordinary indeed.

Nonetheless, Jill was going to look. She had to.

Three

A visit to the studio was in order. Jill flipped though her reconstructed Rolodex, trying to think of someone she knew who worked there. She knew any number of people working on pictures the studio was financing, but she didn't seem to know anyone on the payroll. She had last year. She probably would again next year. But at the moment, she didn't.

Except Cathy Cromartie.

Well, why not? The rule was, that if you met someone outside of group, you had to tell the group about it. That was all.

So Jill called Directory Assistance and got the number of the studio's main switchboard in order to call a fellow member of her psychotherapy group.

She had not been lying when she told Doug that she was a reasonably well-adjusted person. She believed that. And part of being well adjusted was having the sense to realize that when your mother was the sort who couldn't take a Children's Chewable Tylenol without getting addicted to it, that when you had been in the legal custody of a father who, however adoring, had been away on location for weeks at a time, then you might have a few problems.

These few problems had started getting the better of Jill during the first year after her father's death. Her grief had caused something in her psychological navigational system to tilt. Behavior previously unremarkable had become extreme, and finally her friend Susannah Donovan, no stranger to psychotherapy, had put a label on it: "extreme caretaker-ism."

Of all her qualities, Jill had always most valued her loyalty. She was an excellent friend. Most of the projects she spent her time on resulted from pleas from her large circle of friends.

But in the year after Cass's death something had gone wrong. Helping people was exhausting her; she was turning into Horton the Elephant of Dr. Seuss's books. Like Horton, Jill would have sat on the top of a tree through rain and snow, hatching someone else's egg.

She had become unable to say "no." She tried to do everything anyone asked her, but still it seemed like no one was ever satisfied; no one ever thought she had done enough. If she spent eight hours serving dinners to the homeless, why not ten, why not twenty? If she gave ten thousand dollars to a drug abuse program, why not fifteen, why not a million? Everyone had his hand out, wanting her time and her money.

Both Susannah and her mother, the only ones seemingly aware of what was happening to her, had urged therapy. Primarily because she wanted to show them that she wasn't closed-minded, she had a session with a therapist who had immediately recommended she join a group.

It had begun disastrously. She was almost immediately sucked into the bewildering vortex of one member's troubles. This young man was a terrible procrastinator. After her second session, Jill had sat in a coffee shop with him and helped him fill out a job application form, virtually doing it herself. That simple favor — such was her definition of the act — had been an open door to unceasing demands. He wanted help balancing his checkbook. He needed to find new car insurance. He needed someone to call his boss and say he was sick.

Jill instead called the therapist to quit the group. "I don't need this. This is what I'm trying to get away from."

"Ah . . . but, Jill," came the irritating answer, "this is the point."

Indeed it was. Group therapy was not a gathering of seven people each waiting their turn to talk about their current life problems. The group focused on the group itself, on what happened inside that room during those ninety-minute sessions. The assumption was that a member would, given enough time, react to the people in the group as he reacted to the people in his "back-home" social sphere. The therapist and other group members would help him understand this behavior, and then, within the safe confines of the meeting room, he could try to alter it.

Jill had to admit that how quickly she had turned herself into Horton the Elephant did confirm the first stage of the process. So she thought she ought to stay with it and explore the rest.

She had been in the group for more than a year now, and she could see the difference in herself. Had she lost her calendar during her Horton the Elephant stage, she would have been so agitated about disappointing the people who were expecting her to be certain places at certain times that she probably would have had herself hypnotized. Therapy had also helped her recover the warning system that alerted her to people who were snakes and users. Although she still was not great at saying no, she had learned to reframe the questions people asked her. "I certainly could do what you are asking, but my skills are organizational. Perhaps I can help you in that way instead."

She had joined the group on the same day as Cathy Cromartie, another woman also in her late twenties. At that first meeting the two newcomers had sat side by side. They never had again. Jill did not dislike Cathy, not at all, but the dynamics of the group had set up a polarity between them. The contrast had been too strong. Cathy was tiny, dark-haired, quivering with tension, a simmering kettle threatening to explode into a furious boil. Compared to her, Jill was a cool, long-stemmed lily.

The group met at one o'clock. Cathy, an associate vice-president in the studio's production department, came in her business clothes; she wore vibrant power colors and dramatic accessories. As small as she was, Cathy was an intimidating presence. She looked like someone with power. Jill, whose wealth could have given her considerable power if she had wanted it, dressed casually. She was never sloppy or ill-groomed; she might wear an open-necked Egyptian cotton shirt over an eight-gore twill riding skirt clenched at the waist with a wide leather belt, or cuffed silk trousers with a chunky handknit sweater. Her clothes were every bit as expensive as Cathy's; when you're five feet ten with size-six shoulders and hips, expensive clothes fit better. Otherwise the shirt cuffs stop about two inches before your arms do. But her clothes were so understated that their quality was apparent only in the details of construction: the wide, beautifully finished seams, the careful linings, and the fine sheen of the fabrics. Her sweaters had intricate handknit patterns, and her blouses had covered buttons. The pockets of her skirts were never economically set into the side seams. They were moved in a few inches and carefully bound and welted into a slit in the body of the skirt itself. With the pockets placed there, the wearer could tuck her hands and her keys into her pockets without adding eight inches to the silhouette of her hips.

So the rest of the group often reacted to these two expensively dressed young women through the contrast between them. Jill knew that she was popular and influential at Cathy's expense, something she felt rather bad about. This was exactly the sort of thing that a member was supposed to bring up during the group sessions, but so far she hadn't and Cathy hadn't either. Jill had long since noticed that what she and Cathy had in common was much more important than their physical differences. Neither one wanted to be the focus of any of the group's discussion.

Asking for Cathy got Jill through the studio's switchboard; a brief mention of her interest in *Weary Hearts* got her through Cathy's secretary; her name got her through Cathy's assistant and to Cathy herself.

"Jill, this is a surprise." Cathy's voice sounded wary.

Jill could understand that. If someone in the group were to call her, she would be uneasy; even Horton the Elephant might pause before climbing a second tree. "I know," she responded, trying to keep her voice light. *This is no big deal; don't worry.* "I need to ask you a professional favor."

"Yes?"

"I have some questions about the making of *Weary Hearts*. I wanted to prowl around a bit and I wondered if you could open a few doors for me."

"What kind of questions?"

That was an entirely legitimate response. Cathy would be crazy to open doors when she was unclear about Jill's mission. But her question put Jill in a bind.

One of the rules of group was honesty. You were not supposed to lie. Jill obeyed that rule faithfully. She didn't tell the whole truth — not even close — but she told nothing but the truth.

Had anyone else asked her, she would have told one of the assorted half-truths that she had told Ken and Lynette, John Ransome, and the people on Cass's production staff. But she found it suddenly hard to lie to Cathy, even over the phone.

No wonder some groups had a "no outside contact" rule. The rules of the group, its honesty and constant self-scrutiny, were too difficult to sustain in normal human contact.

"It's complicated, but basically a member of the Ringling family has raised some questions about what was in the first rough cut. I can tell you the whole story if you want."

"No, that's all right," Cathy said so quickly that Jill felt like she understood the position she had inadvertently put Jill in. "What do you need me to do?"

"I want to see if there's any footage surviving from the film and I'd like to look at the production files."

"That shouldn't be any problem. Remind me what year the picture was made."

Jill did, and as if they were two ordinary acquaintances, they set a time for Jill to come to the studio the next afternoon.

Cathy's office was a study in feminine

power. The glass slab she used as a desk was sparklingly clean and imposingly empty; it bore only a long, low almond-colored phone and a single file folder. The lacquered credenza behind the desk had a dramatic, almost spiky, arrangement of Peruvian lilies, statice, and viburnum in a marble pedestaled bowl. There was not a family picture anywhere. What clearly marked it as a woman's office were not the flowers, but the color of the walls and the chairs; they were a cool, clear lavender-blue, almost the color of delphiniums.

Cathy's secretary had escorted Jill into the office. Cathy herself was standing behind her desk, her fingertips pressed against its glass surface. Jill had always found her tightly wrapped intensity a little jarring in therapy; she seemed to radiate an unhappiness that she refused to talk about. But here, in her own gleaming office, the intensity seemed appropriate; it came across as energy, purpose, ambition.

"It was nice of you to fit me into your schedule," Jill said. "But first, I want to tell you, I adore this color."

"Do you?"

"Yes. It's feminine without being girlish. It's — " Jill stopped herself from saying "It's great." She didn't want to sound like she was waltzing in here to give Cathy's office the *Good Housekeeping* Seal of Approval. She knew Cathy wouldn't take well to that. "I really do like it."

Cathy waved Jill to a chair and sat down herself. The chair behind her desk had the high back of an executive's but she must have had it custom made in a smaller size. She was not dwarfed by it. Even the black leather sling chairs they sat in during group made her look tinier than she was. In a normal man's executive chair, she would have seemed like a child playing at Daddy's desk.

Jill was grateful that nothing in her life required her to be so image-conscious. When you had several hundred million dollars, you had several hundred million dollars, and it didn't matter what kind of chair you sat in.

Cathy opened the folder on her desk and handed a sheet of paper to Jill. "I asked someone to check the card file on *Weary Hearts*. This is the footage that's in the nitrate vault."

Jill had not expected Cathy to have this information in hand. She took the sheet. It was a computer printout listing by vault number and shelf space the location of every can of nitrate film with *Weary Hearts* material. There were the master positives, a few prints of the complete movie, some copies of the trailers, which were the previews of the movie shown as "Coming Attractions," and a copy of the French version of the credits. As expected, there were no outtakes, no footage marked as trims or cuts, not even a reel labeled "Miscellaneous." For such material to have been stored for fifty years would have been unusual in the extreme.

"I didn't go down to the vaults," Cathy said. "So I have no idea if any of the film is still good."

Another reason why it was unlikely for any of the movie's excess footage to have survived was that prior to the early 1950s, all film was printed on nitrocellulose-based stock, which was highly flammable and chemically unstable. Nearly half of all movies made before 1950 no longer existed in any viewable form, their nitrate film having first turned to a thick, smelly goo and then a fine brown powder. The film manufactured during the forties was particularly unstable, due to chemical shortages caused by the war. Movies such as *Weary Hearts* were seen only because they had been transferred to the safety film now used universally.

"I didn't expect you to," Jill assured her. "I'm impressed that the card file is on computer. My experience with card files is that they are just that, tattered file cards full of lies about what's where."

"The files for the other vaults are pretty inaccurate." Cathy admitted. "But apparently about ten years ago — I just learned all this this morning — after the original camera negative to *Citizen Kane* burned, we turned over all our original nitrate negatives to the Library of Congress. So some outside archivists went through all the nitrate vaults to see what we had, and they organized it. The stuff might all blow tomorrow, but at least it would be burnt in alphabetical order."

Jill was surprised that the records for the vaults had been so recently updated. "This is pretty impressive for a studio that can't even keep track of its scripts."

"Oh, don't think the studio did this," Cathy assured her. "You have your father to thank."

"My father?"

"The studio never would have paid to have this catalogued. The Library of Congress and the American Film Institute wanted them to, but no one around here was that generous-minded. So your father did some quick fund-raising among his friends, and they set up a little fund that paid for the archivists to find out what we had."

Jill hadn't known this, but it was not out of character. Cass had been one of the few history-minded people in Hollywood. This was exactly the sort of thing that would have interested him.

But still, this was all getting curiouser and curiouser. Anyone wanting to help preserve Hollywood's legacy had a choice of any number of truly urgent projects. Given that the studio had taken steps to preserve the original camera negatives, it would have seemed that Cass and his friends might have spent their money to better effect.

Perhaps he, too, had been looking for *Weary Hearts* footage.

Whatever his motives had been, he had hired these archivists and they would have been good ones — film scholars deeply grateful for the chance to catalogue a studio's collection of miscellanea before it deteriorated. If they said there was no miscellaneous footage from *Weary Hearts,* then Jill was willing to accept that.

Cathy went on. "I also called to see what we had on safety stock, and there's only copies of the complete film and some foreign language trailers."

"That's what I would have guessed."

"Here's something that may surprise you then." Cathy leaned back in her chair. Other people tended to deliver dramatic news by coming forward, moving closer. Not Cathy. Jill had noticed that during one of the group's protracted discussions of body language. "There's next to nothing in the script library and all the production files are missing."

"What?" Jill had known about the script library, but the production files? This was where she had expected to find the budgets, the footage counts, all the material that would prove what script had been shot. "Have all the files from that era been destroyed?"

"No, we have more storage space than the other studios, so we've held onto the production files. But there's nothing there from *Weary Hearts*."

"Nothing? Isn't that odd?"

"Yes. But sometime in the fifties someone was interested in the rights — "

Jill knew who that was.

" — and my guess is the files were pulled then, and they didn't get put back. Or they could have been misfiled any time in the last forty years."

Jill nodded and Cathy went on. "Legal does a better job of keeping track of itself. Its *Weary Hearts* files are right where they belong. You're welcome to go look at them." She handed Jill a card with a name and phone extension. "They're expecting you."

Jill took the card. "Cathy . . . thank you. I wasn't expecting you to do all this. Didn't it take you hours?" Jill knew the premium

Cathy placed on time.

"Actually, no. I was assuming it would, but just last week some guy was through with the same set of questions."

Some guy? Jill drew back. "He wasn't named Doug Ringling, was he?"

"I don't know," Cathy confessed. "Apparently whoever it was used to be some hotshot college basketball player, and I wasn't interested in getting involved in an endless discussion about college basketball. The clerk in Legal — "

She broke off, embarrassed. One of her issues in group was her tendency to write off other people too quickly, assuming that they could have no value to her.

Jill wasn't going to respond. This wasn't group; Cathy was entitled to some emotional privacy. Anyway, Jill's own reactions weren't anything she wanted scrutinized.

For the past few days she felt as if she had been rediscovering a trail her father had laid years before. Optioning those rights, paying to have the nitrate vaults catalogued, all that was curious, important because he had done it. Her quest felt urgent, a secret journey into a mysterious land whose dark map only she could ever read.

This was what she felt. But the reality was that she was following a trail made by a former hotshot college basketball player with a face that should have been locked in an iron mask.

"What about stock footage?" she asked Cathy. Surely that was something Doug wouldn't have known to ask about.

In only one case was unused or excess footage saved for more than six months. That was when the studio thought that some other production might be able to use it. Shooting crowd scenes and location exteriors was expensive. If a shot of such scenes did not show any of the principal actors, it might be used in a later movie. So, after a film was completed, the unused footage was sent over to the stock footage department, which examined it, saving anything that might be of use. Stock footage material incorporated into a film made after 1952 would have been printed up on safety film.

"I didn't think about that," Cathy said. "Let me check."

She picked up the receiver of her almond phone with one hand, unclipping her disc-shaped earring with the other. She said a few words, then waited while the call was placed. When the connection was made, she identified herself and asked if a friend of hers could come over and look at any footage they had from *Weary Hearts*. She listened for a moment, then covered the mouthpiece with her hand. Her nails were beautifully manicured, lacquered with a rich burgundy.

"They don't have anything," she said. "Not even a catalogue entry."

"What?"

"Nothing, zero, nada. The outtakes must not have been sent over."

"Are they sure?"

"Oh, yes." Cathy's half-smile was gentle, amused. "Our hotshot basketball player was over there last week."

Jill made a face while Cathy thanked the person on the other end of the phone. As Cathy clipped her earring back in place, Jill spoke. "Isn't that odd? Wouldn't you think the battle scenes and the rides of Mosby's Rangers" — this was all material supposedly deleted from the first script — "would be worth saving?" If it had been filmed in the first place.

"I suppose. You may know more about this than I do. Maybe it just fell through the cracks. Remember, this wasn't Warner Brothers."

That was true. Warner Brothers was the studio that made the trains run on time. Everything was put on paper. People at Warner Brothers clocked in, took regularly scheduled coffee breaks, and generally kept

91

track of themselves.

But this studio had had more in common with Universal. Time and again films went into production without budgets, continuity scripts, or even complete casts. Worried about their next projects, producers had no choice but to leave directors alone. The dislike of paperwork, the disregard for routine, and the resulting chaos allowed for the spontaneous creativity that marked the best of the studio's films. Those conditions also permitted some large-scale disasters.

And what about large-scale deception? Jill still couldn't imagine how a director could dupe a studio about what script he was filming, but an atmosphere of total confusion would be a good first step.

She thanked Cathy, silently deciding that a birds-of-paradise arrangement would be an appropriate thank-you gesture, and set off for the legal department.

On March 10, 1948, the legal department had read the Estimating Script of *Weary Hearts* and had memoed Miles Smithson with two single-spaced pages of concerns. The British Board of Censors, for example, always deleted quotations from the Lord's Prayer. Smithson would either have to have the dialogue on page fifty-nine rewritten or have Oliver McClay shoot alternative protection for Great Britain.

These two pages told Jill nothing. The legal department certainly would have read the approved script; there was no chance the lawyers had been involved in the deception.

On August 2, 1948, the department advised Smithson that on page eighty-seven of a script marked "Revised and Final: Make No Changes," the line "I wish to *God*," should be changed to "I wish to *heaven*."

Jill thought. Yes, about a third of the way through the movie, Phillip said, "I wish to heaven."

The only interesting thing about these files was that they weren't musty. They had probably been aired out a week ago by a former hotshot college basketball player.

Now that Jill had visited her father's old studio, seen his lawyer and secretary, and talked to the people on his production staff, thoroughness compelled her to see only one other person who had known him: her mother.

Melody had been Cass's second wife. His first wife he had known since childhood; they had grown up in the Valley together. Jill had never met Ellen Casler, but knew that she had come from a good Winchester family, that she had attended Stuart Hall and had graduated from Sweet Briar. After this proper upbringing, she had married Cass and had settled with him in Charlottesville.

She had been content to be the wife of a University of Virginia English professor. Life in Charlottesville had been quiet, she had known everyone she had needed to know, she had understood the standards.

But after Pearl Harbor a bad knee had kept Cass out of combat. He had been sent to the Office of War Information in New York, where he first wrote and then edited training films. Handling film had been, to Cass, everything that "gay Paree" had been to other soldiers. After that there was no bringing him back to the farm, even if that farm was the elegant university founded by Thomas Jefferson.

Ellen had, of course, gone to California with him, but she had not been comfortable there. Hollywood had had a different set of rules, rules that Ellen did not believe in. A Hollywood hostess thought that she should never serve the same menu twice. Ellen could not understand that. Her mother had never given a party without serving Aunt Sally's peanut soup, and there wasn't a soul in Winchester who would have wanted her to.

And the people in California had altogether

too much money. Ellen's grandmother had been born in 1867, and at that time in Virginia the nice people *never* had money. The movie business was suspiciously full of talented immigrants' sons, and her husband was turning out to be every bit as talented and energetic as these dark-haired men with their long, strange names. She did not approve.

So, after three years of such a life, Ellen had taken her two boys and gone home. For more than a decade she and Cass had lived separately. She was still Mrs. William Casler, treated with respect, enjoying a far nicer income than any other nice lady in Winchester.

She thought that Cass would eventually come home, but at age fifty-one, he suddenly demanded a divorce. The distinguished, Yeats-loving former professor was going to marry nineteen-year-old Melody Johnson. Melody was not from a good Virginia family. She had not gone to Stuart Hall; she did not have a degree from Sweet Briar. What she had was the best pair of legs in Las Vegas.

A year after Melody and Cass married, Jill had been born. Five years later they were divorced. Melody had moved out of the Bel Air house; Jill had stayed.

Jill knew that it was unfair to say that

her mother had given up custody of her. The accurate statement was larger: Melody had given up.

Cass had been determined to keep Jill, this delicious golden-haired child who lived in clouds of baby powder, white ribbon-threaded dresses, and stuffed bears. With her silver-handled mother-of-pearl teething ring and her bright pink plastic Brady Bunch lunch box had come the sweet pleasures of late-life fatherhood. Cass had let his two sons go back to their native land; this daughter he was keeping.

There had never been any question of attacking Melody, of threatening to prove her an unfit mother. Cass was too gentlemanly for that, and his lawyers too clever. An attack might have roused the defensive lioness in even the frail and shaken Melody.

Cass's silver-haired attorneys, in their white shirts and dark pinstriped suits, had sat across a long table and done something much more devastating. They asked Melody to speak for herself.

"By what criteria would you select her schools, Mrs. Casler? What type of curriculum do you prefer? Who do you envision being her peer group? How do you propose to cope with the psychological ramifications of divorce?"

And poor Melody, who believed the only thing valuable about her were her legs, had given up. Those legs might have gotten her out of the trailer park she had grown up in, but they weren't going to analyze curriculum for her.

Melody had not given herself enough credit. Of course she could have chosen a school. She had taught herself to dress, she had furnished a Bel Air home, she had learned to converse with writers and producers, she had developed taste and acquired interests, all from reading fashion magazines and watching other people. She had, Jill now knew, an enormously retentive mind with an unerring capacity to distinguish between essence and effect.

As much as Jill understood this, she also knew that she had been better off in her father's care. Her mother would have been a fine parent during her good periods, but Melody had an addictive personality. During Melody's bad times Jill would have suffered terribly.

Melody was currently in one of the good periods. Having married two father-figures — the husband after Cass had been George Norfolk, a federal judge — she was, at age 47, married to a son — Dodger third baseman David Ahearn, who was only six years older than Jill.

The previous summer David had embarked on a hitting streak that hadn't ended until he had tied Pete Rose. For all of David's twelve years in the majors, the pressure and the media were almost too much for him. This brought out the best in Melody. She had been wonderful, traveling with David, making his world private and comfortable. Anything she asked for during those long road trips the Dodger organization gave her. They knew she was essential to keeping the streak alive.

This, much more than her stunning legs, was the basis of Melody's appeal to men. She made them comfortable. A gifted director, a well-respected judge, and an intelligent, articulate athlete had found her irresistible.

But she set too high standards for herself. It wasn't possible to make everything in someone else's life perfect. When she couldn't, she believed herself to be failing. She couldn't forgive herself, she couldn't make a few corrections and go on. She would instead turn herself into what she, at heart, believed herself to be: a woman valuable only for her legs.

Jill knew the pattern well. It would start with shopping. Melody would be drawn to a dress, but couldn't decide whether to buy it in amber, periwinkle, or ivory-on-ivory. She would buy them all and then never take them out of the trunk of her car. She, whose body was so easy to fit, would buy suede suits that needed to be altered, even completely recut. Then she would forget to pick them up from the store. She would buy new linens for all her beds and store them, forever unopened, in her linen closets. Her garage would be lined with boxes of dishes and cookware, still in their original packagings.

As soon as Jill could drive, she would spend Saturday mornings at her mother's house, going through her car, her closets, her poolhouse. Saturday afternoon she would drive all over Beverly Hills, through Westwood and along Rodeo Drive, returning things. She would also go through Melody's desk and for those things she couldn't return, she would give her father the bills and he would pay them.

Besides the shopping, there were secret, chemical addictions that Jill knew less about. Never alcohol — drinking too much was what people in trailer parks did — but Valium, diet pills, and such. Jill never really knew for sure how extensive these addictions were, but she was well aware of their debilitating effect.

Her mother's latest setback had come at

the end of baseball season the previous fall. Jill had felt herself sucked back into all the old caretaking patterns, so she had forced herself to tell her therapy group what was happening. It was the first time she had ever disclosed what was happening to her "back home," and the group had responded well, helping her understand how to stand back, how to stop protecting her mother.

Without Jill's protection, Melody came to a crisis quickly. She had been to Betty Ford before, so this time David, acting with the advice of the Dodgers' management, had encouraged her to go to Hazelden in Minnesota. She had come out energetic and determined. She was still with David and once the baseball season started, she had settled down to write an autobiography, the contents of which Jill didn't care to speculate about. But as it was the first time Melody had had some purpose other than making a man comfortable, Jill had to approve.

She dialed her mother's number.

"Jill, darling." Melody's voice was low, the affection in it genuine. Jill had never doubted that.

They exchanged pleasantries. Then Jill asked her mother if she was free for lunch any day next week.

"Lunch? The two of us? What a lovely

idea. Of course, I'm free. Any time. Actually, Tuesday isn't good . . . although I could cancel — but isn't Tuesday your group? You're still going, aren't you? Oh, I'm sorry, I didn't mean to pry."

"It's okay," Jill assured her. "I'm still going. Shall we meet on Monday? Is that all right? The same place we went last time?"

"We could go there if you want. Of course we could . . . unless you want to go somewhere different for a change."

Jill didn't care where they ate. She just didn't want to have an endless conversation about it. "We can go wherever you want. I don't care."

"Oh, I don't either. I just thought that you might — "

Jill hated this. It was clear that Melody had a certain place in mind, but she was unwilling to suggest it herself. She wasn't going to admit that she had any preferences; she wasn't going to risk putting forward an idea that Jill might reject.

This rambling chatter, this inability to be direct, drove Jill nuts. Melody was nervous; she was frantic to please her daughter. It was a sad inversion of the more common parent-child dysfunction: in Jill and Melody's case, the child was the authority figure with love and approval to withhold or bestow.

It was heartbreaking . . . but also reassuring. A nervous Melody wasn't on Valium.

"I just want to see *you*," Jill said. "We can eat a hot dog on the beach, for all I care. You think about it and call me back."

"Do you think you'll want French or something lighter?"

"Mother, I don't care. You decide." Resolutely Jill changed the subject. "How's your book coming? Has Brenda's agent had a chance to read the proposal?"

"Oh, yes. She's sending me a contract . . . but Jill, about Monday, do you know what you're going to wear?"

Jill wanted to scream. Her mother was a high-school graduate, and yet the first agent she had shown her partial manuscript to was accepting it. That was amazing news, something Melody should have been very proud of. But all she could think about was what they were going to wear to lunch.

What difference does it make? So what if I'm in slacks and you're in a suit? So what if I'm in red and you're in coral? Who cares? They're going to let us eat. They're going to take our money.

But Jill knew everything would be easier if she answered. She glanced around the room. The hotel laundry had just returned her dry cleaning. Swaddled in plastic, it was draped across one of the oyster-damask sofas. The garment on top was peach. "I'll probably wear my peach skirt and sweater."

"Your sailor sweater? I really like that. Did you ever get shoes to match?"

"No." Jill wore soft off-white loafers with the calf-length skirt and silk sweater. The skirt and sweater were a pale rosy peach; the sweater's sailor knot and the stripes in its V-neck insert were ivory. So her shoes were fine. Not great, not perfect, but fine, which was enough for Jill.

Her mother, of course, had much higher standards.

The restaurant Melody finally chose was a new place in Westwood. The walls were a washed-pink stucco. The windows were deep and recessed, with shutters that folded back into the walls. The Mexican tile floor was a warm, earthy white while the tablecloth and dishes exploded in the colors of a piñata: red, fuchsia, turquoise, crayon yellow. The cuisine was supposedly nouvelle Mexican, something Jill could not quite imagine.

Melody was waiting for her at a fuchsia-draped table tucked into one of the window recesses. She had had her hair restyled since Jill had seen her last. More platinum than Jill's, it was feathery short, wisping about

Melody's delicate features. Before Jill could say how much she liked it, Melody leaned forward confidingly. "This place will never make it," she whispered. "It looks great empty. But what about when it's full of clothes? Who wants to spend half a morning getting dressed to be outshined by the plates?"

Jill didn't know, since she would never spend half of the morning getting dressed. Even when her childhood friend Payne Bartlett had dragooned her into going to the Academy Awards last month, she hadn't spent that long getting dressed.

Her mother was reaching under the bright tablecloth. "Look what I found. I think they'll be perfect."

She handed Jill a glossy taupe shoebox. Surprised, Jill opened the box. The tissue paper inside was patterned with a teal-green grid. The stores her mother shopped in always had wonderful tissue paper.

Jill folded back the tissue. Beneath it was a pair of peach T-straps. Jill lifted one shoe out of the box. It was piped with an ivory trim.

Jill and Melody had identical feet. Not only could they wear each other's shoes, they could buy each other shoes. When Melody had been married to George and stranded, absolutely *stranded*, among the conservative shoppers of Boston, she would occasionally call Jill for a Care package of shoes.

"The peach is the right color, isn't it?" The flow of Melody's voice had an anxious undercurrent.

Jill held the shoe next to her skirt. They were precisely the same shade. Melody's eye for color was unerring.

The anxiety in Melody's voice grew. "I had them add the trim."

She what? Jill looked at the shoes again. The seam between the soft leather and the fabric lining had been slit open and the ivory piping sewn in place before the seam was closed again. The piping circled the vamp of the shoe, then ran across either side of the ankle strap and up and down the T-strap. Adding that trim would have been no small undertaking. How on earth had Melody persuaded someone to do that kind of work over a weekend? Jill didn't care how much money and leisure a person had; this seemed like a waste of both.

This was the sort of moment Jill did not know how to handle. Across the table her mother looked so eager, so desperately wanting Jill to be pleased with the shoes. *Good God, Mother, where are your values?* But Jill couldn't say that.

So she swiveled sideways in her seat and pulled off her loafers, slipping her feet into the T-straps, crossing her legs one at a time to fasten the tiny silver buckles. She put her weight on her feet, testing the feel of the shoes. "They feel great," she said. Then she stood up, knowing her mother would want to see how they looked. A waiter dodged out of her way. "And they are exactly what the skirt needs. I'm always telling myself that off-white and ivory are the same, but they aren't, are they?" All that was the truth. She sat back down. "But I don't like the idea that you spent so much time looking for them."

"Don't be silly." Her mother waved a hand, happy now, pleased that Jill liked the shoes. She didn't hear the reservation in Jill's voice. "I enjoyed it. Now tell me what you've been up to. I don't think I talked to you all week."

"Did you read about that rally yesterday? I helped Betsy and Lexa on it. But I want to hear about your book. The agent liked the first three chapters? That's wonderful."

"You can't be as surprised as I am," Melody responded lightly. The praise she had gotten from Jill, as mild as it was, was making a tremendous difference in her manner. "She even thinks that there are enough participles and such, that a good, strong editor is all we'll need. I'm not going to have to hire one of those 'as told to' people . . . although Sheila really liked that man she worked with."

"Aren't you pleased? I'm certainly impressed. I don't know that I have enough participles in me for a whole book."

"Part of me expects that tomorrow she'll call and say it was all a mistake." Melody's laugh was clear and bell-like. One of Jill's first memories of her mother was her light, beautiful laughter. "Guess what her biggest complaint was?"

"I haven't a clue." When at ease and unthreatened, Melody was a delicious companion. "If you've got participles, what else could they want?"

"Sex. She's very disappointed that I haven't slept with more people."

"See, there's the problem with customizing your shoes. It doesn't leave you with enough time to sleep around."

"That's what I told her. Middle America can read about sex from anyone. Who else will tell the truth about the agonies of a badly lined beaded gown?"

"Only you," Jill admitted.

"And I think the women who'll read my book are unhappier with their clothes than they are with their husbands."

"That's a nice thought."

"It is if you believe husbands are more important than clothes."

The waiter was hovering near their table, so like two guilty schoolgirls they opened their menus. It was pages long. Jill wondered if she could just order a taco.

Melody closed her menu with a snap and handed it to the waiter. "Surprise us."

He blinked. "I beg your pardon?"

"We're not going to read this thing. Bring us something to eat. We're not fussy."

The waiter backed off.

Jill admired her mother's tactics. "That should put them in a tizzy."

"It serves them right." There was no longer a trace of the hesitant, unhappy woman Melody so often was. This was the charm that three talented, successful men hadn't been able to resist. "They have no right to inflict such a long menu on women who are too vain to admit that they need glasses." She leaned close to Jill again. "Isn't this splendid? I never sat down inside a restaurant until I was fifteen, not even to have a Coke at the counter in the bus station. And now I don't even care what I'm served."

Melody rarely spoke about her past and certainly never in such a light way. Writing about it in her book was making her able to talk about it. Jill was curious.

Interview your family, the Bowenian psychotherapists said. *Find out if your mother faced the same problems you are.*

But Jill's mother had grown up in a trailer park. It took Jill a frantic moment to come up with a common ground. "Do you remember that crush I had on the actor Bix Ringling? Did you ever have a crush like that?"

"Heavens, yes." Melody's laugh had a silvery tinkle. "It was Cary Grant. A dark movie theater and Cary Grant, that's all I needed . . . of course, that's all I had."

Jill hadn't known this, but she wasn't surprised that the debonair, elegant Cary Grant had been Melody's icon through the squalor of her early years. "But you met him, didn't you? Was it wonderful or a big disappointment?"

"I was lucky. Not a man on earth aged better than Cary Grant. All the girls in my high school were in love with Elvis, poor things. And the few times I met my idol, it was always public enough that he was being Cary Grant, so it was quite grand. If he was doing LSD and beating his wife or all those awful things that people are saying now, I never knew about it." Melody's voice trailed off as her interest in her own story was replaced by curiosity about Jill. "Why do you ask? I'm sure Candy Jimenez from my high school sees Elvis two or three times a month. Did you run into Bix Ringling at the Safeway?"

"Almost." Jill started to tell her mother about Doug's visit and ended up telling her the entire story, which surprised Jill very much indeed.

She had never confided in her mother. Melody had always longed for it. Every other Friday afternoon throughout Jill's schoolgirl years, Cass's driver would drop her off at Melody's house for the regular weekend visits. Waiting on the kitchen counter would be a beautifully arranged tea tray with delicate porcelain cups and tiny frosted cookies. The water would be simmering. It would take Melody only moments to bring it to a boil and pour it over the tea leaves. She would carry the tea into the living room, setting it down on a low table. The sofa would be piled high with clouds of pillows. She would pat the spot next to her, inviting Jill to sit down. "Now we can have a nice, long talk."

And her eyes would seem so needy. She would seem so frail that Jill would be overwhelmed and retreat into silence.

But now, for nearly the first time in her life, she told her mother everything, not just

110

the facts of Doug's story, but how Jill felt, how threatened she was on her father's behalf. Her mother's eyes were warm with sympathy. "You don't think Cass would do anything dishonorable, do you?" she finished.

"No, not dishonorable."

There was reservation in Melody's voice. Jill was surprised. Her parents had never spoken ill of one another. "But?"

"Film is a collaborative business. Your father understood that. That's why he was always so productive. He knew you had to compromise. 'We're not Keats here,' he always used to say."

"So you think he might — "

Melody interrupted. That was unusual for her. "I don't think anything. But we don't know if there was a secret script, much less whether or not it was a masterpiece. It seems to me like you've got a long way to go before you can decide what your father's role was. You may be getting a little ahead of yourself."

Ahead of herself? Jill could not believe what her mother was saying. How could having faith in Cass's integrity be getting ahead of herself? That's where she was starting from.

Four

Jill and Cathy obediently reported their off-site meeting to the group on Tuesday. Cathy offered a straightforward factual account, ". . . I did a little research, she came to my office, the meeting lasted no more than twenty minutes."

"So what was it like?" one of the members asked Jill.

"Fine," Jill answered. "Her office is beautiful, and she really did a lot more than I expected. It saved me a lot of time. I appreciated that."

"Wasn't it odd?" someone else asked. "Did you feel like you knew her real well or not at all?"

"A little bit of both." Jill was careful not to look at Cathy when she said that. "But it was fine, it really was. It was no big deal."

Everyone was silent. Jill knew that two or three members were itching to get on to their own concerns and were waiting the requisite number of beats to be sure that this subject was over.

But Bill, the therapist leading the group, spoke first. "I think there's more to be said here."

Now, this was exactly what Jill hated about being in any kind of therapy. She hadn't liked talking about her mother's breakdown last fall, but she knew she needed help, so she had done it. But this, people expecting her to talk when she had nothing to say, she flat-out hated. It was like being back on her mother's pillow-filled sofa. She had met Cathy, had gotten help, had thanked her, and said good-bye. That was truly all that had happened. But six pairs of eyes were staring at her, waiting for her to say more. At least Cathy had the grace not to look at her.

So Jill looked back at the six pairs of eyes, her face as blank as her mind. What did they expect from a woman raised by a proper British governess? Alice had brought her up on cold water and brisk daily walks. Alice had loved her, Jill knew that, but history and geography had been the order of the day, not emotion. Jill could still recite all the kings of England. Did they want to hear that? *Egbert, Ethelwulf, Ethelbald . . .*

In a moment, the eyes all switched to Cathy.

"Why did you do more than Jill expected?" a member asked her.

A touch of distaste flickered across Cathy's face. "I was very pleased that she called," she answered.

113

"Why aren't you looking at her when you say that?"

"Because I was talking to you." Pointedly Cathy turned to face Jill, first looking at a spot near the center of Jill's forehead, then making reluctant eye contact. "I was very pleased that you called."

Do you hate this as much as I do?

You bet.

"Why were you pleased?" someone asked.

Cathy turned back to her questioner. "Because like everyone in this room, I want Jill's approval — "

Jill stared at her, horrified.

" — and I'm proud of the way my office looks. I wanted her to see it."

The therapist spoke quickly. "This is an important issue. Why do we all like Jill? Why do we value her opinion so much?"

Jill had once fallen while mounting a horse and had bruised her tailbone. For weeks, every time she sat down, she felt exactly as she was feeling right now.

"Jill," Bill went on, "why don't you go first? How do you view your role in the group?"

"No," Jill protested, acutely miserable. She wasn't going to go first. She wasn't going to go at all.

But she was. She had gotten a lot of help

114

from this group because other people had been willing to be honest. So she took a deep breath and spoke. "We've talked about our sibling rivalry issues before." Jill knew it was crucial to three members that they get their fair share of the group's attention; they would become agitated if they found themselves ignored. All had several brothers and sisters, and in their plea for the group's attention they were re-enacting their need for their parents' attention. "I was an only child. I don't need to be Bill's favorite, because I've never been in competition with anyone for either of my parents."

The other people were nodding. Jill's comments were often accepted without much question. She supposed that was part of what Bill was trying to explore.

"But it's more than that," someone added. "You're always so interested in everyone else, so open . . . and then when you told us about your mother, that was obviously hard for you."

And it had also been more than six months ago. Jill knew she had been coasting for a long time on that one piece of self-disclosure. She hadn't even told the group that she had lost her house to a mudslide.

Other people were chiming in, now with comments about Jill's intelligence, her insight.

"It sounds like we're back to everyone trying to win Jill's favor," Bill said. "Cathy, you started this. How do you explain it?"

Cathy's eyes met Jill's briefly. Jill thought she saw an apology there, an apology for having brought this up. "I think there's always a magic about people with . . . people who are so very attractive. Jill's wonderful to watch; her movements are so graceful. I adore her clothes. That presence gives people power."

Jill started to squirm; then, suddenly self-conscious about these allegedly graceful movements, she froze.

Bill was looking at Cathy intently. "Is that really what you want to say?"

Cathy looked right back at him. "Yes."

Jill was suddenly alert. Cathy was lying.

She had said, "I think there's always a magic about people with . . ."

With money. That's what she had started to say. *With money.*

Jill's wealth had never come up in group. She hadn't wanted it to. Money could be such a barrier, a reason for people to dismiss who you were or over-value who you were. Jill didn't want to come to group and have to listen to other people talk about her money.

The group knew that Jill didn't work, but two of the other women, married to successful

116

men, didn't either. No one had thought to explore the difference. But Cathy was single and self-supporting. That was a difference that would have interested her. Enough people at the studio remembered Cass's fixation with real estate that Cathy could have gotten the general picture easily.

Yet she hadn't mentioned it. She had changed the subject, conspiring with Jill to hide Jill's wealth. You weren't supposed to do things like that in group, but Jill didn't care. She already had all the attention she could stand.

After ninety minutes of having her popularity and influence dissected, Jill had learned one thing — why most of her friends were actors, writers, and directors. The majority were so overwhelmingly self-absorbed that they never asked her difficult questions about herself.

She was going to be surrounded by these people this evening. Her longtime friend Susannah Donovan was starring in a movie premiering tonight, and the benefit afterward was for a school of therapeutic horsemanship at which disabled children supplemented their physical therapy by learning how to ride. Jill liked this cause. Her Phillip-Wayland fantasies had been important to her; how much more it must mean to a wheelchair-bound child to be John Wayne for an hour. So, when she was reconstructing her calendar, Susannah was one of the first people she called. She bought tickets to many benefits she didn't go to; this one she wanted to attend.

As it was nearly the first of May, the benefit had a Kentucky Derby theme. The school's colors were emerald and white, and the balcony running around three sides of the hotel ballroom was hung with deep swags of emerald and white bunting. The waiters, wearing racing silks of those colors, were passing trays of mint juleps. A small orchestra played Stephen Foster songs, and clustered at the edges of the dance floor were masses of potted plants and a few bales of hay. Saddles, riding tack, and horseshoes hung from white trellises. Red Kentucky Derby roses cascaded out of silver loving cups in the center of each table. As favors at each place setting, the men received silver-plated lapel pins shaped like horseshoes; the women got bracelets made from miniature snaffle bits.

Jill picked up the little box her bracelet was in and held it up questioningly to her friend Mina sitting across the table. "Please," Mina mouthed.

Mina and her husband Bill had two tiny daughters. The couple regularly took home

Jill's party favors so that neither one of the children had to be conned into believing that a horsehead tie tack was as glorious as a snaffle-bit bracelet that jingled when you moved your chubby little arm.

Bill was sitting next to Jill. She handed him the bracelet. He slipped it into the pocket of his dinner jacket, patting the pocket so his wife would know where to find it in the morning.

"Thank you," he said. "It will be well loved. It will be lost, but until then it will be well loved." Then he stopped, shaking his head. "What's become of us? I used to be a kid from Des Moines. Now we give a two-year-old a silver bracelet to lose."

"It's only plate," Jill said.

"But still . . . oh, well, I suppose you were given the Taj Mahal to lose."

"Hardly. My mother might have done something like that, but my father and governess made those decisions." Before coming to America to look after Jill, Alice had taken care of a little boy who was now a Duke. Henry and his sisters had never gotten new toys. If a set of wooden soldiers had been good enough for your grandfather, went that household's philosophy, then it was good enough for you. Alice had seen no reason to deviate from that principle just because

Jill's father was never in the financial straits that Henry's father always was.

Dinner was pleasant. This was one of the few tables in the room where all were capable of enjoying themselves even if no one took their pictures. That's why Jill liked these people. After dessert some of the women at the table excused themselves to go to the ladies' room. Jill went with them, but lost track of them in the crowded rest room. She returned to the ballroom alone, threading her way out of the thicket of askew chairs and chattering people. She was almost back at her table when she heard a familiar voice calling her name.

She turned. It was her friend Payne Bartlett, America's latest heartthrob and one of Jill's oldest friends. They had known each other since the days when their rosy little bottoms had been lined up on the same changing table and slathered from the same tube of diaper rash ointment.

Like Jill, Payne had grown up in the business, his father having alternated between being a studio executive and an independent producer, always successful in either capacity. Unlike Jill, Payne had decided to play on their fathers' field. He had a remarkably successful on-screen career, playing sweetly troubled youths and stirring the hearts of

120

the nation's fourteen-year-old girls.

Payne himself was approaching twenty-eight and, bored with the sweetly-troubled-youth typecast, he had started his own production company to develop different roles for himself.

He held out his arms. "Jill, sweetheart, a new dress. I don't believe it. What brought this on?"

Jill did tend to wear the same clothes over and over. "My mother. What else?" Jill tilted her cheek for his kiss. "I went out to lunch with her yesterday, and we had such a good time that I broke down and went shopping with her afterward."

"That was nice of you." Payne knew all about Jill's difficulties with her mother. "And nice of her. Your clothes are more interesting when you shop with her. It's a great color. Who is it?"

"Versace. The Princess of Wales has one like it in blue, with a different neck. It's a silk shantung and I could have bought a small Chevy for what I paid for it. That's all I know about it."

Payne laughed. "You don't have to be belligerent about it. Is it fun to wear?"

"Yes," Jill admitted, then softened. "Yes, yes it is."

"Then that should be the end of it." Payne

took her arm, leading her through the main entrance of the ballroom. In one corner of the anteroom several rolls of grassy sod had been laid, creating a small green lawn. Three piles of hay were stacked picturesquely next to tubs of rosebushes, and a white board fence formed the back lot line of this mini-pasture.

Jill sat down on one of the bales. The chiffon layer of her golden-yellow dress swirled down with her, coming to rest a few seconds later, falling into drifts around her legs. Payne, formally dressed in a black tie and pleated white shirt, arranged himself elegantly along the fence, one arm stretched across the top rail.

"So, Jill, what are you up to?"

"What am *I* up to?" Where were the reporters when you needed them? Surely Payne asking her about herself was the most news-worthy thing that would happen all evening. "Are you feeling all right?"

"Now, that's not fair," he protested. "You know I'm — "

"And don't feed me a line. I've known you too long."

"Why are you so hard on me?"

"Someone needs to be." Actually, Payne was one of the lesser narcissists of her ac-quaintances. His recent absorption with his new business she found entirely understandable.

A shadow fell across her skirt. "Excuse me, Mr. Webster — "

It was a photographer. Payne rearranged himself on the fence. The photographer stepped back far enough that Jill gathered she was being included in the picture, so she looked up at Payne with an adoring smile that would, no doubt, come across as brainless. It didn't matter. She would probably be cut out of the picture.

As engaging as she was in person, Jill took truly horrible pictures. Her friends in the business — Payne, Susannah, and the others — all looked better, more vibrant, on film than in person. Not Jill. The camera captured nothing of her personality. At best, photographs made her look vacantly pretty; more often she looked subnormal.

The photographer thanked Payne and moved off. "I'll probably be labeled an 'unidentified female companion,' " Jill grumbled happily.

"Oh, come on." Payne dropped his elegant pose. "That happened to you once. You've been dining out on that story for three years. You should look on the bright side. At least they knew you were female. Now, where were we? Oh, yes. You had just finished lecturing me about how egotistic and self-centered I am becoming and were about to tell me why you were at the old studio on Friday."

So that was what this was about. "How did you know I was there?"

"I saw you. But I was being driven, and you, lowly billionairess that you are, were trudging along on your beauteous gams. Now, what were you doing there? You have to tell me. The thought of all that money walking around unescorted makes me nervous."

"I was just poking around. I found out something odd last week. Apparently my father once took out an option on remaking *Weary Hearts,* and — "

"Wait a minute." Payne jerked away from the fence. "Say that again."

"My dad took out an option to remake *Weary Hearts.*"

"Your father was thinking about remaking it?"

"I don't know. It's strange. He never talked to any of his people about it, but he renewed the option a couple of times."

"He did?" All the young heartthrob postures had dropped out of Payne's manner. He sat down next to Jill, an intent businessman. His fans would have never believed it of him, but twenty years ago Jill had seen him engineer some shrewd baseball card trades. "Do you have any idea what his plans were?"

"No, none."

"Has anyone been through his papers? Was there anything about it?"

"Not a thing."

With his thumbs pressed to the wings of his cheekbones, Payne rubbed his forehead with his fingertips. He was thinking. Then he dropped his hands. "Jill, will you do a favor for me?"

"Sure. What is it?"

"Did you speak to anyone at the studio about this?"

Jill thought back on her conversation with Cathy. "No. I did raise it with some of the people who used to work for him . . . and with Ken and Lynette, and my mother. But not anyone at the studio."

"Will you not say anything to anyone else? At least not until I tell you?"

"Of course, but why?"

"You know I have tremendous respect for your father. My dad always said that in that whole crowd, Cass was the best."

Jill did appreciate him saying that. This was what she was used to, Cass being praised, Cass being spoken of as "the best."

Payne went on. "So if he thought *Weary Hearts* was worth remaking, then maybe it is."

Jill blinked. She knew that Payne's new company was looking for material, but . . . "You'd remake *Weary Hearts?*"

"I can't say that. I've known about this for ninety seconds. But I want to think about it. I'd like to look at the movie again, read that old treatment that guy found, see what's what. And I'd rather not have a hundred other people doing the same thing at the same time."

Jill could understand that. She hadn't much cared for having been half a step behind Doug Ringling all week. "I won't say a word," she promised.

Payne gave her arm a quick squeeze. "Then let's get back to our tables. They're about to start the drawing."

Jill had always found it a little odd that people who were worth millions and wore dresses with sticker prices like those of cars had to be enticed to charitable benefits with party favors and door prizes. She was perpetually winning things she didn't want, a Bob Macke dress that she had never worn or a haircut and makeover at a new salon when she was entirely content with the people who took care of her now.

So she paid little attention. Bill, sitting next to her and familiar with her ways, commandeered her evening bag and extracted her ticket. Toward the end of the drawing, he nudged her and passed her the ticket. "You won."

Jill peered up on the little emerald-and-white draped stage where Susannah had been drawing numbers. Susannah was in a beaded gown that must have cost more than a medium-sized Chevy and next to her was a bay horse.

"Oh, my God . . ."

The people at Jill's table pushed her out of her chair.

Jill did not want to win a horse. If she wanted a horse, she could go out and buy one. People living in hotels did not need horses, especially this horse. He was the strangest looking creature with a thick neck and a deep sway in his back. He was so slab-sided that he was almost rectangular. He was probably part draft horse and part . . . well, God might know, but Jill didn't.

She stumbled up the stage steps. Susannah had her arms out, her best lead-actress smile in place.

"Jill!" Susannah's voice came out in a little hiss so that it would not disturb her smile. "You have a new dress!"

They embraced, Susannah keeping her face toward the photographers, Jill happy to hide hers in Susannah's flowing hair. "I'm going to murder you," Jill whispered into the auburn mane. "I haven't won that animal, have I?"

"Goodness, no," Susannah hissed back. "They use him at the school." Then she stepped back, dramatically leading Jill to the odd-looking animal, then spoke loudly enough for others to hear. "You get to name him."

Jill was deeply relieved. Now that she was assured that this horse was not going to be part of her life, she revised her opinion of him. He might look funny, but he had a kind eye that spoke of intelligence. His ears were forward, not laid back suspiciously. He looked like a good, solid, blue-collar horse, the kind that you could roll a wheelchair up to. He wasn't going to bolt when you put a C.P. kid on his back.

Pokey, that was the first name that came to her mind. *Pokey.*

No, that wasn't fair. How could you be John Wayne on a horse called *Pokey?* She had an obligation to wheelchair children everywhere to give this horse a thrilling name. *Killer.* No, their parents might not like that. *Warrior. Daredevil.* She needed something dashing and gallant, full of mischief and courage.

"Let's call him Bix," she said decidedly. "Bix Ringling."

"Would you look at this?" Randy Casler folded back the issue of the *People* magazine and handed it to Doug. "Here's a picture of my Aunt Jill."

Doug fitted a plastic lid on his coffee before taking the magazine. As always he and Randy were at the 7-Eleven, getting their morning coffee. There was a regular crowd who turned up around five every morning: farmers who had finished the milking, the carpenters, electricians, and roofers who had found work in the housing developments in the counties that ringed Washington, D.C. They needed to be on the road early to beat the traffic. Randy and Doug were egg men. They got up early because Randy's three hundred thousand chickens got up early.

Usually everyone took their coffee out into the parking lot, leaning against their trucks, passing the time of day before getting on with things. But today it was raining, and most of the men grabbed their coffee and sprinted back to their trucks. Those heading into the suburbs knew that their long drives from the Valley were going to be even longer.

129

Only a few lingered inside the store, staring at the magazines or scratching off the numbers on lottery tickets.

Doug looked down at the *People*. Three black-and-white pictures were printed in a row above the text. All had been taken at the same party. In the center photograph the actor Payne Bartlett, dressed in black tie, was leaning against a fake board fence, and sitting on a bale of hay at his feet was, according to the caption, "Jill Casler, the wealthy daughter of the late director William 'Cass' Casler."

Randy spoke. "Is it a good picture of her?"

Doug looked at the picture in the magazine again. If it weren't for the caption, he wouldn't have recognized her. In person he had thought her exceptionally attractive; her face had been lively and expressive, her manner unstudied. This picture, however, suggested a person with a personality only slightly north of a glazed doughnut.

"I don't think she's as dumb as this picture makes her look," he said.

Randy took the picture back. "You think this makes her look stupid?"

"Close to brain-dead."

"Oh, well." Randy flipped the magazine shut and tucked it back into the rack. "Guessing a girl's I.Q. was never my strong suit."

Truer words had never been spoken. Perhaps in a reaction to his negative mother, Randy was remarkably uncritical. He was a ladies' man, well acquainted with each year's crop of Young Lovelies. He liked girls who were lively and good-humored. They didn't have to be drop-dead beautiful, as long as they were fun. They needed to be bright enough to read the Pizza Hut menu, but beyond that, Randy wasn't too fussy.

As much as Doug valued discernment in people, he had found the last month of Randy's uncritical company refreshing. He had had enough criticism for the moment. In March he had resigned from his job as head basketball coach at Maryland Tech. This had not been any quiet, discreet parting. If Doug hadn't resigned, he would have been fired.

The path that had led him into a Division I coaching job had been as steady as the path out of it had been swift. He had grown up the Valley's star basketball player. He spent every summer at the Five Star basketball camp. During his senior year in high school he had been named to the second-string All-American team. With grades and SAT scores that matched his basketball skills, he had left Virginia to go to college at Duke University, in Durham, North Carolina.

Duke was one of the shining spots in college basketball. It had an honestly run program with no hint of the scandals that infected so much of college sports. Duke was known as the "Harvard of the South." All its athletes were smart, having SAT scores hundreds of points above some of their opponents' scores. Duke players didn't live in special dorms; they couldn't major in bogus fields like "recreational technology." They had to pass organic chemistry. And every one of the Blue Devils graduated — every one of them.

The school was arrogant about its excellence, and its student body was witty and energetic. After an N.C. State player was arrested for mugging a Domino's pizza delivery man, twenty Domino's pizzas were delivered to the State bench just before the start of the game. Whenever the bald Lefty Driesell, then coach of the University of Maryland, was in town, Duke students came to the game in bald skullcaps. When an opposing player with the last name of Hale was sidelined with a lung ailment, one side of the Duke bleachers shouted "In Hale," with the other answering "Ex Hale" until even the ailing Hale himself was laughing. In the national finals one year, Duke was opposed by the University of Nevada–Las Vegas, which was pretty much the sort of school one would expect to find in Las Vegas. The Duke mascot strutted over to the U.N.L.V. fans with a sign reading, "Welcome Fellow Scholars." Of course, U.N.L.V. had its revenge; they beat Duke by the widest margin of any Final Four game ever.

But Duke had a cheer for even moments like that, one they used after plays by schools like N.C. State, Clemson, or Maryland Tech. "That's all right, that's okay," it went. "You'll all work for us someday."

Doug, quick and articulate, had thrived in this environment. Although the supremely gifted David Lyncton — now center for the L.A. Lakers and known nationwide as "the Lynx," — was his teammate, Doug had been the team leader. He kept practice on an even keel, he encouraged the academic laggards, and he was the bridge between the bench and the starters.

On court he was the defensive star. At six feet four he was tall enough to guard the giants, quick enough to keep up with the little guys. His instincts were superb, and his determination total. "A fellow with four sisters," he was quoted as saying, "learns defense young."

Sportswriters noted his resemblance to the lead character in *Weary Hearts,* and occasionally someone would try to nickname him "the Ranger," drawing a parallel between his defensive skills and Phillip's ride with Mosby's Rangers. The nickname never stuck. Doug's personality was too open and sunny for such a dark appellation.

But, for all this skill, he had one limit — he couldn't shoot. There was no such thing as a routine layup for him, and he was never more than fifty percent from the line. He was always the one who was fouled in the final seconds of a close game. "I really could shoot better," he had quipped, "but then I wouldn't get so much television time."

So there had never been a hope of a pro career for him. After his senior year he had stayed at Duke as a graduate assistant, becoming an assistant coach a year later. His knowledge of the game and his remarkable motivational skills marked him as someone who would soon have his own program.

He was barely thirty when Maryland Tech called. Another school in the state, the University of Maryland at College Park, had received crushing penalties from the N.C.A.A. for such infractions as giving potential recruits a free T-shirt. The state had every reason to worry about the future of Maryland Tech, whose program, many insiders privately thought, was in far worse shape.

Maryland Tech was not the jewel in anyone's crown. It was a large commuter school, and even the best students got only an ordinary education. The athletic department did a startlingly inadequate job. Some of the students on athletic scholarships could not read an airline's in-flight magazine; none of them graduated — not one. They played out their eligibility, then left school after their final game. One a year might go on to the pros. The others had some good memories, but not much else. Certainly not an education.

Doug's mandate was to improve the team's academic standing without impairing its winning record. He did. Some of the kids graduated; the others were reading well enough to get jobs as assistant managers of shoe stores. In each of Doug's first two years the team had come into the N.C.A.A. tournament as a number-fourteen seed. The first year they got to the Sweet Sixteen, the next year to the round of Eight.

Then, in his third year — this year — it all came crashing down. Two weeks before the end of the season, N.C.A.A. investigators came to Frederick. It was the usual recruiting scandal, cash, and cars, but there was a twist — the money and cars had gone not only to the kids or their families, but also to their high school coaches. Influencing the kids' coaches, everyone agreed, was particularly heinous. These were *teachers,* the people who were supposed to be the kids' first line of defense.

Doug resigned immediately, saying farewell not only to his job, but to the fat Nike contract that had come with it. For days afterward the athletic director of Maryland Tech had not pulled his punches, boxing right up to the edge of the slander laws. "Coach Ringling was not up to the challenge . . . you never know what Division I pressure will make a man do . . . we regret that anyone associated with our fine institution would stoop to this."

Doug never answered those charges. He accepted responsibility for everything that had happened on his watch; whether he had known about it or not was irrelevant.

And, in fact, he had not known about the scheme to seduce the high school coaches. He was an excellent recruiter; this was not something he needed to cheat at.

But at any moment it would have taken him about ninety seconds to find out. He had known the alumni and boosters were up to something; he had chosen not to ask what it was. Trying to get the kids to go to class and learn something had been challenge enough. Doug had had a standing excuse for himself; he couldn't deal with everything at once.

His view of the experience was now simple: he had made a pact with the devil, trying to coach clean in a crooked program. Like everyone making a pact with the gentleman in red suspenders, he thought he was going to get away with it. Like everyone else, he had not.

He didn't mind for himself. After all, accepting reality was his strength. He did mind for the kids he had left behind. Each year he had recruited a class better than the school deserved. Then he had abandoned the kids to this large, anonymous institution; he was the captain who didn't go down with his ship. True, he had lost his job and his reputation, but those poor kids were stuck in Frederick. He had promised their mothers they would learn to read. Now there wasn't anyone there who cared about that.

The L.A. Lakers, prodded by the Lynx, his old roommate, had immediately offered him a job as a defensive assistant, but he had been raised by a Southern mother. He knew what a gentleman in the middle of a scandal was supposed to do: drop out of sight. He didn't think that coaching for the Lakers, even as an assistant, qualified as dropping out of sight. Also, he had never wanted to coach in the pros. So he came home, back to the Valley, and was living with Randy in a rattle-trap of a house that had belonged to Randy's now-deceased great aunt.

Randy was twenty-eight, five years younger than Doug. He had his own business because two years before, his grandfather, Jill's father, had died, leaving each of his grandchildren a startling generous trust. So Randy had had the capital to start up right. The egg collection was fully automated, so his labor force consisted of Doug and a few high school kids who came in before school each morning and a few others who came afterward. His henhouse was equipped with full-spectrum lighting that simulated daylight and ion chargers that kept down the dust. His specially developed feed got the hens laying larger eggs sooner than they would have otherwise.

Most egg farms were casual family businesses with the paperwork spread out on the kitchen table and a couple of fat dogs who roamed around eating the broken eggs. Randy had the fat dogs, but everything else was sleek and computerized.

He was interested in every new development in egg production, and on the afternoon of the day he had seen Jill's picture, he asked Doug to read some reports on research done on low-cholesterol eggs.

As the high school kids were helping to load the trucks, Doug took the reports back to the little office in the corner of the barn. They were not uninteresting. It did seem to be possible to lower the cholesterol in eggs, but not, Doug concluded, by enough to justify the expense. People with cholesterol problems still wouldn't be able to eat them.

He set aside the reports and took out a list of all the people in the Valley who had been extras in *Weary Hearts*. He sat back in Randy's chair, put his feet up on the desk, and stared at the list, wondering what else he could do, what other questions he might ask them.

The phone rang. Still looking at the list, he picked up the receiver and answered automatically, "Casler's."

He heard a quick gasp at the other end of the line, followed by a pause. The person calling must not have expected this number to be answered in this manner. Then a woman's voice —

"This is Jill Casler — "

And Doug sat up, his feet crashing to the floor.

" — and I was given this number for Doug Ringling. Is he available?"

"Jill?" The print-out on Doug's lap spilled

open into a long ribbon cascading to the floor. "My God, I never — " He stopped, took a breath, and started over. "This is a surprise. I didn't expect to hear from you."

"Waltz in with a story like that and then not expect to hear from me?" Her voice was light, teasing. "Come on."

"But you didn't believe me."

"No, and I'm not saying that I do now. But I do want to know how you know about stock footage."

Stock footage. So she had been to the studio. She might not believe him, but she had started checking.

This really did surprise him. Usually he was pretty good at sizing up what was happening in a room. It was — or had been — part of his job. Whether the room was a locker room or a recruit's parents' living room, he had to have a sense of what was happening, what direction people were moving in, what kind of push they would resist, what kind they would respond to.

And his sense of Jill Casler's plush hotel bungalow had been of steel shutters locking up tight. She had, he thought, written him off as a complete lunkhead, a good-looking-enough guy, but with carefully stacked lumber where his brains were supposed to be.

140

Clearly he had been wrong. He answered her question. "I did my homework. I read that book about *A Star Is Born*. That's where they found some of its footage. But, tell me, did you find out anything? I just threw airballs."

"I didn't do any better."

He liked her voice. It was pretty and feminine, but direct without any girlish, giggly hesitations. He hadn't paid any attention to it when he had met her. There had been too much else to admire. "Don't you think that's odd?" he asked. "That there was nothing from April, no film, no script?"

"It is a shame about the script. Losing track of it was just carelessness, but the studios are careless. That's the way it is."

"Don't they have any respect for their own history?"

Her laugh was soft and silvery. "That sounds like something my father would have said."

"It's something anyone from Virginia would say. I suppose the people running the studios thought of them as businesses, not museums."

"I don't think it ever occurred to them that scholars might someday be interested in what they were doing. You wouldn't believe what's been lost."

"Tell me," he said. He liked talking to her.

Important films of the silent era had been lost forever, she explained. Warner Brothers had thrown out the cels for its animated shorts to make room for publicity files. In the early seventies a big pit was dug near the intersection of the San Diego and Golden State Freeways, and into it MGM had dumped production files, screen tests, still photographs, and musical scores.

"We would never do that around here," Doug said, then remembered the native sons who were trying to build shopping malls on battlefields. "Well, anyway, what do we do now?" Doug knew that the "we" was a little premature, but he also knew how to build a team. He could take five guys, some from the worst slums of Philadelphia, others from the cushy Washington suburbs, guys with nothing in common except their ability to play basketball, and he could make them into a team. Turning himself and Jill Casler into a little two-man search team couldn't be any harder than that. "I've been talking to the people who were extras, but their memories of the filming are pretty much shaped by what made it into the final picture."

"I suppose that's to be expected. Have

you talked to your uncle again?"

"I've already talked to him three or four times, but it never gets anywhere." Charles was always his helpful, gracious self, but he really didn't know what had been in the script filmed in April. "He wants to help, but he doesn't remember enough. I just get the same stories over and over."

"I wonder if a fresh ear might hear something different. Would he talk to me?"

"Of course. He loves talking about the movie, but he doesn't travel." Charles wasn't exactly an invalid, but he was elderly. As far as Doug knew, he had not left Virginia since the plane crash. "And he's not one for talking on the phone."

"I don't mind coming out there . . . if you could set up a meeting." There was a pause, as if she was consulting a calendar. "The rest of my week is reasonably clear. Anytime after — "

"Wait a minute," he interrupted. Had he heard right? Aunt Jill was coming to the Valley, wealthy Aunt Jill. The Caslers would have gang heart failure. "You're planning on coming here, and you're going to schedule it through *me?*"

There was a pause. "Is that inconvenient?" Her voice was careful.

"It's not inconvenient, it's just out of the

question." Didn't she have a clue? Apparently not.

How was he going to put this? He didn't want to scare her off. If he was going to find out the truth about *Weary Hearts,* he needed her help. On the other hand, a true teammate would warn her about the gang heart failures that would be brought on by her coming to the Valley. She might want to brush up on her C.P.R. "Look" — he tried to keep his voice light — "this Valley is crawling with Caslers. I'm not going to tell them that on Aunt Jill's very first visit she's coming to see the Ringlings."

"Aunt Jill?" She sounded horrified.

"That's who you are, isn't it?"

"I suppose . . . how did you know this will be my first visit?"

"Everyone knows that. Please give me a break here. Call Brad, Dave, Randy, anyone. Let them know you're coming. It doesn't matter when. Charles is always around."

"I wasn't planning on an extensive visit."

What was she planning? To swoop in, see Uncle Charles, and dance off, ignoring the people who had made a tape of her walking into the Academy Awards and who would soon be in the market for group rates on heart transplants? Yes, apparently that had been her plan.

This must be what it was like to be an only child. You thought you could plan things yourself. Two minutes in the Valley would set her straight on that. How should he put this? "Do you know the song 'She'll Be Comin' Round the Mountain'?"

"Well, yes . . . I suppose. I mean, who doesn't? But what does that have to do with anything?"

"I think it captures the tone of what it will be like when you come. May I give you Brad's number?"

"You're really serious about this, aren't you?"

"Yes, ma'am." He grabbed the slim phone book, figuring that Randy didn't keep his parents' number in his office Rolodex. There were now only three Caslers listed — Randy, his father Brad, and his uncle Dave. "It's 703-856- . . ."

"Wait, wait," she interrupted. "Let me get a pen."

Five

She'll be comin' 'round the mountain
when she comes
She'll be comin' 'round the mountain
when she comes . . .

We'll all go out to meet her when she
comes . . .

She'll be riding six white horses . . .

We'll all have chicken and dumplings
. . . sleep with Grandma . . .
wearing red pajamas . . .

Jill did not wear red pajamas. She did not
eat dumplings and she had no intention of
sleeping with anyone's grandmother. The six
white horses were all right, but everything
else was unacceptable.

Calling Doug had been hard enough. But
she had been forced to; she had come to a
dead end. Miles Smithson's widow said that
he had never talked about work at home.
Oliver McClay's widow had Alzheimer's.
Steve Lex, the movie's first editor, had died
in 1950, having never fully recovered from

146

his World War II injuries. Charles Ringling was her best hope.

She had given herself a stern lecture. Doug was not her enemy. She had first assumed that his silence about Cass was craftiness, but perhaps it had been innocence. He was thinking about his own family. Perhaps he hadn't considered what his story implied about hers.

She and he had a common goal, to find the truth. Certainly each wished for a different truth. He wanted his uncle to be recognized as a great talent; she wanted her father's reputation to go unchallenged. But whatever the truth proved to be, nothing less would stop their search. They might as well look together.

So she had called him . . . only to have him want her to make another, even more difficult call. Phillip Wayland would not have done this to her.

It wasn't that she had a bad relationship with her two half-brothers. She didn't have one at all. She exchanged Christmas cards with them, and every time she received a birth or graduation announcement she sent flowers — or had her father's office do so. But that was it.

The older brother, Brad, had come out to California for Cass's funeral. It was, she acknowledged now, the right thing for him to do, but at the time she had been so distracted by her grief that she could only be puzzled by the tall stranger and wonder why he thought he would be any comfort to her. They had stood side by side at the gravesite, and when it was time for Jill to step forward and drop her rose on the coffin, her brother had moved to take her arm. She couldn't help it, she regretted it for days afterward, but she had frozen. She didn't want him touching her. Payne's father had moved up quickly, circling her narrow shoulders with a warm, comforting arm.

And now Doug Ringling was telling her that she couldn't come anywhere near the state of Virginia without making a big production of it with half-brothers, red pajamas, dumplings, and a grandmother who undoubtedly snored.

We'll all go out to meet her when she comes . . . Doug couldn't be right. Why would they be so interested in her? She went from one month to the next without giving them a moment's thought.

As much as she had always thought of the Shenandoah Valley as a magical land, she had never visited it. Doug Ringling wasn't the only one who knew his folk songs. *Oh, Shenandoah, I long to see you, Away, you rolling river* . . . It was a haunting, beautiful song, but it wasn't Jill's theme. She knew the Valley through the movie and through her father's memories. That was enough. She hadn't needed to go there.

What are you afraid of? she could hear her therapy group asking, if she ever raised the issue. *Don't you trust your father's memories? Are you unwilling to test them against reality? Would you rather have his memories than your own impressions?*

That wasn't what Cass wanted. Even though Ellen's unforgiving stiffness had kept him from ever taking Jill to the Valley, she had reason to think he wanted her to go. He had left her a house there. During none of their discussions about his estate had Cass ever mentioned to her a house in Courthouse, Virginia. Yet it had been the one piece of property explicitly mentioned in the will.

"Why did he leave it to me?" Jill had asked Lynette a month or so after the funeral. "Why not give it to Brad and Dave or their kids?"

"I'm sure he had a reason," Lynette told her. "Even though he never went back, he always thought of the Valley as a refuge; maybe he wanted you to have one too."

Jill couldn't imagine herself needing a refuge, or if she did, that she would ever go to Virginia.

Ken, the estate's attorney, had agreed with Lynette. "Cass never said, but I'd bet that he wanted you to have a stake in the Valley. One thing he always felt guilty about was that he never took you back there. Don't sell it until you've seen it."

Jill trusted Ken. As a result, in the two years since Cass's death, she had done nothing about the house. When the elderly widowed relative who had been living in it died, Jill had been occupied with her mother's troubles, so she left it to Ken to work out some arrangement for its care, which she assumed he had done. Even when her own home had been swept away, even when she had indeed needed a refuge, she had never thought of going to Virginia.

Now everything was falling into place. Ellen was dead. Jill wanted to see Charles Ringling; she needed to look at this house. It was simple, perfect. She looked down at the phone number Doug had given her.

If only she didn't have to call Brad . . . What did you say to a brother you had met once?

One danger of being rich was that you could pay other people to do your dirty work. Lynette could call Brad tomorrow morning. *Jill needs to be out on the East Coast this morning, and I'm co-ordinating her schedule . . .*

But Alice, Jill's British governess, had had high standards. A child raised by Alice Hastings had other people do her dirty work only when it would be easier on the person dirtied.

Jill looked back down at the phone. It was still there. She did not want to make this call.

She picked up the phone. She pressed the "one" button, then "seven," "zero," and "three," the Virginia area code.

If she were to say "This is Jill," would he know who she was? Should she say "This is Jill Casler"? or "Your sister, Jill"? "Your sister, Jill Casler"? "Your half-sister, Jill Casler"? "Your half-sister, Jill Casler, the very idea of whom made your mother's skin crawl"?

She hung up.

She wasn't being cowardly, she just needed to prepare herself. She dialed the Casler Properties office. "Lynette, you know my brother Brad . . . what's his wife's name?"

"Louise, I think, but let me check."

Whenever Jill got a Christmas letter or birth announcement from the family in Virginia, Lynette entered its information on a card file. Alice had set up the system. Some of the systems in Jill's life were better suited to Henry and his ducal accumulation of stately homes and debts, but they did have their uses.

Lynette came back on the line. "His wife is Louise, and he has five children: Carolyn, Christa, Stacey, Taffy, and Randy. The daughters are all married. There are thirteen grandchildren. Do you need their names?"

"No." Five children, thirteen grandchildren, and that was just Brad. Dave also had a family. Surely they wouldn't *all* come out to meet her. Or would they? It was an awesome prospect, enough to make a body turn those six white horses around and whip them mightily until all were safe on the far side of the mountain.

"I don't need their names right now," she told Lynette, "but I might in a day or so. Could you type out a list?"

Lynette said she would be happy to do so. Jill thanked her, hung up, and looked at Brad's phone number again.

She dialed quickly. The phone rang twice, then was picked up.

"Hello." It was a woman's voice.

"Louise" — Jill blessed Alice's system — "this is Brad's sister, Jill. Is he available?"

"Jill!" Louise's voice was almost shrill in

astonishment. "Brad, Brad, it's Jill." She must have been so shocked that she hardly moved the receiver from her mouth. Jill could hear her clearly.

It was only a moment before the receiver changed hands. Brad came on. "Jill! What's wrong? Has something happened? What can I do?"

Jill blinked. What could he do? Why was he asking that? If something was wrong, she wouldn't bother him. It wouldn't occur to her. "No, no," she assured him. "Everything's fine. I've been thinking that I'd like to come out to the Valley and see everyone sometime, and I wondered when — "

"Come out here? For a visit?" His voice was blank with astonishment. "You want to come to the Valley?"

"She wants to come to the Valley?" This was Louise's voice. Jill could hear it almost as clearly as Brad's. "She wants to visit?"

"Doug Ringling was nice enough to look me up when he was out here." Jill had jettisoned the idea of saying that she would be on the East Coast anyway. She lied enough about her emotions; she tried to tell the truth about her plans. "That inspired me to come and see the whole family. It would just be for a day or two . . . if it's convenient, that is."

"Convenient? Of course, it's convenient, but you can't come all that way for a day or two," Brad insisted. "We hope you'll stay for as long as you want. When did you want to come? Although any time is fine with us. Any time at all. Just tell us when and we'll come into Dulles and pick you up."

Dulles was one of the airports outside Washington, D.C. Jill wasn't sure, but she thought it was a couple hours' drive from the Valley. "You don't need to do that. I'll rent a car."

Louise's voice chimed in again. "Tell her she can stay here."

"You can stay here," Brad echoed. "We have plenty of room now that the girls and Randy are on their own."

"No, no," Jill protested. "I'm sure I'll be comfortable in a hotel."

"She wants to stay in a hotel," Brad said to Louise.

"She can't stay in a hotel," Louise answered back.

"You can't stay in a hotel," Brad said into the phone.

What followed was a little nightmare. Brad and Louise were determined to do everything they could for her — pick her up at the airport, put her up at their house, feed her three meals a day with a snack at eleven

154

and tea at four. Jill was equally determined to stop them from doing that.

A year ago she would have wanted to keep everyone from going to so much trouble on her behalf. But now her motives were clearer. She really did want to stay in a hotel. This visit might be unbearable; she wanted a sanctuary, a refuge from her refuge, so to speak. She held firm, willing to compromise on the car, but not the hotel.

"Tell her we don't have any hotels in this part of the Valley," Louise said.

"We don't have any hotels in this part of the Valley," Brad said.

"Nothing at all?" Jill asked.

"Just the Best Western off the Interstate, but it's a motel."

Jill spoke quickly, wanting to get in before Louise did. "A motel is fine. It will be perfect. I know it will."

At last he had to give in, and she promised to call him back the next day with her exact plans.

Then he spoke, clearing his throat awkwardly. "I hope you know how pleased the whole family will be."

Jill muttered something and after the phone was safely back in its cradle, she buried her face in her hands.

What had she gotten herself into? How

had a straightforward, understandable interest in a piece of film history led to this, her meeting a group of people who thought of her as "Aunt Jill"? She knew nothing about being an aunt to thirteen children. Except she wasn't their aunt. She was — Heaven forbid — their *great*-aunt.

She felt dizzy, yet blank and flattened. You slap a lid on a grease fire and for a moment the fire stills burns under the lid, out of sight, sucking up the last bits of oxygen, but still there. This was how her mother must have felt when she reached for the Valium.

So far no one had had heart failure, but the Caslers certainly were humming with excitement over Jill's coming. Doug watched it all with great amusement. The old house that he and Randy lived in had one black rotary-dial phone sitting on a shelf in the aging kitchen. It rang more during the next week than it had over the last two months. Randy's mother and sisters called to schedule family events and then reschedule them.

First there was to be a barbecue on Saturday. Then someone remembered that Sunday was Mother's Day. The family always had a barbecue on Mother's Day. Then someone else remembered the Civil War

156

re-enactment at New Market and wondered if Jill might like to see that. So the barbecue was put off to Sunday and a picnic at the battlefield scheduled for Saturday.

Randy was designated to pick Jill up at the airport on Friday since he went into Washington for the farmer's market Friday morning. Then his father, Brad, decided that, as the family's senior male, he should meet her, so he was going to drive in with Randy. Then Louise said that Jill might not be used to riding in pickups. Randy offered to take his new truck instead of the old one. That wasn't good enough. So Brad and Louise were going to drive in to get her in their Lincoln.

Dave's wife, Ginny, then got mad at Louise because Louise wouldn't bring Jill over to Dave and Ginny's for dinner on Friday night. Louise told her if she really felt that welcoming, she and Dave shouldn't go to their duplicate bridge club that was meeting Saturday night.

Randy's sisters couldn't agree about the picnic on Saturday. Carolyn, the eldest, decided it should be potluck. She had made up a list, telling each family what they should bring. Christa and Stacey thought each family should bring all their own food. Taffy thought everyone should bring their own main course and then one dish to share, but that Carolyn shouldn't always hog the dessert, which always got its baker all kinds of attention and praise.

And what should they do about church on Sunday? Did anyone know if she would expect to be taken to church? And what about Monday? She was staying through to Tuesday morning. What should they do with her on Monday? The men would all be back at work.

By and large, the Caslers got along very well. That they weren't at the moment suggested how important Jill's visit was to them.

When they spoke about the visit — and Doug was starting to think of it in capital letters: The Visit — they sounded a little patronizing. How nice it was going to be for Jill to be coming home, to see the Valley where her ancestors had lived for seven generations. How much she must be missing because of being cut off from her heritage, how empty her life must be without family. They were prepared to be generous and supportive. They would rally round and show her the sights.

Yet, for all this gracious talk, they were worried, intimidated, borderline terrified. No one was admitting it, but Doug sensed the repressed anxiety. She might be a very difficult guest — smug, superior, condescending. She was rich, a creature completely different from you and me, a creature completely uninterested in you and me.

He found himself in the unhappy position of being the one person who knew why she was really coming — to meet his Uncle Charles. Charles lived in Winchester with his mother, Doug's grandmother. Doug had his grandmother call Louise Casler to say that Charles wanted to meet Jill; could she come up to Winchester for one dinner? Louise hadn't much liked the idea, but she grudgingly agreed to let the Ringlings have Jill on Monday evening, her last night in the Valley.

Then Doug's sisters got in on things. Like Randy, Doug had four of them, and they were every bit as susceptible to Jill's glamour as were the Caslers. When the four Ringling girls — as they were still known, even though they were all married — heard that their grandmother was having this incredibly rich person to dinner, each one called to invite her husband and herself. Finally Gran realized that she was going to be cooking Thanksgiving dinner in May, which she did not feel like doing, so she disinvited the whole lot, including Doug's parents, even though they only lived across the street.

As two of the Ringling sisters had invitations to the ladies' bridge luncheon now scheduled for Monday, they accepted their exile in reasonably good grace. "You have to tell us exactly what she's wearing," Doug's sister Anne told him over the phone.

"No. I won't. Not one word." Doug knew all there was to know about dealing with sisters. "You'll only end up mad at me. I'm going to say that her skirt was blue, and you'll ask if it was lapis or periwinkle, and I'm not going to know. Hide out at Mom and Dad's and peek through the Venetian blinds. I'll park on that side of the street so you can see better."

The night before her arrival Doug had dinner with his parents. "That poor girl," his father said. "Does she know the number of fatted calves being killed this week?"

"No. She doesn't know anything about the 'Aunt Jill' myth. She honestly thought that she could come see Charles and no one would know about it."

"Your sisters are wondering," his father said — both Doug and his father knew that there was one advantage to living with five women; you could always blame your curiosity on one of them — "if she is coming out to see you."

"To see me?" Doug shook his head. "I wish."

"Now, don't be so sure," said his mother loyally. "You are a very attractive young man."

"So was Uncle Bix."

He didn't have to say more. His parents understood.

It had started when he was young: *my word, he looks so much like Bix . . . doesn't it send chills down your spine . . . dear boy, you can't know . . .* He had been mystified. He couldn't see any resemblance between his skinny self and the grown man in an army uniform whose picture his grandmother had on her bureau.

At fourteen he started to see the resemblance, but, alas, it didn't get him any points with the girls. They had all known him since first grade. They were used to what he looked like and were, for the most part, sick of hearing their parents gush about it. Doug had done all right in high school; rarely did he get turned down for a date. But that was because he was captain of the basketball team, not because he looked like his uncle.

Then came college. He was leaving Virginia, and his father had warned him. "You're going to surprise a lot of people, and you need to decide, when it comes to girls, if you want to take what's really being offered to a character in a movie."

Doug had been an eighteen-year-old male with an eighteen-year-old male's testosterone levels. He didn't do a great job of taking his father's advice. Frankly, he had not cared why what was being offered was being offered. The rigors of practice and classes had inclined him to be faithful to one young lady at a time, but none of the relationships ever led to anything permanent.

As he matured he understood why. His father had been right. If a girl — a woman — was expecting him to be Phillip Wayland, she was going to be disappointed. Phillip was a creature of the nineteenth century. Doug could, if pressed, manage to open car doors and relay a woman's dinner order to the waiter, but Phillip's elaborate gallantry wasn't possible anymore. Not many women these days needed to be protected from Sheridan's hard-riding, battle-worn Yankees. And how would Doug have done it . . . with a basketball?

But his face set up certain expectations, expectations that eventually cursed a relationship. Not all women had as strong a reaction as Jill Casler — in fact, Doug couldn't remember any woman ever having as strong a reaction as she had — but it was a rare one who didn't notice.

He wondered if Jill's reaction was going

to be an issue when she came out to the Valley. Probably not. She wasn't coming to see him.

On the other hand, she was going to be overwhelmed by this family of hers and their barbecues and potlucks and bridge luncheons. She might well need to be rescued, and he had a pretty good idea whom she would turn to when she did —

Phillip Wayland.

Six

Jill slid up the stiff little shade covering the airplane window. As if it were the first flight of her life, she watched the plane take off. The runway sped beneath her gaze, then grew more distant, the view widening to take in the terminal, then streets and houses, the ribbons and cloverleafs of the freeways. The window turned smoky white as the plane passed though the cloud cover. Jill, who almost never initiated conversations on airplanes, turned in her wide first-class seat, wanting to chat with her seatmate, a businessman who did not want to chat.

For the first time in recent memory she ate the airline meal, every bite of it. She paged through the in-flight magazine and went to the bathroom three times, each trip disrupting this unhappy businessman who had used a Frequent Flyer upgrade because he wanted to get some work done. The third time she came out of the tiny cubicle she saw that he had changed seats. That was unusual. Men did not usually run away from Jill Casler and her gorgeous chorus-girl legs.

She sat back down, refastened her seat belt, and twisted sideways in the seat, resting her cheek on the little white bib draped over the headrest. Beyond the double plastic window the sky was blue with little puffs of clouds.

What was she afraid of?

It was true that she didn't like confrontation, but there wasn't going to be any on this trip. What did she and her two brothers have to quarrel about? Whatever their mother had thought of her mother, it wasn't likely that Brad and Dave thought of her as white trash. It was almost a shame; she would have found that funny.

So there was nothing to worry about. Perhaps they would all be stiff and uncomfortable, but that was hardly a problem. Jill was used to people being stiff and uncomfortable around her; it was one price of being wealthy.

She landed at Dulles and rode the boxcar-like people-mover to the main terminal. She recognized Brad immediately, something that she had not been taking for granted. He stepped forward, took her carry-on bag, and introduced her to his wife Louise. He ascertained that she had not checked other bags and led the way out of the terminal. Outside he suggested that the ladies wait while he got the car. Jill never minded walking, but obediently she stopped at the curb and waited with Louise.

Her brother's wife was a thin woman in her early fifties, dressed in a pleasantly upper-middle-class style. She was wearing a pale blue polo dress with neat, tight stitching and a scrolling logo on the breast pocket that Jill did not recognize, although she supposed that her mother would.

"We made a reservation for you at the nearest motel," she said to Jill. "It's only a Best Western. I don't imagine it's what you're used to."

"I'm not fussy," Jill said. "Really, I'm not."

Louise raised her eyebrows. *Then why are you insisting on staying in a motel?* she seemed to say. "It's clean, very clean, I can say that for it. We went over and looked at one of the rooms. We had to as I don't think I know a soul who has ever stayed there. Even at Carolyn's wedding, with all Brian's family in from Newport News, we were able to put everyone up. But we didn't mind inspecting the motel for you. The manager was very pleasant."

Apparently she had minded a great deal indeed. Housing the entire population of Newport News — wherever that was — had been less of a burden than this trip to the Best Western.

Before Jill could apologize, a big, white Lincoln, sparklingly new, pulled up to the curb, and Brad got out, coming around to get Jill's bag. Louise waved her hand toward the front door. "Do ride in front with Brad," she said, the gracious queen, bestowing her throne on the young, blonde usurper.

"No, no," Jill said quickly. "You go ahead."

"You don't want to sit with Brad?"

There was no way to win here, Jill realized. Louise was determined to put her in the wrong. She felt abused because Jill was staying in the motel, but had Jill stayed in their house, Louise would, no doubt, have spent the whole visit feeling taken advantage of.

This was not a game Jill cared to play. She put forth her best copy of her mother's practiced smile. "Thank you. I am looking forward to seeing the Valley."

She opened the car door and slid inside, reaching out to shut the door behind her. Then she stopped, her hand still in mid-air.

Brad smoked. The interior of his car reeked with a tobacco haze.

None of Jill's friends smoked. She was used to no-smoking sections of restaurants and smoke-free suites in hotels. But Cass had smoked, and his clothes and his car had always smelled of tobacco. To this day it was a scent she associated with him. It was rare that she got into a smoky car, but when she did, she thought of him; she would turn, half-expecting to see him next to her.

She heard the door on the driver's side open. She waited a moment, then forced herself to look.

Brad had a narrow face, his shoulders were erect, his hair thinning. He looked nothing like Cass. Jill was glad of that. If it was unsettling to see Phillip's face on Doug Ringling, how much worse to see her father's face on a stranger.

Brad inserted the keys in the ignition and punched in the cigarette lighter. He pulled the car away from the curb. "Do you mind if I smoke?" he asked Jill.

"You should tell him that you mind," Louise chirped from the back seat. "It's such a disgusting habit. The girls and I are always on him to quit."

"I don't mind," Jill said.

She watched Brad take the package of cigarettes out of his breast pocket. With his left hand still on the steering wheel, he shook one free, lipping it out the rest of the way. He pulled out the cigarette lighter and, inhaling, lit his cigarette.

That was exactly how Cass had lit cigarettes. Brad had probably learned to smoke from him. After all, Cass had been his father, too.

Jill's mother had her baby book, full of pictures of Cass and Jill: Cass feeding Jill her strained cereal, Jill riding on his shoulders, Cass twirling her in airplane spins. Cass always gripped her upper arms during airplane spins; he said spinning children by the hands was too hard on their little shoulders.

Ellen had probably had a baby book just like that: Cass feeding Brad his strained cereal, Brad riding on his shoulders, Cass twirling him by the forearms in an airplane spin. No, Ellen would have two such baby books, one for Brad, one for Dave.

Maybe this was what she had been uneasy about on the plane . . . that after twenty-six years of loving, adoring, and being adored by her father, after two years of grieving for him, now she was going to have to share him.

She looked at Brad again. There was so much they could talk about. Brad had been eight when Ellen had brought him back to the Valley. He would remember being Cass's son.

What did Cass ask you? Did he want to know about your imaginary friends? Cass had never seemed to understand that Jill had not had any imaginary friends. She had always

169

thought he sounded like he wanted her to have them so she would desperately try to invent them, but she hadn't been able to. *Did he ask you about the stories you told yourself?* Jill hadn't told herself stories either.

Maybe Brad had. Maybe he had had imaginary friends; maybe he had told himself stories. Jill had inherited her father's money, she also had his charm and his sense of structure. But she did not have what was truly special about him — his imagination. Maybe Brad did.

I know Cass loved me, worshiped me, but sometimes I wonder . . . if I hadn't been his daughter, would he have respected me?

She could barely admit that thought to herself, she certainly could not discuss it with this stranger.

It took two hours to drive out to the Valley, and it was a strained, tense trip. Louise was unwilling to introduce a subject; she wanted someone else to take that risk so she could criticize them for doing so. Nor did Brad have much to say. He knew little about Jill's life. He probably assumed it was an idle one, and he had enough repressed disapproval of professional leisure that he was embarrassed to ask her the questions that would have told him otherwise. Clearly he hated this, having a half-sister, younger than his daughters, to whom he had nothing to say.

Jill, however, could make conversation with anyone under any circumstances. *Your job,* nanny Alice had told her, *is to make other people feel comfortable,* advice that was probably better suited to Henry, now a good, hardworking duke, than it was to Jill, now a recovering co-dependent, constantly struggling with the temptation to put everyone else's needs before her own.

So she encouraged Brad to talk about impersonal things. She learned about the economy and the topography of the Valley, about the ambitious technology of his son Randy's poultry operation, about the textile plant that had polluted the Shenandoah River. Every fifteen miles Louise leaned forward and said, "Oh, Brad, you must be boring Jill to tears. She can't be interested in that." So every fifteen miles Jill had to start all over.

It was still light by the time they got to Courthouse. The Best Western was right off the Interstate, and Brad pulled the car up to the main entrance to let Jill and Louise off, though there were parking spaces only a few feet away. It seemed like excessive formality to Jill, but perhaps this elaborate courtesy was Brad's only way of saying that she was welcome.

What an odd pair he and Louise seemed to be. He, tense and overcontrolled, seemed paralyzed by his high standards and good intentions whereas she was entirely comfortable in her manipulation and schemes. Jill wondered if Louise might not resemble Ellen, if Brad had chosen a wife who was very like his mother.

The motel's reception area was in the center of the sprawling cinderblock building. As Jill and Louise were coming through the double glass doors marked "Registration," Louise let out a little startled hiss.

A man was coming across the reception area. "I know, Louise. I know. You didn't want anyone to come tonight." He was round-faced, shorter than Jill, dressed in casual slacks and a plaid sport shirt. He had an open, cheery look to him. "Forgive us, Jill. We were sitting down to dinner, the kids were about to explode with excitement, and then I realized I was, too. So we dashed over. We'll say hello, and then we'll run right off."

Brad was through the door now. "Jill, this is my brother, Dave, and his wife, Ginny."

Behind Dave was a bright-faced, little brunette woman dressed in a pretty pink track suit.

"No, no, Brad," Dave chided his older

172

brother, "you can't say *my* brother anymore. It should be *our* brother. We're going to need to get used to that."

Until now neither Jill nor Brad had said one word about being related. Jill felt the tendons in her neck easing, the line of her shoulders lowering. Dave's openness was a relief.

She put out her hand. Dave took it in both his and lightly kissed her cheek. "Why are you going to run off?" she asked.

"Louise didn't think it was fair to overwhelm you with family on the first night, that you would be tired after your trip with the time change and all. And she's right, of course. But Ginny and I decided to pretend that you traveled enough so that you could bear a quick grin from us."

He spoke with a warm smile as if he knew perfectly well that he, not Louise, was right. And he was. A flight from the coast was nothing to Jill, and at this point the time change was in her favor.

"Then I'll pretend to be delighted to see you," Jill replied, smiling. How different he was from Brad. It was hard to imagine the two brothers in business together, but they owned their apple orchards in common. "Why don't we all go to the bar and have a drink?"

"Don't you want to check in?" Louise was trying to regain control of the evening. "Aren't you worried that they might give away your room?"

"No," Jill said. Even Best Westerns did not give away Jill Casler's room.

"I'll tell them she's here," Brad said.

So he went off toward the registration desk, and the three women followed Dave into the lounge.

"Do you believe this?" Dave said to his wife as he held out Jill's chair for her. "That Brad and I have a sister who's so beautiful? We've seen your pictures, Jill, and I always thought they were nice, but they certainly don't do you justice."

"I take terrible pictures," Jill replied. "I don't know what it is about my face, but I do look stupid in a picture."

"We saw that picture in *People*," Ginny said in a soft Southern voice. "The one with Payne Bartlett . . . my sixteen-year-old daughter is dying to know if you're his girlfriend."

"No, I'm not." Jill was one of the very few people on earth who knew that Payne was gay. In the name of his career, he had become rigidly celibate. "It sounds corny, but we really are just friends. We grew up together so we feel like — " She stopped.

Like brother and sister didn't seem the most appropriate simile in this crowd. "Like cousins."

Dave smiled. "I'm sure our Heather wishes she had a cousin like that."

"That's not fair, Dave," Louise said stiffly. "Randy is a very attractive young man."

It took Jill a moment to follow Louise's logic. Randy, Louise's son, would be Dave's daughter's cousin. Louise was taking Dave's pleasantry as an attack on Randy. That seemed bizarre in the extreme.

But Dave hardly reacted. "You know I didn't mean anything personal, Louise. Now, where is that waitress?"

Louise pointedly ordered a caffeine-free Diet Coke. Jill, who would have ordered white wine, was not about to be shamed into temperance, She ordered a vodka and tonic. Ginny asked for a frozen apricot brandy sour, which did not sound like the order of a serious drinker, and Dave asked for two beers, one for him and one for Brad, who was approaching the table with Jill's room key.

It was an interesting forty-five minutes. It was soon clear to Jill that Dave purchased his easy charm at a cost — superficiality. He kept saying how wonderful it was to see Jill, seeming oblivious to the fact that they all could have gotten together any time during the last fifteen years. Any questions she had about Cass and their childhoods couldn't be addressed to him either. He would forever be easy to chat with, but impossible to confide in.

His easy questions about her life turned up the fact that her house had been destroyed. Dave was fascinated and sympathetic; Brad was horrified. "Why didn't you call?" he fussed. "Why didn't you let us know? We could have helped."

What's wrong? Has something happened? What can I do? he had asked the instant he heard her voice on the phone.

Brad felt responsible for her. No, Brad probably felt responsible for everyone. Dave was the brother everyone liked; Brad was the one everyone depended on. One of the men in her therapy group was like that — overconscientious a perfectionist, the eldest son of an absent father.

An absent father . . . Well, that was true of Brad, wasn't it? Jill twisted her glass around on the damp cocktail napkin. She had always viewed Ellen as the villain in Cass and Ellen's separation. Ellen had been the one who had left. But Brad and Dave probably hadn't felt that way. Their father had been given a choice between family and career. He had chosen his career. That couldn't have made them feel treasured.

Alice had kept a scrapbook of all the articles written about Cass. From the day of Jill's birth Cass had always mentioned her whenever he could. This was in the days when few men in their fifties had newborns, and Cass was enchanted with the joys of late-life fatherhood. *I have time for her . . . I take her everywhere . . . I really know her.* And the comparison, *It was not like this the first time.*

Jill had thrilled to read those comments, but Brad and Dave, if they had ever seen them, would surely have felt differently. They would have been grown men, but still, Cass's remarks must have hurt. Surely his sons would have read them as being full of rejection.

The real message behind them must have been guilt, Cass's guilt over having put his career first. But it had taken Jill a long time to learn that about her father, time that Brad and Dave never had.

She stirred uneasily. She wasn't used to thinking of Cass as the bad guy, as the one who was less than perfect.

But maybe he was.

Before Jill went to her room, Brad and

Louise laid out the weekend schedule for her. Tomorrow there would be a Civil War re-enactment at the New Market battlefield, which they hoped she would enjoy. A number of family members planned on gathering there for a picnic. Then, after church on Sunday, she could tour Brad and Dave's orchards, take a ride up to Skyline Drive, visit Luray Caverns, or do any other touristy activity that might interest her. In the afternoon the family would assemble for a barbecue. "It is Mother's Day, after all," Louise pointed out, as if to underscore how inconsiderately Jill had timed her visit.

At noon on Monday, Carolyn, Brad's oldest daughter, was having a bridge luncheon for her. Monday evening Jill would have dinner with the Ringlings. Then Brad would drive her to the airport first thing Tuesday morning.

Brad, the ever-responsible Brad, offered to take her to breakfast before the re-enactment Saturday morning, but she excused herself, pleading jet lag. He was to come get her at ten.

At nine the next morning her phone rang. She guessed it would be Brad, checking to be sure she knew how to eat breakfast.

It wasn't.

"Jill, this is Doug. I hope I didn't wake you."

"No, no. But I'm glad you caught me. I was about to go for a walk." Sunshine and exercise were Jill's cure for jet lag.

"Do you want some company? Randy and I are across the street, getting gas."

"That sounds great."

"Then let's meet on the median strip. But I have to warn you — I look pretty weird."

"What do you mean? Do you still look like Phillip?"

"More than ever, I'm afraid."

This Jill had to see.

In the last few days she had thought about Doug a lot. Once she had decided to come to the Valley, she had called a clipping service to see if they had any information, however dated, on a former hotshot basketball player. The packet they sent over was startlingly thick.

Jill had been mesmerized by the articles, profiles, and columns describing his career, detailing the scandal that had ended it. Here was a man liked and admired by other men. When his own athletic director had turned on him, dozens of others had come to his support. "Shoot," the Lynx had been quoted as saying — although Jill doubted that that had actually been his word — "Doug's dad has been G.M.'s top salesman about a hundred times. If Doug had had anything to

179

do with this, would those guys have been driving Chryslers?"

However much Doug might look like Phillip, his personality was his own — relaxed and articulate with a dry self-depreciating wit. His style was one of effortlessness. "Make it look easy, guys," was one of his comments from the sidelines. "Make it look easy." He commanded his troops without the anger or strung-out intensity of other coaches. He led by example; he, too, made it look easy.

Jill liked that.

Determined to get beyond the way he looked, she clipped back her hair and tucked her room key, some money, and a credit card in her pocket. She rarely carried a purse; she liked the sense of freedom, the sense of not needing a lot of things. Her hair was thick enough that it didn't need to be combed very often; her sunblock was strong enough that it didn't need to be renewed. Her one credit card looked ordinary enough, but she could have bought the *Mona Lisa* with it.

She pulled the motel door shut, listening for the locking click. It was a lovely, sparkling day, still slightly cool although the radio had promised the afternoon would be in the upper seventies. The light here was softer than in the West. The blues of the sky and the greens of the meadows and hills flowed together in a swirling watercolor wash.

The motel was in a little commercial oasis. Five or six businesses servicing the interstate traffic straddled the road that was four lanes for a few hundred yards before it narrowed into a country lane bordered by green fields and roadside ditches dotted with buttercups and sweet clover. Among the businesses were a Wendy's and a McDonald's, a 7-Eleven with gas pumps, and across from the Best Western was an Exxon station. Behind its sign, waiting for a break in traffic, was Doug.

He was in uniform, a Confederate uniform. Jill stopped dead. So much for getting beyond the way he looked.

It was a beautiful uniform. Even with the four lanes and traffic between them, Jill could see that. It was made of thick grey wool with yellow satin facings, shining brass buttons, and scrolling gold cording, finished off with glossy cavalry boots and a low-slung leather sword belt.

It was too much. It really was. Jill watched him sprint across the road. Was this what he called looking weird? She had another word for it.

He was across the road now, standing in front of her, the morning sun twinkling off his brass buttons. He was breathing lightly, so well conditioned that his body didn't notice a quick sprint. She heard herself speak. "You look gorgeous. You shouldn't be allowed out of the house in that."

"I'm sorry," he apologized, laughing. "But this is the first time I've done one of these re-enactments, and this getup is borrowed."

"I'm not complaining." Good God, was she flirting with him? She never flirted.

"Well, I am. I feel like a bloody fool. No, that's not true," he said, honesty warming his eyes, crinkling his nose. "I felt like an idiot when I first put it on, but now I'm starting to feel rather dashing. In another hour or so I will be strutting and preening insufferably. But enough about me. Welcome to the Valley. Are you having a good time? 'Not quite yet' is a perfectly acceptable response."

And an accurate one. "I'm having an interesting time. But I committed a terrible *faux pas,* insisting on staying in a motel."

"I know. I heard."

"You did?"

"Oh, yes," he assured her. "Between us, Randy and I have eight sisters. We hear everything . . . no, that's giving us too much credit. We are told everything; we don't always listen."

"You have *eight* sisters?"

"Personally, I only have four, but Randy

has four, too. That's why we deal so well together. Nobody else knows what it's like. He's at the pay phone now. We had a great idea." He was checking the traffic. "Here, I think we can cross now . . . although this uniform does make me feel like I should give you my arm. Anyway, as long as we're on our way to New Market, and you're on your way to New Market, we thought we'd let you hitch a ride with us. Is that okay with you? Randy's trying to negotiate with his dad. Can you bear to change your plans?"

Now, that was one tough decision. She could spend the morning with Brad, who would tell her all about the battle of New Market as clearly and tersely as a National Park Service leaflet, or she could spend it with this man and his gorgeous uniform.

She spoke. "You talk more than Phillip, don't you?"

"He didn't have four sisters." Doug's smile was honey. "I'm making up for lost time. I never got to use the bathroom and I never got to talk. Am I driving you nuts? Back in college, the guys always said I never met a mike I didn't like."

No, he was not driving her nuts. Not in the least.

They were at the Exxon station now. Standing at the pay phone was another Confederate

183

soldier. He was freckled with sandy hair, only an inch or so taller than Jill. His uniform was quite different from Doug's. Torn and patched, it was a yellowy-brown butternut. He pulled off his forage cap, stuck it under his arm, cradled the phone under his chin and reached out his hand to Jill. It was his left hand, so that when Jill put her right hand in it, they were holding hands rather than formally shaking them.

"Yes, Dad," he said, rolling his eyes, instantly creating a little relationship with Jill in which they shared some knowledge about Brad. "I'll be careful. I have the new truck; that will make me careful even if I didn't care about my Aunt Jill whom I now see to be the most astonishingly gorgeous woman."

Lynette's card file had reported that Randy was almost exactly Jill's age. He was the youngest of Brad's five children, the only son. He had gone to college at Virginia Tech in Blacksburg and had been working with his father and uncle when he had received the unexpected legacy from Cass. At least, the legacy was supposedly unexpected, but within two weeks Randy had been at the bank with ambitious plans for his egg production operation.

He was still listening to Brad, his expression

making it clear that he was hearing another round of paternal instructions. Then he said good-bye and, still holding Jill's hand, hung up. "Don't tell me you're my Aunt Jill. I don't believe it. It's not fair. The best-looking girl around is my aunt."

Jill didn't like responding to comments about her looks. Before she could muster a reply, Doug spoke. "What did your dad say? Can we have Jill?"

"If we drive carefully, if we make sure she gets lunch, if we swear to deliver her to the lower meadow at one o'clock sharp."

"So what do you say, Jill?" Doug turned to her. "Do you want to accompany us warriors as we march off to celebrate our Glorious, Noble, Sexist, and Racist Past?"

"I feel underdressed," she said. She was in a short denim jeans skirt and a white knit shirt. "Shouldn't I be in a hoop skirt?"

Randy stepped back and drew Doug with him. He tilted his head sidewards to look down at Jill's showgirl legs, which rose up to meet the hem of her skirt . . . and when you were five feet ten and wore a size six, a knee-length skirt hit mid-thigh. "I think a hoop skirt would be a crime."

Randy's truck was parked by the gas pumps. It was indeed new, glittering with a blue metallic paint. It had oversized tires, so Jill had to hike her short denim skirt up even farther to climb in. She slid into the middle of the wide seat, automatically reaching for the seat belt. Doug, she noticed, buckled his belt, too. Randy did not. The minute they were on the Interstate she decided that that was foolish of him, indeed. He drove at a blinding speed.

New Market was fifteen miles to the south, and during the trip, which was a whole lot briefer than it ought to have been, Doug and Randy told Jill about Civil War re-enactments. It was as if she and Doug knew that the *Weary Hearts* search was only between the two of them, something not to be discussed until they were alone.

"Who participates in the re-enactments?" she asked.

"It varies," Doug answered. "There are some serious students of military history. There are the ones who just want to get out of the house and drink beer — "

"That's the two of us," Randy added. "I just wish there were more girls."

Doug ignored him. "And then there are the serious crazies."

"Tell me about them," Jill said. She had, she was sure, the greatest respect for the serious students of military history, but she was more interested in the crazies.

"They think the South should have won the war. It's like they think that if Lee had had his wits about him at Gettysburg, they would now own Twelve Oaks and four hundred slaves. Although it always seems to me that these are precisely the folks who would be in terrible trouble in a society without a large middle class. Other people really get into the authenticity thing. At least Randy and I have on our own sturdy, white Jockeys. Some of those guys will be wearing authentic reproduction Confederate underwear. Can you imagine?"

Jill could not.

"And you wouldn't want to," Randy added. "The Tenth Virginia has the biggest bunch of beer bellies you've even seen. I always heard that the Confederacy was starving. These guys aren't."

Apparently the re-enactors had gathered at the battlefield the night before, and each army had set up an encampment. Doug and Randy, tied to a morning routine by the habits of three hundred thousand chickens, hadn't been able to come for that. But once they got to New Market and a uniformed Eagle Scout had directed them to park on a grassy meadow, they sought out the Tenth Virginia, and "Private Casler" and "Private Ringling" reported for duty and instantly asked for permission to escort this lady, commonly thought to be a Northern spy, around the grounds.

"Be back for mess," their sergeant told them. "Or I'll put you on report. Private Casler, you still have extra duty from Chancellorsville."

Randy did not seem stricken by this news.

The encampment was permeated with a wonderful holiday spirit. Confederate soldiers were crawling out of their tattered tents, stretching and scratching at pretend lice, boiling Maxwell House coffee over campfires. Besides the soldiers, there were doctors, chaplains, undertakers, and sutlers. Some of the women wore the dress of nurses and camp followers — long, dark skirts and grey blouses, their hair held back by black snoods. Others swept through the orchard in polyester ball gowns, their swaying hoop skirts trimmed with yards of pregathered nylon lace. Mingling with them were the observers, wearing ridge-soled running shoes, carrying cameras and styrofoam coolers, and pushing strollers. Everyone was in good spirits; the atmosphere was gleeful, carnival-like.

Doug and Randy set a brisk pace, striding over stacked muskets, ducking under ladies' fringe-trimmed parasols, plunging down rows of low floorless tents. At one point they got trapped behind a unit of men marching in tight formation. The man directly ahead of Jill had a wooden canteen and a metal cup clipped to his belt; a long-handled frying pan swung behind the seat of his pants.

They watched a precision musket-firing competition, saw a display of nineteenth-century surgical instruments, and stopped at a line of twentieth-century porta-potties. Between the two of them, the men knew an amazing number of people. They were always stopping to introduce Jill to someone or another. No one seemed surprised that Randy had an aunt his own age. Reports about Jill had preceded her. "Oh, right," several people said, "you're the rich one."

"I know that boy," Doug said the first time they heard this remark. "I grew up with him. And his mama would cut his tongue out if she heard him talk that way."

Jill gathered that this was an apology. "Don't worry about it." Even though she hadn't wanted to talk about her money in group, she wasn't ashamed or embarrassed about it. If anything, she was proud of what it said about her father's good sense . . . although his fiscal shrewdness was hardly what she valued the most about him.

Money was an issue at these re-enactments. The uniforms and replicated equipment were expensive, at least by the standards of the participants. Jill learned that the people who were playing clergymen and doctors often couldn't afford to buy the period-style, black-powder muskets used in the battle.

"I can't say I find that too comforting," Doug observed. "Those folks are responsible for the health of my body and my soul, and all that qualifies them is poverty."

The morning grew hotter and brighter. Jill eavesdropped on a "clergyman" showing off a small Bible. It was neither period-style nor a replica — it was genuine. His great-great-great-great-grandfather had carried it through the war.

Jill was impressed. She hardly even knew the names of her grandparents. "Aren't you worried about something happening to it?" She stepped forward to ask.

"I'm careful." Sunlight glinted off his small, round spectacles. "But wait a minute . . . aren't you what's-her-name? Randy's cousin or something? Didn't your father work on the movie?"

Her father had made twenty-eight movies. "He was a director."

"Then maybe you'll know. Hey, guys." He turned, signalling to some people gathering around a nearby tent. "Here's somebody who should know. We were up half the night wondering — how did Phillip get out of the draft?"

Jill blinked. "I beg your pardon?"

"You know, the movie. Phillip. How did he get out of the draft?"

So *Weary Hearts* was "the" movie, as if it were the only movie ever made. Jill liked that. These were her kind of people.

The clergyman was still talking. "He would have to have been exempted from conscription, wouldn't he?"

"I'm sorry. I don't know." Alice's upbringing had left Jill knowing more about the Cavaliers and the Roundheads than about the American Civil War. And during the hundreds of times she had watched Phillip agonize over not being in the army, she had never thought to wonder how he had legally avoided being drafted.

"I figure Stonewall could have exempted him," a woman in nurse's garb said. "The tough conscription law was passed in '62, and he didn't die until May of '63."

Suddenly a group of ten people were all talking about the movie, carrying on discussions that had obviously been going on since the day before.

". . . no, no, you're wrong. Sheridan came through in August of '64 and . . ."

". . . of course, people who started out

191

with Ashby ended up at Appomattox. Rosser took over the Laurel Brigade, and he was there."

"That scene where Booth's at the campfire, that has to be Cold Spring. It can't be Mechanicsville, the sun's in the wrong place for Mechanicsville."

Jill listened, almost disbelieving. She couldn't imagine anyone loving the movie more than she did. Yet these people were looking at it as she never had, opening it up, pouring back into the script all the historical detail that had only been hinted at.

Doug had now joined the group. Jill moved close to him. "Does the movie stand up to this kind of analysis?"

"I don't think there's a mistake in it."

Jill had spoken softly, but Doug had not. The others overheard him.

"Of course, there isn't," one soldier announced. "Our Bix knew his stuff."

The nurse was nodding her head. "It's not like *Gone With the Wind* and that silly lamp."

Jill did not know anything about the position of the sun in the battles of Cold Spring and Mechanicsville. In fact, she didn't even know what state they were in. But she did know about the *Gone With the Wind* lamp, the one that a set designer had placed in

Aunt Pitty-Pat's 1861 parlor even though such lamps hadn't been manufactured until the 1880's.

Suddenly everyone was now defending the virtues of their movie against *Gone With the Wind.* "Just because we didn't have enough money to hire Clark Gable or burn Atlanta."

This was said by someone who hadn't been born yet when the movie was made.

Jill flushed with pride. Her father had given the people of the Valley something they remembered. He might have left, but he had bestowed on them this movie, now a part of their heritage, a story through which they understood their history.

Jill listened to them talk and soon realized that one of the men was looking at her. He wasn't just eyeing her legs; he seemed to be alert for her attention. He was one of the beer-bellies Randy had spoken about. He had a twinkly Santa Claus look about him, even though he couldn't have been much over forty. Being in a very good mood, willing to meet anyone and everyone, Jill smiled at him. Encouraged, he hoisted himself up from the bale of hay he had been sitting on.

Doug noticed him as he was coming over. "Now, this is someone you'll want to meet. This is — "

"Don't waste your breath," the man in-

terrupted. "Everyone knows who she is."
He put out his hand. "Good afternoon,
ma'am. I'm Don Pleasant, the star of this
here movie everyone's talking about."

Jill felt the bones in her hand crumple in
his hearty grip. "I'm sorry. I don't understand. Were you in *Weary Hearts*?"

"Without me there wouldn't have been a
story," he answered. "Doug here may look
like the star, but he's just a period-style
replica. I'm the genuine thing."

"Don played Mary Deas's baby," Doug
explained.

"But the baby was a girl," Jill protested,
then mentally kicked herself. What difference
did the baby's sex make? There had been
no on-screen diaper changes. "I'm sorry. I
suppose people teased you about that endlessly when you were growing up."

The star of stage and screen grimaced. "I
did suffer for that bit of miscasting, but
apparently there weren't any newborn girls
around whose mamas were stagestruck
enough to put them under all those lights."

"But you probably weren't a newborn,"
Jill said. "No one ever casts newborns as
newborns. They're too ugly. Usually movie
newborns are two or three months old."

"February, March, April," Don counted.
"Hey, you're right. I was just coming up

194

on three months old. My God, not only was I playing a different sex, I was playing a different age. Why didn't I get an Oscar?"

"Blame it on Laurence Olivier. He made *Hamlet* that year."

"It was fixed. The voting was rigged, I know it."

"Do you want to hear something worse?" Jill went on. "You know Melanie's baby in *Gone With the Wind*?"

"That ham? That upstart?"

"He grew up and married Raquel Welch."

"No. You're kidding!" Don slapped his forehead. "Raquel Welch? I don't believe it. Wait till I tell Molly. I could have had Raquel Welch, and instead I chose her."

"They did get divorced."

"Molly threatens that too, sometimes."

Jill felt a hand on her arm. It was Randy's. The last time Jill had seen him he had been in the company of two polyester ball gowns. "I don't know why you all are talking about Raquel Welch," he said. "It sounds like a good subject to me, but if I don't get Aunt Jill back to my dad this instant, I will be talking about such subjects in a very high voice."

Jill put her hand out to Don, saying that it had been nice to meet him.

"Same here." He smashed her fingers again

195

and turned to Doug. "I really like her. You should try to keep her around."

"I don't think it's up to me," Doug answered. "But if it were — "

"Come on," Randy interrupted. "We've got to be in the lower meadow in five minutes."

People did seem to be organizing for the battle. The doctors and undertakers had closed up the displays of their equipment. Soldiers were straightening themselves into units. The spectators were streaming out of the encampment toward the meadow.

"My sister Taffy's bringing her new baby," Randy said as the three of them wove their way out of the encampment and through the orchard. "She doesn't want to stay the whole time since he's only a couple of weeks old, but she's determined to have you see him."

"Fine," Jill said . . . and then stopped.

A couple of weeks old . . . newborns don't play newborns . . . February, March, April . . .

"What's wrong?" Randy asked. "Are we going too fast? Blame Doug. His legs are too long."

"No, no." Jill started to move again.

Don Pleasant had been born in February and was just coming up on three months when the company came to the Valley to do the first round of location shots in April.

But there had been no baby in the script supposedly shot then. Jill had read Bix's original treatment. The guilty love story had not been a part of its narrative. Phillip hadn't fallen in love with his brother's wife; they hadn't had the baby together. That had supposedly been one of Cass's brilliant additions filmed in August.

But by August Don would have been seven months old, pounds heavier, very obviously much too big to play a newborn. No, Don's scenes had been shot in April.

Except that the script filmed in April wouldn't have needed a baby.

So the script supposedly filmed in April hadn't been. There could be no question; there had indeed been a secret script. As simple as this was, it was absolute confirmation. That script might not have been a masterpiece — it might have been godawful — but it had existed and it had been filmed.

She had fallen a few steps behind Doug and Randy. She caught up and put her hand on Doug's arm, stopping him. He looked down, puzzled. It was, she knew, the first time they had touched.

"I have to talk to you." She kept her voice low.

"What about it? Is something wrong?"

"Don't you understand what Don said? About his birthday, what that — ?"

"Come on, Ring," Randy ordered. "Hurry up."

Jill could already see Brad approaching them. She knew she had only another moment with Doug. "When can we talk? This is really important."

The first wave of family crested and broke around them. Dave's arm went around her, turning her away from Doug, and there were dozens of faces: Laurie, Carolyn and Brian, Taffy and the baby, Heather, Pete, Pete's girlfriend. She craned her neck around to see Randy pulling Doug back up to the encampment.

"But wait . . ." They hadn't set a place to meet. When was she going to see him? He was the one she wanted to see, not all of these people.

"Don't worry." She could hardly hear his voice over the noisy greetings of the family. "I'll be back."

She supposed that was the sort of thing soldiers always said.

Seven

Carolyn was Brad's oldest daughter. She was in the yellow shirt. Her husband Brian was over by the cooler. Christa, in the straw hat, was the next oldest. Her husband was Ken. After Christa came Stacey in the —

"What do you call that color, Stace?" Dave, who was performing these introductions, called out.

"Melon," Stacey answered and wriggled her fingers at Jill, who wriggled hers back.

We'll all come out to meet her when she comes . . .

Doug had been wrong. They hadn't all come out to meet Jill. Dave's older boy was at college, and only two of Brad's four sons-in-law had appeared. Louise was home preparing for the barbecue tomorrow: her apologies were ponderously passed along by Brad. But everyone else had come, and that was a lot of people — nine adults and more than a dozen children, ranging in age from Taffy's tiny baby to a budding pre-teen wearing a pair of horsehead earrings.

A pleasant chaos prevailed. Everyone was eating. People stretched across one another to reach the chips and stepped over legs and plates to get to the coolers. The watery-looking "tomato juice" served to the adults had been diluted by a generous splash of vodka, and this, too, added to the general liveliness.

They were an affluent, satisfied lot. The four daughters had married a doctor, two lawyers, and a United Airlines pilot. Civil War re-enactments were not their natural milieu; only a few of them had ever been to one before. Their picnics, Jill gathered from the sisters' chat about previous menus, were more often held before the Shenandoah Valley Music Festival or at steeplechase races. They all had traveled. Every child over four had been to DisneyWorld, and Jill heard talk about two-week European tours and Caribbean cruises. The children were in all kinds of activities: soccer and ballet, Brownies and piano lessons. The girl in the horsehead earrings had her own horse.

Jill sought this girl out. She was the oldest of the grandchildren; her name was Allison, and her horse's name was Belle Boyd. She was thrilled to learn that Jill had once had a horse, too.

"Do you still ride?" she asked.

"Sometimes. But you know how it is. If you don't do it every day, you lose your conditioning so fast."

Even at age ten Allison knew what Jill was talking about. "That's what I love about having Belle."

By now the Yankees had massed at the ridge atop a low hill. As the Confederates were gathering around the house and the orchard, Jill had a better view of the boys in blue. She felt sorry for them because they seemed so hopelessly outnumbered.

In reality, Brad told her, the Confederates had been outnumbered. The battle had been fought during the last year of the war, and the Confederates had been so desperate for men that they had emptied out the nearby military academy. Boys of fourteen and fifteen had died on this field. Each year the school commemorated their sacrifice with a roll call, a cadet replying after each name, "Dead on a field of honor."

Jill found this story more chilling than inspiring, but she supposed that was the lure of a re-enactment. It had all the fun of male bonding without the death. Indeed, during the first twenty minutes of the battle, despite all the smoke from the black-powder muskets and the booming cannons, Jill did not see a single soldier die.

Finally a Yankee fell, dropping dramatically behind his line. He did it immediately before a retreat, so the spectators were treated to the sight of the Federal troops moving back up the hill, stepping over his body without breaking ranks. After the army had passed, the fallen soldier stirred. He lifted his head and felt for his legs, needing to reassure himself that they were still there as apparently they no longer had feeling. Unable to rise, he began a dramatic climb up the hill, inching his way along by pulling himself with his forearms. He would stop, still unable to stand or sit, and on his elbow, would load his musket, shoot, then hitch himself up further. He spent the rest of the battle struggling his way up the hill.

"If you think about it, that's pretty grisly," said Carolyn-in-the-yellow-shirt. "I wonder if nineteenth-century medicine could have done anything for him."

Her husband Brian-over-by-the-cooler shook his head. "Probably not. They would have chopped his legs off and his family would have carried him around in a basket. Just keep reminding yourself that that guy's probably a data entry clerk for I.B.M. and is loving every instant of this."

Randy was among the Confederates who stormed the orchard fence. At least, that's what his sisters said. Jill couldn't distinguish him from the several hundred other Confederates clad in their ragged butternut. She scanned the charging ranks for a tall figure in grey, but couldn't find Doug in the first wave nor among those that followed. He must have already died. He had probably had the sense to expire up in the apple orchard where it was cooler.

As the battle drew to an end, the sisters began putting things back in the picnic baskets. Jill collected used plates and cups.

Brad came up to her, holding open a thirty-gallon trash bag. "May I discuss the evening's plans with you?"

"Of course." The biggest surprise of the picnic had been Brad. This reserved, awkward man adored his grandchildren. He had held Taffy's baby most of the time she had been there, and during the battle he had gone behind the line of spectators to play with the children. He had played soccer with a beach ball and three toddlers. He had gone down on his hands and knees to be their horsey. Upright again, he had given airplane spins . . . and yes, he had held the children by their upper arms.

He was at his best with the little ones. With Allison, nine-year-old Steve, and the twins, who were a pair of smart-mouthed seven-year-olds he grew more cautious. It was only in the uncritical company of the youngest that he relaxed.

"I'm afraid," he was saying to Jill, "that I need to get home and help Louise get ready for tomorrow, and this is Dave and Ginny's bridge club night. But the girls are all going over to Carolyn's. She says they'll get a movie for the kids and order pizza. Does that seem satisfactory?"

What could Jill say? It sounded like a fine arrangement, and at any other time she would have gone happily. But right now she wanted to stay here and wait for Doug. He said he would come back, and she wanted to be here when he came.

It was like in the movie when Sheridan and the Yankees came to burn Briar Ridge. Phillip rounded up the horses that the Confederate cavalry needed so desperately and drove them into hiding, knowing that he was leaving Mary Deas to face an invading army alone. He came back as soon as he dared, running through the ruined garden, calling her name, hunting for her, desperately hunting for her, fearing that the Yankees had killed her or taken her with them.

A shadowy figure appeared at the cellar steps. Phillip stepped behind a tree, drawing his gun. It might be a Yankee. Then the shadow took shape, a woman's shape. It was Mary Deas. With heart-stopping joy he ran to her.

It was like that. Doug would come back hot and tired, his uniform ripped and stained. She had to be here. She couldn't let him return to an empty meadow.

"Oh, please, Aunt Jill. Do come." Allison was at Brad's side, her hazel eyes pleading. "You'll be able to see Belle. You'd like that, wouldn't you?"

Yes, Jill would like that. She forced herself to think clearly. This was nothing at all like *Weary Hearts*. The worse danger either she or Doug had faced this afternoon was a sunburnt nose. He had borrowed his uniform; he wouldn't have let it get ripped or stained. Even if she spent the evening with the family, she would be back at the motel tonight. He had found her this morning. He would find her again.

She now became Allison's special property, riding with her in the back seat of Carolyn and Brian's Volvo station wagon. Brian was the doctor son-in-law, and as they were waiting in a long line of cars inching their way out of the grassy parking area, he reached into the glove compartment and handed Jill a map so that, while listening to Allison's equestrian chatter, she was able to orient herself. Luray, where Carolyn and Brian lived, was east of New Market. Courthouse, where most of the Caslers lived, was to the north. Winchester, where the Ringlings were from, was still farther north.

Carolyn and Brian had recently built a house on twenty acres outside Luray. It was a big house, nearly six thousand square feet, and they were clearly quite proud of it. As soon as the children were settled in front of the television and drinks had been offered to the adults, Jill was taken on a tour.

She didn't particularly like the house. It was certainly liveable. The three-car garage led into a pretty laundry room that led into a large kitchen, which, in turn, opened into a family room with a rough-hewn stone fireplace. There were six bedrooms, a finished basement, closets everywhere, and a pool out back. It was an upper-middle-class dream.

But it had no character. The front half of the house was traditional Georgian with an arching, airy foyer flanked by a formal living room and dining room. The back half was Californian, full of light and glass and cathedral ceilings. Atrium doors and Palladian windows were stuck in every available place.

"I suppose you live in some sort of mansion," Carolyn said as they were standing in her eleven-by-fourteen marble bathroom, the defensiveness in her voice reminding Jill that she was Louise's daughter.

"Oh, no. Not at all," Jill assured her. "My

house is so much smaller than this. I have two bedrooms and less closet space in the whole place than Allison has in her bedroom."

Jill's house had been built back in the twenties as the guest cottage for an estate long since razed. It had been a funny little timber-and-stone fake-Cotswolds thing, and as it had been designed as a guest house, it had originally had no kitchen. One had been added later, but to reach it, you had to go through what had been the coat closet. Nor had the house had a dining room; the first floor had been given over to a double parlor with built-in glass-fronted bookcases and —

And it was gone, lost, carried away by the mud. Jill had to blink and hold her eyes open wide.

What was wrong with her? She wasn't going to cry about her house, was she?

She had given Carolyn the wrong impression; she had let Carolyn think that she still lived there. She should tell her . . . not from any grand commitment to the truth, but because self-disclosure was a building block in relationships. Jill had learned that in group, and she believed it. She wasn't any good at it, but she did believe it.

She wasn't looking for a new house partly because she didn't know what she wanted in a house. Carolyn had obviously spent a long, long time thinking about what she wanted in her house; maybe something in her experience would help Jill. Such a conversation would certainly bring the two of them closer.

But the step between learning something in group and applying it to your own life was a big one. Alice had always said, *Don't worry other people with your problems.* Her mother had begged, *Talk to me. Tell me what you're feeling.* Between these two extremes, Jill had felt paralyzed.

So she said nothing.

As they came down the steps, the tour over, they saw Brian closing the wide front door with his foot, his arms full of pizza boxes. Carolyn hurried over to take them from him, and as she took them back to the kitchen, he spoke to Jill. "I hope you don't think we're insensitive."

"Insensitive?" She didn't know what he was talking about. What was insensitive about carry-out pizza?

"About the money, your father's money. You must have been thinking about it when looking at the house."

Jill hadn't been. It rarely occurred to her to ask how people could afford their possessions. "Is that what you did with the money he left you, put it into the house?"

"Some of it . . . although we all, except Randy, set aside college money first. I tell you, Jill, I'm a doctor, and I do fine. But even so, college for four children . . . that's something to worry about. Then, all of a sudden, because of your father, I didn't have to worry about it anymore. I remember lying in bed the night after we had a financial planner work it all out for us, thinking 'I don't ever have to think about the college thing again.' It was heaven."

"That's really nice. I know Cass would be glad to hear that." Cass might have pretended that he had left money to his grandchildren only to make Ellen mad, but Jill had never believed that.

"It was such a surprise." Brian was shaking his head, remembering. "Brad had always made it clear to Randy and the girls that there wouldn't be anything. When Carolyn and I got engaged, he sat down with me and said that if I had heard anything about a rich grandfather — which I hadn't — not to count on it, that he and Dave had been taken care of years ago and that was the end of it. Then he came home from the funeral with this news . . . I can't tell you how stunned we all were. Even Louise didn't know what to say."

That must have amazed the family as much

as the unexpected legacies.

"Anyway," Brian went on, "we put away the college money, got Allison her horse, and the rest we put into the house. We already had bought the land and had had a set of plans drawn up — as I said, my practice does all right. So we used your father's money for the frills — the marble in the foyer, the pool, the Corian in the kitchen, the stable. All that adds up fast."

"What did the others do with their money?" Jill asked, genuinely curious.

"Randy put his into his business, and the others had babies."

"I beg your pardon?"

"My kids have three one-year-old cousins, and your father died two years ago. Put it together. Everybody but us was committed to two-kid families, and then all this extra money turned up, for college, bigger houses, full-time cleaning ladies. All of a sudden, everyone except Carolyn was pregnant. Taffy's on her second post-money baby."

"That's wonderful." A delicious little shiver ran down Jill's arms. A business was good, a new house and a horse were nice too, but what finer thing could extra money be used on than a baby?

Some people in her therapy group believed that all that stood between them and happiness was money. Sometimes Jill was tempted to say, "Look, I'll pay for you to have that housekeeper, that car, that trip, and you'll see, it won't make any difference. You'll still be you." But, clearly, money had made a difference in the lives of these people. Probably because they were happy to begin with.

It also sounded like her father had willed his grandchildren exactly the right amount — not enough to tempt them into idleness or a changed life-style, but enough to make their already chosen lives measurably more comfortable.

Brian continued. "Carolyn and the others all grew up hearing that you aren't supposed to talk about money, so they probably won't say anything to you . . . even though they are dying of curiosity to find out what it's like to have as much as you do. But I wanted to say something, to let you know that we haven't taken it for granted. I know that none of us knew your father, and we didn't have any particular feelings when he died. But it does mean something to me that this man who might not have even known my name, who my wife only remembers meeting once, that he must have wished me well."

Jill was almost in tears. She had loved her father so. "Oh, he knew your name. Don't doubt that for a moment."

The saddest thing Jill had found when cleaning out the Bel Air house had been a small, leather-bound calendar on her father's nightstand. It was a diary-type calendar, listing dates without assigning them to days of the week so that it could be used year after year. Only one kind of information had been recorded on its pages, and all of it had been in Cass's own hand — the birthdays of all his grandchildren, and then of their children. The girls' wedding anniversaries had been marked along with their husbands' names.

It had been right next to the lamp. It hadn't even been inside a drawer. Cass must have looked at it every morning and given a few moments' thought, perhaps even said a prayer, for whoever was having their special day, even though in many cases he had never met that person. Until she had seen that book, Jill hadn't had any idea how strong Cass's feelings were for this family in Virginia. He had chosen between them and his career, and a part of him must have always regretted that choice. It had been forty years, and the pain had never fully eased.

"Oh, I'm sorry." Brian put his arm around Jill's shoulders. "I've made you cry."

"It's all right," she said, sniffing, taking his handkerchief. "I'm sorry. I don't usually fall apart like this."

"It's me. Someone should have warned you. I make people cry. My patients look like raccoons because they've got their mascara all over everywhere."

He talked lightly for another moment, giving Jill a chance to collect herself, and then, his arm still around her, took her back into the family room, now crowded with people eating pizza.

It was as if her tears had cleared her eyes, and suddenly she could see among them signs of her father. Christa and little Matthew had his high forehead. Carolyn and Stacey had had to choose their earrings carefully; they both had his sharply tapering earlobes. Two of the little one-year-olds had those ears as well. The twins and their cousin Steve had Cass's eyes, deep-set and grey-blue. Yet none of them were thinking about him. None of them knew anything about him.

Yesterday she had thought it would be hard to share Cass with her two brothers. Now she realized that this was harder, the knowledge that no one wanted what she would find so difficult to share. "Grandfather Casler" was a stranger who had given them money. They appreciated that. But the important things about him, his charm, his quiet warmth, his remarkable talents, they knew nothing about.

"Aunt Jill?" It was Allison, and Jill looked down at her, searching her face for Cass's mark. "Do you want to come see Belle now?"

"I'd love to."

Out beyond the swimming pool Carolyn and Brian had built a small stable. It was a well-designed little building, picking up some of the architectural detail from the main house. Inside were a small tack room and two roomy box stalls. Allison unlatched the gate to the stall on the right and cooed to her horse.

Jill followed her into the stall. Belle was a bay, finely built, pretty, and small without being at all pony-like. Her face was dished, her ears delicate, her mane and tail flowing. Jill guessed that she had some Arabian ancestry.

Jill held out her hand. Belle smelled it, and Jill spoke to her in a low voice. Then, in a moment, she moved closer and ran her hand down the horse's sleek, muscled neck.

What a marvelous horse. In fact, it was a little surprising how good she was. Brian did not seem like the type who would over-buy. Allison must have tremendous potential as a rider if her parents had bought her such a good horse.

"She's magnificent." Jill looked back at

Allison. "You must love her."

"Oh, I do. I really do. Would you like to ride her?" Allison asked. "Or we could go out together. I could ask Emily if you could take Dodger." Allison gestured over her shoulder at the other box where a friend of hers kept a horse. "I know she wouldn't mind. What about tomorrow? Could you do it tomorrow?"

Tomorrow? Jill thought. She was expected to go to church with Brad and Louise tomorrow, then tour his apple orchards until time for the barbecue. Riding with Allison sounded better than any of that. "I'd love to, but I don't know when. Is there any way of squeezing it in before church?" Jill had a feeling this wasn't going to work. "How long does it take to get from here to Courthouse?"

Allison wrinkled her nose, now looking every bit like the ten-year-old that she was. "I don't really know. I should. We go up to Grandma's all the time. But it's not that long. I'm sure we'll have time. We can — "

The stable door opened and they heard footsteps coming down the short, narrow corridor formed by the tack room. Jill moved to the stall gate, assuming it would be some adult who knew the distance between Luray and Courthouse.

It was Doug. The bright light from the corridor outlined him, shining around the fringed epaulettes at the shoulders of his grey uniform.

Joy gushed through Jill, tingling up her arms, circling through her cheeks. It was like Phillip and Mary Deas embracing in the trampled garden, having found love amid their ruined world.

"How did you find me?" she breathed.

"Hi, Mr. Ringling," Allison chirped.

Allison's warble restored Jill to a measure of sanity. No, this wasn't like Phillip and Mary Deas embracing in a trampled garden. This was not an epic passion . . . at least it wasn't yet. She needed to keep reminding herself of that. She really did like Doug Ringling. Perhaps they would become friends. Perhaps fate would give them a magic, frictionless glide toward intimacy. But it hadn't happened yet . . . and it wouldn't, not if she kept expecting him to be Phillip.

She tried to speak normally. "How did you know to come here?"

"I have four sisters," he answered, as if that always explained everything about him. "In this situation they would all be at Kim's because she had the newest and biggest house to show off."

"I bet he knows," Allison put in, still

216

wondering about the ride with Jill. "How long does it take to get from here to Courthouse?"

"Thirty minutes," he answered. "Twenty if your uncle Randy is driving."

Church was at ten. Brad had suggested she be ready by nine thirty. That would mean leaving the stable at . . . this wasn't going to work. Jill could do it Monday morning, but she supposed Allison would have to go to school.

"Oh, honey, I'm sorry."

And she was. There was so much she wanted to do in the two days she had left. She still hadn't seen Charles Ringling, she hadn't seen much of the Valley, and she did want to spend every possible instant with Doug. "Actually, Allison, I think I'm going to stay longer than I originally planned. What about Wednesday? Wednesday after school?"

"Wednesday? That would be *great*." Allison hugged Jill, her head almost reaching to her chin. "Wednesday's early release, so we'll have loads of time. Let me go fix it with Mom and Emily." She dashed off, stopping at the door to ask them to please turn off the lights when they left.

"Will do," Doug told her before turning to Jill. "This is good news, your staying. Is it just that you wanted to ride or does it have something to do with what you wanted to talk to me about?"

As they left the stable, Jill explained what she had inferred about the movie from Don Pleasant's birthday. "So, I'm not saying that this secret script was a masterpiece, but I am saying that it looks like there was one . . . although I still don't have a clue how they pulled it off."

Doug was shaking his head. "I'd be dangerous if I had a brain. That's so obvious. I can't believe I missed it. So is it safe to say that every scene with the baby in it was shot in April?"

"No." Jill was blunt. "It's safe to say that every *shot* with Don in it was done in April, and there won't be that many. If I remember right, most of the time you don't really see the baby. It would have been a doll wrapped in blankets. But I'd need to look at the movie again."

"I've got a copy. You want to come watch it tonight?" He glanced at his watch. "It's still early. But I should warn you, we live in a real dump."

"We?" This magic glide might have a bit more friction than Jill had anticipated.

"Randy and I bunk together, and we're not the most attentive housekeepers."

"That doesn't bother me. But I don't think we can leave right away. I don't want to offend anyone by leaving too soon."

"Leave it to me."

He had spoken airily. Jill was firm. "I really don't want to be rude."

"Don't worry," he assured her, his face glowing with a wicked little grin. "They have to let me leave first. I parked everyone in."

The house Doug shared with Randy, Jill discovered an hour later, was not a dump. It was a white frame farmhouse which had clearly been decorated by an old lady. Several crocheted afghans were draped across the back of the sofa. White lace antimacassars protected the arms and back of the soil-resistant easy chair. Braided rugs dotted the floors; *Reader's Digest* Condensed Books and *Ideals* magazines spilled from the bookshelves. The lamps had hand-painted glass globes. Only the VCR, the superb stereo system, and perhaps the two fat collies sleeping on the sofa testified to the current occupants.

"Whose house is this?"

"It's Brad's now." Doug shoved the two dogs off the sofa and pushed them outside. "Randy's great aunt used to live here. She's dead."

Jill drew a finger through the dust on one of the glass globes. "I gathered that."

Doug dropped to the floor in front of the TV and started to flip through the video tapes. Jill moved to the sofa.

"No, stop," he called out. "Don't sit there. Not unless you want a terminal case of dog hair. Let me pull the chair over for you."

Jill didn't need a chair pulled over for her. The floor was fine. She sat down in front of the sofa, and figuring that between her white shirt and her own golden hair she was a good match for the collies, she leaned back against the sofa.

Doug slipped the tape in and punched the play button, then came over to her, switching off the lamps. "Are you sure you're okay?"

"I was in the Peace Corps. I don't mind anything this side of raw sewage."

"You were in what?"

"The Peace Corps." The music was starting. "Will you sit down?"

The credits had begun. . . . *presents a Miles Smithson Production* . . .

"The Peace Corps? You aren't serious, are you?"

. . . *Weary Hearts* . . .

"Yes, and I am also serious about watching this movie."

"The Peace Corps?"

. . . Bix Ringling . . . Charles Ringling . . . Alicia Ringling . . .

"I hate people who can't shut up during movies."

"Where? What country? Why?"

"Phillip Wayland would have shut up during movies."

Doug groaned . . . and shut up.

Eight

It was a solid, well-built house, brick and square with twin chimneys and cool, high-ceiling rooms, spacious halls, and polished floors. It sat at the center of Briar Ridge, a horse farm that produced the finest horses outside of Kentucky. Other farms along the curving silver river grew oats, wheat, corn, peaches, and Queen Victoria's favorite apples, but Briar Ridge's rolling hillsides were bluegrass pastures, kept close-cropped by the horses.

Two brothers raised these horses. Booth, the older, was fair-haired and intense, expecting a lot from himself and others. He was a quiet man, a large man, as strongly built as his house, as sturdy as its grove of oaks.

His younger brother, Phillip, was arranged on different lines. Slender and quick, he was a glorious young man, his hair a wild black spill, his eyes full of spirit and reckless laughter. The family intensity, the one trait he shared with his brother, manifested itself physically in him. He was fearless, and his sinewy strength was inexhaustible. He was a born cavalry man, and Virginia had great need for such men.

Mr. Lincoln had already refused to exempt Virginia from the conscription laws and the state had reversed her decision and joined the secession. Booth and Phillip were going to join Turner Ashby and his Black Horse Cavalry Troop, taking a string of horses with them. They were waiting only for the spring foals to mature a little more.

Their mother had been a Morrison, and one of her cousins had married an angular, gaunt-eyed mathematics professor, the now-Colonel Thomas J. Jackson. On his way to Harpers Ferry, he stopped at Briar Ridge. He wasn't known as "Stonewall" yet or thought to be great, but his deep, gentle voice had weight. Booth's young bride served him dinner and afterward let the brothers show him through the well-tended paddocks.

"This is a fine crop of yearlings," Colonel Jackson said. "Who's to train them while you all are gone?"

"Old Pompey here," Phillip answered airily, waving his hand at the grizzled-haired Negro following them. "He's been doing this since before we were born. And we'll not be gone that long. This thing's going to be over in ten weeks' time."

"It may, son. It may."

"But it may not?" the steadier Booth asked.

"It may not. And if you care to serve your country best, perhaps one of you should stay behind."

Even Phillip could see the wisdom of that. The Valley's Germans weren't going to war; they could stay home and farm, raising the corn and the oats that the army might need if there was still fighting by harvest time. But the Germans weren't horsemen. Training a spindly legged foal to pull artillery or lead a cavalry charge was perhaps not work to be left to old Pompey.

Yet it was inconceivable to Phillip that he would be the one to stay. Booth could manage the farm better than he. It was he, not his muscular brother, who had the build of a cavalry man. To stay home when there was a war going on, to miss the glory, the honor, the *fun* of it all . . . it was unimaginable.

But as darkness blanketed the green fields and shadowed the pink dogwood blossoms, as the two brothers stood on the white-columned veranda, leaning back against the red brick still warm from the spring sun, Booth said, "I suppose we'll be needing to flip a coin."

Phillip straightened. "What about Mary Deas?"

Through the open window of the parlor, past the gently stirring white undercurtains, a girl's silhouette moved, slender and quiet in the lamp-lit room, her rich skirts brushing against the mahogany chairs. She was Booth's bride.

"If men used that for an excuse," Booth answered, "there'd be no army."

He pulled a coin from his pocket, a coin minted by a nation they no longer considered themselves a part of. He flipped it in the air. Phillip called heads, his voice confident, knowing that this was an exercise, that Providence could not deny him what was his by right — a place in the Black Horse Troop.

But Providence did. Booth caught the coin on the back of his left hand, trapping it with his right. He moved toward the lamplight and uncovered the coin. Mary Deas's shadow moved across the window, blocking the light for an instant. But the shadow passed, the light glinted against the coin. It was tails. Phillip was to stay home.

Although Mary Deas's soft, dark eyes had been looking at the world for only seventeen years, they saw it clearly. An hour later the light wind that stirred through the upper story windows caught at her white nightdress, teasing it into the billowing netting of the canopied bed. The gentle folds of her lace-trimmed gown, the cream of her magnolia skin shone against her dark eyes and the intricate walnut posters of the bed.

"Phillip wants to go," she said to Booth.

"I can't send him off to die."

"But Booth . . ." She couldn't say it: He might die too.

"I have a chance. He doesn't."

And as little as she knew of war, Mary Deas knew that to be true. Phillip would surely die. Gallant, brave, and foolhardy, he would die in the first battle of the war, long before he would have been of much use to anyone. Booth had a chance, and if he did die, it would be after a long, hard road.

So, three days later, it was Booth who swung himself into the saddle, accompanied only by Pompey and a string of Briar Ridge's magnificent horses.

Phillip would have loved the hot-breathing excitement of a cavalry charge; to Booth, it was mind-numbing duty. Turner Ashby was an inspiring leader, a magnetic white-plumed figure, the first into a battle, the last one out. But he was no manager; his troops had splendid horses and superb skills, but they were disorganized and undisciplined. Booth hated the chaos.

When he got his own command, he forced on it the order and control the rest of the troop so desperately needed. Rain dripping off of his forage cap, he would rub his hands over a whisper of a campfire, always watching out for his men, worrying about the horses, making sure that they didn't outstrip the supply trains. While none of his men wanted to be like him, while there was nothing magnetic about him, they respected him, they cared what he thought of them, and they trusted him.

Phillip's life back at Briar Ridge was no easier. His was Aeneas's part, commanded by the gods to stay alive so that he could found a city. After Manassas in late July, "old Jack" started to seem like a god, and Phillip accepted the covenant. Hold on to that stallion, keep those mares, and stay alive so they can keep breeding.

He knew of a narrow path into the dark bulk of Massanutten. When the Yankees came, he led the horses up there. When they had gone, and Jubal Early, now generalling the Army of the Valley, came back through, Phillip turned over the two-year-olds. But once again he traced that narrow path, leading the stallions and the mares; the now-desperate Confederates would have taken them all. Although every fiber of his soul hungered for a blaze of glory, one chance risking it all, he knew that that was not the part assigned him. As the Valley changed hands time and again, he lay in the swamp, hiding himself like a coward.

He faltered once, saddling up his mare to ride with John Mosby's Rangers. It was a glorious raid, a late-night swoop on a Federal supply depot, which the Irregulars looted and burned, The spring night was crisp, the line of fleet-flooted horses followed a flaming torch. When the dark mass of the depot loomed ahead, the riders spurred their horses and let out the high-pitched Rebel Yell, charging toward the Federal supplies. The stores were profligate — the tinned lobster, the cheeses, the cases of champagne, their corks popping. The light from the burning buildings glistened off the flanks of the sweating horses.

At dawn Phillip returned to Briar Ridge, swinging a loaded blanket off his saddlehorn, hams and cheese rolling across the fading white verandah.

Mary Deas looked up at his soot-stained face. "I've no call to tell you what to do."

He sobered, the laughter draining out of his dark eyes. "No, Mary Deas, no, you do."

"Then there shall be no more of this. If

you must go to war, follow the way of honor. Join General Jackson and take all the horses with you. I will go live with Mr. McGuire."

So Phillip never again rode with Mosby.

Life grew hard and hungry. The colored servants sickened or were swept away by one army or the other. Phillip minded none of it for himself, but he hated that it was also happening to Mary Deas.

"Take care of her," Booth had said, and Phillip knew that he was not keeping his promise to do so. "Take care of her" had been said when the land was soft, not worn lean and bitter by an invading army.

They worked side by side, leading the stallions into the breeding pen, assisting the births, cleaning stables, breaking the colts, Mary Deas doing things that no lady should ever have to do. The girl became a woman, and the reckless cavalier became a man.

Mary Deas had loved her orderly, silent husband; Phillip's laughing gallantry had never attracted her. But Phillip was changing, tempered by the soul-burning anguish of his constant sacrifice.

They said nothing, but sometimes, at night, in the wide upstairs hall, Phillip would pause at a closed bedroom door, his face contracting with pain and longing. But he would always move on, the heels of his worn boots thudding against the exposed floorboards. Inside the room, Mary Deas, her white nightdress gleaming in the dark room, would hear the footsteps stop. Her hand at her throat, she would wait, not knowing what she wanted, for the door handle to turn or for the footsteps to move on.

Then, in August of '64, Sheridan came. Phil Sheridan who was to the Valley what Sherman would be to Georgia.

Briar Ridge was warned. A lean, narrow-eyed rider, one of Mosby's men, found Phillip and Mary Deas breaking colts. They stopped, and while the wind swirled Mary Deas's limp, heavy skirts, they heard about Grant's order to Sheridan, to pick the Valley so clean that a crow flying across would have to carry his own provender.

"They've got orders to burn the barns, but not the houses, and they're supposed to leave folks enough to get themselves through the winter."

"But they aren't," Mary Deas said.

It wasn't a question. The days of courtesy between soldier and civilian were four long summers gone.

"No, ma'am, I don't know that they are."

He helped them gather the ever-decreasing number of horses, but before driving them back into the secrets of Massanutten, Phillip gave him a fresh horse and bade him leave. Mosby's Rangers needed horses, too.

Mary Deas followed Phillip into the barn. He swung a saddle across his mare's back. The air in the barn was ripe with the sharp, thick odor of dung.

Phillip tightened the girth. "Those Yanks can't be as wooden-headed as they used to be. They're going to know that there've been horses here."

In the first summer of the war the Yankees — or so the people of the Valley thought — had to tie their cavalry men to their horses, such inept riders they were. But the years had taught them much. Sheridan's men would know that the horses had been stabled here. They would tear the Valley apart to find them.

"Then we must burn the barns ourselves," Mary Deas said.

They sprinkled benzine on the hay, and as the fierce flames shot between the weathered boards, Phillip took her by the shoulders.

"I can't leave you here. Come with me."

She shook her head. "Maybe I can keep them from burning the house."

"They might hurt you."

"I'll be all right. It's the horses that count."

Phillip settled into his saddle, his face a dark mask, his eyes glowing with pain. He had to choose. The horses were his duty, what he owed to his young country. Mary Deas was his love.

She watched him leave, the horses stirring up a cloud of dust that was swallowed by the smoke. She drove the pigs and the chickens to the creek bottom, the willows brushing against her face, and then there was nothing to do but wait.

At last they came, the Yankees. Spiritless, without even an adolescent's joy in destruction, they moved through the house in blank silence, emptying drawers, slashing mattresses, kicking through linens. Mary stood at the turning of the staircase, her shoulder blades pressed tight against the landing wall. What she saw was their boots, unpatched and thick-soled. Phillip's boots were so worn that his footsteps sounded like he were wearing moccasins.

Through the long dining room windows she could see men on horseback trampling the garden. Others were breaking through the thicket, looking for the creek bottom, for the pigs and chickens. They were organized, intent; a weary captain sat on his horse, watching.

Men came around from the back of the house, sacks of dried apples over their shoulders, hams swinging at their side, food intended for the starving Confederates. The Yankees must not have needed it; they threw it into the angry flames of the burning barn. It was hot work on this August afternoon. They pulled off their thick blue coats, coats that would be warm against a mountain winter.

Those who came into the house did not look at Mary Deas or speak to her. There was no taunting, no Rebel-baiting, no eyes shifting away from hers in half-admitted shame. They didn't care. They were tired, and this was their job, something they just needed to get on with.

It took them little more than an hour. The chimes of the Winchester clock jangled against a clumsy blue shoulder, and the captain lifted his hand in a silent signal. Mary stayed on the stairwell, watching through the fanlight over the mahogany door as they formed into straggling ranks and marched off.

She remained motionless, waiting until she could hear nothing but the ticking of the old clock. Then she walked through the house, touching nothing, only looking at the remains of the joyless plunder, at the scattered linens, the sliced feather beds, the bare sideboard. The cellar storeroom was empty, the thick soles of the Yankee boots having tracked white flour dust up the stairs.

Still in the storeroom, she heard a frantic calling, her name. She moved up the cellar steps, into the sunlight of the ruined garden.

Strong hands closed around her arms. "Mary Deas, are you all right? What have they done to you?"

"They got the pigs and the chickens," she reported, her voice flat. "They rode through the garden and set fire to the fields."

"I don't care about that. Did they hurt you?"

"No one spoke to me, no one looked at me, no one touched me . . . I'd almost rather that they had — "

Even now she couldn't say it. Phillip gathered her up, holding her long and close.

What followed happened only once, but come October, Mary Deas set a cup of the weak chicory coffee in front of Phillip and spoke. "There's to be a baby."

It was a long and bitter winter. There was scant food for the horses, even less for the humans. Mary Deas had little hope for herself or her baby. Phillip heard tell that one of the Germans across the Valley still had a cow. He cut from the steadily diminishing herd three of the best mares, all in foal. They were proud horses, not bred for the plows to which the Germans would hitch them. But Mary Deas had sacrificed enough for these animals; now, Phillip thought, it was their turn.

They saw the rest of the county little that winter. When they did, their neighbors assumed that Booth had come home for one of the "spring plowing" leaves that Confederates so often took.

Lee surrendered in April; two days later Mary Deas gave birth to a tiny girl.

A part of Lee's army, Booth got his parole and began his weary journey home. He was on foot. Of all the magnificent horses that had left Briar Ridge spring after spring, Booth had only one war-worn mare, and he put the loyal, nearly crippled Pompey on that.

At last they turned up Briar Ridge's muddy lane. The stone fences now enclosed fields overrun with blue thistle. The white gates were gone, long since having been used for firewood by stragglers from General Banks's army.

But Briar Ridge was more recognizable than Booth. Suffering had starved his massive strength into a sinewy power. His gaunt face was bearded, his eyes sad beyond all imagining.

"We had best expect the worst," he said to Pompey as they plodded up the lane. They had already seen the charred chimneys and ruined houses, had spoken to women with minds as vague and wandering as their eyes.

They came up over the last rise, braced to find ruin. The big barn was gone, its charred timbers dragged into a makeshift paddock. But the house was there, solidly brick, its twin chimneys still presiding over the ruined kingdom. And coming down the steps of the verandah was Mary Deas.

Booth gripped her silently, engulfing her, lifting his head only when the spring stillness was broken by the cry of a newborn baby.

That there should be any new life in the burnt and desolate Valley seemed a miracle to this weary man. Booth followed Mary Deas to the cradle. She lifted up the crying baby, and Booth touched the child, letting her tiny fist curl around his war-roughened finger. It was not until she cried again, and Mary Deas turned away to unfasten her dress, that he realized that the baby was hers.

So certain that neither she nor the baby would survive, Mary Deas had not thought about what would happen when Booth came home. She loved Phillip. She could hardly remember the girl who had loved Booth. But Booth was her husband, and he had spent four years on ruin's darkest river.

Throughout his first day home, she, in her guilt, was newly conscious of how Briar Ridge had changed. She and Phillip had witnessed the decay gradually, but for Booth the curtainless windows, the scarred walls, and the ruined furnishings had happened in an instant, replacing his memory of warmth and elegance.

It was not until sunset that she could speak. "The house, Booth . . . it's not what you left, and you must think we didn't — "

He shook his head. "It's home, Mary Deas, and it's standing and you're in it. I don't care what it looks like."

His voice was so gentle and weary that she could hardly breathe. "But the baby . . ."

He stood, putting his hands on her shoulders, turning her face toward the fading light. "If she is yours, then she is mine, and we shall never discuss it again."

But he did have one question, which he saved for his brother. In a few days they started clearing the thistle from the field that their great-grandfather had cleared in his day. As they struggled to mend the worn harness traces, Booth spoke.

"It wasn't some Yankee, was it?"

"No," Phillip answered.

And they both knew that that truly was the end of the subject.

Phillip also knew that there was no longer a place for him at Briar Ridge. Surely whatever meager living that could be eked out of the blackened Valley belonged to the men who had fought for her.

Four years before, he had cared nothing about a wife's soft eyes and a baby's warm breath. Now they held joys offering more than he had ever dreamed of. But the woman he loved and the child she had borne him were his brother's. He had to step aside. Donning his old jaunty manner, he cuffed his brother on the shoulder and declared that it was now Booth's turn to stay home — Phillip was off to join the cavalry. He was going to go west and fight the Indians.

But he was going to have to do it in a blue coat.

Nine

Doug stretched forward, picked up the remote control and, with a quick touch, shut off the television's bold glare. The room went dark, lit only by the starlight filtering through the paned windows. In a moment the darkness eased into a quiet gray as his eyes adjusted to the soft, dreamy light.

During the last half hour of the movie Jill had sat forward, pulling her legs in, wrapping her arms around her knees. It was not a position most women would have found comfortable, but most women did not have her lean torso and long legs.

She turned her head to look at him, her long hair falling down over her shoulder. "I was afraid that you had ruined the movie for me."

He linked his hands behind his head. He felt good, relaxed, comfortable with her. He was glad she had spoken. "How so?"

"I tried to watch it after you came to California. I couldn't. I kept thinking about you instead of Phillip."

"But this time?"

"It was fine. I loved it."

"I'm glad," he said . . . even though she

had ruined it for him. He had been more aware of her than he had of Phillip and Mary Deas, more sensitive to her movements and reactions than to anything on the screen.

He wanted to touch her. Nothing much, perhaps just her arm or her cheek. One long lock of her hair had caught on the knit of her shirt. He could lift it, smooth it back into the shimmery cascade spilling over her far shoulder.

He kept his hands resolutely linked behind his head.

She noticed the stray hair. She scooped up the lock, sweeping it back across her neck. Her hand followed the flow of her hair down her body until she crossed her arms around her knees again. Then, almost absentmindedly, she ran a hand down the length of her calf. It was too dark for him to see her legs well, but he remembered them, smooth and golden, with long sleek muscles.

Through his own thick hair he felt his hands grip each other, united in their determination to stay off her. His thumbs pushed tight against the tendons in his neck.

This was not going perfectly. They had watched this movie for a purpose: to locate precisely which shots Don Pleasant's chubby little face had been in. Doug cared about this movie. He wanted to find out what had happened when it had been made forty years ago; he wanted to redeem Bix's reputation. He should have been attentive, he should have been taking notes.

But when Don had come on screen, Doug had paid absolutely no attention. He had been watching Jill.

Perhaps she had done a better job. He could ask her. *So did you get anything out of the baby's scenes?* That was the thing to ask.

He spoke. "I am enormously curious about you."

"Where do you want me to start?"

He did not care. Anything. Everything. He wanted to know it all. "The Peace Corps." The carefully stacked lumber he was using for a brain had crashed when he'd heard that. "Were you serious? Were you really a Peace Corps volunteer?"

She nodded, her hair swinging gently. "I joined after college."

College. More lumber crashed. That sounded so normal, so middle-class, so surprising.

What was wrong with him? Why was he surprised that she had gone to college? She might be rich, but she wasn't from another planet. That's what most young women in this country did, they went to college. Even

241

those whose lumber was less well stacked than his went; those whose earrings were brighter than their minds went. Why should Jill be any different just because she had money? He felt his hands relax their grip. "What country did you go to? What did they have you do?"

"I was in the Central African Republic, and I taught the locals how to build, stock, and maintain fish ponds."

"Fish?"

She nodded. "Fish. But don't ask me why. I said I was interested in animals, which is true. I meant horses, but the C.A.R. did not seem to need a young ladies' equestrian program, so I ended up with fish. But I liked it. It was fascinating, and I did some good."

"Is that why you joined? To do some good?"

"It wasn't that simple."

"Oh?" he invited her to go on.

"My mother has a lot of problems, and I was terribly engrossed in them. I didn't understand it at the time, but the only way I could stop trying to save her was to run off and try to save the world."

Doug was always impressed with people who could sum themselves up so neatly. "Did it work?"

"No. I neither saved the world nor got

rid of my need to save my mother."

"What did you get out of it?"

"Self-reliance. It's one thing to be on your own; it's another to do it in a different culture. Like figuring out how to keep healthy in such a poor country when your body is used to a protein-rich American diet, things like that. I learned you had to take care of yourself before you could help others. You can't build fish hatcheries from an American hospital bed."

Self-reliance. It was interesting that she should have used that phrase.

When he had knocked on her door, he had had some stereotypes about rich kids — that they were selfish and irresponsible without much self-esteem, that they couldn't take care of themselves, that they couldn't survive without their money. Doug wasn't anywhere near as good as his father when it came to assessing people quickly, but he was all right at it, and it had taken him about twenty seconds to realize that these stereotypes did not fit this rich kid.

Had he not known that she was independently wealthy, he would have pegged her as some kind of very successful free-lancer. She seemed too relaxed to be working in a corporate setting, but she didn't seem to have any doubts about her ability to support herself. She was, as she had said, self-reliant.

He said as much to her now.

"Oh, but I have supported myself," she answered. "I put myself through college. Tuition, room and board, books, everything."

"You did?" He was surprised, but he liked being surprised. "Even I didn't do that. I had a basketball scholarship, but my folks filled in the gaps. Why did you do it? Was it late-adolescent rebellion?"

"No, my father was one hundred percent in favor of it. But I did have something to prove. My mother's never been self-supporting, and it's always caused problems for her. I needed to be sure I could do it."

"What did you do? Did you have a regular college-kid job? Did you wait tables, stuff envelopes?"

"Both of those. I even pumped gas one afternoon."

"Pumped gas? Surely not."

"I can prove it. I still get some residuals from that ad. I was a hand and foot model," she explained. "I did all those things with people taking pictures of my hands."

"A hand and foot model?"

She extended her hands out in front of her. Doug hadn't looked at them before, but they were lovely. The skin was smooth, her fingers were long and tapering, her unpolished nails filed into graceful ovals.

In a commercial for detergent, she explained, the detergent might be poured onto a dirty T-shirt and then that T-shirt dropped into a washer. That had to be done by a female hand, a lovely graceful hand with sure, steady movements.

Pictures of her face were flat and uninteresting, she said, but her hands and feet photographed beautifully. She had done countless nail polish, jewelry, and shoe ads. She also had done movie work. Some very talented actresses did not have pretty hands, and close-ups of hired hands had to be cut into their movies. Jill's left hand had been married to some of the sexiest men in Hollywood. She had sat behind a pregnant woman and rubbed lotion on her belly. She had self-examined someone else's breast for an American College of Obstetricians and Gynecologists video.

"Why not your own breast?" Doug asked. "And please note how steadily my boyish blue eyes are fixed upon your face."

"Because hers was nicer, I suppose. She was a breast model, I was a hand model. The era of specialization."

"Just what Henry Ford had in mind, no doubt. Was there good money in it?"

"Very good. But I got tired of how careful

you had to be. You couldn't scrounge around in your purse for your keys for fear you'd scratch yourself and be out of work for two weeks. Of course, I couldn't ride. That was the biggest sacrifice. For four years I didn't ride. And the shoots were pretty boring. You spent the whole time walking around with your hands in the air so the blood would drain. But anyway, I have supported myself and I know I could again . . . although not as a hand model. Two years in the Peace Corps took care of my future in that line of work."

"But surely having all that money's made some impact on you," he said. " 'The rich are different from you and me' and all that."

"People do want to believe that, don't they? Either that I am weak or pampered, or that I must live in a more sparkling world" — she sketched a rainbow in the air with her hand — "a world where all the colors are brighter and everything is dipped in glitter."

"That's pretty much what people around here think," he admitted.

"It's not so. I think that money — and by that I mean real money, not the quick ten million that a flash-in-the-pan producer or junk bond dealer makes — takes away your excuses. 'I can't afford to' slams the door so fast that you don't have to ask yourself whether you really want what's behind it. I think money has forced me to be honest with myself and face things about myself that other people don't have to."

Doug was still trying to wrap his mind around the notion that ten million dollars was not "real" money . . . although he supposed her point was about "quick" money not having the effect of money that's been around, money you can take for granted. "Like what?" he asked.

"Well, I've had to decide that I didn't want to train Kentucky Derby winners or have a coffee plantation in Kenya, because I could have done either one. With more money than you could ever need, you've got to face that your limits are within yourself. I could have twice the money I do and I still wouldn't have an imagination."

Doug tried to imagine himself in her shoes . . . or even in a pair of measly ten-million-dollar shoes. She had a point. Money would eliminate a lot of distractions. He wouldn't have, for example, signed the Nike contract or done as much radio work. Those had been time-consuming, not very rewarding jobs that he had done in the name of asset-formation. But would all the money in the world have given him better shooting skills?

No. Would it have prevented the pickle he was in now? No. Would it get him another job at a Division I college? No. Not unless he bought the school and forced them to let him be head basketball coach.

Suddenly he remembered his manners. It was late. What a long day she had had. He pulled his legs out from under the coffee table and stood up. "I know you're still on California time, but Randy's chickens aren't. They get up powerfully early."

He put out his hand for her. It wasn't necessary. He'd been watching her legs all day, with a coach's, as well as a man's, eye. There was more than enough muscle in them to get her upright. But she put a cool, smooth hand in his, then let him do most of the work. The strength of his arm had to pulse through hers. It was nice.

He picked up the grey Confederate jacket that he had shed halfway through the movie. Swinging it over his shoulder, he thrust out an arm, holding open the screen door for her. The night was clear, and the starlight lit their path to his car. He drove a Chevy Cavalier. He wasn't very interested in cars; he didn't care what he drove as long as it was a convertible.

"Do you want me to put the top up? It's gotten a little cool."

Jill shook her head. "I love an open car."

"Then, here." As they reached the car, he opened the grey wool jacket and circled it around her, settling it on her shoulders like a cape, letting his hands rest on her for a moment longer than needed.

The house was at the end of a little gravel lane. A small stand of cedars marked the crossroads of the gravel and the county blacktop. From there it was no more than ten minutes to the Interstate cloverleaf where the Best Western was. Jill had her head tilted back against the headrest; she was looking at the stars.

The Best Western was quiet and brightly lit. The Valley was a safe place, Doug's common sense told him. The doors to the rooms fronted the parking lot. He could stay in the car and watch Jill's every self-reliant step until the door to her room closed behind her. This was, he knew, what a sensible man would do. *Good night,* he would say, *see you on Monday.* And that would be that.

But his Mama hadn't raised him to heave women out of the car, leaving them to face unescorted the perils of a bright, safe ten-yard walk. He pulled his car into a space, got out, and came around to the passenger side, although by this time Jill had gotten out of the car by herself. Together they walked toward her door. She was still wearing the jacket to his uniform. It was long on her, but not overwhelming so. She was tall.

The doors to the motel rooms were painted royal blue, each one lit by a small torch-shaped sconce. He did not hold out his hand for her room key. Phillip Wayland might have done that; Doug thought it was better if he kept his hands in his pockets. She unlocked the door herself and pushed it inward.

Behind them in the parking lot, a car door slammed. In the quiet night an ignition ground, then caught, the motor revving. Its headlights swept past in a bright arc. The light glittered against the gold braid and sparkled off the brass buttons of the coat around Jill's shoulders.

"Would you like to come in?" she asked. "Room service has pizza."

He'd been afraid she would ask that. He shook his head. "The chickens get up early."

The chickens? That was a feeble excuse. He prayed her to understand. *I have a rule. Never after the movie. I've learned the hard way; I have to live by it.*

There was nothing he wanted more than to go in that room with her. But it would ruin any chance. He knew that better than he knew anything.

"Then you'll be needing this," she said and lifted the coat off her shoulders.

Instead of handing it to him, she held it up for him to put it on. He turned, straightening his arm, catching the coarse-woven cuff of the full white shirt he had worn beneath the jacket. She lifted the jacket up his arms, settling it over his shoulders, just as he had for her. Most women could not have done this for him, but she was tall.

He turned back to face her, and saw the light from the little sconce caught in the clear lines of her brow. She straightened one edge of the unbuttoned coat, then let her hand lie flat against him, half on the coat, half where he could feel her cool fingers through the loose weave of the shirt. She rose on her toes and kissed his cheek.

His hand instantly clamped at her waist, gripping her tightly to stop the trembling. But he did nothing else, willing the message. *Yes, I like this. Yes, this is how I feel, too. I would give anything . . . but I can't be Phillip for you.*

In a moment she stepped back, seeming to understand.

"Good night," she said, her voice free from rejection's rancor.

"Good night," he answered. How he hated this. And he turned to go.

Jill pushed the door shut. It was a fire door, and the metal was cool against her palm. What a day this had been. She looked down at her feet. The white canvas of her shoes was streaked with grass stains and smudged with reddish-brown soil. She pulled down the three-quarter sleeves of her once-white shirt. Dog hair floated from the folds and dust marked the creases.

Doug Ringling was a smart man. She admired him for his caution. The movie's lure was too potent. When her thoughts had turned southward, what had she been thinking about, the hair on his chest, the muscles in his legs? That's what any normal, sexually fervored woman would have thought about. But, no, good old Aunt Jill had been thinking about the silly uniform, the way the rich soft wool would feel beneath her palms, how cool would be the tangle of fringe at his epaulettes, how crisp the ridge of the braided trim. She had imagined the pressure of his brass buttons against her breasts, the outline of his sword belt against her hips.

Jill did not expect romances to be permanent. It wasn't that the idea of permanence frightened her. Indeed, she treasured the thought that her friendships were permanent. But she had long since stopped dreaming of One True Love. She did not have a linear, conventional view of her life in which dating would lead to marriage and children. She never asked a love affair to promise a lifetime of happiness; she never spent the opening steps of love's delicious waltz assessing a man by such a weighty measure.

Nor did she ever knowingly start to dance with the wrong foot. For Doug to have dropped his sword belt at the foot of her bed this evening would have guaranteed the briefest of cotillions. They both knew that.

But this could turn into something quite pleasant. If they watched themselves, if they didn't take shortcuts, everything should be easy.

Hadn't it always been easy when Phillip Wayland had come down off the screen to take her in his arms?

She pulled off her crumpled shirt and showered quickly, rinsing the day's grime off her lean dancer's body. On the nightstand she had left Goren's *Rules of Bridge*. She looked at its red cover uninterestedly and pushed it aside, taking up instead her file on *Weary Hearts*. This was what she and Doug had in common, their interest in how this movie had been made. They hadn't talked at all about the baby's scenes. They needed to get back on track.

Her file included copies of John Ransome's article and Bix's original "war movie" treatment. She reread them both.

In the treatment, just as in the movie, the brothers tossed a coin. Booth joined the cavalry and Phillip stayed home to raise horses and, unlike in the movie, to ride regularly with Mosby's Rangers. Ransome admitted that the twin stories were neatly structured. The brothers' paths would cross, sometimes directly, sometimes more subtly. Swimming his men and horses across a swirling river, for example, Booth noticed that the only other cavalry unit successfully crossing was led by a man on a horse from Briar Ridge.

All the episodes in the original treatment stood up well to historical scrutiny. As a Ranger, Phillip never did anything that the Rangers didn't do, and Booth never rode anywhere that the Laurel Brigade hadn't. "This screenplay," said a Civil War historian whom Ransome had consulted, "was written by someone with the map of Virginia engraved on his heart." But the episodes were only adventures. There was no psychological struggle. Booth had no trouble adapting to command, and Phillip was content to be a guerrilla.

Nor was there a romance. The oddest thing about the story developed in the treatment, Ransome said, was Mary Deas's role. She and Phillip did not fall in love in this version; there was no baby. She had no differentiated character; she was generalized Woman, who stayed home and whined about the menfolk needing to be careful.

It made no sense, Ransome concluded, to have her be Booth's wife. The romantic tension of brother- and sister-in-law living together was never exploited. She should have been Phillip's wife. It wouldn't have added to the overall conflict, but it would have been tighter and might have added some poignancy, as she would have been cautioning her husband, not a mere brother-in-law, against risking his life with a band of irregulars.

Of course, then the casting trick — brother, brother, and brother's wife playing themselves — would not have been as neat. So Ransome wondered why Charles and Bix had not switched parts. The final version had the irony of a broad-shouldered man joining the cavalry in lieu of his lighter, wiry, born-horseman brother, but Cass had been the one to appreciate that irony. Bix's treatment had been indifferent to it. All Ransome could figure is that Bix simply didn't know how to structure a screenplay.

Jill laid down Ransome's article, knowing that there was another explanation. If Don Pleasant's scenes had been filmed in April, then the secret script did indeed develop the romance between Phillip and Mary Deas, and perhaps also developed all the ironies of the brothers' fates. But when Bix wrote the dummy treatment for the "war movie" script, he was trapped. He had to make it conform in all obvious ways to the secret one. He couldn't switch the heroine's husband without someone noticing.

But if the script filmed in April had had the romance, the irony, the psychological struggle, what had been Cass's great contribution in August?

From the nightstand Jill picked up the antique leather traveling frame, one possession that had escaped the mudslide because she always traveled with it. It was a double frame. On one side was a photograph of her father; on the other, where normally would be a photograph of one's mother, was the last stanza of his favorite poem, Yeats's "Easter 1916," written out in his own hand.

Jill looked down at the picture. It was a formal portrait of a man with a high forehead and sharp, aristocratic lines to his cheekbones and jaw. His hair had not thinned with age, but had grown white, leaving him with the look of a courtly Southern judge.

Why hadn't he told her about the secret script — not while she was still in the middle of her mad crush on Phillip, but later? Cass would have known she would be interested. It seemed odd that he should have kept it from her. What could he have had to hide?

Jill looked at her watch. It was nearly two; that meant it was only eleven in California. Her night owl of a mother would be finishing dinner. Jill dialed her number.

"Happy Mother's Day," she said when Melody answered. "I wasn't sure I'd be able to reach you tomorrow."

"Darling, how sweet of you." Melody's low voice was warm with affection. "Are you in Virginia? Is the Valley as lovely as your father said? Is his family making you welcome?"

Making people welcome was important to Melody. It had to do with fresh flowers, the right amount of ice in a drink, a perfectly placed footstool.

"As welcome as they are able," Jill answered. "No, I don't mean that. Brad is stiff, and Dave is a bit too genial, but everyone else seems fine. I had a really nice talk with one of Brad's sons-in-law, and the girls — actually, they are women but everyone calls them 'the girls' — are giving me a ladies' bridge luncheon on Monday."

"A bridge luncheon? Oh, Jill . . ." Melody's laugh was light, silvery. "What a waste. There was a time in my life when I would have sold my soul to be invited to a ladies' bridge luncheon, and here you're probably dreading it."

"Not exactly *dreading* it, but if you wanted to go in my place, I wouldn't object."

"Ellen would love that, wouldn't she?"

"Actually, Mother, Ellen is dead." Jill was surprised Melody hadn't heard that, then remembered she had been at Hazelden when it had happened.

"Oh, dear." Melody's voice sobered. "That's why you should never say anything bad about anyone, for fear that they'll turn up dead. But that must make it easier for you to see her children."

"It does." Louise was difficult enough. "And it also helped that Cass left them all some money." Jill could see that now. It wasn't exactly that her father had bought her way into the family, but those legacies had eased any resentment the grandchildren might have felt about Jill's inheriting so very much.

"I hope you won't worry if it doesn't work out. There's nothing magic about being related. I spent the first sixteen years of my life living in a very small trailer with people I was related to, and I loathed every minute of it."

"I thought part of the Twelve Steps was learning to accept your past."

"I am," Melody told her. "I'm learning that I was absolutely right the whole time. A trailer park and I do not belong on the same planet. I want no part of any place that does not have showers with very clean ceramic tile. That's my minimum; below that I will not go. Those fiberglass enclosures are unacceptable. Thank God you were in the Peace Corps. At least no one can accuse me of inflicting pathological hygiene on subsequent generations. But enough about me, tell me about the Valley. Is it beyond-everything lovely? Your father always said that it was."

"I honestly don't know," Jill admitted sheepishly. "Yes, it's beautiful, but I've hardly had a minute to look at the scenery. It's quiet, gentle, but it's not fry-your-eyeballs-out magnificent like Mt. McKinley. I need more time . . . and I'm going to stay longer than I planned. Did you know that Cass left me a house here?"

"Did he?" Melody sounded pleased. "I didn't know he had property out there. . . .

259

No, no, wait, now I remember. It came up during our divorce settlement. He was such a gentleman about everything, but he made it clear, in the nicest possible way, but still clear, that that house was one thing he wasn't giving up. Not that it mattered, it wasn't worth much . . . although it must have been worth an extraordinary amount to him. I wonder why. What's it like?"

"I don't know. I haven't seen it."

"Oh, Jill . . ." A faint note of disapproval crept into Melody's voice. That was rare. One of the things that made Melody such a restful companion during her good periods was that she truly felt she had no right to judge other people. "Don't you think you should go look at it?"

"I will," Jill promised. "I'll do it tomorrow. Right after Brad's barbecue, I'll go. I'm sure someone there will know where it is."

Church was church, thoroughly tolerable, occasionally moving. The business of running apple orchards was interesting, the apple orchards themselves were enchanting, and the barbecue was disappointing. Jill had thought that she had made such a promising start on Saturday, but assessed in daytime's brighter light, she realized she had felt close to one child and to a doctor who was probably very good at drawing people out. The rest were still strangers. She knew their names and little else.

It didn't help that Louise was now firmly in control. Jill sensed everyone being more careful, watching what they said, where they set their glasses. It was probably an automatic adjustment for all of them, something they didn't even notice, but their cautious politeness became a screen that Jill could not seem to penetrate.

It was all a disappointment, but Jill was determined not to give up. Perhaps her mother was right, and there wasn't anything special about people being from the same gene pool. But her father had clearly thought differently. That small leather-bound diary on his nightstand had made that clear. Each member of this family had been important to him. The bond created by blood was a mystery Jill did not feel fully initiated into, but for her father's sake she was willing to slog along a little longer.

By two o'clock everyone in the family was there except the airline pilot son-in-law and Randy. Louise and Brad were puzzled and upset by their son's absence. Brad continually apologized to Jill as if he feared that she might take Randy's behavior as a personal affront, and Louise sniffed that a person with his own business ought to be responsible.

It turned out that being responsible for his own business was precisely what Randy had been. He arrived at four, dirty and sweaty, with a tale of a cooling system gone awry. Hot chickens, Jill gathered, soon became dead chickens. He and Doug had just gotten the system working again twenty minutes before.

"But we called the barn," Louise protested. "You could have answered the phone."

"I could have," Randy answered, obviously experienced in dealing with his mother. "But I didn't."

"I hope you at least had the courtesy to invite Doug to join us after he spent all afternoon working with you."

If this was another one of Louise's digs, it failed. Randy was ahead of her. "Of course, I did. You know what he always says about your barbecued chicken. He'll be here in a bit. He wanted to clean up first."

Whether or not that pleased Louise, Jill did not know . . . or care. It certainly did please her.

He arrived in another twenty minutes, dressed in khaki slacks and a neat polo shirt, his hair rumpled as if it had been dried by the wind. He went directly to Louise, speaking to her first. Jill didn't mind waiting; she knew that he would come to her next.

She watched him as he talked to their hostess. Now that he was out of that romantic uniform, it was easier to see his build. His height was in his torso, just as Jill's extra inches were in her legs. The result was that you noticed how tall he was only when he was standing next to another man. He did not have the "alpine-tree" look of so many basketball players of whom "tall, tall, tall" was all you could think.

His long-dead uncle Bix had been built this way too. Bix had been notably shorter than Doug, but he had had the torso of a much taller man. That's why he — and Phillip — had looked so imposing on a horse.

Doug finished talking to Louise, then threaded his way through the clusters of people, smiling, nodding, but never stopping until he was at her side. He spoke softly. "I need to talk to you."

"Fine."

He touched her arm, directing her out to the wide, pressure-treated pine deck that spanned the back of Brad's house. The one-year-olds were splashing in a round green wading pool, watched by Dave's daughter and her boyfriend. Doug moved to the railing on the other end of the deck. Jill felt a delicious shiver of intimacy, almost as if they had made love last night.

But his tone, though low, was anything but intimate. "Why didn't you tell me you were my landlady?"

"Your landlady?" Jill stared at him. Then she understood. "Is that the house? You're kidding."

"No, I'm not. Randy told me this morning. Everybody calls it Aunt Carrie's house, but it really is Aunt Jill's."

Jill tried to remember the house. She couldn't. She hadn't gotten beyond the living room, and all she had noticed of it was Aunt Carrie's cluttered furnishings and the blanket of dog hair. But she could understand how Randy had ended up there. She had needed a caretaker; he wouldn't have wanted to take rent money out of his business. It seemed like an excellent arrangement.

"I honestly thought it belonged to Randy's father," Doug continued. "Randy and I just split the utilities, and — "

"Wait a minute," Jill interrupted. "You aren't going to offer to pay me rent, are you?"

"You better believe it. 'Offer to pay' is where we're going to start; 'cram it down your throat' is where we'll end up if we have to."

He sounded like he meant it. Fortunately,

Jill had learned long ago how to get out of such discussions. "If this conversation truly interests you," she said pleasantly, "why don't you have it with my lawyer?"

He blinked, then grimaced. Here was a man who knew when he had been beaten. He groaned. "I really hate it when people say things like that."

She patted him on the arm. "That's why we say them."

She felt someone else's arm go around her shoulders. It was Randy. "What are you doing to this man?" he asked Jill cheerfully. "This is exactly how he looks when he's talking on the phone to one of his sisters."

"She's worse than my sisters. At least my sisters don't threaten to sic their lawyers on me. Would you please tell her that I didn't know the house was hers?"

"Sure. He didn't know," Randy said, clearly not caring if he was telling the truth. "I don't see what he's making such a big fuss about, but it certainly is within the realm of possibility that I forgot to tell him it wasn't Aunt Carrie's. I mean, if Aunt Carrie couldn't remember, what hope is there for the rest of us?"

"What do you mean Aunt Carrie couldn't remember?" Jill asked.

"Just what I said. Apparently she forgot

that Grandfather Casler really owned the place. When she died, since she didn't have any kids, she left it to my dad."

"What?" Jill was gripped by a sudden, sick feeling, as if she were hearing rats' feet scurrying inside the walls of a house. "She left it to Brad? Brad thought it was his?" She hated confrontation, confrontation of any kind. How angry Brad must have been when he found out the house belonged to this half-sister who hadn't even let him take her arm at their father's grave. How hurt he would have felt, how betrayed.

"I'm really sorry," Jill heard herself say to Randy.

But what was she apologizing for? For having been loved?

"Don't be silly." Randy's tone was still offhand. "Aunt Carrie might have been out to lunch, but Dad isn't. I know he's not the most approachable guy in the world, but he knows the lay of the land. He always knew that the house belonged to Grandfather, and he always told us that it would go to you. He never said, but he knows perfectly well that Grandma Ellen loused up his and Dave's chance for a big-time inheritance."

Jill force herself to calm down. "I'd really like to see the house in the daylight. Would that be possible?"

"Sure. We'll take you there when this breaks up. Just don't tell my mother why you want to see the place. I think she's temporarily forgotten that it's yours, and if she remembers, she'll have fits about how dirty it is."

Just as the house was not a dump, it was not truly dirty, Jill discovered two hours later. The two beds on the upstairs sleeping porch weren't made. There certainly was dog hair on the living room furniture, as whoever vacuumed the floor didn't believe in vacuuming furniture. But the floors themselves had been vacuumed within living memory. There was only one meal's worth of dishes in the sink and they had been rinsed and stacked. Nor did the bathroom look like something you'd need a tetanus shot before entering.

The house was, as Jill had noticed the night before, a white frame farmhouse. Set up on a little rise to catch the breeze, it had a wide veranda that wrapped around both sides, giving the square dwelling graceful lines. A porch swing hung in one corner of the veranda, sheltered by a white trellis covered with climbing roses. On the southern side of the house, where long hours of sun would fall, was a large flower garden.

"It was built in the 1880's," Randy told her. "There was another house here before that, but it burnt during the war, and it took people twenty years to get the money to build again. Some of the foundation is from that earlier house."

"Is that what's so special about the house?" Jill asked. "My mother said Cass would have given up everything else he owned before this place."

"It's not the house as much as the property," Randy said. "It's the one tract that's been in the family continuously. We've bought back some of the land that we lost in the thirties, and, of course, other pieces have been picked up or sold off over the years. But this we've always had."

"How long is 'always'?"

"Dad knows the exact date, but I think the Caslers first showed up here sometime around the Revolution."

"The Revolution?" Jill stared at him. "The *American* Revolution?"

"Sure." Randy was as offhand as ever. "I think this was part of what George Washington surveyed for Lord Fairfax."

George Washington. The American Revolution. This property had been in one family for more than two hundred years! It was the family's heritage, their stake in the life of their land, and the sort of property that was to be passed from eldest son to eldest son.

Aunt Carrie's husband, Willston, had been Cass's older brother. He had inherited the property, but had not been able to hold on to it. He had had to sell it to his younger brother, who no longer lived in the Valley. But as Carrie and Willston had had no children, Brad was the eldest male of his generation. In her will Aunt Carrie had tried to return the property to its rightful owner, the eldest male.

So why hadn't Cass, with his sense of tradition, his sense of being a Virginian, done the same? Why hadn't he left it to Brad, his eldest son, who could have in turn left it to Randy, his eldest son?

But he hadn't. The property belonged to her, the youngest child, the daughter of the second wife, who had been in the Valley for a total of two days now. It didn't seem right.

Jill was ready to rush back into town, shrieking for a copy of the deed, imploring someone to tell her where to sign so that she could turn the property over to Brad. But her year in therapy was teaching her to distinguish between generosity and bursts of ill-considered self-abnegation. This little fit certainly smelled of the latter. She needed to wait until her frenzy quieted. If giving the house to Brad was right today, it would still be right next week.

She turned to Randy. "Everyone's been saying that the trusts Cass set up for your generation were a surprise, but I heard you were at the bank within two weeks. Isn't that pretty fast to put together a plan for a business like yours?"

Randy shrugged. "I've always known I wanted to be my own boss, but not apples, there's enough apples in the family. I like gadgets, so I'd always figured if I ever had money, I'd really go to town with poultry."

That didn't answer her question. "So the money wasn't a surprise to you?"

"It should have been," he admitted. "Dad always told us never to expect anything."

But Randy had remembered Cass from the time he had come to the Valley for his mother's funeral — Randy's great-grandmother. "I was just a kid, but I really liked him. I don't know why, but I did. I had this impression that he was the sort who played fair, who would do the right thing. I suppose this will make me sound greedy, but once I got older, it did occur to me that the right thing would be to leave something to my generation. So I guess I wasn't surprised . . . although never in a million years did I think he'd give us as much as he did."

Jill could have kissed him. His impression of Cass had been so accurate. Cass did play fair; he did do the right thing. People in the Valley might not have known that about him, but she did.

That's why it was so hard to believe that he had butchered *Weary Hearts*.

Ten

Having decided to stay longer in the Valley, Jill rented a car and drove herself to the ladies' bridge luncheon that Brad's daughters, Carolyn and Stacey, were holding for her on Monday.

She had been thinking of this luncheon in much the same spirit with which she had undertaken some excursions in Africa: as a bizarre tribal ritual that she was fortunate to be able to observe. Once there, she discovered that her fellow guests found it equally bizarre. They were service-minded women in their late twenties and early thirties with comfortable, busy lives full of kids, station wagons, and dogs.

"My mother used to do this all the time," one guest marveled, clearly pleased to be dressed up and away from her preschoolers in the middle of the day. "I wish I knew how she pulled it off."

"Our mothers all had full-time maids who they paid about two dollars a day to," another guest named Anne pointed out. "They had time to be ladies."

"Do you remember what Grandma Ellen first said when she saw the plans for your house?" Stacey took a silver tray full of mint-trimmed mimosas from Carolyn and started passing the stemmed glasses among the guests. "You know the way the kitchen opens right into the family room so the kids aren't underfoot all the time? Grandma was horrified. 'Carolyn, dear,' " — Stacey was mimicking an elderly Southern voice — " 'You must have a door on your kitchen. Where will the maid sit?' "

"At what I pay my cleaning lady for my six little hours a week," a guest laughed, "she'd better not sit."

Usually this was not the sort of conversation Jill participated in. She wasn't going to pretend that she was worried about the cost of cleaning ladies for the sake of a camaraderie that everyone would know was false. But she hadn't made much progress with her family yesterday. She knew she needed to exert herself more. Observing without participating was her greatest vice. It was a luxury you paid for sooner or later. *Self-disclosure,* her therapist said, *is one of the building blocks of relationships.*

She took a breath. "At least you — "

The room went silent. Jill broke off, startled. Apparently a new verse was needed in "She'll Be Comin' Round the Mountain": *And we'll all shut up and listen when she speaks.*

She struggled on, trying not to laugh. There was such a disparity between the attention she was getting and the significance of her remarks. "At least you all grew up with mothers who had maids. I have friends who have no role model for how to treat household help, and now that they're in a more affluent position, they are very uncomfortable telling people what they want done."

Jill knew several people in this situation, the worst being her mother. Melody tended to cast service people in the role of authority figures whose sole purpose in life was to say "no" to her. She had gone through housekeepers, secretaries, publicists, personal assistants, and interior designers. She didn't control her employees; her employees controlled her. Finally she had given up and now did everything herself except the yardwork and her tax return.

For her own part, Jill had been taught by Alice to manage footmen and upper house parlormaids, a skill that fortunately she could apply to limo drivers, hotel clerks, and head waiters. She understood that these people were not slaves put on earth to do her bidding, but accommodating her was a job they were paid to do, and there was no reason for everyone not to be straightforward and pleasant about it.

As good as she was at dealing with the "servant problem," Jill had less confidence in her bridge skills. She had played in college — shuffling cards was one thing a hand model could do — but little since then. Her fellow guests, however, played just as badly as she did, in large part because no one was paying any attention to the cards.

During the third round the conversation took a turn so interesting that Jill passed on sixteen points so she could concentrate on what was being said. Two of the women she was seated with identified themselves as Doug's sisters, and the former Miss Ringlings were happy to talk about their brother. So when he appeared at the Best Western that evening to take Jill to meet his uncle Charles, she was wickedly well-armed.

"I met two of your sisters," she said as soon as they were on the road.

He shot her a quick, suspicious look. "Which ones?"

"Anne and Kim."

"It could have been worse. What did they tell you?"

That they had told her something — something embarrassing — was not even a question. "Mostly they talked about the love of your life."

"And just who is that supposed to be?"

"Holly."

"Holly?" Doug abandoned all pretense of safe driving and stared at her. "Holly Wallace?"

"I don't think that's her name anymore."

"Did they happen to mention just when this great romance took place?"

"Oh, yes." Jill had not needed Doug's blank astonishment to know how unimportant his high school girlfriend was to him now. "But apparently that was the last great romance they know any details about."

"And can't you see why?"

Jill could. "Actually, what they say is that in your job you attract the wrong sort of women, which I thought was pretty interesting," she went on breezily, "as I have a good friend who always attracts the wrong sort of men. They end up copying her Rolodex and stealing her jewelry."

"It is such a problem," he agreed. "Women stealing my jewelry. I hardly know where to turn. Did my sisters have any answers?"

"They said that your problem is that, in your old job, you traveled so much and were so busy you tended to attract women who were distancers, women who weren't comfortable with emotional intimacy." These were Kim and Anne's thoughts, but not their language. Jill was translating into therap-ese. "But that's not what you wanted, so every spring, when you had some time to develop a closer relationship, everything fell apart."

"I knew that that theory was being floated around."

"Do you agree with it?"

"A man with four sisters never agrees or disagrees with any of them. Did they say anything about my looking like Uncle Bix?"

"No, they didn't," she kept her voice even. "I imagine they're so used to the way you look that they don't think about its effect on others." She took a breath. "But it can be a problem, can't it?"

"It can be."

"I certainly was a ditz about it when you were in California."

"I did catch you off guard," he admitted. "Actually, your reaction was interesting. Do you know what I liked about it?"

"Apparently not the fact that I was prepared to throw my heart at your feet."

He glanced at her sidelong as if to say that had it been *his* feet at which she was throwing her heart, that would have been fine. "It was that you didn't make your reaction my problem. Most of the time when people are surprised by how I look, I have to spend about a half hour consoling them, calming them down, telling them that it's okay. Yes, you reacted strongly, but you made it clear that you were going to take care of it yourself."

"Of course," Jill said calmly as if this emotional adulthood had been something she had been born with.

"I suppose you're in the same boat when people fall all over themselves because you have money."

He had a point there. "Then you're nicer than I am. I'm afraid I don't have much patience for those people."

"I can't imagine you being rude."

"I'm not. But I don't let them work out all their feelings about money on my time."

"That's the difference. Most people have stronger feelings about money than they do about Phillip Wayland."

"Except me."

He smiled. "Except you."

Instead of coming north on the Interstate, Doug had taken a back road, a narrow ribbon of blacktop with dirt shoulders falling off into shallow drainage ditches that sparkled with wildflowers. The road rose and fell with each swell of the earth, sweeping past the stone churches, the sagging, vine-covered barns, the crisp clusters of convenience stores and roadhouses at the crossroads.

They were in Winchester now. The outskirts of town were full of appliance stores and car lots, Pizza Huts and video stores. They drove by a decent-sized mall that had, Doug said, killed the downtown. A few turns brought them suddenly into a small town with narrow streets and old sycamores. This was the historic district. Doug stopped the car in front of a good-sized, square brick house with white trim and a two-story bay window. The yard was fenced in by iron railings.

"This is your grandmother's house?"

Doug nodded. "My parents live across the street. They were going to come this evening, and then my sisters started inviting themselves until it got to the point that Gran put down her foot and told everyone to stay home."

Jill was still looking at the house through the car window. It reminded her of Briar Ridge. Of course, it was smaller than the house in the movie, and Briar Ridge had a cleaner, more Federal look, while the scrolling white brackets that trimmed the porch of this house and the elaborately turned balusters were mid-Victorian Italianate. But the two houses had the same solid Southern feel to them.

Which shouldn't be a surprise. Bix Ringling

had grown up in this house, Jill reminded herself, and if he had indeed first conceived of the story during the dark hours of his confinement in a German P.O.W. camp, he would be drawn to a setting like his childhood home.

The front door, with its large oval of beveled glass, was open. There was a screen door that obviously had been installed much later. Doug opened it without knocking.

"Come in, come in," a woman's voice called from the back of the house. "If I come out and be polite, we'll lose this gravy. Come in and make yourselves at home."

Jill stepped into a square high-ceilinged foyer that took up a quarter of the first floor of the house. A fading Oriental rug was centered on the polished wood floors, and a little spinet piano sat under the bend in the mahogany staircase. Doug drew Jill over to the staircase wall. Next to a dark oil portrait of a stern-looking ancestor was a cheap, black dime-store frame enclosing an intricate line drawing of shooting stars and flowers exploding into peacocks and train cars.

A voice came from the other side of the house. "That was Bix's."

Jill turned. Through a wide arch was the parlor. A man was sitting in a wing chair, his legs covered by an afghan. It was Charles Ringling. He was much older than he had been when he had played Booth — much, much older, his hair silver rather than fair. But there was still no doubt as to who he was.

"Bix was always doodling," he continued. "He'd do it whenever he was sitting down. He had so much energy, he had to pour it out in something. We kept that one because he drew my wife's face."

Doug pointed, and Jill peered at the drawing. Down in the corner, almost off the paper, framed by lilies, was a woman's face. Mary Deas, or as she would be known in this house, Alicia Burchell, Mrs. Charles Ringling.

"She was beautiful." Jill crossed the old Oriental and went into the parlor, taking the hand that Charles extended. He did not rise.

"We did lose something when Bix died," he said.

Jill knew that, before World War II, Charles had trained as a lawyer. After the plane crash he had stayed in his family home and had gone back to the law, opening a small, quiet practice writing wills and doing real estate closings. He had retired a number of years ago.

The furniture in this room was dark and

ornate, upholstered in fading velvets, the tables topped with marble. The pictures on the walls were hunting prints and portraits, framed in deep gilt. A set of pocket doors with insets of frosted glass separated the parlor from the dining room.

"Why don't you offer Miss Casler something to drink?" Charles said to Doug. "Have you ever had Virginia wine?" he asked Jill.

"No, but I'd love to try some. And please, call me Jill."

"I would like that." Charles gestured for her to sit down. "The Valley's been talking for days about your coming. I'm so pleased you could spare an evening for us. I have wanted to tell you how much I admired your father and his work."

"I appreciate that," Jill answered. No one else had said that. This was what she was used to, people saying this first. "I truly do."

"Then I want you to tell me which of his films is your favorite . . . and to show you that I'm not asking for compliments, we shall only talk about the ones he directed."

Cass had been the editor and, along with Bix, the co-screenwriter of *Weary Hearts,* but not its director. "Then, for me it would be *Nancy.*"

"More than *Mustard Lane?*" *Mustard Lane*

won Cass his second Oscar, and most critics considered it his best work.

"It's a personal choice. It was shot in England and I was on location almost the whole time."

Doug returned from the kitchen with the wine. He handed her a glass. "That was the one about the pilot and his daughter, wasn't it?"

Jill nodded. Although it had been made in the early seventies, *Nancy* was set right after World War II. The hero was an R.A.F. pilot, one of Churchill's "few" to whom so many had owed so much. His wife having been killed during the Blitz, he went to the country to pick up his ten-year-old daughter, who had spent the war in a large country house to which she had been evacuated. Even at the time, Jill sensed that the picture was infused with Cass's love for her.

"Did you know that was from an old Valley story?" Charles said. "A Colonel Barnhope, he was with Stonewall at Sharpsburg — what a terrible day that was. His wife died during the war, and he was left with his little girl. I never completely understood why your father changed the setting, but it was a lovely picture. I remember being so saddened by it, wishing that my wife and I had had a child. It might have made her death easier to bear."

Charles still had Booth's voice — slow and rich, promising strength and safety. It was hypnotic to sit amid this worn Victorian graciousness, the late afternoon sun filtering through the lace panels that hung behind the velvet curtains. Jill felt like she was in a dream, lifted out of time. It wasn't quite real, hearing Charles talk about the battle of Sharpsburg as if it had been fought only yesterday. The Civil War and World War II, Charles and Booth, Alicia and Mary Deas, Bix, Phillip, and Doug, they all blurred together. Like a soft Madras plaid, the colors bled into one another, making lovelier, more glowing patterns than when each color stood on its own.

A crisp voice broke the spell. "I do declare," an elderly woman said, coming out from the kitchen, untying her apron, "I've been making gravy for coming up on seventy-five years now. You'd think I wouldn't let it get away from me like that. Don't get up," she said to Jill. "The turkey's got to sit for ten more minutes. Then we'll have Doug carve it."

Marie Ringling had her son's beautiful silver hair, which she wore twisted into a soft, thick knot. She seemed like a brisk, practical woman.

"It was so nice of you to have me," Jill said. "It sounds like you weren't given much choice."

"Don't worry yourself. I had plenty of choice. Doug offered to take us all to a restaurant, but Charles isn't one for going out, not since the old Hotel became a home-less shelter." She sat down on one of the wing chairs. "I'm old enough and tired enough to make a fool of myself. Tell me about all the famous people you know. The nice-looking boy, Payne Bartlett, is he your boyfriend?"

Jill liked people who were direct and so the conversation through dinner was lively. Jill, Mrs. Ringling, and Doug did all the talking. Charles seemed to be listening in-terestedly, but he said little, and Doug functioned as the host, carving the turkey, refilling the wine glasses.

Mrs. Ringling had made a pie for dessert. She brought it out to the table along with the coffee in the plastic pot from the Mr. Coffee machine, which she set down next to an exquisite cream and sugar set.

Mrs. Ringling's china had been nothing more than pretty, her flatware did not have the marvelous heft of the best sterling, but this cream and sugar were extraordinary, or-nately patterned silver with long triangular facets ending in tiny engravings of Oriental faces.

"These are," Jill said truthfully, "among the loveliest things I've seen in a private home."

"Do you like them?" Mrs. Ringling seemed pleased. "My mother's people were Ropers. They're from them."

"Tell her about the dent." Doug handed Jill the sugar bowl, turning it so she could see the large dent in its side.

"When the Yankees looted Charleston — that's where the Ropers are from — they took most everything in the house, certainly every scrap of silver. A neighbor saw these in the gutter and brought them to the family."

"They must have been thrilled to get them back." Jill curved her hands around the sugar bowl, her palm pressing into the dent, perhaps made by a cobblestone, perhaps by a horse's hoof.

"I don't know," Mrs. Ringling replied. "Apparently old Mrs. Roper used to say having them only reminded her of everything that was gone. But she never sold them, and God knows she would have needed the money badly enough. I've always had half a mind to take the thing in to be repaired, but I don't know — the dent adds something."

Charles had his coffee and appeared to be

waiting for the cream and sugar, so reluctantly Jill set the bowl down. She had been so calm about having her house swept away. She had been quite proud of herself, thinking she had been so wonderful and sane. But maybe it was easy to be wonderful and sane about lost objects when you lived in a world where the oldest things were the glasses used on the set of *Casablanca.*

Jill offered to help Mrs. Ringling with the dishes.

"No, no. I've got my own system. You sit here with Charles. I know you all came to talk to him."

Charles watched the kitchen door swing shut behind his mother. "But, alas, I don't know what Charles has to say." His rich voice filled the room. "I know you're interested in Bix's version of the movie, but I never saw his rough cut, and I never read the whole script. I'm an intuitive actor, I work inductively, I build. I don't pay attention to the whole."

Jill noticed that he was using the present tense, he who had not acted in more than forty years. "But surely you knew something was up."

"Of course. In fact, my wife was one of the first to tell Bix that the studio wasn't going to like his script. She read a draft. I remember her writing him a note about it. Of course, we knew what he and Mr. McClay were doing."

"What was it like on the set? Was there an 'in' crowd of people who knew?" Doug had talked about a little group being in the plan. "Were you a bunch of Boy Scouts playing a practical joke? Or were you serious, Cassius and Brutus plotting to kill Caesar? Did it feel like a prank or a conspiracy?"

"I think everyone took it very seriously. The stakes were high; we could have destroyed our careers. But it felt worth it. Everyone involved felt that strongly about what Bix had written."

"How many were involved?"

"I honestly don't know. There was a code of silence about it. No one ever talked about it so you never knew for sure who knew and who didn't. My wife and I, even when we were alone, didn't discuss it. For me, it helped my performance because it made for an unsettling atmosphere, very isolating. It kept you from ever feeling completely at ease with anyone."

"Do you know if Miles Smithson knew?"

"I don't for sure, but I doubt it."

"Then there must have been some sort of mastermind committee." Jill now believed that a secret script had been filmed, but she still couldn't imagine how it had been done. "To fool the producer . . . it would have been such a complicated undertaking. Someone would have had to keep track of who knew and who didn't. All the paperwork, the footage counts, the budgets would have had to be doublechecked. It's staggering."

"You'd have to have known my brother. Bix was as clever as they come. Remember, he outwitted the Germans."

"So you think he was capable of pulling this off?"

"My dear, he was capable of anything."

That was a worthless answer. No one was capable of anything. But whatever the details of the deception, clearly Charles had not been involved.

"We did have one tremendous advantage," he continued. "The studio wasn't paying any attention to us."

Jill thought back to her bridge luncheon. In one hand she had mismanaged her board entries completely, but her opponents were paying no attention, and so had led back to the winning tricks.

But Miles Smithson had not been at a ladies' bridge luncheon. Paying attention had been his job. "How could Smithson not be paying attention? This was his unit. He was responsible."

"*Circean Nights,*" Charles answered. "Everyone in Mr. Smithson's unit was caught up in that."

Circean Nights. Of course. Jill had forgotten that that had been filmed during the summer of '48 . . . and the spring and the fall. Miles Smithson had had a lot more to worry about than the narrative structure of a low-budget war movie.

Circean Nights had been to the studio what *Cleopatra* had later been to Fox and *Heaven's Gate* to United Artists — the swelling, self-indulgent, seemingly unstoppable epic that was threatening to sink the studio. With all the chaos and the heart-stopping costs of *Circean Nights,* who would have paid much attention to a tiny-budgeted war movie being shot in Virginia?

So a little pony named Bix might well have shot between the legs of the thundering thoroughbreds.

"Also remember the political situation," Charles continued. "The House Un-American Activities Committee and the antitrust suits. I'm sure those seemed more important to the studio than what we were doing."

Again he had a point. If Jill remembered correctly, the HUAC hearings about Communist sympathizers in the film business had been held in 1947, so by the summer of

1948 the blacklists would have started. If politically suspect screenwriters wanted to work, they too were having to dupe the studios, using "fronts" to write behind. Moreover, the antitrust lawyers in the Justice Department were pressuring the studios to sell their theaters, to separate production and distribution from exhibition. These legal efforts would ultimately prove the death of the studio system.

As bad as the political situation must have seemed to the studios, the economic outlook was worse. The G.I., who in 1946 was back home, courting, taking his sweetheart to the movies, was by 1948 married, with a baby on the way and no money to spend on a movie ticket.

It could have been Bix's moment.

"But what about the shooting scripts you were using in April?" This was the part of Doug's story that had made the least sense. "Why were they on the plane in August?"

"Alicia was working on them," Charles answered easily. "They were a mess, with pages and pages of rewrites; every one was different. Even the master script didn't have everything in it. When it became clear that we weren't going to use much of it anymore, she wanted to sort through the mess and get one clean copy so at least we'd have a record of what we had done. It was an admirable effort, but clearly we would have all been better off if she hadn't attempted it."

"So there was a lot of rewriting going on during the April shoot?" That was as Jill had guessed.

"Oh, God, it was endless, total chaos. Imagine Phillip writing a movie."

Phillip? Jill could not imagine Phillip writing a screenplay at all. He was a man of action. "So Bix and Phillip were a lot alike?"

"Gracious, yes. We were all up there, playing ourselves. That's what made it such a lark." He shook his head sadly. "We were so young."

But he had just said the atmosphere had been unsettling and isolated. How could he also say the filming was a lark? Jill was filled with a hundred badgering questions — surely he could remember filming some scenes that did not appear in the final version, surely he had some sense of any difference in tone or atmosphere between the two versions, surely, surely, surely — but his tone of gentle elegy made questions impossible.

The kitchen door opened. "I can make more coffee," Mrs. Ringling said.

The men shook their heads and Jill spoke. "But won't you join us? I'd like to hear what you have to say about this."

"What *I* have to say?" Mrs. Ringling shook her head. It was hard to believe that she was well into her eighties. She and Charles seemed to be the same age. "No, young lady, you don't want to hear what I have to say."

"Why ever not?"

"Because I've got no truck with this business of glorifying the war, whether it's those big-bosomed historical romance books or that silly re-enactment thing they had over the weekend."

"You don't approve of that?" Jill asked.

"Approve of it?" Mrs. Ringling snorted. "I grew up in Richmond. We lived across the street from the Confederate Home, and I'd go over there and hear those old soldiers talk. They'd have tears in their eyes, talking about the boys who had died. And we'd go to the cemetery, and there would be children there, fourteen-, fifteen-year-olds, *children*. I can't see having a party to celebrate that."

"People like to dress up in costumes, Gran," Doug said mildly.

"Then let them be witches at Halloween. I see these healthy young girls pretending to be fancy Southern belles, when the real girls were dead of typhus or widows at seventeen. I read in the paper this morning that silly Lonnie Simpson said he had been born in the wrong century. If so, he was right lucky because Lorraine had a terrible time with him, and had he been born in this right century of his, he would have been born dead and would have taken his mama along with him."

"That does take the fun out of it," Jill acknowledged.

"Fun! Beats me why people think the Civil War would have been such fun. I had two boys in World War II, and then Ward went to Korea, and not a one of them came home and said it was fun, but at least they came home. It's been forty years, and I still think about my Bix almost every day, and I can't imagine those Civil War mothers were any different." She blinked almost as if she were going to cry. Then she straightened angrily and started fussing with the coffee cups. "Why did you get me started on this? You know how I hate it."

Doug went over to his grandmother and put his arm around her. "You're a silly old woman." His voice was not as rich as his uncle's. It didn't have an actor's polish, but it was full of warmth and life. This man loved his grandmother. Jill had never known her grandmothers. "It's all right to cry. We won't tell."

Mrs. Ringling blinked harder and tried to shove Doug away, but he was taller and stronger and so kept a grip on her, dropping a kiss on her beautiful silver hair.

"Will you let go of me?" she demanded. "How am I going to get these dishes done with you hanging on me like an overgrown toddler?"

"Do you mind if I show Jill the letters?"

"If that's what it takes to get rid of you."

"I'm serious, Gran. I won't show them to her if you don't want me to."

"Now why should I mind?" Mrs. Ringling was determined to be her stoic self again. "You know where they are."

Doug let go of his grandmother and motioned to Jill. She followed him toward the staircase. "What letters are these?" she asked once they were past the landing turn.

"Bix's. He wrote them during the war."

Doug opened the door to a white-walled bedroom. A walnut dressing table stood between the windows. Doug moved aside the little vanity stool and pulled open one of the table's drawers. He took out a thin packet of letters and handed them to Jill. The envelopes were faded; the top one had red military markings.

She sat down on the bed and took the letter out of the first envelope. The handwriting was tiny, but so crisp and unslanted that it was as legible as typescript.

> Somewhere in England
Dear Mother and Father,
The nice lady —

Jill stopped reading. "This isn't Phillip's handwriting."

Doug drew back. "No, of course not. It's Bix's. He wrote it during the war. It had nothing to do with the movie."

"I know that. But a minute ago Charles just said that they were all playing portraits of themselves, that Bix was Phillip. And this isn't how Phillip would write. His handwriting would be loose and careless, flowing, scrawling."

"You believe in handwriting analysis?"

"Not in the extreme, no. But this — " she gestured down at the letter — "is a very distinctive hand, and whoever wrote it wasn't Phillip. The people at the re-enactment said that Bix didn't make one mistake in the movie. I'd believe that of the man who wrote this letter. I wouldn't believe it of Phillip. Nor can I imagine him mastering the kind of detail necessary to pull off this secret-script stunt."

"Bix did get captured during his first engagement, just like Booth said Phillip would."

"But that wasn't necessarily his fault," Jill argued. "The two wars were different. Bix wouldn't have had a fine Virginia horse to gallop away on. Anyway, Bix got captured before he wrote the movie. Perhaps he was making fun of himself." Jill shrugged. "But I don't know what point I'm trying to make. I'm certainly not claiming I know everything about Bix by looking at his handwriting for twenty seconds."

She picked up the letter again.

"Wait a minute."

She looked up. "Yes?"

"It's funny you should say that about Bix not being Phillip. I know this sounds strange, but I don't really like Phillip."

"You don't like Phillip?" She marveled. "Isn't that heresy?"

"I don't say it much . . . and maybe 'like' is the wrong word. I don't respect him. You meet a guy like him out on the court, and he's a piece of cake to guard. It doesn't matter how good his basic skills are. He has no subtlety. He might as well be wearing turn signals."

"But that was Phillip at the beginning of the movie. He grew, he changed."

"Yes, but it was a matter of making one tough decision and sticking to it. He stuck to it well, but once he had made that choice, he didn't have any others. The last few times I've watched the movie, I wished we saw more of Booth, more about what he was going through . . . but maybe that's just because I'm a coach and so I'm interested in how a group of men relate to their leader."

"Don't you admire Phillip at the end? For leaving?"

"Not necessarily. Who's to say that Booth and Mary Deas are going to be happy together? I wouldn't want a wife who was pining after someone else. Don't you think it might have been more interesting if Phillip said, 'Look here, I was a rat, I'm sorry. I wish it were different, but it ain't. We can't turn back the clock.'? Who owns Briar Ridge and who loves Mary Deas are treated as the same question. She gets turned over like a piece of property."

"Is this a feminist interpretation of *Weary Hearts*? That might have made for an interesting movie, Doug, but not one that I would have loved."

He smiled ruefully. "Maybe that's why no one has ever asked me to write for the movies."

His smile was one Phillip never would have had. "It must be strange to look so much like someone and then not really respect him."

"You've got it wrong. I don't look like a character in a movie. I look like my uncle Bix, and him I respect plenty."

Jill nodded, silently apologizing.

Until now Doug had acted as if his resemblance to Bix was nothing more than an odd wrinkle in his love life. But it couldn't be that simple. What would it be like to resemble someone who had died before you were born? Would it seem as if he had had to step aside to make room for you?

She spoke. "Tell me, when you were growing up, how did you feel about looking like Bix?"

He shrugged. "For the longest time I thought everyone was crazy. Here I was, nine years old. I couldn't see any resemblance between me and a grown man. But it did make me feel kind of a connection with him. Not quite that he was up in Heaven watching out for me, but something along those lines."

"So how do you feel about him now?"

"Now? If he's still up in Heaven watching out for me, he's not doing such a great job. Maybe he needs to visit the neighborhood optometrist."

"Be serious."

"I can't be. I don't know how I feel . . . creeped out that he died at twenty-eight, I guess."

"That is pretty creepy," Jill agreed. She was twenty-eight. "To what extent do you identify with him?"

"Identify with him?" Doug looked a little blank, and Jill reminded herself that he was not in therapy, he hadn't spent a year thinking about these things.

But he tried. "I don't know how to answer that. There are differences. He was an actor, I'm a ham. He was athletic, I'm an athlete. We're both middle brothers, but he had two brothers, I have four sisters. He was Tom Sawyer — people say that over and over — full of schemes and tricks and plans. No one ever says that about me."

Except the athletic director of Maryland Tech . . . he implied that you were chock-full of schemes and tricks and plans.

But Jill was not going to introduce that subject. It needed to come from him. She waited a moment and when he said nothing, she picked up the letters.

Somewhere in England
Dear Mother and Father,

The nice lady at the Red Cross tells me that they notified you that Son #2 is alive, well, and in an English hospital, surrounded by pretty nurses. I'm told I can add little else, just that the Germans

had me and now they don't. Being captured so early in one's career doesn't seem
particularly meritorious, but during basic
they told us that if captured, we were
to cause lots of trouble, and in that, as
you can imagine, I distinguished myself.

I'm fine. There's a little question about
the mobility of the fingers on my right
hand, and so a shy young lady with a
delicious accent is teaching me to type.
Surely piano playing would have the same
effect, but apparently the army needs typ-
ists more than piano players. I hope that's
not a military secret.

I know my little stint as a missing person
left you sick with worry; believe me, it
was involuntary. What do we hear from
Charles?

Love,
Bix

The next letter was typed.

Washington, D.C.
Dear Mother and Father,

What do you think of this fine typing?
A pity it wasn't Charles who learned
to type as his handwriting is so of-the-
moment.

All my moaning about sitting behind a

typewriter is another case of Bix-over-reacting. I would be gloriously happy if that was any way to feel in the middle of a war. I'm working — mostly typing — for Colonel Frank Capra of Hollywood. He directed that movie *It Happened One Night* that we all liked so much and is now making movies for the war effort. Most of the unit is back in Hollywood. I don't know how I slipped in, but I'm not going to ask for fear it was a mistake.

Washington is crowded, crowded, crowded. I share a bed with a fellow who works a night shift. We've not met each other, but he seems a fine sort. I left him some Ringling apples and a few of Mother's cookies so he thinks I'm a fine sort, too.

Love,
Bix

P.S. I wish I could get these cameramen out to the Valley. They don't believe me when I tell them how beautiful it is.

Washington, D.C.

Dear Mother and Father,

I've dispatched a personal ambassadorial corps to persuade Charles that the censorship regs do not prohibit him from writing home. A group of entertainers is off to England to perform at the bases. Some of them know some of us, which is how I met them. Our best hope is a lovely girl named Alicia Burchell, who would, I am told, have a great future except that she may be too tall. I told her that my heroic brother is a great mountain of man, and she promises to look him up . . . providing that the looking will indeed be "up." I've warned her about still waters so she doesn't expect Brother #1 to be the gasbag that #2 is.

What sad news about Willie Roselander. I shall write his parents.

Love,
Bix

"Read this one." Doug handed her another letter; the handwriting on it was more feminine, more dramatic than Bix's. "It's from Aunt Alicia. She wrote it right after marrying Uncle Charles."

York, England

Dear Mr. and Mrs. Ringling,

You must be spinning with questions. "Married Alicia," Charles telegraphs, "letter follows" . . . then he is ordered off and so the letter must come from this complete stranger who is now your daughter-in-law.

But a very happy stranger she is. I met Bix in Washington and knowing that I was headed here, he commanded me to find Charles as the one man who is a good head taller than me. He is that . . . and so much more. I am reeling, desperately, delightfully in love with him. He is such a peaceful person . . . so steady and calm, enduring daily danger with good humor. He's unlike anyone I have ever met . . . yet I feel like I've known him my whole life.

Like so many others, we are legally joined, only to be physically separated. His life on the base is so restricted and there are no quarters for wives (what a lovely word!) so I shall continue with the tour I am on. Please don't think Charles has hooked himself to an exotic dancer who struts about in feathers and under-garments . . . I wear a uniform and sit behind a piano. We are as respectable as people living out of duffle bags can be. I trust I will not discredit the name I'm so proud to bear.

Most sincerely yours,
Alicia Ringling

"What a marvelous letter." Jill shook her head. "I would *die* if I had to write introducing myself to someone's parents. She was no dumb starlet, was she?"

"Hardly," Doug agreed. "Dad knew her . . . no, that doesn't cover it — Dad was in love with her. He had a mad crush on her. He was fourteen the summer they were filming and he's always said that he was moon-eyed the whole time. My grandparents were crazy about her too. Grandpa said she was sharp as a tack, this lovely creature who looked like she had the mind of an angel food cake, when she really had all the sturdy common sense of a kid from a Wisconsin dairy farm."

"I suppose that explains why Charles never married again."

"I suppose." Doug handed her the next letter. It was from Bix again.

Washington, D.C.

Dear Mother and Father,

Some very fine news. The newest Mrs. Ringling (Alicia, that is — this is not a coy way of announcing the creation of a Mrs. Bix) returns to the States next week. I got a note from her. She is routed through Washington and is so eager to meet the family that she is prepared to

305

descend upon you *without an invitation.* Rather than allow her to inflict such a blot on herself, I invited her not only to eat Sunday dinner with the family, but to stay in Winchester for the duration of the war. I know that this is what you would have wanted me to do.

I imagine she will say yes to the food and no to the lodgings. She will probably go back to California until Charles returns. She has a contract with the studio that pays her more than the army pays me.

I'm being allowed time off when she comes so I'll escort her down. It seems overwhelmingly unfair that I should be bringing Charles's bride home, but among all my good fortune, surely the highest is having a brother who does not resent injustice.

Apparently Alicia is quite alone in the world so the idea of cousins, aunts, uncles, parents, and even gasbaggy brothers is a great joy to her.

Love,
Bix

"What nice letters." Jill looked up, hoping that Doug had more. But his hands were empty. "It makes me want to call them up and invite them to lunch."

"I know what you mean. They must have been fun. In fact, as a kid I always heard about Uncle Bix and Aunt Alicia, and I assumed that they were the ones married, not Charles and Alicia."

Jill could understand that. Bix and Alicia had obviously both been bright, articulate people while Charles had been quiet and steady.

She folded Bix's last letter and slipped it back into its envelope. Charles had been wrong when he said they were all playing themselves in the movie. He might well have been like Booth. Alicia's description of him in her letter seemed to confirm that. But Bix hadn't been Phillip, and Alicia hadn't been Mary Deas. She had been livelier, more teasing and witty than her movie role.

Charles had married Alicia. Ward had had a schoolboy crush on her. There had been one other Ringling brother, the middle one. He had sketched his sister-in-law's lovely face. Had her portrait sprung from the idle strokes of his pen or from some warmer stirring of his heart?

Eleven

Tuesday Jill went to group.

That was one of the rules of group; you went. You were charged for sessions whether or not you went. That financial pressure could be considerable incentive; in some cases therapy was the member's second greatest expense after his rent. The fee itself meant nothing to Jill, but she didn't want to appear careless about issues important to others. As a result, the financial incentive ended up working as powerfully on her as on anyone.

She also didn't like it when other people skipped — Cathy Cromartie, who traveled on business, was one of the worst offenders in this regard. The dynamics of the group changed when one person wasn't there. So, on this Tuesday, as every other one, Jill went to group.

She got up at six and left the motel twenty minutes later. She drove two hours to the airport, caught a nine A.M. flight to the coast which got her into LAX, with the time change, at 11:10. This gave her plenty of time to be in Westwood by one.

There wasn't a flight back east until ten thirty in the evening. So she stopped by the office and looked at the mail; went down to the trunk room of the Holmby Court where her clothes were stored and picked up her jodhpurs; and had dinner with some friends. The red-eye returned her to Dulles very early Wednesday morning; she was back at the Best Western by nine. It had taken twenty-seven hours, and as she had flown first class and had been met at the airport by a car and driver, had cost something more than two thousand dollars, not counting the fee for the therapy session.

But as she followed Allison and her graceful little horse down a narrow, wooded bridle path later that afternoon, she knew that it had been worth it.

Young Allison did ride well. Jill noted her good seat and soft hands, how smooth her transitions were. Little logs occasionally blocked the sun-dappled paths; Allison and Belle took them with an easy fluidity.

Jill herself was not doing nearly as well. She had not been on a horse for more than a year, and it was unsettling. Dodger seemed wide between her legs; the movement of his muscles felt unfamiliar. Tomorrow her inner thighs would be sore, and she would be walking in short, jerky steps.

Ahead of her Belle lifted into an airy canter without Allison having done anything that

Jill could see. The girl had thought "canter," and her horse had cantered. It was a mystical communion of human and animal soul, two creatures from different species working as one. Jill had once been able to ride like that. She had sometimes felt that her beloved Willow understood her better than any human.

Alert herd animal that he was, Dodger saw that Belle was cantering and stumbled into one himself, just as Jill was reminding herself to slide her leg back and close her calf muscle. That was how a rider signaled for a canter. But Jill was no rider, she was a passenger.

The shadowy bridle path broke open into a sunlit meadow of clover and thistle. The hazy blue mountains ringed the horizon. Jill drew abreast with Allison, ready to ask her about her teacher. Jill wanted to find the best dressage teacher in the valley and get herself back in shape. First thing tomorrow morning, she wanted to be in a ring, on a horse, being lunged for an hour. She wanted to ride again. She loved to ride. She was going to start again.

No. This was exactly why she had not been on a horse for more than a year. Horses were addictive; they could take over your life. Serious riders devoted themselves to honing a very narrow set of skills. Jill could do that. She could afford it. She could let riding organize her day; cultivating and polishing this physical skill could be her goal. Yet how was it any less self-indulgent a life than the ladies who lived for their clothes, their manicures, and their lunches?

But how wonderful to be on the back of a good horse. The meadow sloped down into a woodland; a soft breeze danced through the delicate leaves of the locusts, the soft needles of the white pines. The two horses were cantering along a thicket of mountain laurel; the flowers were a showy pink, the leaves pointed and glossy. Jill's hair flowed down her back, her shirt rippled against her ribs and breasts. It was coming back to her, the movement of horse and rider. Her body was remembering.

Why did it have to be a choice? Why couldn't she ride once a week? Just a trail ride, no lessons, no time in the ring, no goals. Could she do that? One trail ride a week. Or was that like the deals an alcoholic made with himself? *I'll just have one glass of champagne* . . . This was as delicious, as intoxicating, as champagne. Jill, her mother's daughter, had always assumed that it was as addictive.

Maybe not. She would know soon enough.

And wasn't it better to make the mistake out here so she could run away from temptation if it proved too strong for her?

Suddenly the summer lay before her as sweeping and bright as this green meadow. She would spend the summer here, in the Valley, in this world where the air was soft and clean. On Tuesdays she would go to group. On Wednesday she would ride with Allison. The rest of the time she would explore her father's homeland. She would learn what it was like to live there. She would prowl the aisles of the grocery stores. What kinds of cheeses were sold? Was there enough demand for fresh veal? She would watch the mothers waiting to meet the school bus. She would read all the notices tacked to the wall of the hardware store. She would roam through the dusty racks at the used book store, finding out what people were reading and selling. She would go to the Baptists' Strawberry Festival and the volunteer fire department's Ice Cream Social. She would visit the needlework show at Belle Grove plantation, pick up a coffee mug at the Shenandoah Crafters show. She loved this, poking around the edges of other people's lives. She had adored it in Africa and Peru; she was certainly going to like it here.

How long she would stay, she didn't know.

Perhaps only a week or so, maybe the whole summer, she wasn't going to worry about it. She would set up her own leisurely routine of silvery clear mornings and burnished afternoons, and as long as that routine felt right, she would stay. When it didn't, she would leave.

Back at the stable she and Allison wiped the sweat off the horses' saddle area and curried their coats, using combs and the small circular motion of polishing a car. Jill stepped inside the house to exchange a few pleasant words with Carolyn. Back at the motel she showered and changed. Then she set off to find Doug.

There was something so delicious about setting off to find someone. In California she would have never dreamed of meeting someone without very definite plans. People's schedules were too complex, traffic too difficult, gatherings too large. You could be at the same party with someone and still miss him. But she had a wonderful lilting feeling about this afternoon, about every afternoon in the Valley, that there was a magic in the light wind that made things work out sooner or later, and unlike Los Angeles, it didn't matter if it was later, because one thing that you had in the Valley, that no one ever had in California, was time.

There was no answer to her knock at Aunt Carrie's house. She guessed that if she turned the knob, the door would open, but she didn't want to be inside. The sun was still above the treeline, slanting on the flower beds at the side of the house. Jill swung herself over the porch railing, lightly dropping down onto the clover-studded grass, and followed the perfume of the flowers.

The blossoms of the early spring daffodils had withered to a transparent brown, but the Dutch iris and tulips were blazing, purples and blues, red and golden yellow. Low to the ground were a row of lilies of the valley while the still tightly furled gladiolus thrust up tall. It was an odd garden, its individual beauties arranged without grace, each flower planted in a straight row, more like a crop than a garden. Although not entirely abandoned, it was not well tended.

But the rich soil, the dark glacial loam, from which both the flowers and the surrounding weeds grew, had been in her family for more than two hundred years.

She heard a sound behind her and saw a shadow coming across the grass. It was Doug, just back from the henhouse. He had a baseball cap on backwards, his T-shirt was marked with sweat, and his jeans were stiff where he had wiped his hands.

"Hello," he called out, belatedly pulling his cap off. "Did you have a nice ride? You look happy."

"I am. It was wonderful. And these, the flowers, they're beautiful."

"Aren't they, though? It's almost enough to make you forgive Aunt Carrie her taste in interior design. Randy's in the shower. There's only one, so I have to wait my turn. Can I get you a beer in the meantime? You can sit far away from me."

Jill laughed and followed him into the house. It was dim inside, the dusty venetian blinds cutting off the Valley's lustrous sun. Jill felt the world constricting under the leaden press of Aunt Carrie's clutter, the yellowing recipes torn out of the newspaper, the faded plastic plants, the candy dishes full of rubber bands, paper clips, and pennies.

Jill hated clutter. It was a reaction, she knew, to her mother's compulsive accumulation of objects. But at least Melody's things were of superb quality and rigidly organized. Here, tucked between two brightly painted ceramic birds was a little stack of white envelopes preprinted for church contributions. It was a mess.

Doug handed her a beer. The neck of the bottle was cool, slightly damp. "Do you mind if we go back outside?" she asked.

"Lord, no. This place gives me the willies."

"So why live here?"

"Because I don't mind having the willies."

He held open the front door, whistling for the fat collies. The two dogs rolled off the couch and ambled outside, uninterestedly sniffing the bushes.

Doug dropped down on the front steps, leaning back on his elbows, his legs stretched out. Jill sat next to him, looking down at his legs. His jeans were worn; the knees were soft and slightly saggy. The inner seam was wearing; the denim's white warp strands were pulling away from the seam.

She stretched out her legs alongside his. The concrete steps still held the warmth of the afternoon sun. Even though Doug was easily six inches taller than she, their legs were nearly the same length. His height was in his torso and hers in her legs.

"So have you had any great thoughts since Monday night?" he asked.

"Great thoughts? . . . Oh, about the movie."

"That's what I had in mind, but if you've had great thoughts on some other matter, I'd be happy to listen."

Jill doubted that her analysis of their respective leg length counted as a great thought. "Actually all that junk of Aunt Carrie's did make me think of something. I know it sounds ghoulish, but what do you think happened to Bix and Alicia's things? The stuff from their homes out in California — did Charles bring it all back here?"

"I haven't a clue. Charles wouldn't have brought it; he never went back. To this day I don't think he's left Virginia. But I suppose he would have had to have someone send back his clothes and such. And Bix's place would have to have been closed up too. I never thought about that." His blue eyes glittered bright with interest. "Do you think there might be something about the script among Bix's effects?"

"There shouldn't be. Scripts and all the drafts and notes are technically the property of the studio, but obviously Bix wasn't treading the straight and narrow. He would have to have kept the material somewhere."

"Let me call Gran." Doug drained his beer, hitched his feet onto a step, and rose effortlessly.

In a few minutes he was back with a report. "She's really not sure, but she does seem to recall somebody sending out a box of Bix's things. She doesn't know what was in it, where it is now, or even if any of them ever went through it. But we're welcome to come look in her attic . . . which is a little like saying we're welcome to line up behind General Pickett."

"Behind who?"

"General Pickett. You know, Gettysburg, Pickett's Charge? Good God, woman, where were you brought up?"

"Southern California."

"Well, that would explain it. If you're going to stay around here, you need to brush up on your Civil War history. Anyway, Gran didn't know what happened to Alicia's things but she says she'll ask Charles. I told her we'd come right away. I hope that's okay."

"I don't have any plans." How lovely it was to feel so free, so flexible. She didn't suppose she would want her normal life to be so empty of arrangements, but now it seemed exactly right, to be sitting on a farmhouse step drinking a beer one minute, then in an open car sweeping down a country road the next. Perhaps she should reread Bruce Catton or Shelby Foote.

"This may be a wild goose chase," she reminded Doug as they buckled their seat belts. "Even if the stuff is there — "

"No one would have thrown it away. I know this family, we don't throw stuff away."

She went on. "Even if it's there, the chances of there being anything about the movie are so remote."

"But it's bound to be interesting. It belonged to Bix."

Jill glanced across the car at him. The wind had divided his hair, flattening it against his head. What were they looking for here? Bix's movie or Bix himself?

Charles was not home when they arrived at Doug's grandmother's. "He went for a walk," Mrs. Ringling said. "I don't think he much likes having this all stirred up again . . . but get that guilty look off your face, Douglas. Charles isn't trying to stop you; he wouldn't dream of that. It was just such an unhappy time, none of us likes to think about it. But I can't see that this is any worse than dressing up and pretending to be cannon fodder."

"Did you ask him about Alicia's things?" Jill asked.

Mrs. Ringling nodded. "Her girlfriends closed up their place for him. They shipped his clothes back here, but he had told the girls to keep as many of Alicia's things as they wanted and get rid of the rest."

"He didn't want anything?" Doug asked. "Nothing?" He was surprised. "If somebody I loved died, I think I'd want to hold on to something of hers."

Mrs. Ringling tried to explain. "You have to understand. This was 1948. We were just starting to believe that the war was really over. So many boys had died, and there was so much going through belongings and trying to decide what to save and what to give away. Things were finally starting to seem normal again, and then this happened. Bix and Alicia were the only Valley people on the plane, but every last one of the other men were veterans — every one of them. They'd survived the war, only to have this happen. Some of their families came out, and it was like everything bad was starting up again. I can remember the day they found Alicia's purse — "

"Alicia's purse?" Jill interrupted. "From the plane crash?"

Mrs. Ringling blinked, suddenly aware of what she said. "You know, I hadn't thought about that in years. It was, I don't know, maybe two weeks after the crash — we'd had the funerals and the memorial services, and all the families had gone — a couple of kids found Alicia's purse, caught in a tree. It was one of those things. There her purse was, completely intact."

"What ever happened to it?"

"That I can't tell you. I remember seeing it. It was this pretty green thing, but I don't know what happened to it, or what was in it. I'm not the sort to have a great hankering

320

to look at the lipstick and compact of some poor girl who had just died." She cleared her throat and spoke more briskly. "Now, do you want to go up in the attic or not? All I can say about it is that Carrie Casler's is more of a mess."

"It is?" Jill's heart sank. During the drive over she had thought about clearing out Aunt Carrie's house, getting rid of the clutter, taking down the aging venetian blinds, brightening everything with fresh paint. Whatever she did with the house, whether keep it or give it to her brothers, she would like it to be in good shape. And it would give her a project. As delicious as today's unshaped leisure was, Jill knew that day after day of it wouldn't be healthy. She had given into this temptation before. Observing without participating, as much as she loved it, had a cost, a thousand tiny, almost imperceptible, hammerblows landing on your self-esteem as people with schedules, purposes, livings to earn, came to seem more important than you.

"Oh, lord, yes." Mrs. Ringling started up the stairs. "Carrie was gone forty-five before she finally accepted that she wasn't going to have children. She was always collecting hand-me-downs and old toys. There must be boxes and boxes of the most worthless junk in that attic."

Mrs. Ringling led the way to one of the back bedrooms and opened the closet door. A ladder of one-by-fours had been nailed into the wall, leading up to a square framed opening. Doug went up the ladder first, stopping to slide the hatch out of the way. Jill stood in the closet beneath him, looking at an egg spot at the fraying hem of his jeans. There were still bits of shell trapped in the dried crust.

Finally he angled the hatch out of the opening, and, crooking one elbow under a step of the ladder, handed the hatch back down to Jill. She leaned it up against the closet wall. It was a simple plank of plywood with handles on one side and a batt of insulation stapled to the other. Jill had to pluck some of the yellowing fibers off her shirt, balling them up and tucking them in her pocket. Then she climbed up the ladder herself. Doug put out his hand to help her through the opening. It was one of those maneuvers that would have been easier to do on her own, but she took his hand anyway.

The attic was long and narrow; the steep-pitched roof sloped sharply from either side of the high center beam. Two paned windows under the gables let in the fading sunlight, which fell in narrow slants on the dusty floor. Doug groped toward the center of the attic, his footsteps stirring up the dust. Reaching overhead, he found the chain for a naked light bulb. In its glare Jill could see suitcases, steamer trunks, packing barrels, a rocking horse, a dress form, an artificial Christmas tree, and boxes, dozens and dozens of boxes. They ringed the attic, from under the eaves all the way around to the edges of the trap door.

"Thank God it's not August," Doug said. "We'd die from the heat. Look at all this crap."

"Do we have to open every box?" Jill asked. Why did people hold on to so much stuff? It was nice of Doug to talk about keeping a few mementos of a dead love, but all this? Why?

Because it might be family silver saved from looting Yankees; because it might be a dead son's last manuscript; because some people did find meaning in objects.

She looked over at Doug. He was rocking back on his heels, scratching his head, trying to figure out where to start. What must it be like to have such a history? To be part of a family whose silver was looted by the Yankees?

Wait a minute. She was from such a family. The Caslers had been here since before the

Revolution. She might not know any of the family stories, but she had as much right to them as Brad or Dave.

"Let's assume the stuff's in the original box," Doug's voice broke into her thoughts. "I can't imagine anyone repackaging it. Look for something that might have come from California."

So Jill started on one side and Doug on the other, shifting the boxes about, looking for one with stamps and a California return address. Jill did stop to open a box labeled "Old Purses," but the only green one was a 1960's acid lime.

It was dirty work, and some of the boxes were heavy. As good a shape as she was in, Jill could feel the back of her shoulders tightening and the dust settling in her hair and on her face. She was in a corner where there was little light, and she had to squint at each box: "Susan's College Books," "Scout Uniforms," "Unpack Immediately."

She was tempted to explore the "Unpack Immediately," when she heard Doug let out a whistle.

"Jill, come look at this."

She threaded her way around the stacks of boxes. He was kneeling, almost directly under the light bulb. The light shone on the rivulet that a drop of sweat had traced through the dust on the back of his neck. Leaning over his shoulder, Jill looked down at the box.

It was addressed to "Mr. and Mrs. Samuel Ringling" with a return from Miles Smithson and the studio's Hollywood Blvd. address. The original packing tape had been slit and then the box resealed with masking tape.

"This is bad news," she said, "it being from Miles Smithson." Smithson had been the producer of *Weary Hearts*. "He wouldn't have sent any studio property."

"I still want to look at it."

"That goes without saying. Is it heavy?" she asked. "Can we take it downstairs?"

"Somebody brought it up here," Doug answered. "But I don't know how Gran's going to feel about having forty years of dust tracked through the house."

Jill glanced around for a cloth or a rag, but didn't see one. So she pulled her shirttail out of her skirt and began dusting off the box. Doug followed suit, and the two of them kept bumping into each other as they worked. Then Doug climbed halfway down the ladder and Jill handed the box to him. Mrs. Ringling must have heard them climbing down. When they came out of the closet, she was standing in the bedroom, her hands on her hips, looking at the box suspiciously.

"You aren't going to set that thing down in here, are you?"

"Why don't we spread out some newspapers?" Jill suggested, even though she knew that it was emotion, not dust, making Mrs. Ringling's voice tight. "If you tell me where they are, I'll run get them."

So Doug held on to the box until Jill had spread out a carpet of *The Winchester Star*. He then set the box down and took a folding pocketknife out of his jeans. Jill liked men who carried pocketknives; she liked what it said about the challenges they thought they might have to face, problems that they would have to solve with their hands. Payne always played characters who carried good pocketknives but on his own time he relied on his smile and his brain. Doug's smile was almost as good as Payne's, his brain was perhaps better, but he also trusted his hands to get him out of trouble.

In this case smiles, brains, hands, even the knife weren't necessary. The masking tape was brittle and peeled off the box almost by itself. Doug folded back the cardboard flaps and lifted off a layer of yellowing newspaper, a *Los Angeles Times* dated October of 1948. Beneath the newspaper were file folders, a camera, and packets of envelopes. Doug began to lift the things out, arranging them systematically on the newspaper.

Mrs. Ringling was watching, still from a distance. As Doug took out a packet of envelopes, she stepped forward, then stopped, stiffening. Jill looked at her inquiringly.

"Oh, it's nothing. Just those envelopes there" — Mrs. Ringling pointed — "are the letters I wrote him. Funny, him saving them all neat like that."

Doug handed the bundle of envelopes to her. "Do you want to read them?"

"No." Her voice was brisk. "That boy got his writing ability from his father. I probably wrote about setting out the tomato plants and putting up the beans. They were boring forty years ago; think what they'd be like now." She watched Doug lay out the remaining contents, then left the bedroom, taking with her, Jill noticed, the letters she had written her long-dead son.

Jill looked back at the things arrayed on the newspaper. The camera was initially the most interesting. It was a Leica.

"I don't know for sure," Jill said, "but I think this is a very good camera. Surprisingly good."

"Is there any film in it?" Doug asked.

Jill turned the camera upside down, examining its winding mechanism before trying to open it. "If there is, forty years in a hot attic won't have done it any good."

But the camera was not loaded. Jill set it aside.

Except for a few family pictures, most of the other objects were inexplicable, things with meaning only to people long dead — a silky rabbit's foot, a battered fountain pen, three matchbooks, all with phone numbers inside, a gift enclosure card reading, "Now maybe you'll keep away from ours. With greatest respect, All of us." If Doug found any of it interesting just because it had belonged to Bix, he didn't say.

They went through the papers carefully, looking at each sheet in each folder. All were orderly, none exciting — Bix's discharge papers, his contract with the studio, carbons of his assignment sheets, his 1947 income tax return. Except for the word "writer" on his contract and again on his income tax return, there was nothing to indicate that Bix was one — no manuscripts, no outlines, no notes.

Jill shrugged. "Smithson would have weeded out anything that belonged to the studio . . . and anything that had to do with the conspiracy. He can't have been proud of the fact that he was duped. It must have been quite a scene when he saw the rough cut."

Among the folders had been a manila envelope, labeled in what they guessed was Smithson's hand: "Bix's doodles, October 20, 1948." Doug and Jill rifled through the contents quickly, establishing that they were all doodles, then going back to look at each one carefully.

The doodles were weird and wonderful explosions, some on the backs of envelopes, others on narrow strips that must have once run along the margin of a larger piece of paper, still others taking up full sheets of paper. Doug and Jill sat cross-legged on the bedroom floor, careful not to lean their dusty shirts against the wall or the bedspread, passing the doodles between them. But the artwork was too interesting, too full of detail and energy, not to be talked about, not to be shared. Soon Jill found herself closer to Doug and they were looking at them together, their arms brushing as they laid aside one or pointed out a detail in another.

Miles Smithson had put them in the envelope by size, and the 8½-by-11 sheets were at the bottom. One was strikingly different from the others. It was dense, covering the entire sheet, and rigidly geometric, full of straight lines and darkened boxes marching out from a tight center of three typed words: *Original Screenplay: Untitled.* Centered underneath them were two more words: *Bix Ringling*.

It was, obviously, a title page.

"This is it. I bet it is." Doug pointed to the words. "This is the title page for his script."

"We don't know that," Jill argued calmly. "He could have written dozens — "

No, he couldn't have. He might have done dozens of treatments, but this was the title page for a full screenplay. He had only been at the studio for three years, and he had spent the first year on horror movies, then becoming a men's dialogue specialist. The carbons of his later assignment sheets had shown him assigned to adaptions, rather than new concepts. How many original screenplays could he have done on his own time? There was a very good chance that this sheet had once been attached to some version of *Weary Hearts*.

Doug cursed. "What a bitch. What an absolute bitch — just to have the title page."

"But it's nothing to get angry about," Jill spoke quickly. She didn't think there was any reason for anyone to get angry; she never did. She took the paper from him. "We never expected — "

"Jill, look!"

He took the sheet back, turned it over.

The other side, masked by the density of the doodle, was covered with a dramatic, feminine hand — Alicia's.

Dear Bix,
A million, million things to say. I hardly know where to start. It's magnificent, overwhelming —

"Look at this. I was right." Doug gripped the paper. "It's . . . Charles said that Alicia read it and wrote Bix about it. This is it. This is what she said."

Even cautious Jill agreed. Alicia had read the screenplay, turned over the title page — as anyone would have done — and written her thoughts to her brother-in-law. Bix, after reading her note, must have put the page back on top of the manuscript and drawn a box around the title, and then another box and a line, again and again until the page was covered with this dense, dispirited design. Jill did not have to read Alicia's comment to know that Bix hadn't liked what she had to say.

It made the two of them feel so real, so close.

Dear Bix,
A million, million things to say. I hardly

know where to start. It's magnificent, overwhelming, powerful, every superlative, so much so that the whole question of "Like-dislike" feels trivial.

First, as a person who knows you . . . as your friend . . . I was miserable reading it because it reminded me of what you went through in the war. I know there's nothing about capture and escape in here . . . yet I could see it, and I ached for you and for all the things that you've never told any of us about.

But that's me knowing you. It's not relevant to anyone else . . . I say that, but then I wonder. Aren't there other girls out there who care about men who went through all kinds of things that they're trying to forget? Maybe these are things you want . . . need to say to us, but I don't know that we want to hear. And the ending . . . we — all of those girls who stayed home — can't live with the thought of that happening, that he's really that changed because of the war.

I try to imagine myself as an ordinary girl out in my best sweater on a Friday night . . . is this the movie I'd want to see? The answer to that is no. And I'm afraid that's what the studio would say too.

But . . . Bix . . . I'm not telling you to change it. I can't bear the thought of that. It has to be made this way. I don't know. Do show it to Miles. Maybe he'll have some ideas.

Alicia

"This is exactly what Granddad said." Doug's voice was charged with energy. "That it was too good, too powerful to be commercial."

"That's what Alicia thought." Jill spoke cautiously. The most gifted producers in Hollywood had trouble predicting how good a movie would result from a particular screenplay. Alicia, though far shrewder than her lovely face suggested, was still a young actress, and one whose judgment, Jill thought, might have been seriously biased.

However, this did confirm that the idea of Bix having written a masterpiece was not a story made up out of sentimental nostalgia after his death. The family had thought it at the time. They weren't necessarily right, but certainly that's what they had believed.

Slowly pieces of that story were being confirmed. Dan's birthdate proved that there had been a secret script filmed. With everyone at the studio busy with *Circean Nights,* the conspiracy might have had a chance. Alicia's note was hinting at some of the differences in the two scripts — her talk about the ending suggested that it was different. She lamented how much "he" had changed. Was that Booth or Phillip? This was now another question to answer.

But Jill had to wonder if their search for the secret script wasn't going to uncover another story, one more private, one that Bix would have never wanted anyone to know.

Bix wasn't the reckless gallant Phillip any more than Doug was. But he might have had one thing in common with the role he played. He might have been falling in love with his sister-in-law.

She decided it was time to raise the issue. If this was what they were going to find, she should warn Doug so he could decide how hard he wanted to go on looking. "Doug, you don't have any sisters-in-law, do you?"

He looked puzzled at her change of subject. "No, I specialize in the real thing, actual sisters. But some of my brothers-in-law have sisters, and I know them pretty well. Does that count?"

"I don't know. Read this letter again, trying to imagine it being from a sister-in-law. You know more about families than I do. Is the tone right?"

"What do you mean, tone?"

"Just read it."

He picked up the paper and read it carefully, then again. He bit his lip, then spoke slowly. "No, this isn't right. Last spring, when I was busy shooting myself in the foot, Anne's sister-in-law, who was in my class at school, wrote me a note, which was very nice of her, but the letter was full of 'C.J. and I' — C.J., that's her husband — she was speaking for both of them. It wasn't just her to me. This is so direct. You'd think she'd start off 'Charles and I got this yesterday' or something. But she never mentions him. I think you're right. This is so . . . I don't know."

"So intimate." Jill finished for him.

He drew back. "You don't mean 'intimate' as in having an affair, do you?"

"Not necessarily anything physical. But they were both so bright and articulate, they must have had a lot in common. Then the tone of this letter — "

Doug interrupted. "It wouldn't have been an affair. Bix never would have slept with Charles's wife, not ever."

Jill didn't ask how he knew that. *He* wouldn't have had an affair with his brother's wife. But who was to say what Bix would have done? "Did he have a girlfriend?"

"No, but that's beside the point. Bix wouldn't betray his brother."

"Phillip did."

"But that was during a war. They were facing an invading army. That has to excuse something. And you were the one who said Phillip wasn't anything like Bix."

He almost sounded angry. "That's true," she said mildly. "I'm sorry. I was out of line. I'm being a woman here, turning everything into a love story."

They packed the box back up, keeping out only the envelope of doodles. Doug got fresh tape to reseal the flaps. Then, wearily, they climbed back into the attic, now lit only by the electric bulb, and like two very good scouts, they put all the boxes, trunks, suitcases, dress forms, and rocking horses back under the eaves.

When they were back downstairs Mrs. Ringling offered to make sandwiches for them. There was a bone-in ham sitting on the kitchen counter, and the bread was from her own sourdough starter, but Jill felt too dirty to eat. She sat on one of the spindle-backed kitchen chairs, waiting for Doug. He ate two sandwiches, then looked expectantly at his grandmother, who laughed at him and took a pie tin down from the top of the refrigerator. She cut him a slice.

"You're sure you won't have any of this?" Doug pushed the pie in Jill's direction. "It's dried apple. You won't find pie like this in California, not like me old granny makes."

Mrs. Ringling rapped him sharply on the head with her knuckles. Doug grabbed her hand and kissed it.

"What was that for, young man?" she demanded.

"I was counting your liver spots," he said and threw his hands up to ward off the next onslaught from his grandmother's knuckles. "Come on, Gran, stop hitting me. What's Jill going to think?"

Mrs. Ringling dusted off her hands and returned to her corner of the kitchen. "That we're family."

Jill turned in her chair, looking across the room at Mrs. Ringling. "Did you get other letters from Bix or Alicia? Besides those ones you have in your jewelry box?"

"Oh, I imagine." Mrs. Ringling shrugged. "They were both ones for writing, but I don't suppose I saved them. Those ones upstairs, they were special. He was wrong, you know. No one had told us that he had escaped. He was still listed as missing, so we were waking up every night thinking that he was dead. Then, out of the blue, sitting in the mailbox was that letter. I'll never forget it.

You know, first you almost don't notice, 'Oh, another letter from Bix,' and then an instant later it hits you, what it means — that he's alive. I didn't really need to save the letter. I'll remember every word until I die."

The overhead fixture cast a steady glare on the Formica of the kitchen tabletop; the salt and pepper shakers made squat little shadows. For Jill the news had come over the phone, Ken Sommerston, her father's attorney, calling. But for her the news had been bad — a heart attack, alone in a New York hotel room, no one heard anything . . .

Whatever had been attached to that title page they had just seen couldn't have been a masterpiece. Cass would have never, not ever —

Jill pushed away the thought. "Do you remember any of the other letters?" she asked Mrs. Ringling.

She shook her head. "No . . . it was so long ago."

"Was there anything about working on the movie?"

"Well, now that you mention it, there was that blame horse. That's right. He wanted us to find a starving horse. What were we supposed to do? Go around and ask the neighbors? I can remember Sam trying to figure out what we were going to say, 'It's a right pretty day, isn't it, and aren't those magnificent lilacs you've got there, and excuse me, but do you happen to starve your horses?' We laughed and laughed."

Doug had finished his piece of pie and was now eating straight out of the tin. "So what did you do?" he mumbled, his mouth full.

"Asked the vet. That was Sam's idea. And it turned out that there was this miserable animal who was about to be put down, so they used it. It wasn't the most humane thing to do, keeping the poor creature alive those extra weeks, but they did put him down as soon as the movie people were finished."

"And that would have been Blossom?" Jill asked. "The chestnut Booth and Pompey bring back from Appomattox?"

"I suppose. Though I can't say I've ever seen the movie myself."

"You haven't?" Doug dropped his fork, and Jill stared at her.

"Not many people know that. I suppose I'm the only one around here that hasn't. Sam saw it when it first came out, and he said it was too much like having Bix back alive, and I just didn't think I'd care for that."

Jill shivered. Whenever she thought about motherhood — which wasn't often as she was a little short on good role models — she thought about babies and toddlers. But Bix Ringling was twenty-eight when he died, and his mother's heart mourned him to this day. It was frightening to think about caring that much, that long.

Doug was speaking. "Do you remember whether the scenes with the horse were filmed in April or August? You mentioned the lilacs, so it would have been spring, wouldn't it?"

"I don't know." Mrs. Ringling frowned. "Oh, wait, yes I do. It must have been during April, because when they came back in August, some little fellow was all upset because the poor horse was gone. He wanted to find another one who looked exactly like her. I don't know what they thought, that we regularly keep around a supply of dying horses for the movies."

As they drove south toward Courthouse, Jill and Doug tried to reconstruct the movie's final episodes from memory. They now had two pieces of information — everything with either the horse or the baby was shot in April.

Jill refused to look at the video until she had showered. Doug gave her a towel and a clean T-shirt, which was every bit as long on her as the little denim skirt she had been wearing. It was a bit more transparent, but she knew that Doug would not say anything. If he noticed — and she profoundly hoped that he would — there was a professionalism about him that would set aside those responses as not appropriate to this moment.

When she came out of the bathroom she found him on the floor in front of the television. The dogs were sleeping next to him, and on the screen Booth was leading the weary Blossom home.

"It's pretty clear," he said. "The whole journey must have been shot in April."

"Let me look at it." She pushed aside one of the dogs and sat down. "You'd be surprised what clever editing can do." When Gary Cooper couldn't bat left-handed for *The Pride of the Yankees*, the editor had suggested reversing the number on his uniform, printing all the signs in mirror-image, then having him bat right-handed and run to third base. The editor then flipped the film and made him look like Lou Gehrig.

Doug handed her the remote. "Just don't get near me. You're too clean."

Jill rewound the film to the horse's first appearance. She watched carefully, sometimes using the slow-motion feature. As the daughter of an editor, she knew that Doug was wrong. The journey could have been pieced together from any number of takes. In fact, it almost certainly was. Blossom and Pompey, Booth's black servant, were never in a frame together.

"No." Doug didn't believe her. "That can't be right."

"Look at it again."

And, of course, she was right. Occasionally Pompey was shown on the back of a horse, but almost all you saw of the horse was his reddish-brown mane. In several brief scenes the horse's shadow fell between him and Booth. But when Jill and Doug froze on those frames, both agreed that here were Judy Garland's braids, the thing an editor could do nothing about except pray that no one would notice. This shadow was cast by too healthy a horse, it was not poor Blossom's shadow.

"I'll be damned." Doug shook his head. "I would have sworn you saw all three of them together. That's pretty tricky."

"It's the editing," Jill murmured. Cass's editing.

The phone rang and Doug went into the kitchen to get the phone. Jill rewound the tape again, once again looking at the journey sequence. It really was brilliant editing. It made her wonder why her father hadn't been nominated for an Academy Award on this film. Editing awards were tricky. People had to have some sense of what the original material was like before they could know how creative the editor had been, to know if he had saved the picture or ruined it.

Or just commercialized it.

Doug came back into the living room and Jill twisted around, looking at him.

"That was Gran," he said. "She said she just remembered that there had been film in Bix's camera. None of them had the heart to develop it so Charles had told them to put it in the deep freeze. She hasn't a clue if it's still there, but if we want to go defrost her freezer, it's fine with her."

Twelve

So the next morning found Jill in Mrs. Ringling's cellar, preparing to defrost her freezer.

At first she had been amazed at the notion that a roll of film would have sat in a freezer for forty years. The studio had lost the movie's April script; it had destroyed all the footage not used in the final version; it had lost track of the production files. Why would one roll of undeveloped film still be around after forty years?

Why not? Doug and Randy, both Virginians to the core, had asked. That wasn't so long ago. Who would have thrown it out?

Once she saw the freezer she grew more hopeful. It was a big chest-type without any interior shelves. In a family that didn't unpack boxes labeled "Unpack Immediately," a small object might drift to the bottom and get lost there for years.

Of course, this was not the freezer into which the Ringlings had put the film in 1948. Mrs. Ringling said she had gotten this one during the fifties. "But I moved everything from the old, and I do seem to remember having seen the film a couple times since then. I never knew what to do with it, so I always tossed it back in, but I haven't seen it in ages."

So they started to unload the hulking appliance. The top layer had some supermarket food — Pepperidge Farm Cherry Turnovers, Swanson Hungry Man turkey pot pies, Minute Maid juice. There was meat from a local processor, stamped and wrapped in white paper. The food beneath that was mostly garden produce — corn, peas, and beans — home-packed in white freezer boxes, surrounded by innumerable plastic containers of applesauce. Jill stacked them on top of the washer and dryer, her hands growing cold as she worked. She took out four bags of pecans, two jars of yeast, two packages of bought English muffins, and four wrapped loaves of homemade cranberry bread. Toward the bottom of the freezer were several pounds of coffee packed in the old-fashioned squat cans, some mason jars of homemade soup, and more applesauce. Every layer had its share of leftovers, packaged in foil, tucked into plastic.

Mrs. Ringling shook her head as they reached the bottom of the freezer. "You must think I'm a pretty poor housekeeper." She showed Jill the label on a foil-wrapped packet, "Meat Loaf Leftovers, 4-26-51."

"I don't think any such thing," Jill assured her.

"Valley people always save stuff; I suppose it comes from the wars. Sheridan and then all those children supposedly starving in Europe. It really made us save things."

Jill was starting to get used to the Civil War and World War II existing side by side on the Valley's psychological time line. "Having such a big freezer, you could save things without causing any trouble."

At least, no trouble until it was time to defrost it. Jill's legs ached from riding the day before, her shoulders were tight from moving boxes, and now her hands were very cold.

The freezer was empty at last. They had found no film, but the walls were thick with frost-encrusted ice. Anything might be buried in those glaciers. "Do you have some cast iron skillets?" Jill asked. "I'll go boil some water."

Doug and Randy had been amazed at how willingly Jill had volunteered for this chore. They couldn't imagine her at such a domestic task. But Jill knew how to clean. Alice had made sure of that. It was part of a lady's education; the mistress of a house cannot supervise her servants unless she can properly perform the tasks herself. This was why Alice had taught the duke's two sisters how to clean.

She had approached Jill's lessons with even more diligence. Alice did not trust American money; she had taught Jill to clean in case she ever had to do it for herself. So while Jill could mend aging damask and care for family silver — neither of which she owned — she also knew about oven cleaner and toilet bowl brushes. The irony, of course, was that while Jill could have hired people to vacuum Interstate 81 if she had wanted, Lady Katherine had a charwoman only one morning a week, and her younger sister, the Countess Ives, didn't even have that.

"Boil water?" Mrs. Ringling frowned. "That's sure an old-fashioned way to go about it. Use a blow dryer, girl. It's much less messy and you don't have to run up and down the stairs."

"You blow dry your hair?" Mrs. Ringling's silver hair, twisted into a hair net, did not look like much technology had been sacrificed in its behalf.

"No, but I also use the thing to dust the chandeliers. Doug gave it to me for Christmas a couple of years back. It's right handy."

Alice had taught Jill to dust with feathers and lamb's wool. A blow dryer sounded like quite an improvement. Jill would have to tell the Countess Ives.

There was an electrical outlet in the over-head light fixture, and following Mrs. Ringling's instructions, Jill plugged together three orange extension cords and hooked them up to the Lady Clairol hairdryer. Lady Clairol did work better than the hot water, but even so, the years of ice required considerable patience, something which Jill had in great abundance. Finally she was able to pry the ice off in slabs, and imbedded deep in one of the slabs was a roll of film.

"I sure hope that's the one you want," Mrs. Ringling said. "What a shame to have you go to all this trouble and find yourself looking at Ward's kids standing in front of the Lincoln Memorial."

Jill set the film aside, and since she was the sort who always cleaned up after herself, she finished the chore, scrubbing out the freezer, carrying away three forty-gallon trash bags of elderly food.

Before coming, she had called a friend who owned a photography lab, and he had assured her that exposed, but undeveloped, film should survive indefinitely in a freezer. "It may be as brittle as can be. You'd better send it to someone good."

"I'm sending it to you," Jill had told him. So when she was finally done with Mrs.

Ringling's freezer, she drove to the Federal Express office and shipped the film out to California.

It was just after four as she came to the Courthouse exit, so she turned west off the Interstate, taking the county road to Aunt Carrie's. In the ditches along the side of the road the airy Queen Anne's lace were starting to blossom, and the woodland borders glowed with ferns and vivid masses of the star-like fire pinks. The sunlight was gentle, softening the memory that troops had marched across this ground.

She found the men in the flower garden. A pile of irises lay next to Randy; he was tying them in bunches with kitchen twine while Doug was filling a line of rusty coffee cans with water from the green garden hose. They were working with steady, set expressions, oblivious to the flowers' beauty.

"That's a lot of flowers," she said. "Are you having a party?"

They looked up. "Did you find the film?" Doug asked.

"Did you bring dinner?" Randy asked.

"Yes, to you." She pointed to Doug. "And no, to you," she said to Randy.

Doug cheered and Randy groaned. "It's Thursday, Jill, Thursday. Whoever's out should always get dinner on Thursday; that's our one rule."

"I'll be happy to go get something, but what's so special about Thursdays?"

"Friday's the Farmers' Market," Doug explained. "Randy may look like God's gift to womankind, but on Fridays he's a florist. We spend Thursday evening getting ready."

"Don't laugh," Randy said as he wrapped lengths of string around his forearm. "I didn't have to pay myself last summer, thanks to these flowers and that jam."

Apparently Aunt Carrie's flowers were indeed serious agriculture. From March to October she had sold her flowers at one of the weekly Farmers' Markets in the Washington suburbs. She had made enough to cover her groceries and pay off what was left of her winter heating bill.

"But I only made that much because I sold all her jam," Randy said. "Now it's gone, so I'll be lucky if I can get another year out of these babies. They've survived some intense neglect."

Doug brought out an armful of badly cut tulips, and Randy started to tie them. Jill guessed that they were Cottage or Darwin tulips; they were flamboyantly colorful — scarlet, deep purple, golden yellow, and a lovely pure white — with long stems that tended to droop.

"Do you always bunch them by kind?" Jill asked as she watched Randy wrap the tulips near the heads, trying to make the stems appear straight. "Don't you ever do assortments?"

"We don't know how," Randy answered. "Apparently Aunt Carrie was great at this mix-and-match stuff. She'd get twice as many bouquets because she'd add a lot of weeds."

By weeds, Jill assumed he meant the Queen Anne's lace, the purple violets, the maidenhair ferns and the thistle.

"If you'll let me help," she said. "I can probably do some mix-and-matching." As part of the English-lady's education that she had received from Alice, Jill had, of course, learned to arrange flowers.

Randy instantly dropped his twine and scrambled up. "What a perfect division of labor. You do this and I'll go pick up dinner. I'm much better at picking up dinner than I am at the flowers."

Jill set Doug to work sharpening the knife. Then she hitched a ride down the lane with Randy and, taking a bushel basket from the back of his truck, filled it with ferns and Queen Anne's lace. She carried the bushel basket back up the lane, gath-

351

ering armloads from the flowering shrubs, perfumed masses of delicate lilacs, clouds of brightly colored azaleas. Then she cut foliage, boxwood and privet, magnolia leaves and euonymus.

Back at the garden Doug had finished picking the tulips. Jill herself liked the droop of their long stems and the interesting, natural shapes made once the flowers were arranged. But she knew other people wanted all stems to be as regimented as daffodils so she set Doug to work rolling the tulips, five at a time, in newspaper. Plunged up to their necks in cool water, the flowers would be straight by tomorrow morning.

She hammered the woody stems of the foliage, the lilacs and the azaleas, stripped off all their lower foliage and blossoms, and put them into warmish water. She recut all the flowers, slicing them at a crisp, sharp angle, and then put them in cool water.

Then she lined up all the coffee cans and began to combine the flowers. She mixed some iris with the white Treasure azaleas and some more with the pale pink Cameos. Sprays of lavender Corsage azaleas went with deep purple tulips. She did all-white arrangements, all-yellow, all-lavender. She blended cool, pale blossoms; she grouped the rich, vividly colored flowers. She combined the quiet and the striking. To some she added touches of greenery; in others the foliage was profuse. Every bouquet was different, and she was as happy as could be. It wasn't quite as good as riding, but it was better than searching through attics and freezers, getting permits for other people's fundraisers, better than raising fish.

"You're very creative," Doug said.

Jill looked up from her work. He had finished eating and was gathering up his trash, stuffing it back into the McDonald's bag. Jill hadn't touched her own food; she had hardly noticed Randy's return.

"No, I'm not," she answered. "Creative people write movies. I arrange flowers."

He crushed his bag into a ball and deftly tossed it into her heap of stripped leaves and cut stems. "That's the first time I've heard you put yourself down."

Jill clipped a withering blossom off an iris. Her therapy group often told her that she should stop comparing herself to her father. She didn't think she did it as much as they thought she did. "You're right. I shouldn't have put it that way. I try for a realistic assessment of my abilities. I did not inherit my father's narrative imagination. This sort of eye for domestic, craftsy detail I got from my mother."

"Can I ask you a personal question?"

"Of course."

"It's about your mother."

"All right." Which Jill realized was a step down from "Of course."

"The media makes her out to be such a ditz. That judge . . . they gave him a really hard time when he married her."

" 'Judge Norfolk marries ex-showgirl,' " Jill quoted the headlines.

"She's gorgeous, she's . . . excuse me, but apparently she's had some pill problems, so it's never sounded like she's the strongest person in the world, and no one's pretended that she's well-educated. But then she's married these really talented men — your father, the judge, and now David Ahearn, he's no slouch. He'll probably go straight into network broadcasting the minute he retires. What's her secret?"

Jill considered the few flowers remaining; they were going to make for an odd arrangement.

"You don't have to answer," Doug said.

"No, no, I don't mind." She had spent several years pondering her mother's character. Doug was right. Melody had married some noteworthy men. Jill had been very sorry when she divorced George Norfolk, but had been pleased when Melody returned to David Ahearn after leaving Hazelden.

"She's a nurturer," Jill explained. "She likes to take care of people. Mother's homes are deliciously comfortable. There's always exactly the right number of pillows on the sofa, there's a footstool in the precise spot you want a footstool to be in. Her sheets smell of lavender. Luxury and beauty and comfort matter to her, and she knows how to pamper people. Some men like that."

"Did you?"

"I suppose I found it a little smothering. I also felt like she expected something in return. Here she was, rushing around, doing all these things that seemed motherly, and I knew that there was something daughterly I was supposed to be doing in return, and I didn't have a clue as to what it was. That's what I loved about my horse; I knew what she expected of me."

"It sounds like you feel a little guilty about it."

"I'm trying not to." Jill decided that these last flowers would have to be for their own kitchen table. "Maybe, if she had been a full-time mother, she would have learned that nurturing involves more than physical comfort. But I think she knows that and feels inadequate; that's what brings on the bad times. But I know it isn't my fault."

Jill's voice was more emphatic than her heart. She had often felt totally responsible for her mother's situation. "I was completely uninvolved in the whole custody issue; there was no question of it ever being my decision." She stepped back and surveyed the line of coffee cans. Each week there would be more and more flowers. A few more days of sun would bring the peonies to flower, followed by the hybrid tea roses. In the woods and along the roads would be the daisies, the black-eyed susans, the magnificent tiger-colored day lilies, and the coneflowers. "Now, what do we do with all these?"

"Put them in the truck."

Randy came out to help. "Jill, this is great," he exclaimed the minute he saw all the coffee cans. "Look how many we have, and they're so . . . so done. I'll bet we can get away with charging a buck more a bouquet." He clapped Jill on the shoulder. "I'd hire you in an instant, but I can't afford you, and since the flowers are really yours anyway, it would seem a little silly."

Jill waved her hand, dismissing him. "I don't want your money."

"I know. That's what I like about you."

Randy had brought a red pickup over from the barn. It was older than the one with oversized tires and blue metallic paint. He used this one when he genuinely needed a pickup; the other was reserved for pickups of human blossoms.

The three of them loaded the truck. Some of the cans were so heavy with flowers that they had to steady them with bricks. Then the men laced on a canvas cover, and discussed the weather, deciding that there was no need to back the truck into the barn.

Randy turned to Doug. "I went last week."

"Are you sure?"

"Positive. Because I had this long discussion with Dad about how I should pick up Aunt Jill at the airport since it was on my way home, but he thought she might be insulted if we picked her up in a truck."

"Me?" Jill shook her head. "I wouldn't have minded riding in a truck. And anyway, I didn't want anyone to pick me up in the first place. I wanted to rent a car."

"You don't need to defend yourself to us," Doug put in. "We know what it's like to be told what to do. We have sisters. But if you're really so gung ho about driving 120 miles in a truck, why don't you come with me tomorrow?"

That was not a difficult decision. "I'd love to."

★ ★ ★

Doug knocked on her motel door shortly before five the next morning. He had already stopped at the all-night 7-Eleven to fill a thermos with coffee. Sharing sips out of the red plastic cup, they shot up north on 81 and then cut east on 66. The dark highway was almost deserted except for an occasional convoy of eighteen-wheelers, barreling at such speed that Doug pulled over to the shoulder and let them pass.

More traffic appeared as they approached the city, and the sky was growing light when Doug drove into McLean, one of the wealthiest suburbs of Washington, D.C. The farmers' market was in the parking lot of the town's soccer fields. Doug backed the truck into what had, for years, been Aunt Carrie's space.

They were one of the last ones there. Other vendors had much more elaborate setups. In the space next to theirs was a trailer built like a little house with red-painted half-walls, a white-shingled roof and a space in the center from which the grower and his wife could sell. Other had shelving and awnings, burnt-wood signs. Doug set up an aluminum folding table, put out his coffee cans, and scrawled the new price on a piece of cardboard.

The market did not open until eight; while

waiting, the vendors chatted among themselves, familiar and friendly. Doug and Jill's neighbors immediately noticed their price increase, and it caused a bit of flurry among the others with flowers.

The customers who arrived first seemed to be retired people, perhaps with a lifelong habit of getting up early, now needing someplace to go. Jill could tell who the regulars were; they commented on how different the flowers were this week.

She had a good time. The first few times someone looked at all the flowers and bought nothing, she took it rather personally, but then she managed to disengage her feelings from the process. The retired people wanted to chat, and since she had thought about every bunch, she had something to say.

"These smell better, but these will last longer."

"Once it starts to wilt, dunk the whole thing head first in a bucket of water. That only works with some kinds of flowers, but it might work with these."

"If you want the buds to flower, snip off the old flowers with the sharpest scissors you have."

"That one may be a little tricky to arrange, but the azaleas should hold up the other flowers. If you have any problems, let us know next week."

She saw Doug looking at her oddly. "What is it?" she asked.

"I'm surprised, that's all. I didn't know that you were staying through next week."

"Oh, yes." Guiltily Jill realized that she hadn't communicated her intentions to anyone; she had assumed that Doug, at least, would somehow know. "I think I'm hooked on these flowers, and I would like to clear out Aunt Carrie's house if that's all right with everyone."

"It's certainly fine by me. All those little doily things are driving me nuts. I'm starting to dream about them."

After nine the customers grew younger, and their cars more expensive. They were McLean's mothers, driving Volvo station wagons and Mercedes sedans. Some were in tennis clothes, others in casual, but well-cut skirts. Even those in jeans wore expensive T-shirts, with shoulder pads and interesting collars. In a hurry, none of them cared to chat. As it took only one person to make change, Jill left Doug at the truck while she looked at the other stalls.

When she returned, one customer at the table was wearing a tapestry-covered hair clip that Jill herself might have worn. Jill was sufficiently interested in the hair clip that it took her a moment to notice that the customer and Doug were not on the best of terms.

One end of the metal table was covered with loose flowers. The customer, a well-groomed woman in her mid-thirties, was dismantling the bouquets.

"Look, lady," Doug was saying, "I don't care what color your sofa is. You can't do that."

The woman ignored him. The other customers were moving away.

"Now I'm serious." Doug started to set the coffee cans back out of her reach. "I don't want all these taken apart."

Jill felt the desperate scurrying in the pit of her stomach that she always got when people grew angry, even when they weren't angry with her. She spoke quickly. "Can I help you?" Behind her back, she gestured to Doug, telling him that she would handle this.

"I have already explained." The woman's voice was rigid with stress. "My sofa is yellow chintz with pink, ivory, and lavender flowers. I must have those color flowers." She pulled the deep purple tulips out from the bunch of Corsage azaleas, dropping them to the table. "I'm having a Senator to dinner."

Jill's mother once had a pair of flowery chintz sofas. Melody never would have dreamed of slavishly copying its floral design . . . perhaps because she entertained people much more sensitive to beauty than your average politician. "You might find," Jill suggested mildly, "that the deeper tones would make an interesting accent."

"I think I can judge what is appropriate for my own house." The customer thrust a large bunch of yellow, pink, lavender, and ivory flowers at Doug. "How much are these?"

He was leaning back against the tailgate of the truck, his hands in his pocket. He stayed right there. "Lady, if you're too cheap to order from a florist, you and the Senator had better accept those as our gift."

The woman drew back, startled. "What are you talking about?"

"Your money is not money I care to have."

She stared at him, her lips tightening.

"I mean it," he repeated. "Take them." He gestured with an elbow, not taking his hand out of his pocket. "They're yours."

The woman was trembling. She dropped her flowers on the tables and spun, stalking away.

Jill started to gather the blossoms up, sorting them back out into bunches, mingling them again with the deep-hued rejected flowers.

"What a bitch." Doug was shaking his head. "You get people like that every once in a while. People who think they're such hot stuff because they've got money. I can't stand them."

Jill ignored the slur on people with money. "Don't be angry with her. Feel sorry for her. She was under so much strain. Giving this dinner's got her twisted in knots, and now she does have to go to the florist. She's going to have one awful day, and you certainly didn't help."

"Okay." Doug grinned, a little boy pleased with his own naughtiness. "The people you ought to feel sorry for are those poor bastards who are going to her house. She's going to be such a fun hostess."

Jill had to agree with him there.

They sold out well before the market closed. Doug looked pleased as he counted the money, and Jill, owner of shopping malls and office buildings, of golf courses and avocado groves, was tickled pink.

"Are you in any rush to get home?" she asked Doug as they stacked the coffee cans in the truck and folded up the table. "I could really use some clothes. Is there any decent place to shop around here?"

Whenever Jill traveled to a place with laundry facilities, she took a standard set of clothes — the short, straight navy skirt; a loose, mid-calf denim skirt of a light soft blue so pale it was nearly lavender; a pair of white running shorts; some pleated taupe slacks of washable silk; assorted T-shirts in white, lavender and peach, some cotton, some silk; a cotton sweater, patterned in taupe and lavender; and a fistful of handhammered silver jewelry. The wardrobe all fit into a carry-on barrel bag and would take her everywhere people weren't mourning or wearing sequins and bugle beads. But it wasn't going to do for a week's worth of gardening.

"I don't mind stopping," he answered. "There's a big mall just up Dolley Madison, but I don't know if it's got your kind of shopping, as I don't have a clue as to where people in your financial stratosphere usually shop."

Big malls were certainly not where Jill usually shopped. "We can go there, but let me call my mother. Maybe she'll have some ideas."

"Does she know Washington?"

"No, but she knows shopping. If I have to go into a department store, I'm only going into one, and she'll know which is the best bet."

At one time in her life Jill had truly loathed shopping, a reaction, no doubt, to her mother's binges. Her year of therapy had softened some of the jangling associations, and she could now regard it as a boring chore.

Doug pulled into a gas station that had a public phone at the edge of its lot. As it was nine o'clock in California, Jill caught her mother thinking about getting out of bed. "I don't need anything dressy," she explained. "Jeans and a sweatsuit. A bathrobe and maybe some kind of dress. Except for the dress, I suppose I could go to the Gap."

Jill had never been in the Gap in her life, but some of her friends had been featured in that store's series of celebrity advertisements.

"No, Jill," her mother told her. "You can't go to the Gap. I could shop at the Gap, Susannah could shop at the Gap, but you aren't nearly interested enough in clothes to shop there."

Jill was not offended. She remembered Susannah's ad. Her friend had worn a men's T-shirt belted up as a mini-dress over a mock turtleneck with a chambray shirt buttoned wrong. It had been a great look, casual and effortless. But Jill knew that it had taken the actress a good part of a day and fifteen thousand dollars worth of borrowed antique Indian jewelry to put the outfit together.

Susannah had enjoyed spending the day that way. Melody would have adored it. Not Jill. She wasn't very interested in clothes. She didn't mind wearing the same thing day after day because no two of her days were ever the same. Clothes were not what provided variety in her life. Nor did she need to use clothes to call attention to herself or to satisfy fantasies. If she had an urge for an African safari, she would go on one. She didn't have to use shopping at Banana Republic as a substitute.

"Washington has a Nordstrom's now," Melody told her. "Bloomingdale's has gone downhill, and with all those housewares and luggage, they've never been able to concentrate properly on clothes. I believe there are some Saks stores there, but you know I've never really liked Saks. If you have to go to the local chains, do that Woodward and Something over Hecht's, but try for the Nordstorm's. They are supposed to have the best service in the country."

Jill blinked, overwhelmed by this flood of information from a woman, who, as far as her daughter knew, had never been to Washington. Woodward and Something . . . was she really supposed to buy clothes from the two reporters who had covered Watergate?

"And, Jill . . ." Melody's voice grew tentative. "Why don't you let me send you a dress? It would save you so much time."

A memory swept over Jill, a pile of little dresses, white flannel sprigged with pale blue flowers, trimmed in eyelet lace; cranberry corduroy piped in cream; black watch plaid with hunter green cuffs and collar; daffodil yellow with a golden pinstripe — all for a child who wore a uniform to school.

On the other hand, Jill did not want to spend any more time inside a store than she had to. "Sure, Mother, that would be great. But nothing very dressy."

"I'll remember that," Melody promised.

It turned out that there was a Nordstorm's at Tyson's Corner, the big mall not far away. Doug parked the truck on one of the upper levels of the multi-tiered garage, then turned to Jill.

"I lied to you when I said it was fine if we went shopping," he said. "I really hate shopping with women. I've been fired. I've been captain of a team who had their faces stomped by a bunch of gorillas in the national finals on national TV. Those were both seriously unpleasant, but I would happily endure either one of those again rather than shop with a woman."

"You should have said something."

"I am. I don't mind being at the mall. I'll go to the bookstore, I'll go to a movie, I'll hang out, just *please* don't make me go with you."

Jill thought about her mother, how impossible it was to get her to be this direct about her preferences. What an easy companion Doug was. She reached across the truck and patted him on the arm. "We won't make you do anything you don't want to do."

He opened the truck door. "That's what they always say."

They arranged to meet in an hour. She chose the time, doubling what she thought she would need, in case of lines. Doug shook his head. "That's not very long."

"It's too long for my taste, but I don't know much about the retail collections — what's the difference between Calvin Klein and Ralph Lauren — I should have asked Mother."

But even without that key information, she was at the rendevouz point fifteen minutes ahead of schedule and had to wait for him.

He was clearly surprised to see her. He sat down, noticing that she had already drunk half a cup of tea. "You are the most remarkable woman. Is this what it's like to have money? It makes you able to shop fast?"

"I don't know that it's the money. I just don't like to shop."

"Can I ask you a personal question?"

"Only if you remember it will now be two-zip. You asked me about my mother yesterday. I haven't asked you a thing."

He frowned. "What on earth do you want to know about me?"

"You go ahead. I like this building up credit."

He looked uncomfortable, but when she continued to smile blandly, he went on. "You have all the money in the world, don't you?"

"I wouldn't go that far, but I am very comfortable." Jill knew that "very comfortable" was an understatement, and this was not someone she wanted to dissemble with. "By most people's standards, I really do have a lot, more than I'll ever need."

"Then how do you go about making decisions about things like clothes and such? For my sisters money is such a big part of that. If you're looking at two sweaters and they both look good on you, do you just buy both? Or all three hundred, since everything must look good on you."

"It's simple. I don't have the closet space."

"The closet space. Wait a minute, time out here." He made a T with his hands.

"People who live in trailers don't have enough closet space. People who live in Manhattan don't have enough closet space. But you . . . how can you not have enough closets?"

"I air-conditioned my house. I lost part of every closet to the duct work, and I didn't have that many to begin with." Jill noticed that she was talking about her house as if it still existed — not a good sign. "But it's not only that. I like to keep my life simple. Things have a cost besides their initial price — there's giving them space, thinking about whether or not to wear them, and just taking care of them. So often really wonderful things aren't worth how much care they require."

"For example?"

"Oh . . . linen sheets. They feel great to sleep in, they're so cool and soft, not like silk, which I find too hot and slippery, but — "

"I don't know that hot and slippery is always bad," Doug reflected.

"But the sheets?"

"Good point. I'm sold. Linen it is."

"No, it's not. Not unless you iron them every day. Can you imagine, getting up every morning, knowing that you've got to iron your bed?"

"I don't get up every morning and *make* my bed. I always feel so pleased that I've managed the getting up part that I don't like to tax the system. But surely you could pay someone to do the ironing."

"And that means having someone come into your house everyday, that means finding that person, deciding what degree of her personal problems you're willing to have come in your front door, etc. No set of sheets is worth that. Cotton's easier."

"I'm crushed. What's to become of us boys from the wrong side of the tracks and all our sick fantasies, if the rich girls of the world are sleeping on ordinary sheets?"

"Don't be so quick to call cotton ordinary. A friend of mine just bought a set of cotton voile sheets for fifteen thousand dollars."

"Fifteen thous — That's not possible."

"It was for the whole ensemble."

"I don't care. Fifteen thousand dollars . . . my dad can put you in a real nice Chevy for that."

Now that he had a clearer fix on Jill's plans, Doug cut a deal with his mother. He would produce Jill for Sunday dinner if she could guarantee a No-Sisters event.

"I wouldn't have minded meeting your sisters," she protested as they were driving up to Winchester Sunday.

"I know, but I would have."

That was not true. Doug liked his sisters. But he had seen how Jill operated in a big crowd. She was pleasant and polite, but there was something withdrawn about her. She was holding back, watching, observing, without being involved. When she met his parents, he wanted her to be there, both feet planted, bathing suit wet, the whole works.

By and large, he felt good about the way things were going. Friday had been great, Saturday even better. She had spent the day doing strange but seemingly knowledgeable things to the flowers, and then, without it even being a question, they had spent the evening together, driving into Harrisonburg to see a movie. They weren't kids; they both knew where things were heading.

Then a thought would cut him off at the knees. *This woman is the single richest person that you have ever met.* It was a challenge that might undo more than his knees.

Seeing her with his parents would be a reality check. Doug thought the world of his parents. The whole time they were growing up, he and his sister never understood car salesman jokes. His father was so well respected, so well liked.

Doug knew that everyone in college basketball thought he was a great motivator, but he wasn't anywhere near as good as his dad. Ward Ringling, more than any psychology textbook Doug had read, knew how people went about making decisions. His job, he believed, was not to sell people cars, but to guide them through the decision-making process. Doug had stood on the floor with him, eavesdropping on other salesmen's pitches. "He lost them right there," Ward would say. "He just made the decision too hard." Or — "She's letting them get off track; now they'll have to come in next week. They're going to end up with the Celebrity wagon. They're not crazy people, you can tell that. But now they've got to go home and remember why they shouldn't buy a Blazer."

Every bit of success Doug had had as a recruiter had been thanks to his father. What a kid's family really wanted was not a free Chrysler, but an easy decision. Doug had learned how to make decisions easy for people.

As he turned into his parents' drive, his mother, Grace, was the one who came to the door. She came out onto the porch, putting out her hand to Jill. "I've been hearing such lovely things about you — how you helped the boys with the flowers . . . and defrosting Gran's freezer for her. My girls are writhing with guilt. One of them should have gone over and helped her ages ago."

"No, no," Jill protested. "I didn't do it to make anyone feel bad. I had my own agenda."

"Whatever the reason, it was nice of you. Now, come out back. Ward is fussing with the charcoal."

Actually he was coming through the house, drying his hands on a tea towel. He extended one to Jill. "So you're the young lady responsible for those velvet collars."

Jill drew back. "I beg your pardon?"

"Do you hear that, Grace? All that trouble and she doesn't even know what we're talking about." Ward drew Jill into the living room, telling her a story that Doug knew well.

Years ago a picture had appeared in a magazine of Jill and her father. They had been at a funeral or something, and Jill, no more than seven or eight, had been wearing a little wool coat trimmed with a velvet collar and velvet cuffs. The picture had made its way up and down the Valley with all the young girls swooning over the velvet collar and cuffs. So, that Christmas, Marie Ringling had bought two yards of velvet and made collars and cuffs for her daughters' coats, stitching them on after the girls had gone to sleep Christmas Eve.

Jill was shaking her head. She didn't even

374

remember the coat.

Doug started whistling "She'll Be Comin' Round the Mountain."

"It looked pretty odd," Ward finished, "the beautiful collars on these ratty old coats, but the girls loved them . . . even the ones who were old enough to know better."

"Doug," his mother asked. "Why are you whistling? It's not polite."

"Your mother's right, Doug," Ward agreed. "But it is a good song." He started whistling too. Doug picked up a harmony. He thought it sounded pretty good, a regular church choir. Thinking maybe they could get a three-part thing going, a descant or something, he looked over at Jill. Alas, she and his mother were fleeing into the kitchen.

He and his dad finished a few more verses, did a rousing chorus of "Clementine," and then went out into the kitchen where the two women, sensible people that they were, were mixing drinks for themselves.

"So, tell us, Jill," Ward said as he took over the bartending duties, "what do you drive?"

That was an interesting question. Doug realized he didn't have a clue what kind of car she drove.

She answered. "A Chevy."

He didn't believe her. He was willing to

believe that his father could sell her one, but he didn't believe she already had one.

"Good for you." Ward handed her her drink. "Which model? Do you like it? Is it a good car?"

"I love it. It's a wonderful car."

Doug ran through the Chevrolet's product line in his head. What possible car could she think was so wonderful? Doug felt a stiff breeze whirling about his knees.

He called her bluff. "You didn't say which model." He figured that there was a good chance that she wouldn't know the names of any Chevy cars.

"Oh, it's an old one."

"How old?" he asked.

"Pretty old."

Suddenly this all made sense. "It's not older than me, is it?"

Her eyes rolled upward; she was doing some subtraction in her head. She was enjoying this. "Pretty close." Then she relented. "I have a '57 Bel Air."

A cut lime went splat on the floor. Ward clapped his hand over his heart. "A '57 Bel Air. I don't believe it. Don't tell me, is it a two-door hardtop?"

Jill nodded. "Colonial Cream," she said, naming the paint color.

"That was the ultimate cruising car. My

first boss had one of them. They only made 150, 175 thousand." Ward shivered in delight. "Oh, God . . . would you marry me? What's the mileage?"

"Around forty thousand."

"Forty thousand? How is that possible? People who bought those cars first time around *loved* to drive."

"Apparently my original owner had to sell it to his mother."

"That could account for it. Now, may I ask the sleazeball question? What did you have to pay for it?"

"Nothing. It was a gift."

"A gift?" Ward moaned sadly. "Oh, Douglas, what chance do guys like you and me have when other people go around giving girls '57 Bel Airs?"

"It was a professional-type thing," she explained. "Do you remember the movie *Bob's Drive-In?*" Apparently some friends of hers had produced the movie, and the set had been riddled with drug usage, causing delays that were costing about a thousand dollars a second. The producers called Jill, and she flew out to the location. She claimed she didn't do much. "But they all knew I was the last step before calling the real grownups. So people shaped up. Afterwards my friends gave me this car. It wasn't the one used in the movie. Mine's better. It's never needed restoration. It's still got the original paint job."

"And forty thousand miles." Ward took her hand solemnly. "I meant that, about wanting to marry you. There's no blood test in Maryland. Do you want to go now or wait until after dinner?"

"They've changed the law," his wife told him. "Maryland now has a waiting period."

"Oh, drat . . . well, in that case, I'd better go work on this charcoal."

"I liked your parents," Jill said as soon as the car doors were shut behind them.

"Of course you do. They all do. It always happens. Girls get all gushy about the way I look, but then they meet my dad, and he's the one they fall in love with . . . although you're the first one he's wanted to marry."

"Being part of a strong, stable family is not unattractive, Doug."

"Not unattractive? That's fine, if 'not unattractive' is your goal. Some of us aspire to being major sex symbols. So I have a great dad. What's sexy about having a great dad? Does the Lone Ranger have a great dad? Does James Bond? Does Kermit the Frog?" He backed out of the drive. "Now what do you want to do? Would you like to stop on the way home and see the Reynolds House?"

"That sounds great." Jill was so happy she didn't care what they did. "What's the Reynolds House?"

"How can you know that it's great if you don't know what it is?"

"I always like going to new places." *Especially with you.*

"Actually, this won't seem new. It's where they filmed the exteriors of *Weary Hearts.* It's Briar Ridge."

The house, Doug told her as they drove south, was still in private hands. "They tried opening it for tours, but people were always disappointed since none of the interiors were shot here. The windows are all in the right places, but otherwise none of the rooms are the same."

All there was to identify the house as Briar Ridge was a small plaque fixed to one of the brick columns that flanked the white gates.

But Briar Ridge it was — the lane rising gently past the stone fences, the kitchen garden on the sunny side of the house, the paddocks in the fields sloping toward the road, and the house itself, solid and brick, with its twin chimneys, pillared porch, and the fanlight over the beautiful mahogany door — the whole scene framed in the background by the dark bulk of Massanutten.

Doug knocked on the door although he expected no answer. "I think Mrs. Reynolds usually stays in town after church to eat dinner with her son's family."

Jill was waiting at the foot of the white steps. "Is it all right if we walk around?"

"Goodness, yes." Then he smiled his naughty-little-boy grin. "She likes me."

He came down the steps and directed Jill toward the south side of the house. "This tree line is pretty interesting. If you remember that shot where Phillip and Mary Deas are talking to Mosby's man, you can still see that little grove of English oaks, but Mrs. Reynolds sold the two black walnuts fifteen years ago. It was a shame, but they probably would have been poached if she hadn't done it, so nobody blamed her." He touched her arm, just a light tour-guide's touch, turning her. "And the big chestnut that was over there; it's gone. Apparently it already had the blight when they were filming, though it looked good enough."

Jill thought she knew her father's work well, but even she had not paid attention to the individual trees, and she wasn't sure how truly interested she was in them now.

But it was lovely to be here on this sunny afternoon. The property was not as spruce and trim as in the movie's opening scenes, but nor was it as dilapidated as in the closing ones.

Doug showed her the break in the woods that had been Phillip's path back into Massanutten. "Actually the path doesn't go very far. The clearing that was used in the movie is really a good ten miles from here."

Jill wanted to walk up the path anyway. Two days of working in the sweet limestone soil of the flower garden had made a difference. She didn't feel at home in the Valley — it would not be that easy — but she no longer felt like a stranger. She felt like a welcome guest . . . or perhaps even more than a guest, like someone who has come to stay, a new bride perhaps, learning the routines of the house as both the house and the routines would be entirely hers.

The path followed a little stream through stands of birch and white laurel, past moss-covered stones, delicate ferns, and silvery lichen. The drooping, bell-like flowers of the wild columbine glowed in the patches of sunlight. The trail narrowed, and Jill had to let Doug walk behind her. In another minute they reached a slender birch that had fallen, its crown having caught in another tree so that it was slanted across the path, its feathery limbs, still green, blocking the way. Jill stopped, turning so quickly that Doug had to apologize and step back.

The light here was muted, green and shadowy. The wind was rustling the leaves, and the air had a damp freshness. Doug reached forward as if to pull back the tree's lower boughs. Jill didn't move. Then he didn't, either.

They had walked single file for long enough. The path was telling them to stop, to turn, to face one another.

Doug's hand was resting on the trunk of the tree, just over her shoulder near her hair. She reached up and laid her palm against his face. His skin was warm, still soft after a late-morning shave. She closed her eyes, and all she knew was the smell of the damp moss and the feel of his face against her hand.

He jerked back, stepping away as if her touch were nettle-sharp. "There's no place to go from here," he said abruptly. "We might as well get back to the car."

He started to walk briskly, and Jill followed him, keeping up with his pace. She didn't understand. He had seemed so happy when they left his parents' house. What was wrong? Why had he pulled back?

They went directly to the car, Doug formally opening the door for her. As they were driving down the narrow lane, another car — a large, clean Buick — turned in, then backed out to let them pass.

It was Mrs. Reynolds. As soon as they had turned onto the county road, Doug stopped the car and got out. Mrs. Reynolds unrolled her window and Doug bent down to speak to her. But he didn't hunch over, curving his back, as most men would have. He bent at the knees, balancing with one hand on the car door. His face was level with Mrs. Reynolds, not hung over sidewards.

Jill had never known a man as comfortable with his body as he was. He was fit and strong, moving with an animal's sleek grace. He didn't mind striking awkward poses or twisting himself off balance. He trusted his body not to make a fool of him . . . or if it did, so what?

"That was Mrs. Reynolds," he said when he got back into the car.

Talk to me, Doug. You like to talk. If there's a problem, tell me.

She was a fine one to urge someone to talk, she who sat in her therapy group week after week, never speaking about herself.

They rode silently into Courthouse.

Then he spoke. "You want to shoot some baskets?"

"Sure." She wouldn't have dreamed of saying anything else.

He pulled into a parking lot near a schoolyard. He went around to the back of his car, taking a basketball out of the trunk. Jill followed him past the sprawling brick school to a basketball hoop set at the edge of the blacktop. He dribbled twice and shot.

Jill caught the rebound. Field hockey had been her sport, but she had done her share of running up and down the basketball court. Even after so many years the ball felt familiar to her hands. She dribbled, set, and shot. And missed. Doug caught the ball.

"I'm not going to apologize," she said.

"You've nothing to apologize for," he said. "Your timing's rusty, that's all." He sent her the ball on a one-bounce pass. "Try again."

She did. This time the ball circled the hoop and sluggishly plopped through the net.

"Use your wrists more." He captured the ball again and came over. Tucking the ball between his knees, he took her wrist in his hands, moving it for her.

He came around behind her, following her step by step, motion by motion, retrieving the ball after each shot, flipping it back to her, talking to her all the while, correcting her, praising her. Now he was touching her, changing her grip on the ball, the set of her shoulders, the position of her elbows, but it wasn't about sex, it was about basketball.

And suddenly she understood.

Doug was telling her something. He was using his body instead of his words, but he was telling her that he wasn't Bix. On Phillip's path to Massanutten, he hadn't known whose face she had touched, his or the long-dead face it so resembled. Coaching basketball was what made Doug, and he wasn't going to bed with her until he was sure she knew that.

It's been days since that mattered. When I see you, I see you, not him.

He was behind her, holding the ball out on the palm of his hand, talking about its seams. Suddenly she batted it away from him, pivoted, and shot. Unprepared, he leaped, but not in time to block her shot.

"Try that again," he dared.

She held out her hand for the ball and started to dribble. In a moment he had it. He tossed it back to her. He stole the ball before she had gone a second step. Again and again. She would turn her back, he could reach around her. Sometimes he would wait until she was ready to shoot and he'd block the shot. He could stop it in mid-air, he could snatch it out of the rim. He could, quite simply, do whatever he wanted.

She had no way of stopping him, but she did not feel humiliated. Doug wasn't asserting himself over her. He was asserting his identity to her.

They played on, the light changing from the bright afternoon glare to the slanting rays softening behind the trees. Jill was tiring, but she felt lovely, light and loose, as if Doug had passed to her, along with his knowledge of the game, some of his effortless grace. He was tireless; he sprinted after each ball, never winded, never flushed.

Finally he stopped. He trapped the ball against his hip, one hand dangling free. Still holding the ball, he came to her, and leaning forward, without touching her in any other way, he kissed her. They remained like that, her head lifted, his bent, their kiss glowing, all else motionless, until at last the ball dropped, falling to the blacktop with a small bounce, then rolling off into the grass, and Doug's arms came around her.

It was an embrace that answered the important questions, and in a moment Doug stepped back. With an arm around her shoulders, he led her back to the car and asked the one question that remained. "Is the Best

Western all right?"

"Do you mind if people see your car parked in front of my room?"

"No."

There was no ambivalence in that answer.

He opened the door on her side of the car. Jill slid in, fastened her seat belt, and through the windshield watched him come round the front of his convertible.

As infrequent as Jill's affairs were, she knew that her job would start the minute he opened the car door. That was the point at which she had to start working to make the man comfortable. The minutes between reaching the decision and arriving at the location were often awkward, and Jill knew the whole episode would be far more satisfactory if she smoothed the transition.

But Doug didn't open his car door. The top was down, and he put a hand on the frame and vaulted lightly into his seat. He pulled out his seat belt with one hand while turning the key in the ignition with the other.

This man did not appear to be in the least way uncomfortable. When he turned to back out of the parking space, he rested his hand on the headrest of Jill's seat. Then he took her hand, holding it in a firm, warm grip. He was whistling softly, a little smile on his face. No, he didn't find anything about this awkward at all.

Which left Jill with nothing to say, nothing to do. It was enough to make her feel awkward. She let the quick ride back to the motel pass in silence. Doug took her hand and pulled it over to his leg, flattening it against the sun-warmed denim of his jeans.

It was her experience that upon entering the motel room the two participants retreated to neutral corners and removed their clothing before meeting again in the vicinity of the bed. She started to do that, then noticed Doug watching her, the expression in his blue eyes so interested, so bemused that she suddenly had trouble remembering how buttons worked.

"Do you need some help over there?" he inquired politely.

"I can usually manage."

"Good, then I'd rather watch."

And he sounded so like himself when he said that, so like the man that she was truly fond of, that she then had no trouble at all.

She turned toward the nightstand to take off her watch and earrings. One of the earrings caught in her hair, and it took her a moment to untangle it. As she was laying it down, two strong arms closed around her waist, pulling her against a warm, muscled body. Her shoulders, her spine, the back of her legs basked against his glowing length. The hair on his chest was a soft mat, and where he pressed himself against her, he was hard and velvety smooth.

"You don't have any clothes on," she said, remarking on the obvious.

He kissed her neck, running his hands up and down her arms. Then he turned to strip the spread off the bed. He was clearly at ease with himself, he was comfortable being nude. It made sense. He was, after all, an athlete, used to walking around a locker room clad in a slipping towel.

He was an athletic, imaginative lover. He made love with his whole body. Jill knew that sex could be two pairs of lips touching, followed by one hand on one breast, isolated bits of physical activity following one another in sequence. But when Doug's hands were on her shoulders, his strong fingers searching out the muscles of her upper arms, he was also moving her so that the tips of her breasts would graze against his chest, and his leg was massaging hers and he was kissing her all the while. Or when his lips traveled down, finding her breast, one hand would explore the outer curve of her thigh while his other hand caught in her hair, holding her head firmly, a gesture that made her feel important, even treasured.

Jill found it all wonderful, and yet, as they lay drowsily in bed afterward, watching a narrow strip of sunlight lengthen across the Best Western's royal blue commercial-grade carpeting, she also realized that it was very surprising.

The thought was an idle one at first, then took shape.

All summer Doug had seemed low-key and funny, never demanding, never insisting. He had been moving about a world where there was little at stake; he masked his considerable strength so that it was noticed only by those who were watching. He had been even-tempered and friendly, redeemed from blandness only by his wit. His style was effortless and one of ease.

But style wasn't substance. Not until he joined her in her bed did Jill realize that. He was an athlete. He knew how to become a completely physical being, moving in an intensely physical world, where instinct and experience blended into total, focused, driving commitment.

Basketball was an intense sport, played by men of great endurance and unceasing concentration. Basketball was not a game for the laid-back. It was a game for the fast, the sweaty. It was dig in and try harder. And now, all that drive to win, the determination and intensity of a winning coach, had just been directed onto her graceful, grateful body.

She had to wonder what he did with that ambition and intensity the rest of the time. He had certainly managed to hide them from her. But surely this was the most important thing about him. Doug Ringling was not just a man who resembled a character in a movie. He was a man who played basketball.

Thirteen

The strip of sunlight grew longer, and Jill grew drowsier. Her thoughts about Doug had not been enough to shock her into wakefulness. She might have missed a few things about him, but he was still Doug. As long as they were careful, as long as they didn't take any shortcuts, everything would be all right. She curled up closer to him.

He spoke. "How do you think people will have sex in space?"

"What?" That woke her up.

"If you don't have gravity, how are you going to stay together? Can you imagine, you're holding someone, you're all ready, and she just floats away?"

"I don't know . . . you could use bungee cords. What on earth made you think of that?"

"Bungee cords? What an interesting idea. Boing, boing." Doug bounced his hands together imitating the action of a shock cord. "You know, that might be a lot of fun."

She stared at him.

Doug dropped his hands, pulling her close to him. "I was just thinking about how spatial some of the metaphors for great sex are —

the earth moving, rockets shooting, all that — and somehow I ended up wondering about sex in space."

"Were you thinking about those metaphors for great sex because you were about to say something?"

"No," he said bluntly. "I figure if you've got to ask a woman how it was for her, the answer's probably 'right lousy.' "

Jill agreed with him on that one. "You know, for someone who talks as much as you do, you seem to let your body do the important communicating."

"Are you one of these women" — his eyes narrowed in mock suspicion — "who think that just because she goes to bed with a fellow, she has the right to analyze him to death?"

"Yes."

"That's okay," he said philosophically. "My sisters don't have that excuse and they do it all the time anyway. I'm used to it."

Jill smiled and started to trace a little pattern on his chest.

He dropped his chin and watched her finger intently, as if nothing else mattered but —

"Goddamnit." He sat up so abruptly that Jill lost her balance. "I don't believe it." He clapped a hand over his eyes. "I don't bloody believe it."

"What is it?" Jill sat up, the rats' feet suddenly stirring up the anxious ashes in the pit of her stomach. "What happened? What's wrong?"

Unmentioned diseases, forgotten marriages — no, no, she knew him, she trusted him. It wasn't any of that.

"I can't believe how stupid I am." He banged his head against the wall, disgusted with himself. "I left my ball at the school. It's my favorite one. I've had it for years, and I've never left it anywhere. I can't believe it." He sighed and leaned back against the headboard. "Oh, well, maybe it will be there in the morning."

Jill relaxed. How sweet and funny he was. All he wanted to do on earth was fling himself out of bed and go rescue his beloved basketball, but he had manners, he wasn't going to do it.

"Stop feeling sorry for yourself, boyo," she told him, tossing the sheet off. "Let's go get it."

They dressed hurriedly and trundled themselves in the car. As Doug ground the ignition, he leaned across the car and kissed her on the forehead. "You are a grand sort, Jill. Woman enough to make a man forget his basketball, mensch enough to let him go get it. I think I like you."

And mensch enough not to mind when you get busy during basketball season; traveler enough to go to away games and on recruiting trips; and self-reliant enough not to mind being left behind; rich enough so you wouldn't have to do radio shows and run summer camps.

Except that wasn't his life anymore. What was the point in being exactly the right woman for who he was a year ago?

A couple of ten-year-olds were playing soccer with Doug's beloved basketball, but they relinquished it obediently. Doug restored it to the trunk of his car, then took Jill out for as proper a dinner as could be had by people who weren't wearing all their underwear.

He shook out his napkin. "Now brace yourself, I'm about to motivate the pants off you."

"You've already done that."

He blinked. "Oh . . . I guess I have. I was just speaking figuratively."

"So what do you want?"

"No, no, no. We can't be that direct. We have to point the way" — his hands carved out a little road in the air — "so you see the conclusion yourself before we say it. That way — "

"What do you want?"

He made a face at her, but answered. "For

you to check out of that hideous motel and move into the house, which, although equally hideous, is at least your own property."

"I'd love to."

He blinked again. "Wait a minute . . . you're being too easy. I used to be good at this."

"At what? Getting women to move in with you?"

"At motivation. Of course, my dad's a million times better than I'll ever be, but — "

"You'd be good at selling cars. I'd buy one from you."

"I know. But if you'd buy one from me, you'd buy two from him."

"So why aren't you selling cars?"

"Beats me. Have you ever been to bed with someone who's at such loose ends?"

"Not with anyone who's so proud of it, no."

They spent the rest of dinner wondering how dinosaurs had had sex. Then they went to pack Jill's things, arriving at the motel just in time to grab the phone.

"Jill, darling, it's Jacob."

Jake Steinherd was the photographer Jill had sent Bix's film to. "Did you get the film?" she asked eagerly, waving Doug to sit down on the bed. "Did you have a chance to look at it?"

"It arrived on Friday, and I put it back in the mail on Saturday."

"Oh, Jake, you're an angel. So there were some pictures?"

"There were eight of them. The first seven were of a party. We all guessed that it was the wrap party for that old movie *Weary Hearts*."

"It was on the movie's set," Jake continued, "and a couple of the actors were still in costume. That's how — and I have to admit that it wasn't me — one of my assistants recognized everything. The last picture is of a man and a woman sitting at a table. We think the woman is Mary Deas, or whatever the actress's name is, but we don't recognize the man."

Knowing Jill as he did, Jake had assumed that she was not traveling with a portable fax machine and so was Fed-Exing the pictures to the Best Western. Jill checked out, instructing the front desk to call her the moment the package arrived, and, sure enough, the desk clerk called Monday morning at ten thirty, and by eleven she and Doug were sitting on the curb of the parking lot, ripping open the mailer.

The pictures were indeed of a party on the set for the Briar Ridge dining room. Everyone was eating cake and drinking champagne; costumed actors were mingling with people in street clothes. Alicia and Charles were in costume. Mosby's gaunt-eyed rider, the man who played Stonewall, and Preston Havelock, the actor who played Pompey, were in street clothes; they had apparently turned up for the party. The director, Oliver McClay, was clad in a coat and tie; assorted crew members were less neatly dressed. Of the seven pictures, only two had Bix in them, suggesting that he had taken the others.

Charles looked the best — thin, but calm, proud and glad to be done. Alicia and Oliver McClay looked exhausted. In the two shots of Bix there seemed to be a wariness about him, which could have been either a holdover from his character or a dislike of having other people monkeying with his very expensive camera.

Then Jill flipped to the last picture. As Jake had said, it wasn't the party at all, but Alicia and —

"Good God, it's my father."

Alicia and Cass were sitting outdoors at a table covered by papers. Alicia, as lovely as in the studio's posed stills, was wearing a print sundress, a little caplet falling over her shoulders. She was sitting forward, looking at the camera, a pen in her hand. Cass, his collar open, was lounging back, a cigarette in one hand. There was another chair between them; that must have been Bix's chair. Jill looked at clutter on the table, the glasses, the ashtrays, the papers. Jake had made eight-by-twelve prints, enough of an enlargement to see things that looked like bound scripts.

Jill would have bet anything that those were scripts for *Weary Hearts*.

She pointed them out to Doug. "That's what we're looking for. Those must be the missing scripts, the ones that were filmed in April."

Doug squinted, as if hoping to read what was written on the pages of the open scripts. It was an impossible task. "So you think they're working on the revisions?"

"Wouldn't you think so? It was after the April wrap party. They're sitting at a table covered with scripts. What else would the three of them be doing together?"

Cass was looking directly at the camera, an alert man taking a break from his absorbing work. *What were you doing, Daddy? What did you write on those papers? Why didn't you leave me a clue?*

But how could he have known that forty years later his daughter, the child of a woman he hadn't met yet, would want so desperately to know what he'd done to this movie?

Doug was speaking. "But I thought when

your father took over, Bix was demoted to brainless actor. I didn't realize that they all worked on the revisions together."

That's what Jill had thought, too. Never in any discussion of the film had there been reference to Bix — to say nothing of Alicia — being involved in Cass's reworking of the story.

It was no longer clear to her what her father's revisions were; clearly the love story and the baby, for which he had received credit, had already been a part of Bix's story. But until this moment she had never questioned that whatever work had been done over those summer months, whether it had made the movie better or worse, had been done by Cass. Although only an editor at the time, he was a story man, capable of narrative creativity.

But her father was slow. There was still a certain English-professor quality to his mind. Ideas needed to germinate in his mind. He'd read a book, and for months, even years, think about how to adapt it to film.

The story of the revising of *Weary Hearts* was one of lightning speed. The filming ended in late April; the rough cut was probably available six weeks later. By August the cast was back on location, filming an entirely different story. Cass was capable of completely overhauling a narrative, but in weeks, days?

No.

Bix knew these characters; they had been his companions during imprisonment. He would know them well enough to refashion their story. He had already done it once, flattening his ideas into the clichés of the war-movie treatment found in the studio files. Perhaps he had done it again.

"I don't get it," Doug said. "Why was Bix working on the changes? If they really were out to ruin his masterpiece, why help?"

"So he wasn't Howard Roark," Jill answered. "There's no sin in that."

"He wasn't who?"

Jill explained about the architect in Ayn Rand's novel *The Fountainhead* who had blown up his building rather than let it stand with other people's modifications. "Bix probably knew that the end result would be better if he helped. It was the sensible thing to do."

"I suppose." He didn't sound convinced, and Jill wasn't sure she was either. "I'd always figured he had written it off as a bad bet and had gone on to something else."

"That's what *you* would have done." This was not the first time Jill had noticed Doug assigning his own character traits to Bix.

"I guess . . . although I'm not doing so great in the something else department." Doug picked up the pictures again and started to flip through the ones of the party. "Who's that?" He pointed to the one black in the picture. "It's not Pompey, is it?"

"I think so." Preston Havelock, the actor who played Pompey, was not instantly recognizable. His character was much older than he was himself; he looked relaxed and refreshed, the only one of the principal actors who seemed to have had enough sleep, and he had a beard. He was probably growing it for some other part.

"Wait a minute." She snatched the picture from Doug. "How long would it take you to grow a beard like that?"

"Me? I don't think I ever could. Whenever I try, it's all straggly, and I look like something that comes out of the swamp with bad teeth, a jug of moonshine, and patched long johns."

"Be serious."

He looked at the picture again. "I don't know. Maybe two or three weeks."

Two or three weeks. There had been twelve more days of filming in California after the company returned from Virginia. Preston must have started growing his beard as soon as his location scenes had been complete.

But the wrap party was on the battle-scarred version of the dining room set. In the final version of the movie Pompey had appeared on this set.

So Pompey had not appeared in any of the final scenes in the secret script. Pompey and the pathetic horse, Blossom, had never been in the same shot on the journey home from Appomattox. It seemed likely that Pompey had not come home. "What do you want to bet," Jill said, "that in the first version Pompey died during the war?"

"That makes sense." Doug agreed after she explained her reasons. "Pompey supposedly knew the boys since they were born. He helped raise them. It might have been really hard on Booth if he had to watch him die."

"And if Bix was as good as we're saying, he wouldn't have thrown a character like that away. It would have been a big scene." Jill stood up. "Surely Charles would remember filming that."

Doug looked up at her; he was still sitting on the curb. "You'd think so . . . but I hate to ask him."

Jill pursed her lips, a little irritated. It wasn't Doug's fault; this was the whole family's rule, a part of their code: Charles must not be upset, Charles must be coddled, protected, he suffered such a terrible loss. For forty years this had been going on.

"Well, I don't mind asking him," she said flatly. "You don't have to come."

"No, no, I don't mind."

And an hour later they were sitting on Mrs. Ringling's front porch, talking to Charles.

"Do you remember the wrap party?" Jill asked him.

"Not very well, I am afraid. I remember that there was one, but if you're going to ask me who said what, I'm not going to be much help. It really was a long time ago, and wrap parties aren't very memorable. Everyone is so tired."

Jill was willing to believe him on that. "We found some pictures Bix took of the party. Would you like to see them?"

"Of course." Charles put on his glasses and extended his hand. He looked at the first two, then laid them all on his lap, took his glasses off, and, his expression pained, pressed his forefinger and thumb against the bridge of his nose.

Jill thought it a little too mannered a performance.

"This is very painful," he said. "May I keep these for a few days? Perhaps later . . ."

"Oh, of course," Doug said quickly. "We

didn't mean to upset you."

Jill watched as Charles slipped pictures back into the envelope. That was, she felt, probably the last they would see of them. It didn't matter; Jake would have filed the negatives. Charles started to stand up, but Jill leaned forward, putting a hand on his arm, and he was too much of a gentleman to do anything but wait for her to speak.

"In those pictures Preston Havelock has a beard as if he had not been filming for a few weeks, and we also noticed that he and the horse never appeared together on the journey home at the end of the movie. So we wondered — "

Charles interrupted her. "Well, yes . . . now that you mention it, I do recall that the first time we filmed it, he did die. His death-bed was a wonderful scene — he did such a magnificent job. How odd a thing memory is. How could I have ever forgotten that?"

Jill did not believe that he had. She, usually so patient, was ready to strangle Charles. Okay, he had never understood what the script as a whole was about, but he remembered a great deal more than he was letting on. Clearly, he was not going to tell them anything, not until they had pieced it together for themselves. Then he would pretend to "remember."

She had kept back the picture of her father and Alicia. She held it in front of him now. "Do you know when this was taken?"

He shook his head. "That's your father, isn't it? It must have been taken sometime during the retakes. That looks like a place in back of the sound stage where we used to take breaks. They were probably just chatting." He handed the picture back to Jill and, now that her hand was off his arm, stood up. "But I can't be sure."

He might not be sure, but Jill was. This picture hadn't been taken outside the sound stage; it was in the yard of whatever place Cass had been living. She recognized the drinking glasses sitting on the table; she used to own them. Five years before this picture had been taken, they had been used on the set of *Casablanca*.

But what did any of this prove? What did it mean? Why was Charles lying?

Charles excused himself and went back into the house. On her own, Jill would have followed him, but Doug resisted. Charles was not to be badgered.

Doug's car was parked on the other side of the street, in front of his parents' house. Jill stopped at the curb to let an oncoming car pass, but Doug stepped out into the street, waving. The car honked back, and as it came closer, Jill saw his father, Ward, behind the wheel.

Ward turned into his driveway. "I didn't know you two were coming for lunch. You are coming for lunch, aren't you?" By now Grace Ringling was on the porch, having come out to greet her husband. "Grace, why didn't you tell me Jill and Doug were coming?"

"Because I didn't know." Grace kissed Doug and smiled warmly at Jill, patting her on the arm.

Doug explained why they had come, telling about the pictures.

"I'd like to see those," Ward said. "You know I had the wildest crush on Alicia back then. Poor girl, you have to feel sorry for her. Talk about awkward. Your husband's kid brother following you around like a lost beagle. What a nuisance I must have been . . . oh, well, there's nothing to do about it now. What are the pictures of?"

"There's one you'll love," Doug told him. "Alicia and Jill's father are sitting out in the sun. She looks gorgeous, and, Dad" — Doug's voice dropped conspiratorially — "one of the glasses has her lipstick smudge on it."

Ward clapped his hand over his heart. "Butterfly Pink."

Jill and Doug stared at him.

"Butterfly Pink," Ward explained sheepishly, "that was the name of her lipstick."

"You remember that?" Jill asked.

"Tell them the truth," his wife ordered.

Ward's face screwed up in the funny little-boy grin that he had obviously passed on to his son. "I stole one from her. She left it sitting on the library table Mother used to have in the foyer. I picked it up to give it back to her, and lo, temptation struck and I kept it."

"Do you still have it?" Jill asked. A week ago it never would have occurred to her to ask someone if they still had a lipstick purloined four weeks ago — much less forty years ago — but since then, she had learned a lot about other people and their attachment to objects.

"I haven't seen it in years," Ward answered. "I mean, I would never throw it out. To this day, I suppose if you found it and asked me if I wanted to take it in the one box of personal effects allowed in the nursing home, I imagine I'd find room for it. But I can't begin to know where to look." He turned to his wife. "Any ideas?"

"If it's anywhere," she answered, "it would be in that old cigar box with all your other treasures."

"So it would, but where is that?"

"If we've still got it, it's in the basement, probably in the box with my wedding dress. I can look for it."

Doug pulled open the front door. "I'll help."

So they all went inside, Doug and his mother disappearing down the basement steps. Jill turned to Ward. "Do you know when you took the lipstick? Was it around the time of the movie?"

"Definitely. It was the first time they came out, in the spring. I felt so guilty about it that when I heard they were coming back again, I thought about giving it back to her, but I didn't."

At last, here was someone who remembered what happened when.

"Actually it was on the last day of their stay," he went on. "There was some sort of confusion in train connections, and everyone had come back to Mother's to hang out. It wasn't a party, everyone was just milling around, drinking coffee, listening to the radio, and talking. It was raining, I think, so no one could go outside. That's probably why the trains were off schedule."

Doug emerged from the basement, carrying a cigar box tied with string, and in a moment his mother followed, carrying a parcel of white tissue paper.

"I don't feel any need to see my rival's lipstick," she said, "so if you'll excuse me . . ."

She started upstairs. Ward stopped her. "Where are you off to, Grace?"

She looked down over the bannister. "To try on my wedding dress." And with that she marched upstairs.

Both her son and husband watched her round the landing, and when she had disappeared, they glanced at each other, their eyes laughing.

They turned their attention to the cigar box. "Now you sit over there, children." Ward waved his hand toward the sofa. "I don't know as how everything in here is fit for young eyes."

Ward untied the box and, a light glowing from his face, opened the lid. He looked inside, touching nothing, just wearing a deliciously secret half-smile as he stood there contemplating his treasures. How healthy and well-adjusted he seemed; the past wasn't anything that frightened him.

Then he began to stir things around, and, suddenly, from around the lid of the box flashed a gold-toned tube of lipstick.

Jill reached out and took it; the label indeed said Butterfly Pink. Carefully she uncapped it and examined the cap. Then she extended the lipstick: heat and time had turned it into a sticky stub, a sticky stub of Butterfly Pink lipstick.

That's all it was, a lipstick. However rich a talisman to Ward, it told Jill and Doug nothing. No two-hundred-page script was rolled up into the cylindrical top. It was just a lipstick, and it told no tales.

"Oh, and look at this . . . how could I forget this?" Ward was smoothing out a handkerchief. "She blotted her lips with this." He passed it over to Doug. "Now tell me, son, isn't this the single most erotic thing you've seen in your life?"

"Without a doubt, sir."

Ward sighed. "I guess you had to have been there." He picked up the lipstick again. "Butterfly Pink. I used to think that those were the loveliest words in the English language, but now that I think about it, I can't rightly say I've ever seen a pink butterfly." He put it and the handkerchief back in the box. "I'm sorry," he said. "I'd hoped it would tell you something."

"That's all right." Doug grinned. "It told us all kinds of things about you."

Ward wagged a finger at him. "I've spanked you before, young man, and I'd be happy to do it again."

"Do you remember anything else about

the day?" Jill asked. "What anyone said?"

"No. I imagine they were all fussing about the train. But, you know, the same time I picked up the lipstick, I also took that doodle of Bix's that Mother has framed in the stairway. I fell into full-scale kleptomania that day."

Jill and Doug stared at each other. A doodle of Bix's.

They were across the street in a flash. The house was unlocked, but quiet. A stray beam of sunlight caught at the gilt frame of the stern ancestor's portrait and reflected off the glass covering the doodle. Doug lifted the cheap black frame off its hook and side by side they sat down on the stairs. He flipped up the little wire brackets that held the frame's cardboard backing and pushed at the edge of the cardboard to get a finger underneath. It popped up.

Don't talk.

The words jumped off the top of the page. Again the back of a doodle was covered with writing. *Don't talk* was in Alicia's hand, hurried, but still dramatic and loopy, followed by Bix's tiny, precise penmanship. The two hands alternated, a dialogue written between the two of them in the corner of a crowded room on a wet spring afternoon.

Don't talk, Alicia had written. *They can hear.*

Bix — Do you like the idea?

Alicia — *My part's a million times better. It will make my career.*

What about the girl on Friday night in her best sweater?

Jill was puzzled for a moment, then remembered Alicia's response to Bix's early treatment of *Weary Hearts*. In her concern for the project's commercial value, she had wondered how much ordinary young women would like it.

She'll love it.

Bix — *But you don't?*

No, it's wonderful. Then Alicia's handwriting slowed into a stately dignity as if she were writing words that she had never spoken. *I do not know that it is wise to act so many love scenes with you.*

That was all. Even the lively, verbal Bix had no answer.

At least none that he had put into words. Jill was sure that there had been a look, a glance, that had spoken all that neither of them could allow themselves to say.

They had loved each other. Jill had no doubt.

Jill turned the page over. Down in the corner of his intricate drawing, Bix had drawn Alicia's lovely face, her hair swirling out into a pattern of vines and lilies. All three

413

Ringling brothers had loved her. Young Ward's devotion would have been a tender embarrassment, something Charles and Alicia could have secretly smiled over. But Bix's passion might have been close to sin.

When had it started, their love? That day during the war when he had taken her to Winchester to meet the family? During those first years when the three of them were struggling to make names for themselves in Hollywood? Or perhaps they had only been friends until the movie. Perhaps, like Burton and Taylor, playing lovers had made them lovers. Perhaps Alicia did not want to act love scenes with Bix because she had already lived them.

What would it be like, Jill wondered, to be engulfed with a forbidden passion? She never had been. Her own relationships had always been tidy; she had never felt anything that she should not have felt. Yet, all of a sudden, she was drawn to the notion with a dizzying swirl . . . to feel that strongly, to be lured by dreams that overrode good sense and reason? What would it be like? The idea made her own life seem so pallid.

Doug was sitting close, rereading Bix and Alicia's dialogue. Did she want him to be forbidden to her? Would that make her feelings more intense? No. She was glad how easy this was. She was grateful to him for being so straightforward and sane. She really was. She slipped her hand through his arm and rested her cheek against the sleeve of his shirt.

He pulled his arm tight against his body, holding her hand close to him. "I wonder if this was the first time that they . . . you know, that either admitted caring about the other."

A shadow appeared at the front door. "Who cared about whom?" It was Ward. He came inside, the screen door swinging shut behind him. "What are the pair of you talking about?"

Jill straightened and waited for Doug to speak. This was his family.

"We've gotten to wondering," he said, "if Bix and Alicia didn't start caring for each other a little more than they should have."

Ward whistled. "I hope you aren't planning on spreading that up and down the Valley. It would kill Charles."

"We know that," Doug said instantly.

Jill did not know that at all. Charles might well be the most rugged man in the Valley; he was certainly the most adept at getting what he wanted.

"What put this notion in your heads?" Ward asked.

"We've seen a couple of their letters. They seemed so compatible. The tone was so frank and honest. They seemed to have a lot in common."

"What do you think?" Jill asked Ward. "Are we crazy?"

Ward shrugged. "I'm the worst one to ask. I idolized them both. Of course, it never occurred to me that Bix might be falling in love with her, since I was so similarly occupied."

"But she met Bix first," Jill pointed out. "Why didn't she fall in love with him then? Why care for Charles first?"

"That I can explain," Ward answered. "Remember the time. It was during the war, and she'd just lost her parents before it started. If you felt like the world was turning upside-down, I don't know as how Bix would be the man you'd want at a time like that. He was the sort to turn everything sideways, whereas Charles was always so upright, so magisterial. He was the oldest brother . . . and that meant something then, even though there wasn't any great property to go with it. There was a certainty about Charles that must have been enormously comforting. Bix could see everything twenty-six ways from Sunday, and during the war Charles's simple 'this is how it is' must have been appealing.

He must have seemed so safe to her, such a rock."

"That's not how he comes across now," Jill said honestly and waited for the standard Ringling line about Charles's Terrible Loss.

"You've got to remember something about Charles," Ward said. "He turned his back on the one thing he had a talent for. That doesn't do a body any good. I remind myself of that every time someone tries to move me up off the sales floor."

Jill's glance drifted toward Doug, now fitting the cardboard back into the frame. Here was another Ringling turning his back on the one thing he was good at.

Doug stood up to restore the doodle to the wall. Jill asked Ward one more thing. "You're sure that this doodle was done in April, not August?"

"I'm positive. Bix was a terrific brother. I don't know that he paid more attention to me than Charles did, but he was more fun. With Charles I never forgot how much younger I was. I did with Bix. When he was missing during the war, Mom and Dad tried to act hopeful around me, but I knew they were figuring he was dead. So when he came back . . . and then died again, I spent a lot of time remembering him and — " Ward broke off. He had to clear his throat before he began. "This happened in April. Trust me. Now, come back to the house and let's see what's for lunch."

Jill and Doug followed Ward back outside, but on the front walk, Jill touched Doug's arm, slowing him down. "You realize what this means, don't you? Bix didn't help my father just during June and July; he was planning the revisions while they were still in production the first time. They still had almost two more weeks of filming back in Hollywood, and he already knew they were going to need major revisions."

"I know." Doug had come to the same conclusion. "But I don't get it. Could the studio executives have nixed stuff before they were even done filming?"

"If they had had those kinds of reservations, they would have shut down production. Two weeks of filming costs a lot. They probably didn't know. But Steve Lex, the first editor, was already assembling footage; maybe he was passing along his own doubts."

"We don't know." Doug started back down the walk.

Jill didn't move. "Well, there's one thing we do know," she said flatly. "It was Bix who figured out how to save the movie, not my father."

But Cass had gotten credit. He had been

listed as co-screenwriter. If the big ideas had been Bix's, then Cass wasn't entitled to that. So why did he get it?

There was an easy answer — because Bix was dead. Alicia was dead, the important members of the crew were dead, Charles was paralyzed by grief. Who was around to speak up for Bix? To defend his achievement?

No, that wasn't possible. This was where Jill was going to draw the line. Her father honored the dead. He, alone of all his circle of Hollywood friends, faithfully went to funerals. He would send a car to the gates of Jill's school, and Alice would help her change out of her uniform into a dark dress. They would meet Cass at the church or synagogue. At the gravesite afterward, Cass would put his hand on Jill's young shoulder, and she would smell the scent of tobacco that clung even to his overcoat.

Cass's favorite poem, Yeats's "Easter, 1916," was a commemoration of the dead. This reverence was, he had always said, part of being a Virginian. He would never steal credit for the work of a dead man.

But stolen or not, he had gotten that credit. It didn't make sense. It was so unlike anything she could ever imagine him doing. Was it possible that she didn't know him? That the image he had presented to her was false? If so, it was time to revise her image of him. But what was she going to replace it with?

Ward was already across the street. Jill and Doug caught up with him, following him inside the house. Grace was in the kitchen, fixing lunch.

"Did your dress fit?" Ward put his arm around her waist.

Jill couldn't remember her father ever putting his arm around her mother's waist.

Grace Ringling fixed her husband with a stare. "You'd better believe it."

"Why didn't you leave it on?" Doug asked. "I would have loved to see you in it."

"Because I tried it on for myself. If the rest of you get your jollies out of seeing a sixty-year-old woman in a dress made for an eighteen-year-old, then you'll have to go elsewhere."

Fourteen

On the way home from Winchester, Jill remembered that it was Monday. "I'm not going to be around tomorrow," she told Doug.

"Fine. What are you up to?"

"I need to go back to L.A."

"Back to L.A.?" His eyes shot to hers, his brows lifting in surprise. Then the surprise drained away to be replaced by a dark, shuttered look — Phillip Wayland standing in the hall outside his sister-in-law's bedroom. "I'm sorry to see you go," he said formally.

He was assuming the worst. She slapped his arm with the back of her hand. "Don't be a goat. I'm not leaving. I'll be back first thing Wednesday morning. I'm just going for the day. I'm in a psychotherapy group and it meets on Tuesday. I went last week. It's no big deal."

"You went all the way out to California for a meeting? An hour meeting?"

"Actually, it's ninety minutes." As if that made a difference.

"Isn't that — No, no." He stopped himself. "You don't have to explain yourself."

421

"I don't mind. One of the rules of group is that you go, and I always try to play by the rules."

"So you plan on going every week?"

"Absolutely."

Doug drummed his fingers against the steering wheel. "Then I have a question . . . although I don't suppose I could answer the equivalent question if you asked me, and even to ask it implies — "

Jill interrupted. "What's on your mind?"

He made a face at her. "You scoff, but this may be a tricky question."

"I can handle it."

"All right . . . when you say every week, what are we talking about? How long do you plan on being here?"

Yes, that was a tricky question. "What do you think the answer is?"

"I don't know. I mean, my instinct is to say that everything is okay, that we're all on target here. But I worry that we're from such different backgrounds, with such different rules, that I, even in all my wisdom, could be completely off base."

"Our backgrounds aren't that different," she argued. "Yes, I had money, but my father never lost his basic middle-class way of looking at things. I'm not a careless jet-setter. The money doesn't have to be an issue between us, Doug. Not unless you need it to be."

"You didn't answer my question."

"Yes, I did. You know I did. I'm going to stay here until we both want me to go."

Doug's eyes flicked across the car again. Then, tactile man that he was, he touched her arm. He needed a physical confirmation of her sincerity.

Reassured, he settled back in his seat, driving with one hand on the wheel, the other elbow bent out the window. "You'd better not count on me *ever* wanting you to go."

That night Doug worked out a great plan for Jill's traveling to and from California. She would buy one one-way ticket and then a series of SuperSavers, whose low fares required staying over Saturday night.

"Here's how it would work," he told her. "This week you'd fly out on ticket number one and then come home on the one-way ticket. Next week you go out on ticket number two and come home on number one so it looks like you've been there over a Saturday. The week after, you go out on ticket three and come home on two, and so on through the summer."

It was a grand scheme, but she looked at him blankly. "Why would I want to do that?"

"Because you'd save so much — " He stopped, remembering whom he was talking to. "Because it would be such a good exercise in keeping track of airline tickets, because it would remind you what a beetlebrain you're sleeping with . . . I don't know." They were in the kitchen. He leaned his chair back on two legs until it hit the wall with a satisfying little crash, followed by the noise of his head connecting with the plaster. "I hate to think what this is costing you."

"Have you ever talked to anyone about this head-banging problem of yours?" she inquired politely.

"I didn't even know I had a head-banging problem," he groaned. The phone started to ring. "You get that. I can't. I have to stay here and bang my head."

She got up, ramming her hip against his arm. She meant to do it lightly, but as he was, at the moment, trying to bang his head against the wall in new, unusual, and painless ways, she knocked him off-balance. The chair crashed to the floor, leaving the chair sideways and him sprawled on his back.

"I'm sorry," she mouthed as she picked up the phone.

He lay on Aunt Carrie's green-flecked linoleum, watching Jill pick up the phone. Still on his back, he squirmed over so he could look up her skirt.

A slender, dusty foot came down over his eyes. "Hello," he heard her say.

He thought about doing something weird and sexual with her foot, but she had been walking around the kitchen barefoot and he and Randy weren't exactly wizards in the Mop 'n Glow department.

"It's for you." The foot lifted and light flooded back into his eyes. Jill had her hand over the receiver. "Are you too stupid to stand?"

"Unquestionably."

She dropped the receiver to his chest. Still supine, he picked it up. "Hello, this is Douglas W. Ringling." One of the dogs padded over and started to sniff his ear. Doug pushed her away.

"Hey, Ringo."

It was the Lynx's soft, thick voice. Doug cheered into the phone. Of all the men he liked, this one, his college roommate, was the one he liked the most.

"It sounds like you've got sisters in the house," the Lynx said. He knew Doug's family.

"Actually not."

"Oh, my man . . . do tell."

Jill had sat back down at the kitchen table. From his spot on the floor Doug could see only the long line of her fabulous legs. "I can't. She's right here."

"That bad, huh?"

"No, that good."

Jill leaned over and looked at him under the tabletop. "Do you want me to leave?"

"No, stay here."

Even if she were out of the room, Doug didn't know what he would say about her. Her "trophy" qualities embarrassed him. He was crazy about the way she looked — although in bed, he supposed that her degree of fitness was as important as her looks — and he was fascinated by her money. He didn't covet it; he wasn't wallowing in gold-digger fantasies. He was just curious what it was like to have so much. God knew that the Lynx had plenty, but even he wasn't in Jill's league. Moreover, the Lynx's money was that "quick" money that she had been talking about the other day. Every morning, Doug knew, the Lynx woke up expecting it to be gone. Jill was calm about her money. She had always had it. She always would.

But to tell another man, even one he knew as well as this one, that she was rich and lovely put the wrong spin on things. This wasn't about her being rich and lovely; it was about her being her.

"Do your folks like her?" the Lynx asked.

"Are you kidding? My dad wants to marry her."

"She should snap him up. He's a lot better bet than you are." The Lynx had met Doug's parents on the first day of their freshman year at Duke. Raised in the woman-dominated culture of the inner city, the eighteen-year-old Lynx had been mesmerized by Ward Ringling, unable to believe that guys actually had fathers like this. Within twenty minutes Ward was calling him "son," an appellation he had before used only for Doug.

"He just wants her for her car," Doug said. "She drives a '57 Bel Air with no miles."

"A '57 Bel Air? Is that for real? Ask her if she wants to trade."

Doug reached his leg under the table and poked Jill on the ankle. She leaned back down, her hair falling almost to the floor.

"That Lynx wants to trade cars with you."

"What does he drive?"

"A green Jag."

"I don't like green cars," she said and disappeared back above the tabletop.

"She doesn't like green cars," he told the Lynx. "And anyway, why do you want it? It's a real white man's car."

The Lynx chuckled. "So perhaps I can offer her what no white man can."

"Good point. I'll ask." Doug kicked Jill

427

again and when she appeared, he relayed the offer. "The Lynx says he'll fulfill your every sexual need for a week if you give him your car."

"A week?" She shook her upside-down head. "No, it would have to be a month, minimum."

"Oh, pity. He doesn't have that kind of stamina."

A sharp oath burst from the phone, followed by a steady gush of profanity. Doug took the receiver away from his ear and let the Lynx curse into mid-air. Jill, whose face was turning pink from hanging upside down, listened appreciatively for a moment, then disappeared back up the rabbit hole. Doug kicked his shoe off and ran his foot up her ankle. She reached down and pulled his toe . . . hard.

"Ouch," he complained. "That hurt." Then he went back to the Lynx. "Are you done with your temper tantrum?"

"I don't say things like that about you," the Lynx protested.

"How wise you are. No one would believe you."

The Lynx started cursing again. "Why do I put up with you?"

"Because you want my parents to adopt you. You probably ought to call their bluff.

There really is a good chance that if they had to choose between us, that they — "

The Lynx, who had roomed with Doug long enough to know that the only way to stop him sometimes was to interrupt him, interrupted. "Tell me, has this lady gotten you off that movie thing?"

"No, she's a part of it." The Lynx had not understood Doug's interest in *Weary Hearts*, but as he readily admitted, he didn't know what it was like to resemble an uncle. The men he called "uncle" were usually paying his mother money for an afternoon of her time. "She's got a stake in it too . . . not that we've found what we're looking for."

"So you're giving up?"

"No."

"There're lots of jobs, Ringo." The Lynx's soft voice was suddenly urgent, sincere. "Just say the word. I don't know of a team in the N.B.A. who wouldn't want you."

"Oh, man . . ." Doug sat up and ran a hand over his face. This was not the sort of conversation to have sprawled out across sticky, green-flecked linoleum. "We've been through this. I'm a teacher, an educator. I don't belong in the pros."

"You wouldn't be there forever."

Doug shut his eyes and rounded his spine

back against the wall, remembering just in time not to bang his head, and listened while the Lynx, for about the forty millionth time, outlined his future. He was to do a couple years penance in the pros while everyone in the N.C.A.A. forgot that he was supposedly something between Simon Legree and Benedict Arnold.

But he didn't want to coach in the pros. It was so different. The players all had lives and families and investments. They were businessmen who came to work each day. The schedule was so intense, there wasn't time to do any teaching. You coached a game and then got on a plane.

But in college you knew the kids. It started with recruiting. You went to their homes, met their parents. You knew who they were, where they were coming from. Then you saw so much of them, working with them on the court, hanging out in the basketball office. Maybe it was an ego thing on his part, but a coach was so important to a college kid. So many of them wanted to be like you.

Doug suddenly felt weary. He didn't want to think about this. He interrupted the Lynx, speaking lightly. "Isn't this my part? To badger people into doing what's good for them?"

"I don't seem to be doing much of a job of it. When can I call you again?"

When can I call you again? Where had the Lynx learned that particular telephone trick? "Come on, man. You're my friend. You can call me whenever you want."

The phone sat on a little shelf midway up the wall. Doug said good-bye to the Lynx and stretched his arm back over his head to hang the receiver up. He crossed his arms over his knees, rested his forehead on them for a moment, then peered up at Jill, his chin on his arms. She was still sitting at the table.

"You're a silly woman. You passed up a chance to have the Lynx attend to your every sexual need."

She raised her eyebrows. "You want to talk about silly? It sounds like you passed up a chance to coach in the pros."

He groaned. "I'd be lousy at it."

"Would you, really?"

Her gaze was clear and steady. This wasn't a pair of eyes you could lie to. "No. I'd be all right. Depending on who I was working for. Nobody's offering me my own team."

"Is that what you want?"

"Not in the pros." *Fill in the blanks, sweetheart. I had what I wanted. I was head coach at a Division I school, an A.C.C. school. Every kid's dream. And I blew it. Blew it bad.*

"Doug." Her voice was soft. "What happened at Maryland Tech?"

He grimaced. "Do we have to have this conversation?"

"No."

He looked at her suspiciously, but her eyes remained clear. She was telling the truth. They did not need to have this conversation. They could go on, boinking each other like cheery little bunnies; they could blaze as brightly and briefly as crumpled newsprint, leaving behind no sustaining embers, only the faintest grey ash. No, they did not need to have this conversation. It was his choice.

"All right . . . what do you already know?"

"That if you had had anything to do with it, those people wouldn't have been in Chryslers."

He groaned and banged his head against the wall. "The Lynx never says anything quotable. You couldn't get a sound bite out of him if his life depended on it. So why, tell me, why the one time he has to say something worth repeating, it would have to be about me?"

"I also heard that you weren't up to the challenge." Of all the lies that were told, that was the one that had bothered him the most. She knew that.

"If I'd failed," he said, "I'd have been the first to admit it."

"I know that."

"But I was guilty," he pointed out. He didn't want this to be a Whitewash-Doug-Ringling session. "Everything happened on my watch. That makes it my responsibility."

"Did you know that it was happening?"

"No, but only because I didn't want to know. It would have taken me about ninety seconds to find out if I'd chosen to."

"Why didn't you?"

"I made the classic stupid mistake. I thought that the end would justify the means. I wanted to turn Maryland Tech into Duke. That was impossible." Doug thought back to all he had done. The coaches before him had enforced study halls and had required weekly notes from professors. Doug had gotten rid of all that Mickey-Mouse stuff. That wasn't the way to make kids learn; these kids were experts at maneuvering their way through a system. How else could you get into college without being able to read? So there hadn't been a system. Doug had motivated the team leaders, then expected them to motivate the others. He was proud of what he had accomplished there academically. "Combining that with coaching was enough. I figured I'd deal with the stench of our recruiting program in a year or two. Me and Scarlett O'Hara, think about it another day."

"Is that the whole story?" Jill asked.

"Well, no," he admitted. "I made some enemies."

Even though the uninterested commuters who attended Maryland Tech would never be like the witty pranksters who went to Duke, Doug had wanted the student body more involved in the basketball team. He wanted cheering students, not the rich, silent alumni, in the courtside seats. He had wanted to phase out the athletic dorms so that the rest of the students knew the players. None of this had met with the approval of the athletic director.

Then he had failed to recruit a local star. K. C. Preston, a high school All-American out of Baltimore County, got scared off by Doug's talk about academics and signed a letter of intent with Clemson. "He was white," Doug explained. "Our alumns would have killed for a white player, but he was so blindingly stupid — we're not talking bad education here — this guy was truly dim. His elevator just didn't make it to the top floors. Frankly, I didn't want him on the team. I already had enough players who couldn't remember the plays."

"So what did your enemies and young Mr. Preston have to do with your starting summer vacation in March?"

Doug ran his hand up and down the leg of his jeans.

"There is a story you're not telling," she said.

"It's not my own ass I'm covering," he said.

"I never thought that."

"And it's not even the guys who gave out the cars."

"So it's one of the students?"

How right she was. But wasn't it obvious? Who else would he go through this for? He didn't say anything for a long time. He had never told anyone this story, no one, not even his parents. "When the N.C.A.A. started to investigate the cars and all, I took this real open stance — you know, come in, look at anything. There's dirt, you find it, we'll clean it up. Not only did I want to clean it up, but my best hope for avoiding major sanctions was to be cooperative."

Halfway through the investigation two of the players came to him and told him that they hadn't taken their SAT tests. As marginal students at a drug-infested high school, they hadn't fully understood what the tests were. Someone had talked to them, and then they got their scores. It wasn't until coming to college that they realized they had skipped a step.

Doug remembered the horror he had felt when they had told him. He knew what would happen to them. The N.C.A.A. always came down hard on the kids. These guys would be out of college ball. They'd lose their scholarships; they would have to leave school.

Then they had told him something worse. Professors were being paid to change grades.

"It has to be the single worst thing I've heard. There were always rumors that some coaches pressure professors, but we're talking flat-out cash. Frederick used to be this sleepy little place, but now it's development city around there, and some of the alumni have made a mint of money. The faculty are paid garbage, and these guys are offering cash. Take some kid off the bench from a 'D' to a 'C' and suddenly your family has two weeks at the beach you weren't going to be able to afford before. Raise a starter from an "F" to a "B" and you're looking at a down payment on a split-level."

Doug had been in a bind. His two players were juniors with hopes of graduating, but to do so, they had to hold on to their athletic scholarships. But this black market in grades could not continue.

"I felt we had to fess up to the grade-selling ourselves and pray to God that the N.C.A.A. wouldn't blast us off the face of the earth. If they discovered it on their own, Maryland Tech basketball would be history."

Doug had taken the boys' story to the school's athletic director. The A.D., although unhappy with Doug over the K. C. Preston matter, said he would investigate the professors publicly, taking his chance with N.C.A.A. sanctions, but would keep quiet about the false tests. "The price was my resignation, which wasn't out of line. I should have realized that something was wrong with their SAT scores. They were too good — I mean, they were godawful scores, but they were too good for those kids. I guess I was so relieved that I didn't want to question it."

So he had resigned, giving up his job, his reputation, his fat endorsement contract with Nike, and — pouf, nothing happened. The N.C.A.A. seemed happy to confine its investigation only to the Chryslers; no one ever said anything about the false tests or bribed professors; and the team's academic advisor, who must have known about the grade scheme, was promoted to assistant dean. The A.D. had done nothing. "So, my dear woman," he concluded, "you are looking at the chump of the century."

"Aren't you angry?"

"At who? Myself? Actually, I probably got off easy. I figure I made two pacts with the devil — first, in trying to coach at a place like that, ignoring the sleazeball recruiting, and second, in trying to protect those kids. After selling my soul twice, I ought to be frying in hell, instead of sitting here looking at the best pair of legs off the Kentucky Derby track."

Jill ignored his pleasantry. "Do you know which professors took the money?"

"No, but, again, it would take me about ninety seconds to find out."

"Why haven't you?"

He shrugged. "What would be the point, just to drag everyone down with me? I'm going to live up to my side of the deal."

"And then what?"

He shrugged again. He had no answer for that, no answer at all.

Tuesday night Doug missed Jill a whole lot more than he was entitled to. When he got back from the henhouse Wednesday afternoon, she was out riding with her niece Allison. So he prowled restlessly around the dim, cluttered house until she appeared in her jodhpurs, hot, gorgeous, and happy. His impulse was to call for an immediate retreat to the front bedroom they were now sharing, but Randy was knocking about, and such open hijinks would be unseemly. So the three of them ate dinner and then, as Doug was sufficiently obsessed with sex that he couldn't plan any other activity, they mopped the kitchen floor.

But pleasure deferred was not pleasure denied, and he was sleeping like the dead when the phone's faint jangle pierced his brain.

He woke like a shot, fumbling for the phone. What was it this time? Drunk driving? Those were the middle-of-the-night calls. Who this time? Doug couldn't find the phone.

Of course not. He wasn't in Frederick. He was home in the Valley, and Aunt Carrie had only one phone, down in the kitchen.

Jill was already across the room, calling back over her shoulder. "Don't get up. It's for me."

He was fully awake now. She was right. The phone wouldn't be for him. He wasn't a coach anymore. If one of the kids were in trouble, the call would go to someone else. He listened to Jill's footsteps run down the stairs, then across the living room. She swore as she tripped over one of the dogs.

He wasn't going to be able to go back to

sleep. That was the trouble with calls in the middle of the night. They shot you so full of adrenaline that you were up for good. That was fine when you were a coach, when the call left you with things to do, problems to solve. It wasn't so great when you were just some guy collecting eggs for a living.

He waited for another moment, then got out of bed, pulling on his jeans, going downstairs. The kitchen light slanted into the dark living room, and as soon as he rounded the turn of the stairs he could see Jill in the kitchen.

"Yes, Tim," she was saying. "I can hear how upset you are."

She was stuck. The floor-mopping expedition had left the table and chairs on the other side of the room. The phone had such a short cord that Jill couldn't reach them to sit down. She had snared the coffee percolator, but it was dangling uselessly from her hand. She couldn't get over to the sink to fill it.

Doug came into the kitchen and took the pot from her. He pulled a chair close to the phone, then filled the coffeepot, plugging it into the wall outlet nearest the phone, leaving it chirping away on the now-gleaming floor. He brought her a mug, then got an afghan from the living room. He shook out the dog hair and draped it around her narrow shoulders.

It was nearly an hour before she came back upstairs. He was still awake, reading.

"You're nice to me, do you know that?" she said.

"Only because you have money. Was that call anything you can talk about?"

She rolled her eyes. "I know some strange people."

"Tell me."

"Actually, it's not that interesting. I do get some odd calls. This was pretty straightforward."

Her caller was Tim Salterstahl, a publicist romantically involved with the editor of a new, but highly visible, magazine, and he had gotten his girlfriend to agree to a "cover or nothing" deal for one of his clients. "Cover or nothing" meant that if the personality was not featured on the cover of the magazine, the article would not appear at all, the assumption being that for this celebrity anything less than a cover was an insult and it would lessen his or her chances for a cover on another magazine.

Jack Nicholson and Mel Gibson, Jill said, deserved "cover or nothing" deals. Tim's client did not. Indeed, as the romance waned, the editor invoked the "or nothing."

"So why did he call you?"

"Because he was too angry to sleep. He wanted me to come home, talk to Brenda, force her to change her mind. I was to insist that she put his client on the cover and insist that she stop making such a big deal over him not wanting to give her a key to his apartment."

"So what are you going to do?"

"Talk to him tomorrow, talk to Brenda. For this client inside coverage is far better than nothing. They'll both see it," she said confidently.

"What about the apartment keys?"

"That I'm not going to get involved with."

He laughed and slung his arm around her shoulders, pulling her to him. "Do you know who you remind me of?"

She shook her head, her soft hair tickling his chest. "No, who?"

"Your brother Brad. Everyone is always calling him when they're in trouble. He'll do anything for anyone."

Jill winced. "So the pathology must be hereditary."

"I don't see what's so pathological about it. You're two loyal, generous people."

"Who may be enabling other people to be very weak. But loyal and generous is my goal," she acknowledged. "We could go five years without seeing each other, but if you called at three A.M. needing guns, money, or lawyers, I'd recognize your voice and get you what you needed."

Doug didn't think much of the idea of not seeing her for five years. "Orthopedic surgeons were always what I needed at three A.M."

"I know the one the Lakers use."

"That's good information to have. Do you know what you should be when you grow up?"

She tilted her chin back to look up at him. "No, what?"

"An athletic director. You'd be great at it."

"I probably would be. Late-night bad news is one of my specialties."

"College athletics has plenty of that." Actually, Doug was semi-serious. What an asset she would be to a college program. Some coaches had wives who contributed whales to the teams, helping in the recruiting, mothering the troubled players, looking pretty on camera. If you could just hide how much money Jill had, as that would be a barrier, then she —

This was a truly profitable line of analysis. What was he planning to do? Fix her up with some of the guys who still had jobs?

He tightened the arm around her shoulders. "Tell me one other thing. All these people who call you at three A.M., what if you called them? Could they get you guns and orthopedic surgeons?"

"I don't know . . . I've never tried. I generally don't need things at three A.M."

"Neither does Brad."

The next day Doug left the barn at lunch and drove to the Radio Shack in Woodstock, bringing home yards and yards of phone wire. He deftly fished it through the walls, installing phone jacks throughout the house.

He was working in the front bedroom when he saw, turning up the lane, something that had probably never visited Aunt Carrie — a Federal Express truck. He didn't know they came out here.

He stepped out of the window, onto the roof of the veranda. "You can leave it on the porch," he called out to the driver.

The brown-uniformed driver stepped back, shielding his eyes with his hand. "I need a signature."

"Throw it up."

Throwing a clipboard and pen up twelve feet seemed like the simplest of acts to Doug. He was continually amazed at what klutzes other people were. The clipboard struck the underside of the gutter.

"Oh, hell," he muttered, not wanting to go inside, through the house, down the stairs, out the front door. So he sat down at the edge of the roof. He twisted, lowering himself down, holding on to the facia board for a moment so that, with his arms extended, it wasn't much of a drop to the grass.

The package was addressed to Jill. He signed for it, then carried it around to the side of the house where she was working in the garden.

Except she wasn't working. She was standing there, slapping her gardening gloves against her leg and grinning wickedly.

"You could have come around front and signed for it," he pointed out.

"And you could have come down the steps like a normal person. What is it?"

"Beats me. It's for you."

She leaned around his arm to look at the address. "Oh, shit."

Doug had never heard her use naughty words before. "What's wrong?"

"Nothing . . . or at any rate, nothing new. It's the dress my mother said she was going to get me."

He couldn't see what was so scatological about that. "Open it."

She slit open the packing tape with the

blade of her pruning shears. Wiping her hands on the seat of her jeans, she folded back the tissue paper packed inside and pulled out a dress.

It was pretty. No, it wasn't just pretty — Doug's vocabulary started to fail him — it was elegant. A pale brown, sort of a to-bacco-y color, it reminded him of a French Foreign Legion uniform although it was really rather simple, with a double row of low-set silver buttons and a pair of welted pockets at the hip.

Jill lifted out the layer of white tissue paper that had been padding the bottom of the box. She checked the box, seeming surprised to find it empty. She shook the tissue paper and then looked around to see if something had fallen out. She was looking perplexed.

"Are you missing something?" he asked. "Here's the card."

He read it over her shoulder. *Jill dearest, I do hope you like this. I assume you're traveling with your silver jewelry. It should work well. You may have to pick up some ivory or bone shoes.*

Jill was now looking dumbfounded. "I don't believe this." She was shaking her head. "This is not like my mother."

"How so?"

"She sent a dress, just one. No shoes, no

accessories, no nothing. Ivory or bone shoes! She has this thing about shoes. They have to be exactly right. Ivory or bone — that's not like her. It's just not like her."

This was much too technical for Doug. "I'm not sure I follow you here. Is this good news or bad?"

"It's the most amazing news in the world. Mother could have spent the better part of a week looking for exactly the right shoes, tobacco piped in cognac, something like that. I asked her to send me a dress, and she sent me a dress — one."

"Did you think that she might send you more than one?"

"I honestly wouldn't have been surprised if there had been four or five."

"Four or five?" He was astonished. "Five new dresses? Are you serious?"

"Oh, yes. My mother is a compulsive shopper." She looked down at the one dress again. "Or she used to be."

Doug finally understood. "So this is very good news indeed." He couldn't imagine what it would be like to have a mother as troubled as Jill's.

"It is, indeed," she said lightly. "I may never have to shop again."

Life was becoming remarkably pleasant.

Of course, Aunt Carrie's house was not comfortable. The mattresses were lumpy, and the sofa was covered with dog hair. The water was so hard that Jill had to use twice as much shampoo to get any kind of lather. The electrical wiring couldn't handle the simultaneous use of the toaster and the clothes dryer. In the bathtub every morning was an offering of what Randy and Doug called caraway seeds, but was, of course, mouse droppings. But comfort wasn't important to Jill, or she wouldn't have joined the Peace Corps. Nor would she ever visit Henry, whose magnificent ducal home was always a freezing minefield. Since none of the antique-filled rooms at Bickering had enough electric outlets, the floors were always a tangle of extension cords.

Fortunately privacy also didn't matter to Jill. The bathroom was right off the kitchen. Doug and Randy never folded their laundry and so were forever sprinting nude across the kitchen and down the cellar steps to dress out of the dryer. Moreover, they had a combined total of eight sisters. Not a day went by when at least one sister did not appear, bringing half of a lasagne, part of a cake, some early garden produce. Randy's sisters had been the most frequent visitors, but with Jill and Doug openly gallivanting about together, his curious sisters started appearing more. All eight sisters felt entirely at home in the house. None of them ever knocked. They opened the front door, called out "Hello," and without waiting for an answer, walked in.

Randy was the youngest in his family, and his sisters still babied him terribly. In Jill's mind this accounted for how cavalier he was with the feelings of the innumerable Young Lovelies he dated. Doug, on the other hand, had been the middle child — "think of a vicious volleyball game from the net's point of view" was how he described it. His sisters treated him with an easy-going, off-hand contempt. It was clear from the way they spoke about him behind his back that he had long since earned their respect, but they never let that admiration pollute their manner of dealing with him. They kept the boy in his place.

No wonder he had thrived amid the pressures of college coaching. Being caught between the team's starters, the non-starters, the athletic department, the administration, and the alumni must have felt normal.

Every morning Jill went to the 7-Eleven with Doug and Randy for coffee. She loved it. She liked the little routine of pouring one's own coffee, selecting from one of four cup sizes. She liked how neat the stainless steel counter stayed; the customers threw out the little cream containers and mopped up stray drips with paper napkins. She also liked the people she met there — working men, all of them, quite different from the affluent, professional Caslers and Ringlings.

If Randy was shorthanded, she'd spend the day in the henhouse, working in the thick, sour air. Otherwise, she'd work in the flowers or clear out the house. She called Alice, now comfortably retired in a cottage on one of Henry's estates, and had a transatlantic refresher course on the difference between nosegays and bouquets, between cottage gardens and country gardens. The flowers now arrived at market with deliciously English labels that left the suburban Anglophiles swooning.

On Memorial Day she had gone with Brad and Louise to put flowers on family graves and then asked if either minded if she were to clear out the house. Brad had protested at her even asking. It was her house, she should do what she liked.

"I don't think that the contents are mine," she pointed out. "I really have no right to throw them away."

"I don't think any of it has much quality," Louise said.

"That's what I thought." Jill was surprised that Louise was being gracious about something.

"So you're asking if any of us want or need such shoddy items?"

Randy later told Jill that his mother and sisters had already been through the house, taking everything that they wanted. For three weeks she determinedly dragged bags and bags of trash out to his truck. She vacuumed the dog hair, pulled up the carpets, and took down the heavy, dusty drapes. She had the floors sanded and bleached, the walls painted. She washed the windows and left them uncurtained. She persuaded the volunteer fire department to come take half the furniture for their annual sale. She picked up a few things at local crafts stores — some willow baskets, a pair of pine rockers, a simple pottery lamp. Soon it was looking like her — clean, simple, sparse, but with enough of her mother's touch that it was comfortable.

Every Friday she and Doug went to the Farmers' Market. Every Wednesday she rode with Allison. Every Tuesday she went to group.

After her third trip the twenty-seven-hour journey started to feel like an ordeal. The problem was that, because few people wanted to arrive in Washington between midnight and dawn, the commercial airlines had no eastbound flights scheduled for late afternoon or early evening. So Jill chartered a twin-engine Lear Jet with its sexy swept-back wings. It could take her in and out of Winchester, which saved the long drive to Dulles and brought her back east at her convenience. She could be back in her own bed as early as one or two in the morning. It was staggeringly expensive — truly breathtakingly so — but she didn't care.

One Tuesday after the meeting had finished, Cathy Cromartie stopped her in the parking lot. "Is something going on?"

"What do you mean?"

"For the last five weeks you've come wearing the same clothes, but arrived with a different car and driver. That struck me as a little odd, that's all . . . but I'm sorry. It's really none of my business."

"Sure it is," Jill said breezily although, in fact, this was the sort of thing Cathy should have brought up during group, not after hours. "Except the truth is even odder. I seem to be spending the summer in Virginia. I just come back for group."

"In Virginia?" Cathy was amazed. "What's in Virginia?"

"Cooler air, and remember that hotshot former basketball player who was interested

452

in *Weary Hearts*? He's there."

"Jill! You're not in love, are you?"

In love? Jill had never phrased it so directly. She pulled off her sunglasses. "You know, I think I am. Yes, I am. I really am."

"Oh, Jill!" And suddenly Cathy — rigid, controlled Cathy — embraced her. "That's wonderful. So am I."

"You are?" Jill stepped back, delighted. "How splendid. Tell me everything. Who is he?"

"You're going to die. It's stranger than someone from Virginia. He's a carpenter."

"No." Cathy was, Jill thought, the original success-snob. "How did you meet him?"

"He was doing some custom built-ins. He's not just a carpenter . . . no, no, I don't mean that. I'm trying not to think that. He is a carpenter; that's really what he plans on doing with his life. He has a Ph.D. in history and he makes a good living at carpentry, and it leaves him time to read and think and meet me for lunch. It's just wonderful to be with someone who isn't crazed about his career. Now, what about your basketball player?"

"He's not as clear about what he's doing as your carpenter, but he'll get there," Jill said confidently. "He's a marvelous man, funny and kind, warmer than I would have ever dreamed a man could be."

"Is he weird about your money?"

"I don't think so. He jokes about it, but he doesn't pitch a fit every time I pay for something."

"And he's not going to run up a lot of bills on your credit cards?"

"Lord, no."

They were both smiling, laughing. Cathy started to shake her head. "We're really terrible group members, aren't we?"

She was right. They really were. This was unconscionable, such an intimate conversation outside the group. "Are you going to report back?" Jill asked.

Cathy wrinkled her nose and very nearly giggled. "No."

"I'm not either."

There was some turbulent air in the Midwest, and Jill got back to Courthouse the next morning just as Doug and Randy were leaving for their morning coffee. She went along with them. As soon as Randy had drifted off to talk to other men in the parking lot, she turned to Doug.

"I love you."

He folded the sports page back to the box scores. "It looks like David Ahearn hit a triple last night."

"Did you hear what I said?"

"Of course." He went on reading the sports page. "But it's old news. Your stepfather hitting a triple, that's hot."

It might be old news to him, but it wasn't to her. "Do you love me?"

"Would I be here if I didn't?"

"Yes. You're too lazy to make your own coffee. Of course you'd be here."

"You don't need to be so literal."

"And you don't need to be so blasé."

"Blasé?" He looked at her over the newspaper. "Am I too blasé for you? Then how's this?"

He sent the newspaper flying over his shoulder and knocked both their coffees to the ground. He grabbed her, and in the best Phillip-Wayland fashion, bent her over backwards, kissing her long and hard. Over the ringing in her ears, Jill could hear the men in the parking lot cheer.

Fifteen

When Jill was in California on Tuesdays, she tried to find out more about *Weary Hearts*. She located an electrician and an assistant cameraman who had been part of the crew. Neither remembered anything of the scripts, but they confirmed her sense of the mood on the set: serious, intense, a silence charged with noble purpose.

The assistant cameraman knew that something had been going on, that secrets were being kept from the studio. How extensive the secrets were, he did not know.

"Didn't you try to find out?" Jill asked him.

"No. Except for Mr. McClay — and we knew he was doing what Bix was telling him — we were all vets, even Miss Burchell had done her part. A soldier either trusts his lieutenant or he doesn't. We trusted Bix. We had a real 'us against them' attitude, us being those who had fought, them being the guys in suits at the studio."

"Why didn't any of you ever say anything over the years?"

"Because it was still us against them. Bix and everyone dying didn't change that. And what was there to say? I didn't know what was going on. Maybe they were just padding expenses . . . although I'd never believe that of Bix, not in a million years. He was really something, that kid. It's a shame you didn't know him, Miss Casler, a real shame."

Doug came out to California with Jill a few times, but even their combined efforts produced nothing. A little more material turned up in the studio files. Sketches of the sound-stage interiors and of the costumes were found, as were the notes of the lighting designer, but there was nothing about the location work, not even the expense records. Nor did the collectors have anything. Collectors were secretive, passionate, often eccentric people who were devoted to owning movies although generally they could acquire them only illegally. Jill had sent discreet inquiries on their underground grapevine, but no one had come forward with any material.

"I just don't get it," Doug said as Jill came home on the third Tuesday in June, again with no new information. "How can there be nothing?"

"I told you," she answered patiently, "that Hollywood never had any sense of history. It makes you sick when you think about all that has been lost."

"But this is so complete. Sure, some stuff

might fall through the cracks, but you'd think we would turn up some kind of scrap of something."

She had to agree. In all those other searches for lost footage, people had found something: the cutting continuities for *Lost Horizon,* the sound track for *A Star Is Born,* the silent footage for *Lawrence of Arabia,* the home movie of the *Wizard of Oz* "Jitter Bugs" dance. Even when no footage had been found, there were production stills: the "Triumphal Return" sequence from the *Wizard of Oz,* the slaves' share of the Twelve Oaks barbecue in *Gone With the Wind.*

But of the material cut from *Weary Hearts,* there was nothing, not a single photograph, not a stray call sheet, not a loose expense record. If Doug's grandfather had not told him, no one would ever have any idea that there had been a secret script.

And Hollywood was usually not that good at keeping secrets.

"It's just too clean," Doug insisted. "It feels deliberate. Like nobody wanted us to know what was in the script."

"Are you saying there was some kind of cover-up?" Part of Hollywood etiquette was — or used to be — to keep silent about all conflict that happened during production. But Doug was suggesting something far larger, a cover-up by the studio executives to suppress the existence of Bix's fully filmed script. The scripts weren't lost, the production records weren't misfiled, the stills not routinely winnowed. He was suggesting that it had all been deliberate, so that no one would ever know that any of this had happened.

"I think we ought to consider it. It's not out of the question, is it?"

"But to what end?" Jill was perplexed. Certainly none of the studio executives would want to admit that they had been deceived, but no one person, not even Miles Smithson, could have engineered such a cover-up just to protect his job.

One theme had emerged from everyone who knew anything about the production — almost all of the crew had been World War II veterans. "What were Bix's politics?" she asked Doug. If Bix had written a script that glowed Red, the studio might have tried to protect him and itself by destroying all traces of the script.

"I don't really know for sure," Doug answered. "A Harry-Byrd Democrat, I suppose. That's what the family tended to be. He probably would have voted for Truman, but Stevenson might have been too liberal."

"He wasn't a Communist sympathizer?"

"A Red Ringling? I doubt it. And if that

had been the problem with the script, Alicia would have said something in that note, wouldn't she have? Her objections didn't sound political — I don't think that's what the girl in her best sweater on a Friday night would have been worried about."

Jill agreed. "So much for the cover-up theory."

"Not necessarily. Maybe they had some other reason . . . like they didn't want anyone to know how good Bix was."

"No." Jill shook her head, silently reminding herself that they still had no proof that Bix's writing was that good. She now longed for it to be true almost as much as Doug did. Bix had such personal charm, he was so well liked, that she hated the thought that he might have been a two-bit con man. But unlike Doug, she still remembered that they had no proof of his abilities. "The studio executives were businessmen," she went on. "*Weary Hearts* made plenty of money right from the start. It's not like anyone needed to justify a bad decision. From the bottom-line point of view, the studio most likely made the right one. Who on earth would benefit from a cover-up?"

Doug didn't answer. There was something soft in his eyes, something it took her a moment to identify — concern, pity.

She sat down. "No."

"I'm lucky," he said. "My father, all my coaches . . . I've never felt betrayed by any of them, and I can't imagine — "

"No."

This was getting worse and worse. But Doug had a point. If Cass had stolen credit for the revised script, then such a cover-up would have been necessary.

Cass had revered history. Jill had grown up hearing him talk about the cathedrals bombed and the art lost during World War II, about the family homes burned in 1864. His anguish had been genuine. He felt a responsibility to the future, a sense of stewardship about the past. He was a Virginian. He never would have destroyed a dead man's work. He was a gentleman, a man of honor.

But maybe his anguish for these lost artifacts had been guilt over what he had destroyed. Maybe his reverence for the dead had been expiation for what he had stolen from a dead man.

Jill felt Doug's hand lightly pass over her hair.

"Sometimes I regret ever having brought this to you." His voice seemed to be coming from a long way off. "It's turned out that there's a lot at stake for you."

Yes, there was. On the line was her whole

sense of her father, the one person whose love she had trusted.

"But then" — Doug was still speaking, his voice infinitely gentle, infinitely kind — "if I hadn't, we never would have met, and I can't endure the thought of that."

Jill couldn't either. He was still stroking her hair, his hand warm and light. Why did it feel like a choice? That having Doug meant losing her father?

When nitrate film deteriorates, the picture goes first. The image discolors and then fades, growing fainter and fainter until the film stock is nearly clear. Jill closed her eyes, unable to look at the picture of her father on the nightstand. Was his image fading too?

The next day was dark, the sky charcoal and low. Bursts of sharply slanting rain tattooed against the windows. It was no day for Jill and Allison to share their weekly ride.

Jill was disappointed. The loose rose-lavender clusters of the purple-flowering raspberries were now blossoming along the stream banks. But it was too wet. She and the men didn't even drive to the 7-Eleven. She brewed coffee and Doug scrambled eggs at home.

When the men left, Jill pulled down the

attic stairs that slid smoothly out of a framed opening in the ceiling of the upstairs hall.

Jill had worked in the attic once before, and she had seen instantly that Doug's grandmother had been right. Aunt Carrie's attic was far worse than Mrs. Ringling's. The convenient access had been a curse. Had Aunt Carrie needed to climb a vertical ladder to reach her attic, she might not have saved all those boxes of used Christmas paper. The sliding stairs made it too easy.

Jill had already found some fascinating things: someone's naturalization papers, someone else's World War I uniform, a faded quilt with a note pinned to it: "yellow flower — my Sunday school dress; green stripe — Mother's summer housedress; solid blue — shirt T. ripped at Memorial Day picnic." The pin had left a rust stain on the quilt and there was no explanation of who any of the people were. Jill laid it aside, hoping that Brad or Dave might know.

There was also a tremendous amount of junk, the saddest being the children's things. The toys were worn out and battered, many of them looking as hopeless and weary as Aunt Carrie's dreams of motherhood.

But they were old enough to have been made out of metal and wood. The little trucks were of a quality that even Jill's wealthy friends had trouble finding now. So Jill felt like she needed to sort through them, keeping out the ones that could still be played with. Such was her project for this rainy day.

The several boxes labeled "Old Dress-up Clothes" were disappointing. The garments were flimsy, postwar synthetics with a sleazy gleam to them that sent shivers up Jill's spine as she tossed them into the forty-gallon trash bags. One of the boxes had accessories: shoes, belts, purses. Jill decided some of the costume jewelry was worth saving, but the rest she threw out. The only thing that had been well made was a green clutch; the other purses and shoes were —

A green clutch. Jill stared at it. It was scuffed; the soft emerald-dyed leather was stained with water spots. She touched it gingerly, feeling the shape of objects inside.

It was a pretty, green thing . . .

Could it be? Alicia's purse had been green. Might Aunt Carrie have picked it up, not knowing whose it was and stored it all these years as a plaything for the children who never came?

Jill snapped open the tarnished clasp. The light from the overhead bulb glinted against a compact, softened on the lawn of a white handkerchief. She took out the compact. Once silvery, it was now dulled to gunpowder grey.

Jill tilted it to read the swirling monogram: A. B. R. — Alicia Burchell Ringling.

Alicia's lovely face flashed into Jill's mind — the warm smile of her publicity portrait; her dark, troubled eyes as she stood next to the white, billowing drapes of her bed, listening to Phillip's footsteps outside her door; the tiny line drawing Bix had done of her.

This was her purse, she who had once been alive. She had bought herself this handkerchief, she had laundered it. She had touched up her face in the mirror of this compact. She had written herself notes, put money in this wallet. She had married one brother and fallen deeply, desperately, in love with the other.

Carefully, respectfully, Jill emptied the purse, item by item. The handkerchief had a scrolling "A" embroidered on it. The comb was clean. The lipstick was "Butterfly Pink." There was a wallet, a notepad, some postcards.

The wallet had forty dollars in it, which would have been a lot of money back then. But Alicia had been a woman traveling without her husband; Charles stayed home to regain the weight he had to lose for the movie's final sequence. The postcards — pictures of the Valley — were blank; Alicia must have bought them to send and then never had. The notepad had a list — "pick up mail, call Evie, key" — all the routine chores she was planning on doing when she got home.

Only Alicia had never gotten home. Evie, whoever she might have been, had gotten a very different sort of call.

Jill turned the page of the notebook.

Don't talk.

They were the same raw, startling words as before, Alicia's handwriting again hurried and irregular. Then came Bix's answer.

Chas said you wanted to stay.

It was another dialogue, notes they had written back and forth, perhaps while they were on the plane.

Alicia — *Yes. But the screen test. He said I couldn't miss that. But I should have stayed. This is a mistake.*

Bix — *What have I done that you don't trust me?*

Alicia — *It's not you I don't trust. It's me. Bill or someone can take me home.*

Bix — *My brother asked me to see his wife home. I can do that.*

Alicia — *No.*

Bix — *How can we be in the same family if we can't trust ourselves to be alone?*

Alicia had no answer to that. She must have flipped the notebook closed, tucked it back into her purse and snapped the clasp shut, almost certainly among the last acts she had performed on earth.

Jill reread their dialogue, the meaning becoming clear. As yet there had been no physical intimacy. Jill was sure of that. These two bright, gifted people, who must have longed for each other so keenly, had not slipped into physical sin. But now they were going back to California without Charles, and he had asked Bix to drive Alicia to an empty house. The two of them would be alone, a continent away from Charles, from Virginia, from all the traditions that sustained them. Bix believed that he could do it, that he could escort his sister-in-law as surely and safely as if she were nothing more than his brother's wife. Alicia doubted her own resolve.

Slowly Jill repacked the purse and took it downstairs. The rain had let up for the moment although the sky was still heavy. She went down the lane, across the county blacktop, and around the stand of cedars to the long, low building that housed Randy's chickens. She found Doug on one of the wooden walkways between the rows of stacked chicken cages. He was on his knees, tinkering with the conveyor belt that caught the newly laid eggs. She held the purse so Doug could see it. His brows drew together for a moment, then he understood what it was. They went toward Randy's little office. The hens stirred as they passed, clucking irritably.

As soon as the office door closed, Jill handed Doug the notebook. She watched him as he read the dialogue. When he looked up, his eyes were distant and troubled.

Just as Bix's eyes must have been.

"Do you think they wrote this on the plane?" she asked.

He nodded. "Charles said he drove them to the airport and waited until the plane took off. They wouldn't have talked about this in the waiting room with him there."

"What do you think would have happened that night?"

"Nothing. Bix wouldn't have. Not with Charles's wife. Not ever."

He was certain, but how could he know what Bix would have done? All he was saying was that *he* wouldn't have.

She spoke calmly. "They didn't know what would happen, so we can't possibly know. What I wonder" — she took the notebook back — "is whether or not Charles saw this."

Doug drew back, startled at the thought. "He couldn't have. The way he talks about them . . . he couldn't have known. He wouldn't have gone through the purse. Remember what Gran said. If it was too painful for her, think what it would have been like for him."

Jill did not agree. For all of Marie Ringling's brisk and unemotional manner, Jill suspected that her emotions were keener, more intense than those of her dramatically grief-stricken son. "He says he's an intuitive actor. If he's as intuitive as he says, he had to have some sense of what was going on."

"But he has remained so loyal to their memories."

Jill no longer believed the picture of the steadfast, long-suffering Charles. "I think we need to go talk to him."

"You aren't going to show him the purse, are you?"

"Why not?"

Doug blinked at her crisp tone. "Because it would — " He stopped, as if sensing that Jill didn't want to hear this. "There's no point in needlessly humiliating anyone. Let's take the notebook out and pretend we haven't seen it. It's not like it tells us anything about the movie — and that's what we're supposed to be interested in, the movie."

He said a few quick words to Randy, and they set off for Winchester. They disagreed on how to handle Charles. Jill, as much as she hated confrontation, was in favor of sticking the purse under Charles's nose and waiting for a reaction. She hoped to startle him into honesty. Doug, on the other hand, wanted to make it easy on him.

"This was his wife," Doug argued. "She died on the day she was carrying this purse."

Jill was not going to quarrel about this. It was his family. She gave in.

So when they arrived in Winchester, Doug spoke gently. "Sit down, Uncle Charles. We have something you may want to see although it might be painful."

Jill was watching Charles carefully. She could feel the actor's mask falling into place. She had seen this preparatory moment before, the blankness, the waiting. She had seen it in Payne, in Susannah, in countless others whose skills, although perhaps not better than Charles's, were sharper.

And indeed, Charles's reaction was an elegantly understated grief. He touched the purse, remembering the green dress Alicia had died in, how she had worn her hair that day, how —

Jill felt a tiny spurt of anger. This man knew things that he wasn't telling. She was sure of that. Here she was, not knowing if the father she had always adored had lied to her, had stolen from the dead. Here she hardly knew what kind of person her father was . . . and this man would not tell her the truth. And Doug, this was so important to him. It was as if finding Bix's lost script was going to help him find a script to replace the lost one that had detailed his own life.

She forced herself to calm down. *Anger won't get us anywhere; it accomplishes nothing; it never does.* These words were almost a mantra for her.

Her troubled image of Cass was not Charles's problem. It wasn't fair of her to expect him to help her. But Doug was another matter. Charles did have some responsibilities there.

She looked at Doug. He was sitting on a low stool in front of Charles's chair, sitting forward, his hands between his knees, listening, listening sincerely. No wonder he had been so good with players.

He wasn't Bix. Bix was an intriguer, Doug was not. If Bix were Tom Sawyer — clever, controlling, crafty — then Doug was Huck Finn — open, endlessly good-hearted.

How she loved him.

So, for his sake, she was going to do something she didn't think she had ever done before, not even on the playground of her grammar school; she was going to break a confidence.

She sat down across from Charles and waited for a moment when she could break in. "Charles, let me tell you why I'm interested in *Weary Hearts*. Have you heard of an actor named Payne Bartlett?"

Charles nodded, untroubled by the seeming change of subject. "He's the son of Graham Bartlett and Gloria Upham, isn't he? A fine young actor."

"He's interested in remaking *Weary Hearts*."

She had her eyes on Charles, watching a quickening interest flash across his face. She heard Doug's sudden intake of breath, but she didn't dare glance at him. She was too amazed by what she was seeing in Charles's face.

He liked the idea. With the swift instinct he had always claimed to have, he approved.

He was sitting forward now, looking at Jill with more vigor in his eyes than she had ever seen. For a moment it was like looking at Booth, a man capable of leadership and action. "Which version does he want to do?"

"I don't know." Jill knew that she was making Payne's plans sound more definite than they were. "He hasn't heard anything about the script we're looking for."

"But he'd want to play Phillip, wouldn't

he? He'd want to be Bix, not me."

"If he goes to all the trouble of producing the movie, then he would almost surely want to play the lead." Jill's "almost surely" was a lie. There was absolutely no question that Payne would cast himself in the lead.

"But he's wrong for that part." Charles was shaking his head. "He's too big. He's built like me. That was the whole point. Bix was a born cavalry man, and I was not, but I was the one who joined. No, no, he'd have to play me."

Jill didn't answer. Physical credibility would never stop Payne from taking the lead in his own first production.

"He'd be good as me, wouldn't he?" Charles was on his feet, pacing the room, a nervous energy about him that Jill had never seen. "I liked him in *Mountain Ash,* better than when he was doing comedy in that thing last year. How are his horse skills?"

Something was happening here. Jill was bewildered by Charles's enthusiasm. Having played Booth was his entire identity. It was everything in his life; it was even the lens through which he viewed his wife and brother, best able to remember them as Phillip and Mary Deas. So why would he want the movie remade? Wouldn't that be sacrilege?

Apparently not. Clearly he wanted this to happen. She could not imagine why. All she could do was answer the question he asked about Payne's horse skills. "We were in a Pony Club together as children although I don't know what he's done since then. But I'm sure he'd work very hard."

"That might not be enough. He'll have to be very good to play me right."

Charles was acting as if it were all settled, that Payne was going to remake the movie, taking Charles's former part. "I still think he'll probably want to play Phillip," Jill cautioned. "He'll want to be the lead."

"Of course, of course." He waved his hand, dismissing her objection. "Don't forget. In the first version, I — "

He stopped.

Jill stared. What was he saying? "In the first version, was Booth . . . were you the main character?"

The actor's mask fell back into place, shuttering his face. The energy was gone. He was again the languid, elderly gentleman. "My dear, I have told you. I never paid attention to the script as a whole."

Sixteen

"This is incredible." The front door was hardly closed when Jill started to speak. "I don't believe it. Is it possible that Bix had Booth as the lead? You said you wish there'd been more about him, about — "

She stopped, horrified.

Doug was angry with her. There was no doubt about it. His jaw was rigid, his brows lowered, the only movement in his face the snapping of his bright eyes. He was furious.

All thoughts about movies and lead characters and remakes drained out of her. This was so awful. How could he be mad at her? What had she done?

She knew. She had not told him about Payne. She hadn't even thought; not speaking had been so automatic. She covered her face with her hands; she couldn't even speak. *Dear God, please don't let him be angry with me. Please. Please. Please.*

"Jill, what's wrong?" She felt his hands close around her shoulders. She looked up at him. They were standing so close that the whole world was his eyes; she could see nothing else, just the deep-set crystal blue, the low dark brows. But the anger had gone.

She had reacted so strongly; shock had driven his anger away. He was gravely concerned. "What is it? Are you all right?"

She stepped back, embarrassed, almost ashamed. She had overreacted. More than overreacted. She had fallen apart. But his anger had surprised her. If she had had a chance to prepare herself, to arm herself . . . but she had been caught blind . . . and by him.

She pushed down the flurries of rats' feet. She had been wrong, but she could make amends. She would get everything out in the open so that he would never get angry again. "There's more. My father optioned the right to remake the movie. The only reason Payne's interested in remaking it is that Cass was . . . and that's also the only reason I came out here." She wanted to be sure he knew everything. "The story you told me in L.A. was the most unbelievable thing I'd ever heard, but then I found out the one thing that made it a little more believable — that Cass must have known of some reason to remake the movie."

"Why didn't you tell me?" He didn't react to the news about Cass's owning the rights. Her keeping a secret was what mattered to him. "Have I given you any reason not to trust me?"

Those were almost the same words Bix had written to Alicia. "No, no. It's just that Payne asked me not to say anything. If it got out that he was interested, then — " She stopped. Doug would not have run to *Entertainment Tonight* with the news. "I keep my promises. I don't betray my friends. If someone asks me to keep a secret, I do."

"So why now?"

"Because we're stuck. We know about Bix and Alicia, but we aren't any closer to knowing what was in that first script than we were days ago. Charles is lying to us, and I don't know how else to make him talk."

And because this is important to you. I'm starting to understand that you have to find out about this before you can do anything else with your life. I want to help you. For the first time, the very first time, I sacrificed one friend to another. This probably won't hurt Payne, but even if it were to, I still would do it because you're more important to me than he is. You're more than a friend. I love you.

Until she met him, Jill had never understood what it meant to love a man. Friendship was all she had known. Friendship was her biggest dream.

Haltingly she tried to explain. These were things that had to be said. "When you don't have a family, you have to create your own.

477

That's what my friends are for me, and it works because the strong prop up the weak, the orderly help the chaotic, the joyful ease the way of the gloomy. But it's not as clear as in a family — there's no center, no roster of who belongs and who doesn't. So you have to have a code, and — "

She quit. He didn't get it. According to the terms by which she lived, in her emotional currency, she had done something important. Never before had she chosen a lover over a friend. But Doug didn't understand. He couldn't. All this had always been easy for him. He had a family, a wonderful, wonderful family who loved each other. She could explain and explain and explain, and even if he understood intellectually, it would be like a literal translation of a poem: the magic would be lost.

What he could see was what her actions would have meant in his own life, that keeping secrets was a hostile act creating, preserving distance. He wasn't going to be angry with her — he had seen the consequences of that — but he wasn't going to understand. He couldn't.

They were in his Chevy now, its convertible top up because of the rain. The air inside the car felt humid and close. The low canvas roof seemed to be pushing down on them.

"Tell me again," he said, "about these rights and options."

She did, explaining everything — how Cass had taken out an option and then had kept renewing it for years and years. As she spoke, she heard how it must sound, that Cass was planning on profiting from the cover-up. When everyone had forgotten about Bix's secret script, he would film it, calling it his own.

No, no, that couldn't be. If there had been a cover-up, Cass would have been an unwilling participant. What could he have done? He couldn't have kept the cut footage; it was the studio's property.

Frantic for comfort, Jill fumbled for Doug's hand. His was cool. She searched his eyes. They weren't angry, but there was a blankness to them, a numbness, a distance. This was what he must have looked like during his final days at Maryland Tech.

In the hours, in the days that followed, that look never left his eyes. Jill didn't understand it. Something was slipping away from her, something precious, infinitely dear. She was powerless to stop it; it was like the tide slipping back down the beach. At least she understood the tide and the gravitational pull of the moon. This she couldn't understand. Some dark gravity was pulling the laughter out of Doug's shining eyes.

What had happened to this relationship she thought was going to be so easy? There was no open conflict; there was nothing to have open conflict about. For seven days life went on. They continued to go to the 7-Eleven with Randy each morning. They continued to work on *Weary Hearts,* now interviewing all the people who had been extras. They even continued to have sex.

But it wasn't like before. Especially the sex.

As physically exhilarating as sex with Doug had been from the beginning, Jill had not been entirely comfortable. It had felt a little too intense, a little too intimate.

"Too intimate?" He had stared at her, bewildered, the one time they had talked about it. "I don't get it. How can sex be too intimate? I thought intimacy was what it was all about. What do you mean? Be specific."

That had been hard. "Well . . . you look at me." She had winced, knowing how lame that had sounded.

"Who the hell am I supposed to look at?"

Jill hadn't said, but some men didn't look at anyone. They buried their faces in the pillow toward the end and everyone attended to his or her business in privacy.

She had given up. This was Doug's style: Huck Finn in bed. He couldn't picture the alternative: a discreet, pleasant meeting of the genitals in darkened rooms with laundered sheets and the low hum of an air conditioner. He wasn't likely to change . . . and did she really want him to?

That had been before she had told Charles about Payne. Now she could hear the rattle and click of the electric fan over the sound of his breathing.

She had trained him well.

One afternoon she was in the kitchen, unhappily cleaning vegetables for dinner, when she heard the men at the back door. Randy blew her a breezy kiss and disappeared into the bathroom for his shower. Doug stood at the door, surprised.

"I didn't expect to see you here," he said.

"Why not?" she was instantly defensive. "Where else would I be?" Did he want her to go? She said she would stay until they both wanted her to leave. Was he ready for that?

"It's Tuesday."

Tuesday. Tuesday was group day. She had forgotten to go. Oh, God, she had forgotten to go. How could she?

Sick, she looked at the clock. There was no point in calling Bill, the therapist. He would be in another session. But she had to talk to someone, she had to say something. Trembling, she dialed the studio.

People missed group, she told herself as she waited for Cathy to come on the line. It happened at least once a month that someone was not there for one reason or another.

But they always told everyone in advance, or if there was a sudden emergency, they left a message for Bill, and he would say immediately, "June had to go to a funeral" or "Rob's boss is sick, he had to go to a sales conference." Never once in the year Jill had been a member had anyone simply not appeared.

Until now.

Cathy came on the line.

"Cathy, it's Jill." She could hear how urgent her voice sounded, how distraught.

"What happened?" Cathy's voice was flurried too. "Are you all right? Jill, I was worried . . . those little planes . . ."

"I forgot, Cathy. I just forgot."

"You forgot?" Cathy sounded blank, disbelieving. "How could you forget?"

"I don't know." Jill was truly miserable. "Did anyone say anything?"

Of course they had. She could picture the scene, people wondering where she was, glancing at the door, not quite sure whether to start.

"If you want the truth, Jill, everyone was furious. They were tremendously angry."

"Angry?" Jill's voice cracked. "At me?"

She hated anger. There was nothing she hated more. She remembered her parents before their divorce. Her mother had trembled when angry, her face pale, her hand shaking as she reached for the pills. Her father had withdrawn, tense, white-lipped, sucking the flames inward, a fire burning so hot that it could not blaze, there being no air for flame. Nothing had frightened her more.

And now her group had gotten angry with her. "What did Bill say? Did he — "

"He let it happen. Jill, he's not an idiot. He knows what terrible patients you and I have been, how we've been withholding. He's been waiting for the group to sense it. They've been repressing it, denying it, because everyone wants so much to have your approval . . . but when you didn't come, it hit. They felt so betrayed."

Jill didn't betray people. That was her strength, she was a perfect friend.

"I've been just as remiss as you," Cathy was saying. "I was honest with everyone about that. And I'm determined to do better.

We need to talk this through in group, with everyone, not by ourselves."

But Jill didn't think she could go back to group. She couldn't face the anger, the hurt. Not right now, not when things were so bad with Doug. Why did this have to happen now?

That was why it had happened now. If she hadn't felt estranged from him, she never would have forgotten to go.

Heartsick, she tried to wrap her misery in around her, folding it like the wings of a black opera cape, but the satin was too heavy; she couldn't manage it, she couldn't move. Alice had taught Henry how to move in the heavy ducal robes he would have to wear at the next coronation, but Jill was American. Her burden was emotion, not tradition, and Alice had been no help.

What could she do? Who could she talk to? Not Doug. This was about him. In ways she didn't understand, this was about him.

Without being conscious of deciding, she watched her fingers dialing her mother's number. *Be there, Mother. Please be there. I need you.*

"Hello."

The voice was so musical, so low that, for a moment, Jill thought it was the answering machine. When the greeting, now faintly puzzled, was repeated, Jill choked, unable to talk.

"Is anyone there?"

"Oh, Mother . . ."

"Jill, dearest, my baby — what's wrong?"

It all flooded out: Jill's misery inchoate, muddled, the desperate feeling that she was losing Doug, and she had no idea why.

This was what Melody had always longed for, and she listened and listened, murmuring soft words of warmth and comfort until Jill pleaded for help. "Mother, what can I do? I love him so much."

"Darling, maybe there's nothing to do. I know this is hard to hear, but this may have nothing to do with you. It's his problem."

"He doesn't have any problems. He's the strongest, sanest person I know."

"Everyone has problems," Melody said gently, her voice as feathery as her thick down comforters. "That it seems like he doesn't suggests that he's denying something."

"I don't know . . . what's he denying?"

"That he's hurt about losing his job."

"Oh, that."

"He probably needs to grieve about his job. He's lost his reputation, his career, his direction. No wonder he's marching in place. He needs to mourn that before he can move on."

Jill knew the theory behind this, but she listened as her mother repeated it, speaking with the insight of someone who had been, if not right there, in some place just as hard. Elizabeth Kubla-Ross had traced the stages a dying person goes through. A person first denies what is happening, then is angry, and later tries to bargain his way out of it. This is followed by depression and finally by acceptance. People going through any kind of loss go through a similar process, and Doug had lost something indeed.

He was still at the first step, entrenched in denial. There could be no question about that. He could joke about what had happened, but he couldn't talk seriously about it. He probably didn't even think about it. He was refusing to make plans, refusing to even admit that he needed to make any.

This was why he seemed fine; his manner was composed, he was witty and self-depreciating, open-hearted and manly. That's why none of his family or friends were worried about him. He must have seemed like the old Doug to everyone.

But he wasn't fine. He shouldn't be unchanged by what had happened. He was beating himself into a mold to make it appear that he was. He needed to break out of that mold, out of his denial, and move through the other stages: anger, bargaining, depression, acceptance.

Anger.

Jill stared down at the phone that she, a moment ago, had been using to speak to her mother.

Anger.

That was what was next. That was what Doug needed. He needed to get angry with the miscreants who had arranged those students' false test scores; he needed to get angry with the alumni who had given recruits those cars; he needed to get angry with the professors who sold grades, with the athletic director who had gone back on his word, with the N.C.A.A. investigators who had been happy with the simple story. He needed to get rip-roaringly pissed off. He needed to curse and holler, stick his fist through a wall, kick the water cooler, whatever it was that angry people did.

But that wasn't going to happen, not around Jill. She had made that clear on his grandmother's front porch. Not only did you not get angry at Jill, you didn't get angry around her. No wonder his eyes had gone so blank. All summer, anger had been trying to crack through his shell, a healthy, healing anger, but every time he had threatened to express it, she had rushed in, soothing and forbidding, and he stopped being angry. But the price had been emotional retreat — this blank, polite relationship in which the electric fan made more noise than they did.

Jill could handle all the latter stages of the grieving process. During the bargaining she would listen to a partner, not judging, letting him realize on his own how irrational his bargains were. During depression she would neither blame nor pity; she would neither impatiently insist that he shape up nor treat him like a child. At acceptance she would accept too, not ringing in with foolish hopes. None of it would easy, but Jill would do far, far better than most people.

But anger?

Jill's goal in life was to get people to stop being angry. That's what she did, calm everyone down so that things could get done. But there was nothing Doug Ringling needed more right now than to get angry.

It didn't matter what the anger was about. It could start with anything — a woman who wanted to buy only yellow and pink flowers, the people covering up Bix's script, it didn't matter. Sooner or later the fury would boil over into his own life . . . at least it would have if Jill hadn't been such a vigilant little fire marshal.

There probably wasn't a woman on earth

more wrong for him than she was.

She tried to explain this to him.

He looked at her blankly and said exactly what ninety-eight percent of all American males would have said. "You've been reading too many self-help books. That's not our problem."

"Then, what is our problem?" She could hear the sharp snap of exasperation in her voice. "I'm sorry, I shouldn't have spoken like that. How would you define the situation?" At least he wasn't denying that there was a situation.

"That we're not leading a normal life. I mean, we eat breakfast at the 7-Eleven every morning. We're living with Randy. That's not normal, to be living with another guy."

Jill blinked. She had never expected that answer. What did Randy and the 7-Eleven have to do with anything? She could get up and make eggs, bacon, waffles, and hash browns every morning, and that wouldn't get them anywhere but on the road to Cholesterol City.

The irony was that this was the most normal routine she had ever shared with a man. She had never lived with anyone before. She had vacationed with, traveled with, slept with, but hadn't lived with.

Yet Doug did have a point. Randy was living here, too. He wasn't around much, but he was an issue, someone who could walk in at any moment. She and Doug were guaranteed privacy only in their bedroom, and even then, they could hear Randy slam the door as he came in, hear him whistle as he bounded up the steps.

Jill sat down on her side of the bed. Maybe having Randy around was important to her; maybe that was what made it possible for her to live with Doug. His presence forced onto the relationship a formality, a distance, a barrier, that she probably felt comfortable with. After all, she was a child raised by a governess. Alice had loved her, Jill truly believed that, but Alice had to draw lines to protect herself because Cass could have fired her at any moment. A bit of distance in a relationship felt normal to Jill; Randy allowed her to recreate the lines that Alice had always drawn.

Doug switched off the lamp on his side of the bed, and reluctantly Jill followed suit. Her hand dropped slowly, brushing against the leather traveling frame with the picture of her father.

Her eyes had not yet adjusted to the darkness and she could not see the frame, but in her mind flashed an image, not of her father's picture, but of the handwritten poem that faced it, the last stanza of William Butler Yeats's "Easter, 1916."

In 1916 Irish nationalists revolted against the British government, a heroic failure that ended with the execution of some of the leading nationalists. In the poem the speaker is first repelled by how the rebels' commitment to the political cause has changed them; the sweet have grown strident, the beautiful, haggard. Then, in the last stanza, he grows to understand and commemorate them.

Jill loved the poem because her father had. Its attitude toward the dead — that the living must remember, must honor the dreams of the dead — always brought back the memories of going to funerals with him, standing close to him under his big black umbrella, feeling his arm around her childish shoulders, listening to the minister say the final words.

But as the words of the poem marched through her mind on this dark Virginia night, she felt as if they were a comment on the way she lived. She had no single, central passion, and she didn't understand those who did — the Iranians who had thrown themselves into Khomeini's grave; the homeless activists on hunger strikes until death — there was a fervor and intensity in those lives that Jill didn't understand, that she didn't want. But it wasn't a choice. She was incapable of such passion.

This poem made her aware of the cost. Her life, so pleasant, so full of kindness, comfort, and friendship, lacked the vividness, the intensity, the terrible beauty of the Irish Rebels.

There was more to life than she had ever dreamed of, a huge, crystal lake, icy cold on a humid day, a lake in which people were swimming and playing, in which they were finding happiness. Staying on the shore were other people, some unable to swim, some hating the way they looked in a bathing suit, unwilling, unable to join those playing in the water.

Jill was on the shore. She had built a nice, pleasant life for herself, but always with her back to the lake, not admitting that it was there. And, worst of all, she had persuaded Doug to join her on the shore.

But life was better for the people in the lake. How was she going to get the courage to jump in?

Seventeen

In June of 1863 the seventy thousand men of the Army of Northern Virginia, under the leadership of Robert E. Lee, crossed the Potomac River and invaded the North. With the long shadows of the Blue Ridge screening their movements, they marched up through Hagerstown into Pennsylvania. On July 1, in the rolling hills surrounding a small town, they met the Army of the Potomac. It was there at Gettysburg that the South lost the Civil War.

Much was planned to commemorate this most momentous battle of that long-ago war. Doug and Randy, Jill had long since learned, were the most casual of re-enactors, occasionally linking up with Randy's brother-in-law's unit. They had done nothing since New Market. Brian, Randy's brother-in-law, was urging them to come to Gettysburg.

"We need numbers," Brian declared. "Last year it was crawling with Yankees. Don't you want to be a part of Pickett's Charge — the high-water mark of the Confederacy?"

"Yes," Doug answered. "In a blue coat." Earlier in the summer, in the days when they were still laughing, he had presented

Jill with the Doug's Digest condensed version of the Civil War: Robert E. Lee had had only three bad days in his entire life; unfortunately, they were all at Gettysburg.

"Why don't you go?" she said. "You'll have fun." He must miss the company of other men, the afternoons spent in the gym with his players, the evenings spent in coffee shops with his coaching staff. As little as he might have in common with the other re-enactors, they created a masculine world.

Randy was shaking his head. "It's too long a trip for one day. We can't leave — "

Jill interrupted. "I'll take care of the chickens. You've been saying all summer how good this group of high school kids is. We'll get them to stay a little longer. I know the routine; they do too. We'll be fine. Go on the day before so you can camp out with everyone."

So, after the eggs were loaded later in the afternoon on the first Friday in July, Doug and Randy came back to the house to prepare themselves to invade the North. This time Randy was the pretty mama's-boy, putting on the dress uniform with the gilt braid and brass buttons. Doug was too tall for the tattered butternut that Randy had worn at New Market and so Brian had dropped off a battle uniform of plain grey.

Jill walked out to the truck with them, watching them sling their haversacks into the back. Randy was bombarding her with last-minute instructions.

"Shut up," Doug told him flatly. "She can handle it. You know that. And if she does kill them all, she can buy you new ones."

That was enough for Randy and he went back into the house for the ice chest, leaving Doug and Jill alone. Doug was suddenly busy with something in the truck. Jill watched his back as he worked. She liked this plain, neat uniform, the grey collar stiffened by rows of stitching rather than satin facing. He slammed the tailgate and turned around. He was facing her, not quite looking at her. "Randy trusts you, but it's all — "

"I know." How could she ever have confused Doug for Bix? Now she was so aware of the differences. Doug was taller. The soft lower lip that they shared was more sensual in Bix. Bix's cheekbones were sharper, his eyes deeper set. Bix's face was more dramatic, Doug's more open. She had had a mad crush on Bix; Doug she loved.

He put his hands in his pockets. Jill wasn't sure what to say. He drew a line through the dust with the heel of his boot. How awful this would be if they really were soldier and sweetheart, parting perhaps forever, with this sad grey mist between them.

He scuffed through the line with his toe. "I know I don't have to say this, but you will be here when I get back, won't you?"

Jill's eyes flew to his face. Would she be here? How could he ask that? "Of course I will be."

"I know. I know," he spoke quickly, apologizing. "I didn't mean that. Really . . ." He tilted his head back, squinting up at the afternoon sun. "I believe in you, I do. It just doesn't make sense, your being here, selling flowers and sorting eggs, not with your money."

"If you start thinking that way, then it's hard for anything to make sense. What should people with money do? The money lets me be where I want to be, and, at the moment, that is here with you."

His arms came around her, pulling her close to him, tight and hard. His kiss was a soldier's kiss, full of glaring light and sun-hot passion, but when he stepped away, the grey mist was still there.

Randy came back outside, balancing the cooler on one shoulder. He heaved it into the truck and in a moment the doors were slamming and the engine was churning. Jill watched the truck rumble down the lane, the tires spitting pieces of gravel. Then it turned onto the county road, disappearing a moment later over a rise.

She wasn't going to leave. Not just this weekend, but ever. He wasn't going to, either. They were both the most loyal of people; they would be together until one of them died. What was at stake was not their relationship, but the quality of it. She knew that they would be together. Would that togetherness make them happy?

Right now, no. Things were not working. There was compatibility without intimacy. Holding them together was the sense of how close they were to something truly fine. Beyond the grey mist was a land of beauty and willows, a land lovelier than anything Jill had dreamed of. The perfume of what might be echoed lilac and lavender; it was a perfume speaking of a time when the moon would glow more golden, when the wild roses would smell sweeter.

Wasn't this what she had wondered about, a love stronger than reason? She had never understood her friends who stayed in relationships that weren't working, relationships sustained by hope's promises and nostalgia's lies. She understood now. She and Doug would stay together for their lives, bound by an illusion that was too precious to give up.

As she stared at the empty blacktop road — a dark ribbon rising between the cedars and the fields — Jill felt she was at a crossroad. She had the sense that this was the last possible moment to turn the other way . . . but however much she knew she was at the crossroads, she could see only one way — the straight line ahead.

She went back into the house, letting the screen door close behind her. Then, as if the screen alone wasn't quite enough protection from the future, she dropped the little hook into the latch eye. She crossed the kitchen into the bathroom, showered, and then went upstairs to dress.

The last bit of afternoon light threw a slanted rectangle of brightness across the planked floor of the front bedroom. Jill dropped her towel, and as she reached into the closet for her clothes, she caught sight of herself in the mirror Doug had hung on the closet door, a glimpse of the perfect ectomorphic build that she had inherited from her mother.

Why did she always think that? Whenever anyone praised her willowy neck, her delicate wrists, her slender arms and shapely legs, the elegance of her hands and feet, every time, every single time, she always mentioned her mother. Why?

Because of the price her mother had paid for this lovely body. Was that it? Had she always dreaded that the legacy had come to her with the same curse?

But it hadn't. She had set herself a test this summer and had passed it so easily that she had forgotten that it was even a test. Every Wednesday, week in and week out, she had gone riding with Allison. She had loved it, but she had done it only once a week. It was possible. She was going to be able to ride again, letting horses be part of her life, knowing that they wouldn't take it over.

She did not have an addictive personality. She had survived the bleak days after her father's death, she had endured the dull ache of her failure with Doug without giving into any obsessive behavior. She hadn't drunk more than usual, she hadn't taken pills, she hadn't cleaned too much, worked too hard, had too many manicures.

Her body wasn't booby-trapped. It was exactly what it appeared, a graceful human form, a blessing not just for its beauty, but for its health. It was a gift, not something that she was going to have to pay and pay for. Her mother had already paid, and she had passed it along to Jill, unencumbered, unmortgaged.

A pounding on the front door broke into

her thoughts. "Jill, Jill." The screen door rattled in its jamb. "Jill, are you there? The door's locked."

It was Doug.

She pulled a sundress over her head and ran down the stairs. Through the mesh of the door she could see him, still in grey battle dress, his hair rumpled and wild.

"Come on, hurry," he was saying. "Charles found it, the script, he found it."

Jill fumbled with the hook. "He found it? The script? Where?"

Doug pushed open the door, and in his hand was a script bound in tattered, faded blue. "I don't know, among some of Alicia's things, somewhere. We were supposed to pick him up. He said he wanted to go to Gettysburg, but when we got there, he'd already gone. He left this with a note, saying that he'd decided to look once more."

The edges of the script's blue paper cover were tattered. "Weary Hearts, Final Shooting Script, April 14, 1948." And then, in neat lettering, behind the typescript had been written, *for Miss Burchell,* and around her name was a Bix doodle, another Art Nouveau-like tangle of peacock feathers and flowering vines.

This was it, what they had been looking for all summer.

"But surely Alicia would have taken — " Jill stopped. The report that Alicia had taken all of the scripts on the plane with her had been Charles's, and Jill was now sure that that was as false as nearly everything he had told them. She rifled the script's yellowing pages. The margins and the backs of the pages were covered with Alicia's flowing handwriting.

"What's in it?" she asked. "You read it, didn't you?"

"I tried. I sat down on my grandmother's front steps and tried, but I couldn't make any sense of it. I guess I was too excited and all the 'cut to's' and 'fades,' and then everything Alicia had written, it was too much. I couldn't. But you'll be able to read it, won't you?"

Jill nodded. Already she was looking at the cast of characters. As would be expected, it was exactly the same as in the dummy treatment that John Ransome had found. She turned to the first page of text. Doug moved closer. His shadow fell across the page.

"I can't do this with you staring at me," she said.

He winced. "Okay, I'll be inside."

Already reading, Jill moved across the porch and lowered herself into the swing.

"You'll call me the second you're through?"

She waved him off.

As experienced as Jill was at reading screen-plays, it took her several pages to get the rhythm of reading this one. There were more details about camera angles and sets than in screenplays written today, and the handwritten notes were distracting. Most were in Alicia's hand, but some were in Bix's and a few — jolting, jarring, shockingly — were in Cass's. This script must have been sitting on that table next to the glasses from *Casablanca*.

Jill forced herself to ignore even her father's notes, and by the end of the first scene it would have been painful to do otherwise, so completely was she caught by the power of the script.

The basic plot was similar to the final version. Booth and Phillip tossed a coin, Booth went to war, Phillip stayed home. Phillip fell in love with Mary Deas and, as Jill had always guessed from the date of Don Pleasant's birthday, together they had a child.

But this was not a story of their love. Their romance was one tiny strand, hardly more than a few scenes, in a dense tapestry about heroism — Booth's heroism. He was indeed the leading character.

Booth rode to war, a quiet man with an

orderly soul. Yet he was no isolate; there was a vigor about his movements that connected him to others. He loved his wife with a passion of both the body and the soul. He was at home at Briar Ridge, entirely suited to his life there, master of the horses and servants, partner to his brother, lover of his wife.

But war forced out of him acts of unimagined courage, both physical and moral. His choices were hard ones, requiring him to send men, some of them faceless, some of them loved, to nearly certain death. Agony came when he had to lead a retreating army to safety knowing that he was leaving a wounded Pompey to die alone on the battlefield. Leadership demanded a constant return to some inner well, drawing from it again and again, until the ice from this underground river froze the rest of his soul. The physical vibrancy that had been his bridge to others chilled into solitary grandeur as the coiled vigilance that his command required engulfed his being.

The screenplay told a dark story, haunting and poetic. Echoing through the screenplay were the words of the half-surviving Confederates whom Marie Ringling remembered from her girlhood in Richmond, and its message was that, in the end, heroism ruins a man for normal life.

But Phillip and Mary Deas were not judged harshly for their betrayal of Booth. They were ordinary people, and ordinary people needed to love. Booth had become a hero and in so doing had lost his capacity to love.

The Booth of this version did not ask Phillip his question about Mary Deas's baby, "It wasn't some Yankee, was it?" That was not something this Booth needed to know.

It was not that he wished her to have been mistreated, he was not hard-hearted or unfeeling, but what Booth needed to know about someone was not what had happened to him; everyone had suffered, and only the details of their stories were different. Booth cared whether or not a person was surviving. Mary Deas loved her baby tenderly, fiercely. That was survival. What path had led her feet to that road did not matter.

He could see that Phillip and Mary Deas loved each other, and he could see that she was still lovely, that her eyes were still dark and warm, that her daughter was lovely, too, the first violet flowering in a Valley stripped of its blossoms. But he saw all that from a distance, through a veil of hard rain and dried blood. He could not love. The war had done that to him.

He accepted his limits as other men had accepted their physical losses — the hands, the legs, the arms gone with no getting them back. He bore his suffering with dignity, but endurance was not enough; he had to act. One morning Phillip came into the sagging chicken coop where he had stabled the last two horses to find Booth saddling his.

In this version, Booth left. It was Booth who took up the blue coat, going west to fight the Indians. He was a good cavalryman, that was all he was, and Virginia had no need for cavalrymen anymore.

Mary Deas came out of the house, crossing the weed-choked lawn. Her heavy, limp skirts were tied up, her eyes were puzzled by the saddled horse. Booth swung into the saddle, and, in a sad sketch of a cavalryman's jaunty salute, waved his battered hat to her and bid his horse into a gallop. Phillip caught her, his arm around her shoulders, stifling her questions. Together they watched Booth ride off, a man and a horse growing smaller and smaller, fainter, until they were only a cloud of dust, and then not even that.

The script fell shut in Jill's lap.

In the final version Phillip's decision to go west had been noble, a man's decision to step aside, but there was no such bittersweet consolation about Booth's action. He made no choice; this was inevitable. What did a hero do when his world no longer needed heroes?

She could have sat for hours, thinking about what Bix had written, about all that it said about men and what war did to them, about all the things that they did not tell women, but Doug was waiting for her inside. She made herself get up. At the first sound of her footsteps crossing the porch, he was at the door, pushing it open.

"What's it like?" he was asking. "Is it garbage?"

Garbage? Had he been worried about that, worried that they would find, when all was said and done, that Bix was a fraud, a smooth talker, a con artist?

Jill didn't doubt for an instant that Bix was a smooth talker and a con artist, but he was no fraud.

"No, Doug, it's magnificent, better than we ever dreamed."

Doug reached for the script, a light flooding his face. "Will you help me read it?"

"Yes."

They sat side by side on the porch swing. At first Jill talked through the story, setting each scene for him, letting him read the dialogue for himself, and then soon he was able to do it on his own.

She glanced at the pages as he turned them. Already the words of the script were burned into her memory, as vivid and enveloping as if she had actually seen it filmed.

No wonder Bix had gone to such lengths to make this movie. There must have been a compulsion, as urgent as any craving that Jill's mother had ever felt. And no wonder the young veterans he had picked for the crew had cooperated, no wonder they had all been willing to risk their careers. Although it was set during a different war, this was to be their movie, their statement of what it was like to come back home. Amid all the clamor that the boys were back home, here was one voice, saying, "Wait a minute, we've changed. *The Best Years of Our Lives* was fine, but it didn't go far enough."

But this voice had been stilled, and no one spoke these words again until after Vietnam.

Doug was nearing the end of the script, and Jill watched him read the final scene, his face growing bleaker. At last he closed the script with a shiver.

He was silent for a minute and then — "What was it that Alicia said, about aching for him? I feel that."

Jill understood. If she felt isolated, if she

felt like she was standing at the edge of the lake, watching everyone else, how much more withdrawn was Booth? There was no hope for him, and he had once been one of the swimmers, he had once known their joy. And this character, his knowledge and his pain, had come out of Bix's soul.

Doug turned back to the title page, looking at the intricate drawing Bix had penned around his sister-in-law's name. "At least he fell in love."

Yes, that was a comfort. Bix wasn't Booth. Surely there were times during the writing when he must have felt as if he was, when he must have felt that what the Germans had done to him had left him — as Yeats had written in Cass's favorite poem — "changed, changed utterly."

But he had recovered enough to love again. It was not a happy love, but it was love. He had died, but he had been in love when it happened. His soul had recovered.

"Would it really have been such a flop?" Doug asked. "Would they have lost that much money?"

"I don't know," Jill answered. "There's nothing for the blood-and-guts fans and there's certainly not much love interest."

Phillip and Mary Deas's romance really was a tiny part of the script, and Booth's story had nothing to do with loving a woman. His choice was never between the Confederate cause and the woman he loved. Women were beside the point.

But women had been beside the point in *Butch Cassidy and the Sundance Kid,* and people had gone to see that.

"It might not have been a big success," Jill guessed. "But how much money could it have lost? It couldn't have cost that much to make."

Bix had written the movie carefully. Part of the growing sense of the inevitability of Booth's fate came from almost documentary detachment of the camera. There were few close-ups, shot/reverse shots, and glance-object cutting, a narrative technique that required fewer of the time-eating camera set-ups. Bix had saved tight, intense camera work for the battles. There were no big panoramic spectacles with thousands of men and horses. Battles were shot in intimate detail — sweating faces, campfires, and trenches. He had clearly learned from the horror movies he had worked on how to evoke a great deal of atmosphere without spending much money. The alternation between the two styles would have been powerful . . . and enormously cost-efficient.

Jill was perplexed. "This makes less sense

than ever, Doug. *Circean Nights* was draining cash out of the studio, cash and people. It was derailing the schedule of every other production. So why add more complications by refilming this movie?"

"Maybe they just did it as a sop to your dad and Bix, trying to keep them happy until things calmed down." Doug looked down at the script. "Except I can't see how making any changes to this would have made anyone happy. I'm no critic, but what were you saying a while ago, about that guy who blew up his building?"

"Howard Roark in *The Fountainhead.*"

Back in May, she had thought it all right that Bix had not been Howard Roark. Co-operating with the studio had been realistic, practical, and Jill was, above all else, realistic and practical.

But now that she had read the script, she felt differently. Bix should have refused. There was a time to stop being practical. This script had grandeur to it; it was worth every risk he had taken for it. Why had he let them turn it into a love story? Why had he helped?

Doug was turning the pages of the script. "Maybe Charles will have some idea."

"Charles?" Jill could hear how thin her voice sounded. She didn't know what the truth was, but she did know that Charles wasn't telling it. He had said that there had been endless rewriting during the spring filming, but if that had been so, this script would have been a rainbow of colored pages, each color indicating a different draft. There were no insertions, no major deletions in this script. Jill wasn't surprised. Bix had been too organized, too controlling, to have let a director near anything that hadn't been thought through completely.

Nor had Alicia taken all the scripts on the plane so that she could make a clean copy, as Charles had said; there would have been no reason to. All the copies would have been clean. Whatever the history of this particular script was — Jill imagined it had been among the things Alicia's friends had shipped back from California — Jill was sure Charles had known all summer exactly where it was.

There was no point in talking to Charles. He would only lie more.

"He's on his way to Gettysburg," Jill said. "We'll never find him. Let's read what Alicia's written on the script. That might tell us something."

The notes were interesting and bewildering. Alicia had done her work on the script in two stages. The first was in the spring, when she was preparing her part — although surprisingly many of her comments were about Booth's character. Perhaps Charles was able to be such an intuitive actor, Jill thought nastily, because his wife did the analysis for him. Her understanding of his complex, tragic character was rich indeed.

Alicia's other comments were written during the summer, during the preparation of the new script. Certainly most of the rewriting had been done on fresh paper, but there were a number of notes such as "Cut this" and "Don't forget Pompey's still alive." Bix's comments ranged from, "That's the ugliest dress I've ever seen," which was probably a comment written about her calico costume during the spring filming, to quick "big love scene here" remarks. There were a few doodles, but no intimate dialogue. Bix and Alicia had not conducted their romance on the pages of her shooting script.

Cass had written little, only an occasional note here and there — things that he had started and then crossed out as if he had suddenly realized that he was writing on the wrong piece of paper.

But right in the middle of the script, upside down on the back of one of the sheets, he had written a list:

The Living Stream, Too Long a Sacrifice,

A Stone of a Heart, A Terrible Beauty, Wherever Grey Is Worn.

Jill recognized them instantly; they were all from Yeats's "Easter, 1916," Cass's favorite poem, another work about the cost of heroism . . . although, of course, in that poem about Irish rebels, the phrase had been "wherever *green* is worn."

He must have been playing around with them as titles to the movie . . . although these titles fit this script better than the final version. Maybe he too had liked the first script better than the one he was helping to write.

She explained all this to Doug. "I really like 'Wherever Grey Is Worn.' It just fits in millions of ways, since even though Booth will be wearing — "

She stopped. All this time everyone had been searching for film labeled *Weary Hearts* and found nothing, not a trace of anything.

But suppose there had been a cover-up, suppose that for some reason the studio executives had been determined to destroy every trace of this script and the footage filmed from it, and suppose that her father was determined to save the footage, what could he have done?

He could have stolen it, keeping it in his private files. No, other people could have stolen it. Cass couldn't have. He would have found some other way, some legal, honorable way, to preserve it.

Like filing it under another name.

Eighteen

Jill called her brother. Doug urged her to. Brad's your family, he had said, not just yours, but Randy's, too. What's family for?

Jill had no idea what family was for, but she wanted to learn. So she called.

She and Doug needed to go to California, she told Brad, tonight if possible, but she had committed herself to take care of the chickens through Sunday.

Brad was thrilled. He didn't ask what wild impulse was sending her flying across the continent; he didn't care. For the first time in her life, she needed his help; that's what mattered to him.

He'd be delighted to take care of things, he assured her. He had done it for Randy before. It was no problem. Really his pleasure. Any time. Did she need a ride to the airport? Help in making her reservations? Anything at all?

No, no, she told him. This was enough.

Was she sure?

Yes, she was. "And, Brad . . . thank you. It's good to know you're there."

"Jill, I will always be here for you. You're my sister."

This was the first time he had used that word. She thanked him again, then hung up and hurried upstairs. Doug was already in the bedroom, packing. She pulled out the parachute-silk duffle that she had brought with her, laying it on the bed next to his American Tourister carry-on.

It took them ten minutes to pack, then two hours to get to the airport. They had to wait another two hours for the last plane to the coast. Jill spent most of that time on the phone. She asked Cathy Cromartie to get them into the studio vaults; she called the hotel to tell them she was coming. As she talked, she noticed the odd looks Doug was getting.

He was still in Confederate uniform. He had forgotten to change.

On the plane they read the script again. It was awkward to try to balance it on the first-class cabin's wide armrest. Doug's arm was in the way, so he lifted it up, resting it lightly on her shoulders. After a few pages more, she leaned against him. His heart beat with an athlete's low, steady rate.

With the time change, they arrived in Los Angeles at midnight. Uncertain about what the taxi situation would be, Jill had asked the hotel to arrange for a car and driver, and a quiet Mercedes sedan — she did not like limousines — took them directly to the studio.

Cathy had left their names with the night guard at the gate and he waved them on through. The grounds were dark, and Jill was soon disoriented. The park-like campus she had known from her childhood was gone. The curving, palm-shaded walks had been paved over for parking. The low, Spanish-style bungalows had been replaced with mid-rise office buildings. They had to go back to the guard and ask for directions to the vaults.

The studio had dozens of storage vaults for film footage. The sound department had vaults for sound track film and magnetic tape; the stock footage library had its vaults; there were the negative storage vaults and the storage area for library prints, the copies kept for the studio itself to use. There were vaults where bits and pieces of miscellaneous printed matter were kept, such as trailers, costume tests, and foreign language titles. Doug and Jill wanted the nitrate storage vaults.

Not only did nitrate film decompose rapidly, it was also highly flammable. Chemically it was much like dynamite. Burning nearly twenty times as fast as wood, it ignited at half the temperature at which wood ignited, and the older it got, the lower a temperature it would start to burn at. In the New York heat wave of 1949 there was a rash of fires in storage vaults started by rolls of nitrate film spontaneously igniting simply because of the hot weather.

Thus nitrate film had to be stored in fire-proof bunkers. Each bunker was divided into small vaults about the size of a prison cell, holding no more than one thousand cans of film. The exterior wall of each vault was fitted with a blow-out panel, a flimsy, loosely fitting sheet of asbestos. If a fire started in an individual vault, the blow-out panel would explode open, drawing the flames and gases outward so that only the material stored in this one vault would be lost, not everything in the whole storage facility.

A guard met their car at a low, flat building that looked like a cinder block chicken coop. He unlocked the steel fire door and curled his hand inside to flick on a light switch. A dusty concrete corridor stretched out in front of them. Pairs of fire doors, each leading into a vault, faced one another along either side of the corridor. There were perhaps thirty vaults in all. "No Smoking" signs were posted every twenty feet.

"Be careful now," the guard cautioned. "This stuff is like gunpowder. Keep all the doors closed, except for the vault you are in, and if something starts to burn, get yourself out. There's no point in trying to put out the fire."

The doors to each vault were latched with steel bolts. Jill turned the heavy metal handle on the one closest to the entrance. A noxious smell slapped at their faces.

Doug drew back. "What's that?"

"Nitrate film decomposing. It really has an awful smell."

They flicked on the light inside the vault. Along the walls were ceiling-high steel shelves. Lying flat on the shelves were rusting cans two inches deep and ten inches in diameter, each able to hold two thousand feet of film, although some, Jill knew from the smell, would now store only fine brownish powder.

The archivists whom Cass had raised money to pay had organized the material alphabetically by decade. The cans were identified by fading adhesive labels. Even the ones put on by the archivists were now almost twenty years old. Neither Doug nor Jill recognized any of the titles. "This must be from the thirties," Jill guessed. "Let's find the forties."

They carefully closed this vault, making sure that the door was latched, so that if a fire started, the door would not explode open.

They tried the next vault, and the next, squinting at the titles until Jill recognized *Accommodation,* a film made in the early forties.

The cans were organized alphabetically. Jill scanned through her father's list of suggested titles, picking out *The Living Stream* as the title first in the alphabet. Doug was already moving along the shelves, looking for the "L's." But this bunker ended with *The Good Hereafter.*

They moved next door. *Life Worth Living* was followed by *Lost Prizes.* No *Living Stream.* On to the next bunker. *Stockings of Blue* was followed by *Stormbound.* No *A Stone of a Heart.*

It was a work of moments. *A Terrible Beauty, Too Long a Sacrifice, Wherever Grey Is Worn* — nothing.

"Perhaps it's stored a little out of order," Doug suggested.

That wasn't likely, not if Cass had chosen the archivists. But they looked anyway, searching ahead and behind where each title should be. Still nothing. The archivists had known the alphabet. Then they looked for other key words from each title: *stream, heart, terrible, long, sacrifice, grey.* Nothing. Then they looked at each label of each can in the forties. Nothing again.

So they tried the other decades. They looked in the L's, S's, T's, and W's in every single nitrate vault. Still nothing. They looked again. And again. Every vault had the same acrid odor; the gases released by the decay of the film smelled strong and evil.

Jill had no idea what time it was. Her watch said something, but she couldn't remember if she had reset for California time. And it didn't matter. These dark vaults had nothing to do with the sun and nature's day. The clock ticking down in this underground world recorded only decay.

The cans, the floor, and the shelves were dusty, and Jill herself felt coated with a fine grit. She ran her hands down her face, feeling the dirt ball up under her fingers. She was tired, she was dirty, and she knew that this was pointless. She knew it, and so did Doug.

She went back into the hall, away from the worst smell, and slumped down to the floor, leaning her head back against the cinder block wall, feeling more tired, more dirty, than she had ever felt even in the Peace Corps. She shut her eyes.

Everyone was right. There was nothing. Maybe her father had saved the footage, and someone else had gotten rid of it. Maybe it had decomposed so badly that the archivists had destroyed it without being able to tell what it was. Maybe Cass hadn't saved it. Maybe he had unthinkingly discarded it; maybe he had deliberately destroyed it. She wasn't going to know.

She heard a door swing shut and latch. Then Doug spoke. "So we've wasted two fucking months."

Her eyes opened like a shot. "Oh, Doug, no, we haven't. How can you say that? Think of what we have found, the script, the — "

She stopped. Here it was, happening all over again. Doug was growing angry, and as disappointed as she was, she had set aside all her own feelings and was desperately, frantically, trying to coax him out of his anger. And she could, she knew that. In fact, they could go their whole lives with her stifling and choking off his normal reactions.

She took a breath. She wasn't sure what to do. She, so expert at soothing, did not know how to incite. But she had to try. "Except Charles could have given us that script any time. He knew all along where it was." She said this flatly. She believed it.

"If that's the case, then we've been real jerks."

The consoling answers tumbled into Jill's mind instantly, automatically. *Your family has a myth about Charles, and you accepted it.*

Family myths are powerful; they can't be gotten around easily. But she wasn't going to say any of those.

"No, Doug, Charles isn't the issue. If you've wasted two months, if you've been a jerk, it's not because of what you have or haven't found. It's because you're looking for the wrong thing. You're not responsible for Bix's dying. You aren't obligated to clear his reputation. You're so involved in this because you don't want to think about yourself, your own reputation, and your own future."

He was staring at her. She had never spoken like this before. "What's gotten into you?"

"I'm getting sick of it, that's all." She stood up. "You ought to be thinking about yourself and what you're planning on doing with your life; you should be working on that, and instead we've been obsessed with the movie. I'm sick of it. Let's tackle what really matters."

She was lying. Jill, endlessly patient Jill, was not sick of him or the movie or even the unwholesome smell of these vaults. But, as she spoke, she realized that she should be telling the truth. She should be sick of this.

"You're being supportive." Now he was angry with her. "We're all truly grateful."

The rats' feet scuffled as they struggled

to break out of their cages, their beady eyes glowing with a harsh yellow light. Jill refused to give in to them. "You're damn right. I'm being more supportive than anyone you've ever known or ever will know. I've been in therapy for more than a year now. Yes, I've read too many stupid self-help books, but I've also read the best psychology written. I know a lot. And if you don't want to take advantage of my help, then you don't deserve it . . . and you certainly don't deserve to get out of the hole you're in."

She marched out of the bunker, letting the fire door crash shut behind her. She blinked against the harsh glare of the morning sun, then marched on, flipping her hair back over her shoulders. She didn't stop; she didn't listen to see if the door was opening, if his footsteps were following.

The sidewalk turned at a stand of palm trees. In their long shadows the harsh July light was cool, muted. Jill stopped, the combative energy draining from her. She leaned back against a tree, her hand to her throat, trying to catch her breath.

She had never done anything like that, provoked a confrontation, let someone be angry with her, then walked away, knowing that his anger would fester and intensify. It had been horrible; she had hated it.

But she could do it again if she had to. She could hate anger, but she didn't need to be afraid of it. She was going back to her therapy group. She was going to face their anger, she was really going to work, and she was going to learn how to do this.

She started toward the car, but she was barely to the parking lot when she heard her name. She turned. Doug was coming out of the building. At the sight of her he broke into a run.

She watched. His run was magnificent, the effortless, long-legged lope of an athlete. The grey battle jacket of his Confederate uniform was open, swinging free. He was in front of her in moments, breathing harder than this exertion required. He gripped her shoulders, his arms and hands as dirty as hers, his eyes glowing with life.

"It's not you I'm angry at."

How wonderful he was, how sane, how normal. Other people took years to get to this point. It had taken him four minutes. "I know that," she answered.

"I don't know who it is, but it's not you."

"It doesn't have to be anyone." As bad as she might be at the practice, Jill did know the theory. "You can just be mad because it's a lousy situation."

"Oh, no." He turned her toward the car,

starting to walk with one arm loosely around her. "There're villains in this piece. There're plenty of them."

"So get mad at them."

A light rap on the window woke their driver, who brushed aside their apologies. He was, he said, happy to have people pay him for sleeping.

Doug said little on the ride back to the hotel, but there was an energy about him, an alertness, a growing purpose. Until this moment Jill had known only negative things to come from anger, but Doug wasn't stewing, he wasn't fretting — he was getting ready to act. He was using his anger as a signal, a sign that it was time to do something. It was remarkable, thrilling.

The hotel was ready for them. The concierge hurried from behind her desk, ringing for a bellman, gesturing to registration for Jill's key. Jill took the key, murmuring Doug's name. And she knew that, within moments, someone on the hotel staff would be trying to find out who this man in dirty Confederate battle dress was.

The bungalow was fresh with bowls of flowers and a basket of fruit. "I need to clean up," she said to Doug as soon as they were inside.

"I should, too."

She had not taken a bath the whole time she had been at Aunt Carrie's; the morning's deposit of "caraway seeds" had restricted her to showers. She filled the hotel's large whirlpool with hot water, and the pounding jets left her so relaxed and limp that she could hardly put on her own almost-forgotten bathrobe. She found Doug in the living room, hanging up the phone, still unshowered, his chin stubbly. But his eyes were sparkling.

"This is great. The Lynx is in town; he'll be over in twenty minutes."

"That's great. I've wanted to meet him." That was true. She had wanted to meet Doug's best friend. She just didn't want to do it now. She was so tired. She approved of Doug's anger in theory; she was confident that, by working in her group, she would get better at it herself; but in the meantime, it was hard.

Doug hardly noticed how quietly she spoke. He was flying, a man brought back to life. "I ought to change. But I kind of like this, meeting him in a Confederate uniform. He can call me Massa; it will be good for him."

"He can call you whatever you want." It was wonderful to see him like this. She was sorry she couldn't share his exuberance, but it didn't matter. There would be so many other times. "But if we're talking about one

527

person buying and selling another," she pointed out, "he's the one who could buy and sell you."

"That's true," Doug admitted cheerfully. "They are paying him a ton of money."

Jill roused herself enough to order breakfast, which arrived at the same time as the Lynx, a very tall, very quiet, very black man. The room-service waiter recognized him instantly.

Jill greeted him pleasantly, but as they sat down to eat, she didn't feel like she was making a good impression. She was hardly saying a thing. Then she realized that she didn't have to. Doug and the Lynx had been teammates, and that brought a certain way of thinking. Doug loved her; that was all the Lynx needed to know. Everything else would come in time.

She picked at an egg, but it seemed tasteless after the newly laid eggs they had eaten all summer. The men ate everything, even the parsley off the platters. Then they decided to go horse around in the Lynx's private gym. They invited Jill, but she begged off, offering them her car as a substitute for herself. "The hotel has it garaged."

The men grabbed her keys eagerly and, fighting about who was going to drive, left the bungalow. The Lynx had to duck his head as he went through the door.

Jill drifted through the day, sleeping a little bit, lying on the chaise on the secluded patio, hoping that the sunlight would restore her spirits, but the California light seemed harsh and straw-colored. Her eyes had grown accustomed to the Valley's soft light, its gentle colors. She had grown up near a pounding ocean, but in the early days of this summer she had given her heart to the narrow silver river.

The hotel staff had tried to make her bungalow welcoming, and it was comfortable, much more comfortable than Aunt Carrie's house had ever been. But Aunt Carrie's house was home.

And if it were ever carried away by the mud, if blue-coated Yankees ever burnt it down, Jill would now have the sense to mourn.

Late in the afternoon Doug called, wanting her to meet them for dinner.

"Are you having a good time?" she asked.

"I'm having a glorious time. After dinner we're going to meet some guys the Lynx knows. Just because you got a good pro contract doesn't mean you don't mind being cheated of an education in college. The Lynx says a lot of guys are really pissed off about it, now that they see what they missed. He thinks we can get them to say something, and with their reputations, then . . ."

Jill let him go on, and when he finally remembered why he had called, she told him she'd stay at the bungalow. "It sounds like you two will want to talk shop."

He laughed. "Yes, but when we're done, I promise I'll read a dorky self-help book or two. You're right. I spent the summer looking for the wrong thing."

She was in bed when Doug and the Lynx came in, and drifting in and out of sleep, she listened to their voices. She heard words: *press conference, those bastards, what they deserve.* Doug was going to come out of the corner slugging.

She woke sometime later to silence. Doug must have gone to sleep in the other bedroom. She peered at the illuminated numbers of the digital clock. It was nearing three. Awake, she sat up against the headboard, pulling her knees up, wrapping her arms around them. After a bit she switched on the lamp on the nightstand and looked for something to read.

And realized that, for the first time since his death, she had forgotten to pack her father's picture.

The top of the nightstand looked empty without it. She felt very, very distant from him.

She wrapped her arms around her knees, resting her chin on her hands. It had probably been necessary, this distance. Idolizing her father had kept her from loving a man as she now loved Doug, and her love for him was better, righter, truer.

But the cost had been high, and it need not have been. That was what was so sad. There was a middle ground between the idolatry she had once had for Cass and the feeling that she had now, the feeling that she no longer knew who he had been, the feeling that she could no longer trust him.

She leaned back against the headboard and let her thoughts wash over her — troubled, tumultuous thoughts, coming even with a little spurt of anger that she should have to feel this way.

She watched the blinking digital clock: 3:12, 3:12, 3:12, 3:13, 3:13 . . .

This was the time of night that people called her, desperately needing her help. No one would call tonight. No one knew that she was here.

3:13, 3:14, 3:14 . . .

She swung her legs out of bed, fumbling for her robe. Tying it as she walked, she crossed the bungalow's living room. The door to the second bedroom was half-open; she could hear Doug's breathing. Only it wasn't breathing. It was snoring; he and Lynx had been drinking. Doug always snored if he drank right before going to sleep.

She whispered his name.

He sat up, instantly alert. She came into the room and sat down on the bed next to him.

"What's wrong?" he asked.

"I don't know. . . . Yes, I do." She took a breath. "Doug, I need to go on looking for that footage."

"But I thought — "

"I know, I know," she interrupted. "*You* don't need to, but I do."

"Your father?" he asked.

He understood.

It was true that this whole matter had nothing to do with her father's love for her, but it did suggest what kind of man he was, if his first big opportunity had come from deceit and conspiracy. She felt like she had to know.

It was too early to go to the studio, but they left the bungalow anyway, driving out to the beach, walking up and down, hardly speaking, feeling the damp wind in their hair, listening to the ocean, peaceful in its endlessness, frightening in its power.

As it grew light, they drove back into town, Doug stopping to buy coffee and doughnuts for the guards. The same ones were on duty, and even though Doug and Jill's names had not been left on the day's roster, they were let in.

There was no point in going back to the nitrate vaults. Jill knew that. Rather at random, she chose the vault under Sound Stage D.

Only it wasn't at random. This was the vault where most of the miscellaneous printed matter was stored. This was the vault where John Ransome had found the flashback sequence that Cass had reluctantly cut out of *Nancy*.

As only safety film — film that was not so flammable — was stored in this vault, it was one cavernous space, more than an acre in area, lit by bare bulbs dangling over the dusty concrete floors. Bank after bank of metal shelves formed narrow aisles. Again the movies were in aluminum-coated cans, marked by fraying adhesive labels. But no archivist had come in to reorganize them. They were simply in the order in which they had been sent into storage.

Jill groped through the racks, finding the films made during the seventies. It took her a while, but she found *Nancy*, the film of her father's that was her second favorite. The labels on the cans had started to fade, but they were informative. *Nancy, 1973 — outs; Nancy, 1973 — Reel #3, trims; Nancy, 1973 — costume tests; Nancy, 1973 — flashback, answer print, Do Not Discard or Destroy.* Other movies had the title slapped on the side, usually without a date, sometimes even with the title misspelled. But Cass had left things in order. She went to find *Mustard Lane.* It was the same.

Doug's voice came from the end of the aisle. "These don't seem to be in any order. Where should we start looking?"

"I don't know."

It wasn't going to be possible to look at every title on every can. All they could do was walk through the aisles, their eyes swinging back and forth, hoping they would subconsciously hone in on key words. They split up, Jill starting at one end of the vault, Doug at the other. They met in the middle, neither having found anything. Each then paced through the aisles the other had searched. Again nothing. Then they just roamed.

Jill's eye kept catching similar titles, drawing her to *The Living Dead, Two Long Streets, A Grey Wedding,* and *The Old Millstream, The Long Journey, Living Hearts,* then *Two Long Streets* again, and *Grey Wedding.* It was pointless, useless, yet utterly necessary.

She kept coming back to *Nancy*, and at last she stopped, exhausted, letting her eyes fall shut and her face drop forward, her forehead resting against the cool metal of the shelving that held material from the film that had won her father his first Academy Award. She felt Doug's hands close around her shoulders.

There really was no one else she could stand to do this with except him.

She stared at the cans in front of her. That's what mattered, she told herself. *Nancy*. As it had been filmed during the summer, she had been on the set much of the time, traveling with her father to the locations. She had known even then that this story of a widower and his daughter was their story. Nothing that she and Doug had learned about *Weary Hearts* could take that away.

Yet for some reason — no, it was impossible, it couldn't be — she thought she smelled nitrate decay.

She looked at the cans in front of her. *Grey Wedding*, which her eye had been drawn to so often, was right next to *Nancy*. It had two kinds of labels; half had a blue stripe, the others were plain. Peeking out from under the plain labels were the corners of older labels; the cans had been used before. Idly Jill slipped a fingernail — one of the indestructible almond-shaped nails she had inherited from her mother — under one of the corners of the newer labels. The label easily peeled off the metal of the can, then more slowly where its adhesive had adhered to the label underneath.

Jill dropped the top label and rubbed her finger across the lower one, gathering the adhesive into little balls, blowing them off, working idly at first, then more quickly, urgently, feeling suddenly that something was at stake. Her hands almost shaking, she pulled the can out of the rack and held it up to the light.

WHEREVER GREY IS WORN.

She squeezed her eyes shut and looked again. The label was tattered, parts of it having been ripped off with the outer label, and the ink was faded, but it could be read. *Wherever Grey Is Worn.*

In her father's handwriting.

Instantly everything was confirmed. There had been a cover-up, a conspiracy to destroy every trace of Bix's script, but Cass had been a reluctant part of it. He had secretly saved the cut footage, storing it under a false name. He had meant it to be found. She had understood him completely, she had looked in the right place. Someone else had mislabeled the cans, had put them in the wrong vaults, but Cass had certainly sent the footage into storage, intending that someday it would be found.

Daddy, did you know it would be me?

She tried to open the can. She couldn't. Doug took it from her, his knife already out of his pocket. He used the can-opener blade to pry open the can. The lid popped and clattered to the concrete.

But that he needed the keys already told her the bad news. Film cans should open easily. The goo of decaying nitrate film seals them shut.

The gas odor was stronger now. Jill looked down at the can in Doug's hand. The film was a mass of gooey bubbles. A sticky brown froth covered everything that had been stored in the can.

He looked down at it and then back up at her. "It's ruined, isn't it?"

She nodded.

"Oh, Jill, I am so sorry."

She was too. But Cass had saved the film. That was what mattered to her. She would never know why he had had to resort to subterfuge, but at least he was still the man she had always known. She would no longer idolize him; he was not perfect. But he was her daddy.

She watched as Doug snapped the lid back

in place and put the can back on the rack. It looked out of place, the tattered *Wherever Grey Is Worn* label in the middle of the *Grey Wedding* cans, but the *Grey Wedding* label was a little white ball on the dusty concrete floor; there was no way to put it back on.

"I suppose we ought to look at the rest of the cans," Doug said. There were perhaps ten more of the plain-labeled cans. That seemed like a lot to Jill. A whole movie was about eighteen cans.

Doug struggled with the next can. Its contents were in worse shape. The bubbling goo had dried into a fine brown powder. Looking down at it now, Jill could scarcely imagine that this gritty dust had once held the lush images of Bix and Alicia, Booth and Pompey, Mrs. Reynolds's chestnut trees, the rolling white fences marking off the pastures. Now it was dust.

She felt a tiny spurt of anger. Not just about this film, but for the nitrate film everywhere that was deteriorating, all the glorious movies that had shaped the culture and the consciousness of the nation, and that was now decaying. The silent movies, the newsreels, the World War II public service announcements, the cartoons — these shouldn't be allowed to turn to dust. Half of the movies made before 1950 were already lost.

She felt her anger stir, and Jill, relentlessly even-tempered Jill, wanted to kick a shelf. She wanted to hear the cans rattle against each other; she wanted to see some of them clatter to the floor. She wanted to pound her fist on the uprights.

Then she remembered what Doug had done with his anger. He hadn't vented it in violence. He had acted, he had done something.

So, if she was angry about this, she could raise money for film restoration. This would be her own project, not one that a friend had called her in on; she wouldn't be doing it because someone else cared about it. She would be doing it because she cared about it, because it mattered to her.

And in this dark dusty vault Jill felt the tide coming in, the edge of the lake curling around her toes. The rats were gone and she was going to splash in the water.

She looked at Doug gratefully, enraptured, feeling like she owed this to him. What a good life they were going to have together, marrying, living wherever his job took them, but with the Valley always at the center, the kind of life she had never dreamed of having.

She wasn't going to make her father's mistake. She wasn't going to tell her children how beautiful the Valley was; she wasn't going to tell them how fine it was to be a Virginian. That wasn't enough. She would take them there; every summer they would go there, to the land that had been in her family since before the Revolution. They would have family there — cousins, aunts and uncles, grandparents, Ringlings and Caslers, all driving Chevys.

She sat down on the floor, leaning back happily against the shelf, listening to Doug opening the cans. He was in the middle of the plain labels now. He picked up a can and, holding it level in his left hand, started to slip his blade, crowbar-like, under the lip of the lid. The lid flew off, clattering to the floor.

"Jill, look at this."

She scrambled up, already alert. The lid shouldn't have come off that easily. "Doug, what is it?"

He held out the can. Instead of a gooey mass she saw a black waxed bag, the kind that film came back from a lab in. She eased the bag open. There, tightly wound around a yellow plastic core, was a roll of film, still crisp, still whole, gleaming in the light from the overhead bulb. It was safety film.

She lifted the roll out of the can, unrolling the first twenty feet, holding it up to the light. There was Charles Ringling's face, a tight close-up, repeated in frame after frame, spooling down into the wound footage on the roll.

Someone had transferred the *Weary Hearts* footage to safety stock. No, not "someone" — Cass. It was his handwriting on all the hidden labels. He had had it done.

That's why this material had been stored in the seventies; that's why it was stored next to *Nancy*, which had been made when the film community was becoming aware of the need to copy nitrate stock. Cass must have taken the *Weary Hearts* footage out of the nitrate vaults and sent it into the lab under *Nancy*'s budget code. But it had all come to the vault at the same time as *Grey Wedding*, and some well-meaning clerk, knowing that there was no *Wherever Grey Is Worn* in production, had relabeled the cans.

Cass must have thought that they were lost. That, Jill was sure, was why he had never told anyone what he had done. That was why he had had the archivists inventory the nitrate stock. He was looking for the original footage, hoping perhaps it could be copied again, but it had been put in here mistakenly. Nothing had been found. He must have assumed that his efforts had been wasted; that's why he would have let his option lapse. There was no longer any record of Bix's script. There would have been nothing to remake.

But there was a record, the one Cass had saved. This was it.

"Are we going to be able to look at it?" Doug asked eagerly.

Jill nodded. They needed a projection room. But it was Sunday. Cathy, who could have arranged everything, would not be at her desk until tomorrow, and Jill didn't think she could stand to wait that long.

"Let's see if anyone's at the editing department," she suggested. "At least I know where it is."

Jill searched for a guard, wanting to sign for the film, but she couldn't find anyone. So she and Doug picked up the six cans and carried them outside. Such lax procedure was why the studio kept losing things.

They hurried across the studio grounds, carrying all six cans of film. Even though it was Sunday, the studio had come to life. People were moving along the sidewalks, some in suits, others in overalls, still others in running shorts and loose T-shirts. Trucks and paneled vans were carefully maneuvering through the narrow roads. This was the world of movies.

A guard presided over the narrow lobby of the building that housed the editing department. Jill marched up to his desk. "My name is Jill Casler," she said, "and I need to use a Steenbeck."

The guard looked at her blankly. "Do you have an appointment with someone?"

Jill tried to remember the name of an editor likely to be working here. All her father's friends were dead or retired.

"Excuse me."

Jill turned at the sound of a voice behind her. It was a young man, wearing plaid bermuda shorts and carrying a bag lunch. He had been waiting to sign in.

"I'm sorry," he said, "I couldn't help overhearing. Did you say your name is Casler? As in Cass Casler?"

"He was my father."

"Then if you need a Steenbeck, you can use mine."

Jill touched his arm, grateful not just for his help, but for his remembering Cass. "That's very, very kind of you. I don't think we'll be long."

He signed them in and escorted them to a small editing room. It was dominated by the Steenbeck, a flatbed editing table three feet deep and eight feet wide, with a small screen behind it and two chairs in front of it. A rack for cans of film was within easy reach of the chairs. Trims — bits and pieces of film — were taped to the wall.

"Do you know how to work it?" the young man asked.

"I believe so," Jill answered.

"Then I'll leave you," he said, but at the door he paused. "Your father, Miss Casler . . . his work meant the world to me."

Jill looked up from the machine. The young man, probably an apprentice or assistant, was blushing, almost overcome by this closeness to Cass. "Thank you. It did to me, too."

It had been years since Cass had let Jill play with a Steenbeck, teaching her how to splice footage, how to synchronize a sound track. But she found she could still load it.

The film was an answer print, a positive print used to check the technical quality of the negative. A little squiggly line running down one side of the film was the sound track. Cass had done everything he could to ensure that whatever images were on this film would be preserved.

She flicked off the lights. "Now this may be difficult to watch," she cautioned Doug. "There's a sound track, but there won't be any music and it may not be in any order — " She stopped. No, it would be in order. Cass would have spliced the trimmed footage into sequence. She was sure of that. "But it will be bits and pieces of the story. Anything they used in the final cut won't be here. It's not going to be a movie, just footage. It may not tell us a thing."

"I don't know how much I need to know now."

That was true. How ironic that they hadn't found it until they no longer needed to. Jill started the machine.

Several feet of blank film whined by, then the screen flowered into life. It was from the opening scene of Bix's script, Booth in close-up, the camera dollying back to show him on a horse, reining up as he approached Briar Ridge. Jill felt Doug take her hand.

And in another minute or two everything was clear. All their questions were answered.

The first reel carried them only through Booth's first battle. The film ran through the machine, the loose end flapping around and around, the little sharp slap breaking the silence of the room. Jill leaned forward and switched off the machine.

Charles Ringling could not act. As fragmented as this footage was, that was clear. His talents had been adequate for the light romantic secondary parts he had prior to this one, but the drama and intensity of *Weary Hearts* had been beyond him. Booth's silent strength came out wooden; Booth's sturdy masculine sexuality had Charles preening.

The film had been unreleasable, not because it was a masterpiece, but because the lead actor had spoiled it. Bix's brother had ruined his movie.

Jill looked at Doug. His face was tight. This must be hard for him. He had grown up with a special bond with Bix, a bond based on this astonishing physical resemblance. But Charles was his uncle, too. Charles was the one he had known.

She spoke mildly, not wanting to tamper with his feelings. "I'm surprised that the studio let it go on so long. Under other circumstances they'd replace an actor in a day or so."

But these circumstances had been unique — the alcoholic director, too grateful for work to question; the producer, overwhelmed, exhausted, turning a deliberate blind eye. That had been the price Bix had had to pay for deceiving the studio; he had deprived himself of Miles Smithson's wisdom and experience. Miles could have replaced Charles. Bix could not have, not ever.

Doug spoke. "But Bix and Alicia — they would have known."

"Yes."

Had the knowledge of Charles's incompetence been something that they had realized in an instant or had it dawned on them, slowly, inexorably? Had it made their falling in love feel like an even greater betrayal? If Alicia had left him, she would have left a man with nothing, not even a talent.

"So that's why they were already planning retakes in April," Doug said, referring to the dialogue written on the back of the doodle now framed on the wall of his grandmother's staircase. "They already knew that Charles had made a mess of it."

"They had other options, you know," Jill said. "Actors die during production. It's awful, but you can work around it. Cass was the editor on *Twice Seen* when John Reynolds died; his scenes had to be reshot with another actor. *Twice Seen* was before *Weary Hearts*. I'm sure Cass would have suggested that to Bix."

Doug shook his head. "He wouldn't do that to his brother. It would have killed Charles. Bix had to choose between his film and his brother, and he chose his brother. And you know this cover-up idea we had, that someone was deliberately getting rid of everything?"

Jill nodded.

"I bet that was Bix's idea."

She had to agree. There was nothing in this footage that would damage anyone but Charles, but it would have destroyed him. Bix, guilt-ridden about his love for Alicia, was going to do all that he could for his brother. Hiding every trace of the first script left Charles with his dignity. And yes, Cass would have cooperated in that cover-up. He, too, valued family and would have assented to destroying everything, secretly holding on to only one bit of evidence as history's due.

Jill now understood why Cass had consented to receive credit for the revised script. He probably hadn't liked it, but he understood that Bix's need was greater. For his brother's sake Bix needed to pretend that the new script was being forced on him. And how could he show Charles the new love scenes? How could he say, "I wrote these," when they were so much like life?

Which brother had done the greater injury — Charles by ruining Bix's movie or Bix by loving Charles's wife? Jill did not know.

"Why did you think Charles gave us the script?" Doug asked.

Jill had wondered about this. "Think about the timing. It was after I had mentioned remaking the movie. Remember how insistent he was that Payne play Booth, not Phillip?"

Doug nodded.

"I'm sure he's thoroughly convinced himself that the first version was not commercial enough. But on some level he must have suspected his incompetence, and if Payne remade the movie, playing Booth as he should have been played, Charles could point to Payne's performance and say 'that was me, I was that good.' "

"So what do we do with this?" Doug gestured at the cans. They weren't going to watch the other five reels. There was no reason to.

"We have to get rid of the nitrate. It's like a growing cancer down there. You're never to store nitrate with safety. The escaping gases will damage the safety stock and if it burns, it could take everything with it. But this . . ." She gestured at the cans they had brought with them. "That's up to you."

"I don't want anyone to see it." Doug's answer came immediately. "At least, not as long as Charles is still alive."

"Why are you protecting him?" she asked. Her sense of justice urged that he be exposed, that he suffer, that he undergo the humiliation from which his younger brother had rescued him at such a high price.

Doug had an answer. "He's weak, he's a coward, and he's a quitter, but he's family."

Jill could accept that. Anger wasn't all she was going to learn about from him. She was also going to learn about family. She had her own family — Brad, Dave and their children — and she would have Doug's family — his frank, down-to-earth grandmother and his delightful parents.

And his four sisters. Four sisters — the thought was a little overwhelming.

Jill looked through the young editor's supplies, found a pen and labels, and added a third label to the cans. "*Weary Hearts, 1948.*" She and Doug carried them back to the vault, putting them next to *Grey Wedding,* simply because that's where there was room for them.

They took the cans of decaying nitrate footage out with them, carrying it across the studio grounds to the nitrate vault. Outside the entrance to the bunker was a burn barrel, a fifty-gallon drum with a heavy lid and "Highly Flammable" labels. They put the cans in the barrel, knowing that, within the next twenty-four hours, the film would be disposed of.

So the search for the lost footage from *Weary Hearts* was over, a search that had begun with a story a young man had told himself in a German prisoner-of-war camp and that was ending here, on this Sunday morning, with this couple who had learned that once you start to look, you may find more than you ever dreamed.

Payne Bartlett

August 3
on location in some sulfurous hovel

Jill darling,

The business first — how can I thank you for sending me this script? It's everything that you said it would be; Booth is the part of a lifetime. I showed it to Pete; he's aching to rewrite it as a Vietnam story, although I'm not sure it should be tampered with. It's perfect as it is.

Nonetheless, I'm not going to make it, and you shall shriek at the reason —

It's not commercial enough.

Even if we kept the Civil War setting, it would be a Vietnam movie — the themes are so universal — and that market is played out. And setting it in the Persian Gulf seems too chancy. My money people say that for our first few pictures we've got to do some sure-fire hits, Payne Bartlett, the sweetly troubled youth. Payne Bartlett is not sweet, he is certainly not a youth, but he is profoundly troubled by decisions like this.

If we get in a position to do some less

commercial properties, I'd love to see the script again, but I'm confident that someone else will pick it up long before then.

But, again, thank you.

Now for the personal — you're getting married!!! Jill, Jill, Jill. How middle class, how wonderful. And to the new defensive coach for the Lakers. I see great tickets in my future.

Susannah reports that there have been a number of public sightings of the Lynx in the company of your intended, and that he is to be the best man, and as a result, that everyone is begging to be the maid of honor, but that you're having your mother???? To your old buddy Payne, that does have the smell of very good news. But why are you getting married in Virginia? I'll come, we all will, but why there?

Susannah also sent me some clippings about the future Mr. Jill Casler's testimony in front of the state legislature about college athletes. It sounds like you have a clear-sighted, level-headed chap on your hands . . . not that we would have expected anything less of you.

Susannah is, of course, incapable of operating a Xerox machine — God only knows why she is still doing things like that herself — so the copies were lousy, but amidst the blur, it sure does look like you've gotten yourself engaged to Phillip Wayland. So you're going to trust your heart to a cavalry man!

All love always,
Payne

The employees of THORNDIKE PRESS hope you have enjoyed this Large Print book. All our Large Print titles are designed for easy reading, and all our books are made to last. Other Thorndike Large Print books are available at your library, through selected bookstores, or directly from us. For more information about current and upcoming titles, please call or mail your name and address to:

THORNDIKE PRESS
PO Box 159
Thorndike, Maine 04986
800/223-6121
207/948-2962